forever young

One woman's journey into the next phase of her life, a future she has chosen to ignore.

Billy Corass, a mature-aged long-distance runner, is in shock after a fall during her most recent event finds her 'temporarily' placed in residential care.

Also by Wendy Glassby

Between (2021)

A dedication

IF THIS DEDICATION OFFERS a moment of thought, then it is addressed to you, regardless of age or gender.

To each of us who have reached that phase in life where we begin to convince ourselves we no longer have purpose, let us set fresh parameters for our latter years.

This part of our lives could well be the right time to seek out ways of contributing to others; interacting socially with others every day; living each day with a larger purpose or goals in our own lives; and embracing an open mind, curiosity and optimism.

Guaranteed is that if we choose to so enrich our older lives, the benefits most definitely will spread throughout our communities. Without doubt, we ourselves will benefit most.

forever young

a novel
Wendy Glassby

Lily Ellen Publishing

First publication in Australia 2025 by Lily Ellen Publishing PO Box 1095 Booragoon Western Australia 6954, an independent publisher.

Typeset in Adobe Garamond.

Cover designer Cathie Glassby

Editors L.Schickert AM, N Muir, C Nott, J White

First edition May 2025

ISBN 978 0 6488341 2 0 Print/978 0 6488341 3 7 eBook

lilyellenpublishing.com

Contents

In the wild

1

AS I EMERGE FROM what feels like deep sleep, tendrils from the out-side world intrude into my consciousness, bringing with them an awareness of an inexplicable void. Within the gentle act of waking – the deep and slow intake of oxygen and the rapid expulsion of carbon dioxide – comes the pungent smell of dust and earth. Immediately, my brain sharply registers that the strength of these odours means their sources are unnaturally close to my nostrils. This is an oddity that requires an explanation. My eyes fly open in response.

What a surprise to find that only my right eye has any range of sight and my left is blocked by soil. Completely awake now, it's clear that it's not only my face that has fallen into an awkward position, but the rest of my body is also twisted. Something has forced me to dive into the ground, and with no recall except of the few seconds since waking, it's a mystery.

Unexpectedly, I find a small degree of comfort within the limited view afforded by my right eye, its narrow perspective delivering my first – and so far my only – certainty. What little I'm able to see is familiar. I know this place. I've run along similar tracks – perhaps even this one – many times. I'm accustomed to this geographic region and its specific challenges. In a sudden flash of clarity I also know why I'm here today: I'm competing in an event, and somewhere along this trail is where I'm supposed to be. This revelation fills me with optimism. Perhaps now I may be able to convince myself the fuzziness of my mind is only temporary.

My relief is short-lived. I'm unable to overlook the oddity of lack of recall and the definite absence of my usually quick and effective responses. The extraordinariness of my situation is causing a squishy mass somewhere in my chest to pulse and expand. Is this panic? This is an emotion foreign to me, because, after all, I'm Wilhemena Rose Corass. I know myself to be a woman who remembers everything, especially when it comes to long-distance running. I've been competing most of my life, and I pride myself on my thoroughness and my diligence to protocols. Where are those strategies now? This lack is inexplicable. I've improvised before. All I need is my confidence in my experience. Yes. That's what will get me through. If I am to find a solution I need to first find calmness. The rest will follow.

It's all well and good to tell myself this, but it's not working. And knowing why my self-lecture has failed doesn't help, either. Instead, my honesty is shouting that I'm out of my depth. I can't lie to myself as comfort. I can't deny nothing within my database of possible solutions fits. It only tells me I'm in trouble, deadly trouble. Even in my confused state it's apparent the least of my concerns should be about what I don't know. The damning truth that I must accept is my accident has happened in an extremely remote location. No help will be coming. Plus, as any experienced extreme sportsperson knows, ultimately, in situations like this, an athlete must become her own saviour. My emotions are my weakness. And that too is not normal. Instead of calming myself, I've become ultra-aware of the implications of not being able to remember details, convincing myself without them I have no tools with which to work. What I should be telling myself is that as I flounder and guess at solutions, I'm losing precious time. This procrastination might in the end sign my death warrant. I could well die out here. I need to focus on getting myself up and moving. To do that, first I must reign in my thoughts.

My lack of self control is devastating. Nothing is working. My body is stuck in this awkward position; my mind uncooperative.

Come on, girl. You've made a start. You've not lost it altogether. Obviously it's an accident, and they're usually not too hard to handle. Having a mishap or two especially in these kinds of events is not abnormal or a sign of failure. Your fifty years of experience tells you that. You know you've fallen before, become unwell during an event before, and survived.

My pep talk falls on infertile ground. Why can't I remember? I always remember. I feel vulnerable. My mind is stuck on repeat. All my careful planning and accumulated knowledge is useless without recall, because you can't plan around not remembering. And you can't fix something if you don't know what needs fixing.

Slow your breathing. Panic won't help. Settle yourself.

Yet, how can I not be agitated after finding myself face-first into the earth? Or waking up mid-path? This is particularly unnatural. When we athletes take naps – because sometimes there's a need – it's very controlled. We mostly only allow ourselves fifteen minutes in a safe spot to the side of the trail. There's no disputing I'm mid-path, so this is definitely not a controlled occurrence. Reinforcing the conclusion that this was not planned is my body and how it feels. After a mid-event nap, I would wake clear minded, refreshed, and ready to continue. After today's nod off, accidental or otherwise, I'm far from settled, restored, or able to move on. Instead, I'm sluggish and dull, and I've one of those headaches I get when I've slept too deeply or too long.

Rattling around in my head is a haunting fear I'm heading into unknown and deadly territory, one in which my survival no longer relies on me saving myself but solely on the need to be rescued. That one almost certain conclusion – the need to be rescued – is the rock I can't get past. I've never before needed assistance, so this unavoidable inevitability is shattering my view of myself as an independent and competitive athlete, and in seeing myself as less capable permits other doubts to enter my thoughts. These days too often I hear warnings from those who care and no doubt want the best for me and yet know so little about my abilities. My son Brandon for example, and close friends. They worry about the dangers I might be putting myself in by continuing running 'at my age', but I believe their fears are based on an external view of my body that disregards the proof of my continuing abilities. I still get up and do regular training and in events I enter I often win in my category. Yes, I admit, my body takes longer to recoup, but I factor this into my training and planning. Whatever my doubts and fears about being rescued might be, the bottom line is, even if my survival depends on rescue, it's highly unlikely anyone will know of my need and, if that miracle happened, they would also not know where I am because even I don't know.

What I must do is keep calm and stick to the one fact I know: I've had an accident. The few other facts available to me are inconsistent with normal outcomes. This tells me two things: there's a lot I don't know, and what I do know is unreliable, so I can't fall back on the set of routines I have used at other times when things have gone awry. Since waking, I've attempted to flick through my usually reliable solutions and discarded them as not fitting my present situation. If those strategies were in play, I would begin by checking for injuries and assessing how I might mitigate them so I can push on to reach the next check point. And there it is, that little puff of pride I feel when I remind myself that in past events inevitably I not only make it to the next checkpoint but push on to the finish line, all the while gritting through the pain of injuries and putting off doing anything about them until I'm in recovery. That's what stubbornness and determination can achieve. But in the here and now, nothing is normal.

My first step must be to persuade my body to unfold itself, to somehow get my face off the ground. I will my body to cooperate, but it's not complying, seemingly content to remain in its awkward position. My weak will takes the easy route by searching for reasons to punish itself for bringing about this disaster. You've let yourself down; you haven't followed your protocols; you missed the signs. There's no denying that in some way or another I have been at fault. Who else is there to blame? But casting blame and labelling will get me no where, except to increase my internal pain, and this mental self-flagellation cuts deep into my psyche sharper than any wound caused by hitting the ground. None of this is me. I'm the perfectionist. I'm the one who drives herself forward, who follows the rules, who dots the i's and crosses the t's. I'm the one who works hard to get everything right. In my lengthy running career not once have I had a total failure.

Meditation might help. Breathe in, hold, breathe out. I do feel a little calmer.

The calmness is temporary. The noise is back. Now my brain has settled on the possibility that I've had a breakdown, either physical or mental. This is the moment accumulated knowledge and experience of my sport is detrimental. I could scare myself into a stall if I keep scratching at it. I know breakdowns happen. I know some are short-lived, requiring only hydration and rest to fix, but there's one that I fear, one that is not out of consideration as a possible cause because it's early warning symptoms can be confused with the usual pain and discomfort of a long-distance run. As I can remember nothing before waking, how would I know if I experienced above average fatigue, shortness of breath, and weakness in my leg muscles? I don't want to think about it. So terrified am I of what comes with this, my mind only accepts the acronym AKI, but its official name is Acute Kidney Infection. I've seen my peers, capable and experienced runners, go down with AKI during past events. They hit the ground like a sack of potatoes and stay down. I've assisted in their rescue. I'm aware of the consequences. Neither the breakdown nor the rescue is easy, and every part potentially deadly. I continually worry about my risks of becoming a victim to this, thus measures of avoidance and awareness of AKI are embedded into my contingencies. Then, just to make sure, I double up by being super-vigilant of my fluid and salt intake. Overkill, without a doubt, so if by chance my downfall has been AKI, and oh my God I hope it's not, I'll not only suffer the long-term effects of damaged kidneys but I'll also need to admit to the multiple failures of each of my over-indulged avoidance plans. It's my weak spot. And, yet, as fearful as this threat might be, and my desire to rule it out, if I am seriously attempting to find solutions, I can't let myself off the hook.

It's too easy to persuade myself that I or any other athlete might over-look warning signs of AKI. This sport is about endurance. Struggling with a sore body, cramping muscles and pain is the normal burden an athlete carries through a long run. In coping with these, we long-distance runners fight a continuous battle to maintain a fine line between endurance and risk to health. We put ourselves through an endless series of questioning, asking ourselves if what we are feeling should be ignored because pushing a little more will ensure success, or is it time to accept the body has reached its limits. This questioning and responding becomes natural and invisible, and because we need to trust our instincts, we rarely question our choices. But for me, as I face my life-or-death situation, should I be making a call based on instinct by admitting the probability I have missed the clues? Should I demand myself to bypass any desire to identify what has occurred and adopt the far more practical option of accepting one important fact: the seriousness of my situation? I feel a deathly weight fall on me. I must concede no good can come from nam-ing the cause, because reality is no-one knows where I am, and no help is coming. There will be no rescue. And I haven't moved a centimetre. I'm still face-down. My biggest error so far is that I've wasted precious time debating with myself.

Briefly – if I'm truthful to myself – and even I can see I'm wafting away from realities – I don't have enough information to be certain of anything, therefore I have nothing to use to motivate myself. That's the first problem of not remembering. There's no certainty.

The second problem is I've no clues to show the cause of my amnesia. There must be a reason. Forgetting is not usual.

I need to slow my mind and work to gain control of the situation.

Take a deep breath. Hold. Now release it slowly. Calm yourself. Go through what you've learnt since becoming aware you're in deep trouble.

I woke suddenly and I'm face down.

And yet I don't remember going to sleep.

With the waking came the instinctive response of opening my eyes. I remember this because that's the moment I discover my left eye can see nothing. It won't open. Only my right eye can provide me any information through sight, and that's only whatever it can see close-up and short-range. This makes undeniable my abnormal state of landing. Being face-first in the soil gives me another fact. I was not in control at the time of my fall. Ergo, an accident, as already determined.

None of this is jogging my memory. I'm stalled.

One-eye sightedness isn't helping me, either. If my right eye could see the sky or the wider landscape, I might assess how far along the trail I've come, because part of my planning means I've calculated approximate optimum locations for various times of each day. From my right eye's position close to the ground, it sees only granulated orange sand, a highway of ants scurrying around stunted stick-like vegetation and small round stones the size of a kid's marble. The ants aren't troubled by a human face planted in their territory, so this tells me I've probably been in this nose-first position for enough time for them to find my presence non-threatening. If that's so, I need to consider what likely disaster would cause me to fall asleep for many hours or, more likely given my dramatic landing position, what would bring about me being knocked unconscious.

Okay, let's say I was running and something happened that caused me to fall and be out of the world asleep or unconscious for many hours – what use is this information? There's nothing to tell me what that something might have been.

My ability to recognise the sticks as desert grass and the balls as clay gravel gives me some reassurance. It's with confidence I can claim they are both common to the inland desert area through which the course runs, some part of which I was scheduled to reach at the end of my first day. Together, they tell me that at least I met one goal, but the desert run is vast and the place where my efforts were dramatically cut short could be anywhere within it.

As small a glimmer as this is, I'm clutching on to it, and taking it as a positive step forward.

Back to my assessments. My left cheek is stinging. I've an urge to run my fingers over it to check the extent of the injury. That's when I register my hands aren't free. They're trapped underneath my body. My first step should have been to try to release my arms. I need them to help me in other ways, such as restore me to an upright position. This is something I haven't done yet, though obviously I should have already done so, so now's the time. My mind says this should only require some perseverance and energy. My body does not agree. It disobeys my mind's order to move by remaining in its compromised position, huddled into the soil. Apart from my cheek, I feel no stand-out pain beyond what I might expect after a fall. I register a little stinging or burning here and there, not dissimilar to how my cheek feels. I distrust this. The abnormality of my fall hints I've damaged myself more than I have so far identified. To not register pain might mean I'm suffering from shock. If that's the case, it would explain my lack of recall, my body's unwillingness to move, and my general vagueness.

I'm falling back on what I consider my most valued asset, which is the wealth of knowledge and experience I have accumulated over fifty years. Misfortunes and missteps can't be fully covered in any contingency plan, but this stored knowledge may find something that stands out for me to work with if only I can push aside my demons, like blaming myself or allowing my fears that perhaps the crusaders for my retirement have a valid point.

I definitely need a checklist. What might I have injured? Does the diminished pain mean I've done no serious damage, or am I in shock? Or, please no, don't let it be that I'm partially paralysed.

Come on now, what's the first rule of my contingency plan? Stay calm, be realistic, and concentrate.

Okay, let's have it. One, my odd landing does lean heavily towards this being an accident, as I assessed when I awoke. However, I can't completely rule out something more sinister, such as one form of breakdown or the like.

My only dependable information relies heavily on the vision of the local world I'm seeing through my right eye. As I've already figured, by recognising the grass and orange sand, I'm in the desert sector of the run, thus I feel safe to guess this incident happened toward the end of the first day. However, creating doubt about how long I've been asleep or unconscious – whether one night or two – is the resident insects' obvious familiarity. The latter is a possibility that makes me anxious.

Back to the potential causes for my fall. Gravel suggests one probability, as its risk to runners is well known. One awkward footfall, and before I would have had time to remind myself to take care, I'd be on the ground. I have known this throughout my running career, so if I slipped, what caused me to be less observant?

Except for the faint possibility of slipping in the gravel, there's nothing from which I can create a story to explain the 'why' except perhaps dehydration and energy depletion – and if this is the cause, it can only come through a failure on my part to follow my own protocols. But countering this is my observation, reliable or not, that I am comparatively mentally aware. Depletions would mean I would be less so.

If I knew what came before the crash, I'd be better able to assess.

Let me shut my one good eye and think back. One million and one contemplations and remembrances are flashing by. If one person is estimated to have 60,000 thoughts in a day, then mine must be rapidly catching up on any I missed when I was sleeping. Can I snatch out of the crowd one or two that might help me salvage my situation? Like a flip book phi phenomenon, where images flash by as the pages of a book are flicked, I can picture myself running along familiar routes, bordered by landmarks I've passed regularly over the years. Beyond the images, I can feel my thighs itch, an affliction for many runners as it is for me, and vibrations running up my legs as my feet pound, working like they should in a rhythm, up and down. I note that on each side of my body, my bent arms are swinging in time with the beat of my runners. Memory? Maybe, or maybe not. This should happen on a run, so am I re-visualising the actual running or recalling embedded habits? The only definite in this picture is that when I am competing, this must happen for efficiency, and in my present state the rest must be conjecture.

I'm hanging any interpretations on one half-solid but instinctive starting point, which is that I'm on the second day out. Although I can't remember, I know from 'The Plan' the first day starts early and leads from the coast to the inland. By nightfall, I should have been some way into the desert area. I'm certain I can remember this but, honestly, can I be sure of my recall? I've run this part of the trail many times. It's familiar. Could my imagination be replaying previous runs, not yesterday's? Or ... oh God, no. Please let it be that the start has been yesterday, that I've only slept through one night. I can't bear the notion I've lost a whole day and a night longer than I've assumed because if that is the truth, the seriousness of this accident would need to be weighed as much higher. That's terrifying.

Let's say it was yesterday. Let me again close my one good eye and indulge myself by expelling from my mind the frightening possibility and conse-quences that, first, my recollections are of another run on some other day. Or, second, I have been 'out of it' for two nights and one whole day. Let it come. I'm stepping out and moving comfortably forward, well into my rhythm, one foot down followed by the other. What a relief that my recall shows the fluidity of my movement. That's me, running in a style I aim to. I measure the passing of time by recalling fleeting images of familiar landmarks as they appear and disappear, and as I remember seeing the trekking of the sun to its peak and then its fading into evening. I've a strong memory of when my eyes are focused on the horizon and, through the deepening blue of approaching night, the sun drops into the earth, with no hills or ranges to shorten the journey. If this is a reliable memory, it confirms I was still running at dusk on the first day. I'm sticking to this and praying I'm right.

When I tell myself my analysis relies on the belief that anything unexpected would stand out, it's because I train myself to recognise those moments and act on them, with the surety that ignoring them could be fatal. I couldn't, wouldn't, forget. Yet, trying to go back in time doesn't feel solid, and the only positive I can take from this attempt is that at least I've enough wherewithal to recognise my befuddlement. If I think about it, I can understand why I'm confident I'll recognise an unnatural happening. It's because in long-distance running the actual and the habitual blend. We long-distance runners train ourselves to run on automatic. These events cover hundreds of kilometres. Fatigue is a certainty. To fool our bodies, we break the course into sections and focus on each one, pushing thoughts of the next one and the one after that into the background. How we approach each area is pre-determined, scientifically ordered and defined to achieve ideal performance over the whole course. Certain phases that cover relatively easy terrain might be marked for pace, and more rugged ones, or those that come at a particular time of day, might suggest restraint to conserve energy. Habits are set for each pattern of running. Our brain acts as our body's autopilot, tracking breathing, ensuring continuous movement, and being ready to alert us to any needs, such as toilet breaks, or hydration stops. To break the monotony and free our minds so they can concentrate on their responsibilities, we let our mind have free-range, much like drivers do when travelling long distances. Mine is often to prepare a shopping list, which I promptly forget. Has that detachment caused me to forget the actual or to stop being observant? If that's so, then my breakdown may be emotional, a case of mental exhaustion, though this has never happened before, never, not even in my training days.

I'm frightened.

Stop speculating, woman. Remember: life or death, here. Rationality is required, not rambling thoughts.

By sticking to my belief something out of the ordinary would stand out, I can convince myself I would have remembered if my brain had shouted that I needed to rest, had rolled an ankle, or there was a drop in my blood sugar levels likely to cause me to faint, and then I would have acted by choosing a safe location beside the trail to rest. Yet the truth is I'm lying to myself, and the extent of my delusion is impossible to measure, except to admit that in the seconds after first opening my eyes, I felt fear. That's not me. I am a 'see-the-need-and-act' person, not someone who usually panics. Feeling fear is what I've been pushing to the back of my awareness.

When my right eye opened and registered the abnormality of the situation, it noticed – and this is what I've been pushing to the back of my mind – that the little critters, whose private space I'd intruded, were illuminated by a flood of soft white. This is when my accumulated knowledge of extreme running kicked in. My instincts told me I'd awoken early in the morning before the full colour of the rising sun had bloomed. My experience reminded me that here, in this northerly desert, the day's dawning is followed by the sun's full vengeance as it rises higher and higher. I knew that unless I moved quickly, I would find my present awkward but not uncomfortable ground-level sleeping accommodation, turn into one I wouldn't want to be in. My baffled, overactive imagination, not able to pull together what I could see with what I instinctively knew, weirdly painted in my imagination such a future outcome as something not dissimilar to falling asleep on the bottom rack of my overworked oven on Christmas Day. Right away, probably because my fear had silenced my logical thought, I had pushed that terrible prediction into some corner of my mind when, instead, it should have driven me to take urgent action.

For some inexplicable reason at the time of waking, my responses were delayed, maybe because I had found myself unable to move, or had instinctively recognised I lacked sufficient energy – or maybe I was uncharacteristically scared of what I might uncover. If it's any of those, all I'm doing is adding to the negatives by being in denial. Now, as I come out of the fog of shock, I've no choice but to concede what a deep well of trouble I'm in and, yet, despite my full awareness, I'm still unable to focus. It's like I'm drunk. My mind is wandering. I could be delirious. That's not out of the sphere of possibilities. I can't see the sky, only soil and ants, but I'm imagining how I might look to a desert hawk plunging and rising, up there in the deep blue sky. Not its usual prey, but a beige bump, bum in air and nose buried, a sight enough to make a hawk curious. Imagining myself as the hawk, this creature I see on the ground is searching for water, as any sensible animal would do out here. As I should do with some urgency. I should shift my body as well as I can, and be looking for my canteen, which should still be attached to my backpack. I need free arms to test if it's still there.

Trying to move my legs and arms and turning myself over is how I will locate my canteen. Push, push hard, damn it. Well, there's no avoiding reality now. Every part of my body is in protest; in my left shoulder I sense sparks of nerve pain, my arms are cramping, and my legs scream to be moved. I know these spasms. A runner's life is never without some body pain. It makes sense my shoulder will rebel, as it would have felt the full impact of my landing. As if suddenly attuned, or more likely, the shock has worn off, severe pain shoots down my leg from my back. It feels serious.

I must ignore the hurt. If I'm to survive, I need to disentangle myself, measure what parts of my body will probably cause problems so I can deal with them, and my most important goal is to find that canteen.

Finally, I'm on the flat of my back, arms spread-eagle and legs not entirely straight. I barely remember the effort. I must have passed out. The sun's heat has gone up. I still need to test my body and find water.

I can feel myself slipping back into sleep despite the warnings blaring in my brain.

2

I'm still on the ground, energy depleted. I can barely remember turning over. I take this to mean that, once again, I've been out of this world for a while. It's likely I haven't increased my fluid level, as my water canteen isn't in my hand and that means I didn't find it. No water means I'm truly in big trouble. To add to my dehydration, now, I'm pretty sure I can't move. The main change is I'm no longer face-down.

As I'm now face-up, I'm exposed, open, and ready to absorb every one of the sun's glorious but deadly rays. The only thing left for me to do is wait to die.

Strangely, there's a sense of acceptance washing over me. This is how it is. Regret will do me no good. It's too late. I surprise myself by facing my imminent death calmly. There's no disputing my ongoing determination to compete in ultra-runs has put me in a situation, and now I've arrived at this result where I'm facing this solitary departure from this life, I ask myself if, given the opportunity, would I have changed my life choices? For example, would I have chosen another sport, one with less obvious risks? I can't offer the excuse of ignorance. Every ultra-athlete is aware of the risks, and yet to engage in this sport requires a balance between awareness and confidence in your own abilities and knowledge. Otherwise, this is not the sport for you. If we ultra-runners let the fear of the risks get into our heads, we'd never take part.

Do I blame myself? Despite my earlier self-inquisition, no, I don't.

So, probably the answer to regretting my choice of sport is, 'No.' This sport, gruelling as it may seem, feels natural. I feel whole when I'm running. While I never expected an end like this one, this is how it is. Nothing I can do to change it. So be it.

The irony is by ending in this way I'm gifting all those naysayers the opportunity to offer their great advice in hindsight, such as 'She was warned.'

Annoyingly, I won't have the chance to respond, but if by some miracle I could, what I'd say would be, 'I could accidentally find a solitary death as close as in my own home by slipping in my bath.'

As I have nothing else to do but wait and think, that's what I'll do. As my last hurrah, and while I'm still able – and that's questionable even now, because everything is fuzzy and confusing, as dehydration sets in – I'll indulge myself by reviewing my perceptions about my obsession with ultra-sport.

Soon after my seventeenth birthday I became involved. That was when my father broke his own strict rule about the roles of women in society to grant me permission to go along with my brother Graeme on each Saturday to athletic training. My little brother Grae. Who I loved very much. Grae had been privately passing on what he'd learnt in the two years before I joined him, when 'lady athletes' were taboo, so I was ripe and ready. Though we shared a love of running, soon I discovered we did not share the same physical and intellectual attributes. Grae was like a rocket, with the ability to compress energy and then spend it in a sudden burst to achieve the shortest time to the finishing line. He was a sprinter. My assets were patience and endurance. People love the drama and quick highs of a sprint, with successes measured only in fractions of a second. As a sprinter, Grae had adopted the persona of a rockstar. I'm certain distance or ultra-athletics are not viewed similarly. I'd hazard a guess long-distance running is almost a mystery to anyone outside the sport. Why, people might ask, would any sane person want to put themselves through so much pain and agony? Anyone wanting to be involved in this sport must be nuts. Yet, once, in a historic past, distance running was an essential skill for travel or to warn a distant neighbour of danger, and a skill also required in the search for shelter and the daily scavenging for food.

Grae was one who could never understand the mind-set required to be a long-distance runner, nor the demand required by the sport. His view of the sport was probably based on his view of me. He saw me as obsessed and driven, and to succeed, I needed to be almost punishing myself. He was gifted, so he saw sprinting as a natural occurrence. He trained, took part, but for him events came and went. That was it. He saw how I needed to invest so heavily to prepare, engaging in a complex, all-encompassing pre-event preparation such as the perpetual measuring of food intake and waste evacuation, part of a never-ending battle to manage a body that must cope with intense duress before, during and after each outing, and couldn't understand why I would want to ask that of myself. These rituals and disciplines, coupled with aerobic and mental demands, were beyond his understanding.

There are many varieties of long-distance or ultra-athletics, including marathons and the ultra-cross-country style I love. I had often tried to explain to Grae that all varieties, whether casual or invested, required the same effort. You can't go out there and hope to survive without the prep. And just as there are many versions, there are also a wide variety of dedicated spectators, who I believe are held captive by the evidence of effort and perseverance of athletes, winners or not. Ultra-sport is rarely a competition between several athletes, but an athlete's individual battle between specific environmental challenges or circumstances, and their own body. At the core, it's one athlete challenging her own mind and body within set parameters.

All forms are addictive. Once the bug enters the bloodstream, there's no going back. The body hungers for the challenge. The mind cries out for the sanctuary of solitude that stretches over the hours (or days) of the course. Hours are devoured internalising, by continuously engaging in a conversation between the collected pragmatic acceptance of a sport's demands and the ability to tone out the urgency of the pain signals from various parts of the body. Which need is par for the course, and which genuinely demands immediate attention? This continuous decision-making is centred on the goal of not giving in needlessly. Tolerating more pain might be all that's required to succeed. Endurance. Persistence. Control. Awareness.

I'm convinced this philosophy has made me strong beyond my sport even if engaging in this sport means I will die here on the track as I concede I can see no possibility of being saved.

3

The earth tells me someone is—or several someones are—coming toward me. I can tell by their footfall he, she or they are drawing nearer. I assume these are rescuers sent by the event organisers. A miracle.

But how embarrassing.

I have spent years running long-distance and have never been in this situation. My pride is burning more than any muscle, tendon or joint.

That's their job, these rescuers. To do the rescuing. And hopefully not to make a judgment. And please, may they be kind and considerate. Can they be reminded extreme sports often include unexpected or unplanned incidents?

Can I make one last effort and sit up? That might make me feel less humiliated.

The gravel grunts, though the sound tells me they're still some distance away. I imagine their heavy boots, fluoros, and eyes scanning the ground between tufts of desert grass and boulders. As if me, an alien in this landscape, would not be visible among the low vegetation. But maybe not. I should be grateful, not dismissive. It sounds like a considerable number, so it's more likely the emergency squad. Oh, damn them for being a prolific group. One or two would have been fine by me, and darn less embarrassing. Don't be dismissive, young lady. Remember: no rescuer could well be fatal; embarrassment is never so. The voices are indistinct, but I can tell it's still at the conversational level, probably chatting about the footy or the heat or what they will do when they complete today's task. That means they haven't seen me yet. Do I call out?

There's a change of pace. A couple of them are quickening their steps. Well, that's it. I hope they understand how a proficient sportsperson might feel when she needs to be rescued.

Is that her? Is she naked?

For God's sake. Is that going to be the headline? My last shred of pride will be flushed down the toilet. 'Rescuers report their success. Aged woman. Found naked. In the bush.'

Nah. Singlet and shorts, mate. Athlete.

I was wrong. It wasn't the event organisers who sent them out. Otherwise, they would know they were looking for an athlete. Someone else raised the alarm. But who?

An athlete? At her age? Oh, look. She's moving. That means she's alive.

Now, we are discriminating, are we? Yelling back in protest isn't in my best interest. I'd be prematurely declaring myself a lunatic. But my need to shout is strong. 'So? What the … mate?' And how I wish the gurgle of a laughter that trailed after he declared 'she's alive' might catch in the throat of this so-called liberator and choke him. Don't they train them these days to watch their p's and q's? You'd think so, in this time of PC-everything.

Are you sure she's an athlete? Can you think of the names of athletes who would run out here? It's dangerous. And getting herself into this situation means she makes my point for me. Look at her. You know she might have dementia and merely think she's an athlete. Got out of the Aged Care Home and ended up here. It's sounds unbelievable, mate, but I've heard that once they decide on something, there's no stopping them. Super-powered in their determination, these oldies.

Shut up, Chris. She's an athlete. Look, a number on a bib. You know? Like Shirley Strickland.

Nah, mate. I know about Strickland. She's a sprinter. You wouldn't sprint out here.

Yeah, well, I'm no expert. I'm sure she could tell you. Just glad we found her. Oh, look, she's turned her head. She's awake. Mam, Mam. Are you Missus Corass? Wilhemena? He told us we could call you Wilhemena.

I'll nod my head. It's time to be gracious despite my shame. They can call me Wilhemena. Only people I trust get to call me Billy. What competent saviours these are. Not. I'm drawing on sarcasm again, to hit back. It's a useful tool when I need to vent my frustration, and they're making me angry with their assumptions. The only valid one they have made is that I am alive, and that's obvious. I didn't plan this outcome. Can't they find the word 'accident' in their dictionary rather than attach all those negative possibilities? And what has age got to do with this? It's about ability and experience. You two idiots know squat about me. I have a solid urge to stare down these two. Still, it's about survival and finding the proper timing for any challenge, so I'll keep it locked inside. For now, at least.

Did they say 'he' told them to call me Wilhemena? Who is the 'he'?

4

Thinking about surviving here, in the desert, brings me to think about other ways I have been drawn to thoughts of surviving at other times. I used the word survival when questioned about why I left a career in which I was excelling, at a time I'd reached a distinctive level (even though that was likely to be about as high as I could aspire without a full-on battle with my male counterparts).

People who know me say they don't understand why I chose to retire when I did, but it's not about understanding. It's about denial. Theirs, and probably of most of us. Everyone knows the truth. We all know, deep inside us that at some point we each will face the decision: do I hang on or is it time? When the moment comes to decide on retiring or staying on, the spotlight falls on the whatever dismal future we may picture for ourselves once we enter the 'ageing phase.' Only the minority approach this with gusto. The rest of us all fear that future, knowing that death is the only thing that can save us from it, and none of us are looking forward to that option.

This is how I see what happens in adult life. We all need money to survive; after all, we live in a consumer-driven, capitalistic – not socialistic – society. As employed individuals, we need adequate payment to compensate for the big chunk of our 24-hour day that being employed gobbles up. If we are smart with our decisions or lucky, we get to do a job we enjoy, or one that makes us feel that, as we earn our living, we also contribute to society, if only in a small way, thus our employment provides us an opportunity to feel of value. But most of us aren't so blessed. Regardless, the job usually takes over, and eventually work-life balance barely exists. In some ways it feels like we live to work and get paid, rather than its original purpose, to live we need to be paid for work. Why the workload can't be spread more thinly, I don't know. The old excuse was that some individuals have more skills than others which equates to skills being unequally shared, thus the ability to carry out specialised roles can be done only by a few individuals. In my way of thinking, if more are given an opportunity to learn more skills, we could share the load, and this would mean a better life/work balance for more of us. Hey, but that's just me waffling, and this has only a small influence on my use of the word survival.

When I made my decision to survive, several factors collided. I had passed the sixty-year mark in my life, a close friend several years younger than me had died suddenly despite seeming fit and healthy, and the company I worked for chose to adopt a cost-down exercise and indiscriminately fired people without notice, individuals who for years had been excellent, contributing employees. My elevated position meant I had the tough job of delivering the horrible, life-changing news to long-standing friends and peers. I was angry. The cost-down policy nullified the 'we value our people' slogan plastered everywhere in our office and spouted at every meeting and conversation between management and employees. This destructive process and my role within it began to kill me slowly from the inside out.

Then I had an epiphany. Realistically, how many more years were ahead for me? By continuing to work, am I wasting the inevitably short but precious future in which I would or could remain fit and energetic? Time, a commodity that cannot be recovered, was being devoured unnecessarily by a career going nowhere and no longer serving its original purpose, and, frankly, was getting me down. Sixty-something is the new forty-something, I declared, and I'd passed it, so I chose survival.

5

The rescuers are hovering, and I'm trying not to let my face reveal that pain is grabbing me again. It's probably my own fault. Allowing myself to become angry has probably caused my muscles to tense. Or equally likely, the almost nude singlet these two find so shocking did not provide enough protection. I have probably lacerated or bruised my whole left side and the little amount of movement I've engaged in is aggravating the wounds.

Why am I becoming so uptight? I do know the reason but the anger I'm feeling fits me snuggly right at this moment. My ears, attuned as they are, hear every word they say as being sung to the same tune as I've been listening to since my late teens, when I first became involved in long-distance running. In my mind I bitterly recreate their assumptions. 'No wonder this old woman is in trouble. Extreme running is a man's sport.' The men I ran with in the early days, made sure a woman knew this. For them, female inferiority demands exclusion. Same old arguments, same old statements, same old shoot-down of women. These guys aren't saying that exactly, but they've grown up absorbing the same paternal conventions and I don't fit into what seems normal in their view of the world. Plus, I have now moved into the firing line for being in a particular section of the female population. An ageing woman, with a body whose external appearance loudly announces she has entered 'that phase' of life. Someone they can write off as no longer having a purpose, no longer able to add value to society. I'd hoped the invisibility of ageing would allow me a passage to avoid that, but apparently not. I'm invisible unless I'm forcing my presence into zones that are perceived as out of my purview.

No surprise these idiots can't think of any women who are long-distance runners. No one talks about female athletes. Their achievements go almost unrecorded. But they should know them. These athletes are legendary. They stepped out of their expected roles in life and challenged people who said that what they wanted to do wasn't available to them, like the modern-day mothers who fight their way into professional sports previously designated to men. And they have succeeded and continue to do so, so many of them, despite their private disadvantages. What about runners like Deb DeWilliams. Or Sue Hobson? Or even Adrienne Beames? You idiots. Haven't you heard about Beames' controversies? They – men – branded Beames a cheat. A cheat! No thought or suggestion given to the argument around Beames except it was more about not fitting men's rules. Or did these guys miss the news about Turia Pitt? Morons. Pitt hit the headlines for all the wrong reasons. If they'd read further into the articles they would have noticed the word 'running' appeared often. Poor, poor woman. But like all powerful women, she's risen above it all.

Anyway, the rest of this mob is here now. I can only hope this means I'm in safe, if inconsiderate, hands. Let them think I'm dumb. Let them see me as a helpless old woman (helpless old and naked woman), so long as I can get out of here, take some time to recover, and then get back into it again, ready for the next competition.

Lap it up, girl. Salve your wound. Take this information into your next run. Plan better. And aim to learn from the experience so you can do better next try. Let it go.

> One foot down. Lift the other. One
> foot down. Lift the other. One foot
> down. Lift. Forget the pain. Forget
> the distance. See the bush. Run to the
> bush. See the rise. Run to the rise.

Wilhemena, Sam's the name, Mam, and this is Chris. You had us a little worried there, Mam. But we've got you now. You are safe. Don't move. Not yet. Are you cold? Here, let me wrap this around you.

Sam tucks his silver blanket around me like I'm a baby. I have had no one do that for me since, well, since, oh, never, as my mother wasn't one of those tuck-you-into-bed types of people, nor my dad. In our home, you learnt early to take care of yourself. And Mitch, my ex, would never have thought that as part of his husbandly duties, even if I was ill.

Let me look into the eyes of these idiots and examine the people upon whose care I am dependent. First in view is a broad forehead softened by a knot of untamed hair hanging over it. Stone-coloured eyes surrounded by wrinkles. This is Sam, I'm guessing. An ordinary face to go with an everyday name like Sam. His words are his only grace. They help make him sound like he might be the kinder of the two, if only marginally, so I'll reward him with a smile. Let's hope it looks like a smile and not a grimace when it reaches my mouth. Otherwise, they'll be convinced they are right about me. But Chris, where's he? Someone should tell that Chris guy he's in the wrong profession. Shouldn't let idiots out on rescue missions, or if they are that short of staff, they should first educate them about keeping their opinions to themselves. Even if I am senile, he should be a little more benevolent.

Is this Chris? Oh, for God's sake, a smile that stretches out dimples. A flippant joker, I'll bet. But a charmer all the same, a charmer who usually puts his foot in that broad, white-toothed smile. No brain. I have been conned by charmers all my life. I hope this Chris is so biased he sees only the blinking eyes of a stupid old woman, not all my pent-up resentment and the anger behind the retinas.

Hi there, honey. I'm Chris. Good to see you are awake. Let us get this brace on your neck, and then we can see about a drink. You might be a little thirsty.

That'd be a fair assumption, and needed no smarts to conclude that, eh, Chris? I won't say those words. It's such an obvious need I don't wish to put Chris off. My tongue is telling me my lips are scaly. Dry. Tight. Like the thorny devil lizard, I ran past yesterday. Was it yesterday? So, it's no intelligent guess by Chris. There's no doubt I need fluids, as I couldn't locate the canteen earlier, probably still underneath me, so don't bite the hand that feeds or the one that lifts the mug and straw closer to your mouth, young lady. This is what Chris is doing. His other is supporting the back of my head. Or should that be, don't let your lips curdle any offered sustenance? My confused thoughts are telling me loud and clear how seriously I need that water. I can't deny I am rambling.

Sam's silver blanket is doing its job. I'm warm now; I've stopped shivering. I'm floating, half awake, dreaming, but that's only my body. My mind is racing; I can't keep up with it. One minute, I'm back home going through my pre-event preparation, and the next, I'm back with my ant friends. I need to get a hold of myself. Meditate, breathe in, hold, release; in, hold, release.

Chris has lifted me almost, but not quite, into a sitting position. 'To get some more water in,' he says. Now, I can see the rest of the crew. Have I been perceived as so frail, or less likely, a sufficiently important being, to justify this number? And where's the boss? Hallelujah. It's a woman. Doing what women do best: quietly and calmly managing. No fuss. There's hope for this world. I can let go now.

Again, I wake suddenly, unable to remember falling asleep. There are gaps in my memory. Did I drift off again? Now, there's a vehicle, I'm guessing, less than 100 metres away. I must have been coming close to the road when I fell. That's more embarrassing than having an accident in the middle of nowhere. I'm not sure why it feels so, but it does. Another lot of hi-vis uniforms are coming across the red soil. They are carrying a stretcher. Chris and Sam offer comforting words, but I can't make sense of them. I am being shifted over onto the stretcher by several hands. Chris and Sam seem to have the authority to continue their roles as rescuers, as they take the lead to carry me across to the vehicle.

I close my eyes, then open them. Above me, contrasting the blue sky, brown and black feathers dip and dive, the desert hawk is once again casting judgment over this stupid woman who has made a mistake and now is suffering in more ways than physically. I'm dying here. Not mortally dying, but spiritually. I'm mortified. If I were my younger self, I would be bolstered by the knowledge that accidents happen, and afterwards, when you have healed, you get up and bounce back. That's what's missing here, the surety of a future. All those doubts about my age with which others sandblast me at every opportunity are being enlarged and expanded by my present situation. It's so unfair to use my external appearance to label me as incapable, especially when I have displayed no signs their concerns are valid. Well, not until this accident, which could have happened at any age. I do privately admit I won't be able to hold back my inevitable decline for ever.

On that topic, I have a personal theory, something I never broadcast because I know without doubt it'll be challenged no matter how strong my stance. My sport is helping me stave off that moment, keeping my body fit, my mind agile, and my attitude open to changing situations.

I disagree with the premise of my so-called counsellors and carers, but I continue to hear gruesome stories from them of those who ignored the signs of ageing and ended up in the Emergency Department, which led to residential care because 'old bones don't mend.' As eagerly as I try to bury the predictions, I admit if I let myself think too much, I'll frighten myself. Who wouldn't? Facing head-on what is awaiting in the 'last phase' is terrifying, even if logic says it's everyone's future. Like most of us, I'm not ready for it. I prefer to bury the absolute knowledge there are no guarantees in life, except that there's a beginning and an end, and depending on your beliefs, only God or Fate can prediction the duration.

I feel the diesel's start-up vibration and the vehicle rocking as more people than Chris and Sam clamber in and take up the side benches. Not your regular ambulance, it would seem. We rock and roll as the vehicle juggernauts over the rough terrain. I must have drifted off again. I'm awake but can remember no transition from bumpy to smooth, though there has been a change. I sense, more guess, we are now onto the sealed semi-rural roads that lead toward the outer suburbs. This suggests we must be close to the city. The tyres are humming rather than thumping. I can hear other vehicles passing. I have travelled this route many times. I can picture the wide-apart homes of the outer suburbs. I grab an estimate out of my befuddled mind, convincing myself my thoughts are more capable than they probably are, and decide we still have an hour or maybe longer to travel, regardless of which hospital they have chosen for my destination. Thinking about hospitals makes me panic. I have only been in a hospital once in my life, and that was to give birth to Brandon. This is a downward step that has sneaked up on me. There's a knot in my gut.

More stops now, and I'm guessing these are for traffic lights, then I'm startled by the roar of a motorbike, which I assume is impatient to be past us. We aren't travelling fast. My sarcasm generates a flippant explanation. This is what I'm good at doing: creating an internal protest at the status quo. Maybe the driver is being careful with the fragile cargo of an old and naked woman. Even that attempt at rebellion cannot lift me. Blasted motorbikes. One of the standout trials of my life is sharing the road with them. Those bike riders have no respect. They sit back on their charges and take everyone on. No wonder so many meet their deaths on the roads. The rules are there only for other drivers, not bikers.

Our vehicle is slowing and taking corners more carefully. My companions must know we are nearly there, as there are changes to their chatter and more laughter. I hope I'm not the subject, but I can't maintain the rage, even if I am. I am drifting again, fighting an urge to educate this lot on my favourite topic. Yes, yes, yes. Did you know about Roberta (Bobbi) Gibbs? 1966. Women could not register, but Gibbs competes as a non-registered runner and becomes the first woman to finish the Boston Marathon top third ahead of about 375 men. Yes. Go, girl! A year later, Kathrine Switzer registered to run using only her initials because officials still barred women athletes from competing. Race officials tried to tear her number from her back. Not only should women see themselves as equal to men, but they also require more passion to get into a race.

Did I say those words loud enough for my companions to hear? Will they think I'm losing my mind? No one is looking alarmed. Sam is on his mobile. From the snatches of words, I figure he must be speaking with Brandon, my son. Was Brandon the 'he' who sent them out there? Why would he be following up on my lateness? He never shows interest in my running except to lecture me on the risks, always has, and now more so, because 'Mum, you're old and should take more care.'

Sure, sure, Mr Corass.

Mr Corass. That's my little boy, now a fully grown man. The love of my life.

Yeah, yeah, mate. Nah. She's okay. We are taking her to the hospital for a check-up, and you can catch up with her there. Nah, mate. Now, don't go getting yourself all uptight. She's good. Just one of those things. They're accidents. Not intentional. Some fluid, some rest, and she will be as good as.

6

Mitch, my ex-husband, left me when Brandon was four. That's why I possessively declare Brandon as 'my' son. He was mine to raise, mine to spoil, and mine into whom I could pour my heart. Not that Mitch didn't care for Brandon. The reason was not dissimilar to why he didn't choose to be married to me anymore. He didn't want to tackle me, or anyone else, on any subject, so it may have been easier for him to walk away from Brandon, too, to avoid any chance of conflict.

About our marriage, if I wasted my time and analysed why it failed, I might suggest Mitch saw me as too competitive. I put it to him once, questioning if that was so, but he said he didn't mind, just that he didn't have the energy to keep up with my ... what did he call it? 'Energetic drive'? He found interests elsewhere. And not just in the running. Mitch presented well. He was attractive, fantastic body and build, and magnetic personality. He was a man no one could dislike. That side of him hooked me, and many other women. Some women might see the sum total of his appealing attributes as a measure of a 'good man'. I did. But in marriage you see the inner man. Mitch was a good man, but despite his assets, he was an insecure one. He needed to be idolised otherwise he crumbled. I have convinced myself his mistake was choosing me. I'm probably wrong. Maybe what he saw in me was that I could carry the heavy load for him but also flatter and dote on him, mistakenly believing that's the woman I am because of how I responded to my brother, another charmer. Mitch might have seen me as someone I could never be, but it was my mistake for not realising I needed a different type of a husband, not a replica of Grae.

Knowing what I want in a husband came as hindsight. I have learnt it the hard way. Three husbands – one legal, the other two partners only, so I learned something from being married to Mitch – and finally, by the time I'd almost lost interest in male companionship or lost hope, whichever way you want to see it, I can say what I like. My perfect partner is exactly that, a partner, someone willing to share the load and not over-write his wants on mine. We all want to be seen for who we are, so this ideal man – I know it's a man – in our perfect relationship will 'see' me and I will 'see' him. He won't be devastated when his partner, me, expresses views that oppose his. We would be two individuals who love and respect each other. So much for fantasy.

As I fought my battles to include women into ultra-running, often vocally, Mitch never disapproved. But he also never came right out and said he supported me. Mitch, like Grae, was a sprinter. We met through Grae. Some- times, I'd see the male sprinters gathering after an event and they would laugh and look my way, my brother included. Those moments made me worry about Mitch's small betrayals, maybe him making light of my continuous challenge to the status quo, but I have no proof. However, if I were pressed, I would credit him for never openly standing against me as I fought my battles for equality in my sport because that's what I want to be the truth. To have him actively oppose me would be the worst betrayal, far greater than him moving on to another wife, though that shattered me immensely. He may have moved on, but I still hold a warm spot for him, though I admit it to no one, not even to his son.

7

I have been pushed and prodded, rolled and turned, placed into one machine and then another, and between each action, spent hours on a hard and narrow bed, body barely covered, and provided only the most basic privacy behind a curtain. Now this is what I call 'almost naked': my butt overly exposed by my daggy running undies and a gown that does not quite reach around the areas that require the most privacy. Each of us who share this space suffer the same ordeal. Every sigh, groan, or telephone conversation can be heard by any of us who isn't unconscious.

I have been delivered an endless string of questions, often the same ones, and my responses sometimes surprise me. Some questions seem to bring an unexpected answer from me, as if I hear them somehow differently each time, even simple ones that, generally, at other times about which I might be precise. The question, 'Have you ever...', comes with a sense of demanding answers that carry life and death importance. I have spoken to my resistant self about the benefits of being helpful so the medical staff can fill in the blanks. Still, my reasoning is being beaten down by the intensity of the mood of uncertainty within this space. Everyone is at a low ebb in their life, fearing the worst and hoping for something else. A sense of helplessness pervades despite the apparent professionalism and good intentions of those caring for us. This brings me to see myself as being perceived as a confused person. I have answered their questions as best I can, but who carries around records of what caused your parents' deaths or their age at the time? In all honesty, I usually would know these details.

From my side of this interaction, I am still waiting for answers to my many questions, or if not definite answers, a sign of where this is heading. Have I broken any part of my body? Is the damage superficial or internal? Will there be long-term health concerns? My fear is exaggerated by having such little experience, only and in and out visit to a hospital for the birth of Brandon. Apart from scrapes, grazes and bruises, an occasional respiratory illness and the usual childhood experiences, there have been no major health incidents to highlight the inner workings of my body, so until now they have remained mostly a mystery. They work okay, I do the right things, and that's it. After all this workout, someone somewhere must know the hidden secrets of my body and have recorded their findings in those written notes that have followed me. It seems inconsiderate not to share. This is simultaneously both reassuring and unsettling, being taken care of but with a hint that something might be too difficult to discuss. I am being repeatedly told, 'just sleep and relax'. I want to relax but can't let go; there have been too many interruptions. It seems late, but that notion is unsupported because, throughout this continuous activity, I have seen the same faces above hospital scrubs. It may indeed be late. If it is, these professionals have worked long shifts. If I'm tired, they must be exhausted.

Through a few curt words from one of the many impersonal people who fill this space, I learn I am being moved. Same bed, same state of undress, but now we are thundering along tight corridors, past more tired faces, and people like me, holding some part of their body and wearing expressions of worry, possibly heading to the places I have recently been, like to the X-Ray or Ultrasound departments.

Where am I going? What's been decided about me? What's happening?

Settle down, Mrs Corass. No need to fret. For the moment, you are being taken to a ward. A doctor will be along later to answer all your questions and explain. Now, just rest and don't worry yourself, please.

If I was worried before, I am more so, now. Being taken to a ward infers an extended stay, much longer than the check-up via the Emergency Department that I'd expected. What could be so severe that it requires me to be 'in the ward'? My head is whirling through the many possibilities. Did I have a heart attack? Is that the cause of the blanks in my recall? Have I broken something? Maybe it's not as dire as I imagine. Maybe the many voices I've been hearing are speaking the truth, that essentially this stay in the hospital is to ensure I get the rest I need. I'm suspicious. So far, I haven't received enough evidence to convince me.

The orderly and nurse who accompanied me seem keen to return to the ED, if I judge by the swiftness of the parking of my bed in a space already prepared for me. After our silent outward journey to the ward, they are now chatting as they jointly steer the empty bed elsewhere. It must have been sitting in the area the ED bed now fills. I'm not alone in this room. There are three other occupied beds, all filled with sleeping women. The ward nurse comes over and gives me a steely eyeball. I want answers. I open my mouth to question her, but she's not giving anything away. She shuts me up with plain words.

You need sleep, Mrs. Corass, but you might be hungry after your long day. Here are a few sandwiches. If you'd like a cup of tea, I can organise that.

I nod and breathe deeply, ready to start my interrogation, but she's not finished.

The best thing you can do is relax. Please try.

She turns and firmly grabs the curtains. I'm back in my cocoon of simulated and ineffective privacy. End of conversation. I look at the sandwiches, wondering if they are leftovers from someone else's meal, which suggests they will be less than the freshest. Still, my belly wants something in it, so I lean over and bring the film-covered plate onto my chest. It takes plucking and tearing to get into the food. I don't even worry about the filling, proving to myself that I am hungrier than I believe. Egg on one and tuna salad on another. The usual unimaginative variety. I return the plate, its crumbs and the wrinkled film to the side table as a young man, with a giant smile, pushes through the curtains carrying a cup and saucer.

I hope you have milk because that's what I have brought you, and here's some sugar if you need it. If you don't mind me saying, you look like this is precisely what the doctor ordered.

He leaves his gift on the nightstand in the space where the sandwich plate had been before he picked it up. His smile must be a permanent fixture. I manage a weak 'thank you, all good' but no smile, and then he's gone, and my personal space is once again empty except for me and the bed. I am overwhelmed with a desire to sleep, but the tea has appeal, so I struggle to sit up and reach for it. I manage a few mouthfuls before giving in and falling back on the pillow. I'm too tired to worry about the diagnosis, prognosis, or whatever else is ahead of me.

I doubt my sleep did me any good. I had weird dreams. A mixed-up memory of when I was a kid when my brother and I first became involved in running.

8

Dad was Victorian in his style of upbringing. No. That's an understatement. Dad was very much the Victorian man, meaning the son was the focus, not the first-born daughter. Grae could go to the Athletics Club. I itched to belong, too, but that wasn't considered ladylike by Dad. I had to put up with second-best, which was waiting until Grae came home and found the time to run through all he was learning about exercising for strength, the best positions for starting, and what practices should be followed to achieve the best results.

As Graeme's skills grew and his successes went up, Dad, who mainly did not involve himself in his children's activities, became interested, and eventually permitted Mum and I to attend events. There were rules. We could not be rowdy in our support. No 'Go Graeme' shouting, no jumping up when Graeme won, as he often did, and no chatting with other parents supporting their sons. We were two ladies seated quietly in the grandstand, dressed in our best, with hands folded in our laps with the only exception being the need to raise them sometimes to clap Grae's winning streaks. My dream last night was a medley of those outings and the one that accidentally gave me an entry into athletics. My dream wasn't close to the reality of the past. In it, I acted far more aggressively than I remember being at the time of the actual event, a time when I had been barely able to foresee the future my dream so confidentally offered .

The entry opportunity into athletics came about through a man Dad held in high esteem, a Mr Iannello. In the long-past real-life event now revisited in a fragmentary manner in my dreams, we are sitting high in the grandstand, waiting for my brother's event, when Mr Iannello waves to Dad, shuffles his way along the row below us, and stands to face my father with his hand extended. The courtesy handshake over, a nod to Mum and a lesser one to me, he hides his hands in his pockets and adopts an odd-looking stance where the top half of his body leans back slightly, seeming as if he instinctively chooses to maintain a certain distance from Dad to show respect.

Hello there, Bill. That boy of yours is gifted. He may be on his way to the Olympics.

Dad's face remains blank. He doesn't even nod. My father would never admit to such high hopes, despite the likelihood that opportunity might be on Dad's wish list.

Mr Iannello wastes no more words on Graeme or his successes.

This your daughter? I've got a girl about the same age. Is your girl interested in athletics?

Mr Iannello must not know Dad well, or maybe he does and is willing to ignore Dad's conservatism. Dad can barely contain himself, his face dissolving, before returning to its almost unreadable state. Dad had strong social rules, and knowing them, I'm sure his response to Mr Ianello's question would have been of shock and disbelief. 'Fancy this fellow thinking a daughter of mine would be interested in a man's sport.' Mr Iannello doesn't seem put out by Dad's lack of reply. If he noticed the clenching of Dad's jaw and the squinting of his eyes, he ignores the external signs, but as his gaze is fixed on some indefinable spot behind Dad, it's likely he is oblivious to any response from the man to whom he's addressing, as he continues his spiel, revealing his real purpose for speaking to my father, and his true focus which is his daughter.

My daughter is talented. They tell her she could be an Olympian, too, in the years ahead. The trouble is she needs to invest in training. But she's reluctant. She's one of a few females allowed to engage in Athletics.

He pauses, and this time, he holds Dad's gaze before continuing. He's at the crux of his delivery.

If your girl was involved, then they could support each other.

Of course, my father offers no response other than a penetrating stare and a weak smile, as if to say, 'Your problem mate.' No doubt this is the moment that my father, like me, recognises Mr Ianello isn't showing respect but is seeking benefits, and that possibly when his gaze had been fixed beyond Dad's face, he was imagining future glories, not considering he might need to work a little harder to persuade a conservative man like Dad to help him out.

My dream has distorted the actual events. That wasn't the exact moment that changed my life, but it was the pre-step, the seed-planting moment, the one that cracked opened the door to a later opportunity and a miraculous, never-believed-possible chance to break through Dad's prohibition. Many months later, extreme running took over my life.

9

My dream rattles me. I can only interpret it as showing I am more troubled than I will admit. Why am I remembering this incident? I never think about it. It's as if I'm torturing myself. Dreaming of 'the beginning' only presses home the reality that I may have reached 'the end.' This infers all those 'wise' voices I have been trying to ignore may have been correct. I am doomed by growing old.

There's a disturbance in the ward. My companions, who earlier seemed to be comatose, are stirring. A flurry of people is crowding the ward entrance, some distinguishable as staff by their generic green attire, and a tall, blonde suit-wearing male, intently listening to what he's being told.

Brandon.

10

Mum, Mum. Oh. My God. I'm glad they found you.

My boy has moved through the mass formed by a group of hospital staff attempting to confer with him at the entry to the ward. He pushes his way through them and strides across the ward floor toward me. I don't see the 188 cm tall, broad-shouldered man with arms extended in my direction, ready to hug me. He's still my little boy, slightly terrified and panic-stricken after a fall off his bike. The bicycle had landed in the ravine. He was injured, and yet he pushed aside concerns for himself to worry about the lost or busted push bike, probably because I had drilled him repeatedly about the expense of buying the bike and the need for him to take care of it. The man of today seems equally emotionally perturbed.

They tell me your injuries are not severe. Tough you, eh?

Does that mean I can leave?

Ah, maybe not, Mum. You need to settle your thoughts. It's only a result of dehydration or too much sun, but they want to monitor you for a little while. It'll do you good. You are always flying around doing something. At least here, they'll nail you to the bed. And don't give me that scowl. Sometimes, you need to be ordered around rather than you being the one issuing the orders.

My boy is stroking my hair and smiling into my face. I can read there's more to the situation than he's saying, and I vow to uncover it. I know from experience that pressing him for an answer right now will only dig him in deeper, a trait he inherited from me. I must discover this myself because that's the only way to get ahead of the game. I'll play 'nice' mum for a while, and he'll put that down to me not being myself.

Brandon has some small talk to share. I barely listen. He must be paying attention because he surprises me by suddenly pushing himself upward, readying himself to leave.

You need that rest, Mum. That's why I'm not staying long. I'll be back soon. Remember, Mum, rest is the key.

He kisses me on the forehead, a soft, slightly moist peck as only an offspring can achieve, loving but not overly emotional. He turns toward the ward door, waving on his way out to the staff, and disappears into the corridor. He's right about one thing. I need rest. I can feel myself slipping down into the darkness of sleep with not the slightest protest.

11

My body may have finally caught up with real-time. I have slept through the night. Breakfast is being delivered, and I'm surprised by my keenness to secure a tray. Thank goodness the former patient, who would have ordered breakfast for this bed space before being discharged, chose scrambled eggs and toast with apricot jam. I could have ordered nothing better had it been me who filled in the form the day before.

Lifting myself up and puffing my pillows, ready to dig in, I note a definite reduction in my pain. However, my body is still showing signs of stiffness. Brandon reassured me last night I have suffered little damage because of my incident. What a relief.

My appetite is sated, and an empty teacup is ready to be returned to the tray. Now, my bladder reminds me to attend to it. Feeling much better, I enthusiastically push the mobile table down to the end of the bed, heave the bedding off, and swing my legs over the side of the bed.

In a flash, the ward nurse is there, beside me. Her facial expressions are tight.

Excuse me, Mrs Corass. What's going on?

I dip my head to indicate the direction of the shared facilities in the corner of the ward and continue to lower my feet to the floor.

A minute, please. Can you wait? I need to get the commode for you.

I suppress an urge to scream, 'Just going to the toilet,' because I can see the distress I'm causing. Instead, I tell myself to relax and try not to show my thoughts, though I may have given a tiny shake of my head in her direction. The curtains are hauled around until there's barely enough space for the nurse to wheel in a disgusting chair with a hole in the middle, something possibly used on Noah's Ark. No longer can I restrain my look of disbelief. I raise my hand and point towards the bathroom, uttering 'But, but it's just there, the bathroom, just over there ...', only to have my words ignored. This woman is determined. My bladder is no longer patient, so I give in, slide off the bed, grasp one arm of this monstrous chair while roughly repelling the nurse's guiding hand on the way down. I land heavily on the seat, and madly grab the edge of my unflattering and immodest gown, pulling it up out of the way with one hand while yanking down my undies with the other. In a rush I do what I must.

Humiliation and embarrassment. My good spirits have now been dragged down into a commode.

Back in bed, I check the wrap-around for accidental wetness, given the unceremonious manner of my landing on the commode, then tuck it under me. With my chin lowered and eyes hooded, I try to banish into oblivion the confidence-destroying experience. Conflicting messages are being relayed to my brain. Brandon: 'Not too much damage, Mum.' Ward nurse: 'No, you mustn't, Mrs Corass. Can't take the risk. Commode.'

In a final, if weak, act of rebellion, I bury myself under the bedding and turn my face into the pillow, hiding in the darkness behind my tightly closed eyes. I have taken the wrong path and fallen, not accidentally as I did in the desert, but subconsciously, guided in this fall by circumstances beyond my control to an undesirable location where decisions are being made for me by others. Analysis of the cause and outcome of the fall in the desert eventually will arrive at a logical conclusion. This deviation from the designated path is different. I'm the bewildered ewe within a mob, all clambering down the race, being categorised by age, value and destination by the farmer. Open this door, and you go that way. Close this door, and there's no going back. But where am I heading? The ewe's potential fate may be the slaughterhouse; I can only see mine ending equally disastrously, though I haven't any notion of what form it will take except to say, I doubt it's likely to be anywhere near what I might choose for myself. While this imagined dire conclusion is devastating, worse is the realisation that somewhere along this short journey, I have lost my ability to stand up for myself. I've become a different me in the short space of a week or two.

My plunge into the darkness of my future is interrupted by a hand shaking my shoulder. I hear Brandon's voice. He's back, as promised.

Mum, what the hell are you doing? You are curled up like a baby in there. What's the matter? Don't you feel well?

My mouth opens to utter the words that will explain the cause of my withdrawal. Can I rely on this man's knowledge of his mother to count on his understanding of the situation and its impact on me? I wasn't even permitted to take myself to the toilet, Brandon. That's what I want to say. He doesn't wait for a response, already moving into one of his uninterruptable lectures, adult to child, son to mother, which have become increasingly frequent. On and on, he goes until I reach a point where his words become blah-blah-blah. If only he'd let me speak, even if hearing my opinion doesn't change his view. Then I might see worth in hearing what he has to say. If only.

Mum, I don't understand. You have always been so capable. You are intelligent. You must realise it's time to adjust your style of living. You can't do what you always have done. Why can't you be like others your age, settle down, and live your best life at a slower pace? Go shopping, go to lectures, or stay home and read, garden, paint, or whatever you wish. But stay in one place for more than five minutes. Take this last week as an example. You might have died out there. I know you tell me how you go about your preparations. But I don't believe it. It's like I must watch you all the time these days.

If only I may say, 'I want to be heard, so shut up, for goodness's sake.' Instead, I keep my shouting inside me.

I've no doubt my accident has frightened Brandon and that his sermons come from a place of caring. But their tone is out of tune. He's scared for me, but embedded in his rhetoric is a stereotypical view that overrides the nuances of an individual's personality and capabilities. Aside from being demeaning, it's as if, one day, something triggered him to change how he sees me. Maybe he glimpsed his own mortality, or a friend's parent died. He went from caring son to almost a dictator, as if he suddenly learned the weight of responsibility for my fragile future had landed on his shoulders. Usually, this shift in the balance of relationship between parent and offspring comes about when a parent becomes ill. Barring this recent sporting accident, we have had no major event to explain Brandon's over-concern. The intensity of his outpourings has gone up gradually over a long period, spreading across all parts of our relationship like a fungus. I want things to go back to how they have always been. The contrast between how life between us had always been and this expanding and enlarging need of his to take away my rights is soul-destroying. Throughout most of his adult life, he has lived his life independently, as I have lived mine. Perhaps I can see how he might have a right to become somewhat anxious, given the terrifying predictions of ageing we all hear constantly, but is it too much to ask for reciprocal respect? As I have complete confidence in his decision-making and choices, isn't it reasonable for me to expect him to display the same confidence in mine, or at least discuss and negotiate?

As Brandon rattles on with his lecture, I have an epiphany. I remember. I know what must be said to my son. This clarity and its urge to speak rarely happens. Where I'm articulate with others, attempting to present an argument to my son stifles my fluency, maybe because too often of late I'm dumbfounded with his constant spiel. If he would listen – but he won't. It's pointless to try and change his perspective. Besides, I usually can say to myself I'm doing it my way, so just let him get it out of his system. Unfortunately, and annoyingly, he's become noticeably more insistent. I could provide him reassurance if he would permit me to speak; I could show he's worrying needlessly. If only I could get a word in. This is especially true when the subject is my involvement in running. He doesn't believe I'm still capable; he doesn't let me explain my acute awareness of risk, how I always prepare with my safety in mind. Without a solid basis for his case, he has convinced himself of my risky behaviour and stubbornly insists my engagement in this sport must stop.

Against all odds, this time, I interrupt.

If I was so negligent, Brandon, how come you knew I needed help? Tell me that? And how were you able to pass on my chosen route to the rescue crew? Yeah. No preparation, or a flawed prep, my arse. As always, I prepared my plan scrupulously and left you with a copy, including a map of my planned route. I also left a copy with my neighbour. Are these forethoughts the action of someone no longer capable? And when help was needed, who was it that pressed the emergency button on my Personal Locator Beacon, to inform you I needed help? Or for that matter, who was it that acquired these devices in case there was a need, without which neither you nor the rescuers could have found me? The same 'incapable, ageing' person. Me. Thanks for worrying about me, my boy. I genuinely mean that. I know it comes from love, but this is not on me; this is not about insufficient planning due to my incapable brain. Don't let your concern for me – for which I am genuinely grateful and for which I love you dearly – be your measure to define me. Don't you dare suggest that this outcome resulted from failing to enact my usual diligent prep. My prep was spot on. I considered everything, including my age. This was an accident. Nothing more. Your criticism implies you see me as no longer capable, and I reject that. I'm hurt by that. Ageing, yes, but not fully dependent yet, thank you.

12

The Economic and Industry Standing Committee conducted an inquiry into the 2011 Kimberley Ultramarathon RacingThePlanet, an event in which Turia Pitt and others were badly burnt in an out-of-control fire. Aside from defining who was liable to compensate several injured competitors, the retrospective scrutiny highlighted many flaws in organisation, such as those where competitors were put at risk by shoddy or half-arsed organisational decisions. I read it and was guided by it. What I got out of it is the need for emergency communication for all endurance runners, and nothing to do with me being perceived as 'past it.'

Competitors in long-distance events come from a broad range of backgrounds with equally diverse skills so there can be vast distances between the leaders and the stragglers, and one form of protection might not suit all. Organisers often provide Personal Location Beacons or PLBs to a handful of competitors, chosen for their likely placing within the whole field. Based on recorded previous performances, three or four are given to those expected to be part of the leaders, a couple might go to those likely to run within the middle of the field, and several to the newbies likely to be the tail-enders. I'm in the 'grey' area, not a pun referencing ageing. I am a woman who's often been a leader, but now is best described as a leader of the middle. My age and gender may contribute to why I'm rarely gifted with a PLB, but I have no proof. I overcame this by hiring a set of two. One regularly hangs on the opposite side of my backpack to my water canteen.

Had I found a way to speak to Brandon rationally, rather than blurt out an emotional response, I could have shared these facts with Brandon, reassured him of my awareness of the guidelines and their influence on me to hire the PLB pair, one for him and one for me coded for a one-push emergency call from mine to his. Why is debating with my son so difficult? But how dare he dismiss my ability to comprehend.

One of the gaps in my memory centred on my attempt to roll on my back. Until today, my recall has been fragmented, but my retaliatory response to Brandon's lecture is providing a rush of memories, not only of the PLB but also of that last moment before I passed out.

I am on the ground, face-first. I'm aware of the need for action. I need water. The canteen is under me. I push my trapped arms hard into the earth and grit my teeth to overcome the pain. The weight of my body is impeding me, but I don't give in. I push and push until gravity helps my body to topple over. Every muscle and joint are screaming. I am weary and know I'm almost out of energy. As my body is flipped, I feel a whack of something hard. My canteen. I need water. In my last waking moments, ignoring the pain in my arms, I extend my hands to search for my canteen. When my fingers latch onto a likely object, hard and rectangular, I draw it closer to my eyes and see it's not my canteen but my PLB. My last recollection is my finger pressing the button.

13

My ineffectual but emotional outburst is over, the words of explanation so articulate in my head mostly remain unspoken, and now I'm spent. I flop back onto the pillow and turn my face away from my son. If I lose control of the tears building up inside me, their flow down my face will rob my words of credibility. The woman in the next bed is staring back at me. Her eyes and her mouth are open wide. I've shocked her. Oh dear. I shouted, didn't I? Very childish behaviour. But why not? I am fucking angry.

I hear Brandon's deep sigh. I hear his words, 'I'll let you rest.' Without turning back to face him, I know he has left. In my imagination, I paint him with his shoulders slumped to acknowledge his mistake. I would need to look to confirm this, but I already know I am wrong. He would hold his body upright and be as confident in departure as in his arrival, still sure that he is right about me and my situation.

14

Another morning and I'm still here. I can see a rectangle of light being cast over the end wall. Sunlight is streaming through the window on that side of the ward. It's a stab in my side. The outside world is teasing me, hinting that I might enjoy the day in the fresh air if I wasn't imprisoned. The strength of the reflected light tells me of the day's brilliance. If I wasn't here, I might be alone in the remoteness of the desert, where I feel happiest. No inane conversations to rattle me. No politics, predictions or predicaments raising their heads. Instead, I'm here without a word about why I am not free to go, except for the directions 'to rest'. From being a child, rest has never been something to aim for. My conservative parents were not ones to sit and contemplate. Sitting, that some people consider as resting, only happened for partaking in meals, writing, and reading the newspaper. This last activity never took more than a specific and relatively short period. Mother took her long afternoon naps 'to ease her migraines', but they were never labelled 'rest'. When she did so, I was banished to the kitchen with our housekeeper, Mrs Kelly, who indulged me as she prepared meals, baked scones and cakes and cleaned. She would participate in what must have seemed for her a continuous game of Fe Fi Fo Fum. Thus, the word 'rest' only encourages in me a sense of exclusion, taking me back to my childhood. I always felt myself to be the child who was only ever able to be a bother when someone else needed to 'rest', or the noisy nuisance during the time Mum's troubles were at their peak before Graeme's birth. Afterwards, when the focus of my parents was only on the newborn, I felt as if I was only worthy to fetch-and-carry. It's strange how these small perceptions of so long ago continue to linger, little bruises your common-sense says you should let go, but you can't quite do it.

A new morning and a fresh start. I am determined to get to the bathroom on my own. More than one staff member is taking care of the latest arrival. Women have come and gone, so this must be an emergency overload ward.

That there is no movement out of here for me, as there has been for others, is troublesome. I am anxious and feel a nervous twinge somewhere deep down in my gut. Still, I'm confident that I can handle whatever is causing the logjam. I intend to take further action. The first mission, however, is the bathroom. Ideally, given I've no street clothes, a fresh wrap-around would be good, but I recognise the need to keep the target for today low. I wait for my moment, which is when everyone's attention is on the new arrival. I slip off the bed, steady my feet on the floor and focus my eyes on the bathroom door diagonally opposite the bed of the new patient. For a few seconds, I test my ability to stand by letting go of my hold on the bed. All good. First, I step out with my right foot and then follow with my left. There's a spike of pain down my left side, but I ignore it. Right foot again, and then left. I'm about half a metre from my bed when I hear a quiet but firm order.

Stop.

One word silences the ward. The less than ten of us in the ward, staff and patients included, do that. Stop. Each set of eyes is on me. I'm the culprit to whom the order was directed.

Mrs Corass, if you're determined to use the bathroom, let me get you a walking frame.

She moves across to a storeroom and reappears with a frame. A wry smile stretches across the ward nurse's face as she hands the walking frame as if to say, 'I know you're one of those kinds of patients.' She takes her hands off the frame and watches as mine grip it.

Please do not be the patient who's too proud to buzz if she needs help. Best wishes, Mrs Corass.

I'm a chastised child, with my head bowed, but my hands firmly gripping the frame as if my life depends on its support, which it might. I cross the ward to the bathroom, right foot followed by the left, a vague reminder of my regular chant when running: one foot down, then the other. It may not be so, but I feel every set of eyes within that room boring into my back. I force my muscles to do their job. They're stiff and complain at every movement;

the protests of my left side at having to bear my weight are undeniable. For no reason will I give in. I grit my teeth and continue until I reach the door and face my next obstacle: how to wrangle holding onto a frame while simultaneously trying to open the door. I hear the ward nurse's thoughts, 'That'll keep that troublesome patient quiet for a while.' Only after the bathroom door has oozed its way shut, controlled by the suppressor fitted to it, do I relax. I did it. Beads of sweat are on my forehead. Crossing those metres feels almost as demanding as achieving the first few kilometres of a big run, the second hardest section of an event. The most challenging segment is the final run. In those dying moments, when your body feels like there's nothing more to give, comes the finishing kick, a last spurt of energy that carries an athlete across the finish line. I might need a finishing kick to get me back to my bed. Showering and changing might take more out of me than I expected.

The phenomenon of the finishing kick that has come into my mind at this moment is something that has held my attention since first learning of it during my extreme sport research. I've been intrigued. Scientific studies have proven the existence of this protective mechanism, hardwired into the human brain. No matter how a person tries, access to this only comes when a body is about to stop, a worthy point of which to be aware when engaged in extreme sports. Or as is relevant today, when pushing yourself to show you're not dependent.

I have almost reached the shower when the ward nurse bursts in and hands me a fresh gown and some knickers.

These might make you feel better.

There's no time to say thanks before she's out the door and once again it whispers to its closed position.

Back in bed, I feel like a champion. With a clear head, I scroll through the lay of the land. That Brandon has not brought in any clothes for me to wear is not negligence but deliberation. He knows his words won't stop me from trying to follow my will. But he also knows I won't be willing to embarrass myself. Equally so, I know him, probably better than he knows me. His need to do this tells me my son knows something I don't about my health, or he plans to steer me into a life he sees as suitable for me. While his case may sound valid, he is overlooking my rights, denying that it's my life he's organising, not his. This is hurtful. Once he became an adult, I did not control his life. I respected his ability to make his own choices. Yes, I had opinions, which I shared, though not always did he accept my views. Even so, I trusted him to put in play his choices and be capable of putting them right if they turned pear-shape. I expect the same respect.

Why do I seem to have lost that right? Is this about life expectancy? A sense of mortality? Or that a young person doesn't see an ageing future for themselves, assured they've all the time in the world to make mistakes and bad decisions and still have time to put right, but grey hair means you haven't that luxury? Is Brandon fearful I no longer have that time, hence his determination to ensure I make the right decisions, according to his judgement? If I can still make decisions but am not trusted to do so, I might as well be dead. I don't want to be seen as no longer able to make the right calls. When I reach the stage of dependence, I want to be the one to choose how that will play out. What hurts is that Brandon needed no proof of my abilities or lack thereof. Even the implied excuse that he's acting purely out of love and care can't overwrite his unconfirmed assumptions. His changed attitude is written over every action. It's clear he no longer trusts my abilities, and maybe, but I hope not, he can only see me as a burden. This is breaking my heart. I don't have the words to tell him how I feel. They are stifled by emotions I wish I didn't feel about this boy, this man, my son, who has my whole heart. I'm angry and I'm sad. My heart is heavy that it's come to this. I fear if I try to explain, whatever I say will be distorted. I don't want that to happen. I don't want to risk my relationship with my darling boy.

I tell myself it's time for a change in approach. The questions I have put to any staff member I encounter, again and again, about the outcome of tests and my prognosis, have received various forms of the same answer: the doctor will tell me. What doctor? I have tried to obtain an answer to that question and have narrowed it down to the one to whom I was referred by ED. He has an office nearby but is only available on certain afternoons. I suspect this is yet another attempt to distract me.

15

Today's the day. I realised early I wouldn't be able to 'frame' my way there, so yesterday afternoon, after my bathroom revival, I befriended one of the orderlies who had entered the ward to pick up a departing patient. I convinced him I needed a change of environment. He received permission from the ward nurse to take me for a spin to the canteen this afternoon. Meanwhile, focusing on presenting myself as capable and clear thinking, I have listed my questions on the back of the order form for the next day's meals. I'm taking my corporate self on this journey. However, it will take some effort. The only clothes I have is this wrap-around plus there's the need to be seated in a wheelchair, a position that puts me at a disadvantage. Projecting a position of power requires placement at a level preferably above the other stakeholder, in this case the doctor. However, it's these concessions I need to accept if I'm to make this happen.

It won't be the first time I've stood tall in the face of overwhelming opposition. While there's considerable evidence of women making it in a generally male-dominated world, there are far more who, whether capable or not, are not provided opportunity to prove themselves. The sheer numbers of males with whom they are competing, men who take positions of power, whose loud voices trumpet over any perceived confrontations, valid or otherwise, or who may feel threatened by the promotion of the opposite gender. It's a challenge to them personally. My corporate career has taken me as high as I could go without breaking the glass ceiling, and I loved my job, but it was fraught all the way. This meeting could also be a challenge of a different kind.

Neil, my orderly, and his wheelchair are right on time. He helps me tuck in the loose gown to keep my modesty, and we set off. I have noted from his demeanour Neil may have a touch of the rebel in him, and I congratulate myself on the luck of the draw. I gamble by telling him my story and plan, and there's a twinkle in his eye when he agrees to go along.

Yes, missus. Let's stick it to the man.

Neil and I have assumed the doctor is a man. It's a woman, and luck is on my side because the door is open when we arrive at the doctor's office, and she's the only one there.

I lean forward in the wheelchair, asking if she is the ED specialist. She nods her head. She also agrees to a conversation. Neil wheels me in and nods to indicate he will wait outside, closing the door on his way out. I open my folded meal request form and begin my list of questions. I become carried away with my spiel about the circumstances that have brought me to ED and how it's time to learn what has been uncovered in the many tests to which I have been subjected to so I can manage my future. However, as I am rattling through this, I notice the doctor reaching for a file on her desk, its label a surprise. 'Wilhemena Corass, refer Brandon Corass (guardian son).' I mentally protest. Brandon is not my legal guardian. He holds only my Power of Attorney. These are two documents with differing powers. The guardianship is an area I've intended to deal with but haven't yet done so. Obviously, when a son presents as a guardian, what reason would there be for anyone to check the validity of the claim? Curiously, though, in my mind I question why she would have my file there, at the ready? She had no inkling I was coming to see her. Has she only recently conversed with Brandon? Yes. That would explain why she needed to have my file handy on her desk.

Mrs Corass, you presented in a highly dehydrated state. I concluded this led to you becoming confused and dizzy and inevitably falling. I noted bruising and abrasions along your left side, possibly due to the fall. They are not substantial and require only care and time to heal. You may have temporarily displaced your hip. It's back in position but will take some weeks to heal completely. Meanwhile, you will need help in daily life.

I remain silent. I can't disagree with her diagnosis. That's about how I see it. I still haven't figured out what went wrong to bring me down, but that's irrelevant here. The dehydration might explain the bits and pieces I can't recall. I nod. By the tone of this woman's language, it is clear any opinion is neither expected nor permitted. But I can't always control my mouth, even when I know better. I hear the doctor's findings as accusatory. I can't help myself. I need to explain.

Excuse me Dr Eagan, but this wasn't the outcome of flawed planning or the decision-making of a crazy old lady incapable of taking care. This was purely an accident. Accidents are inherent in extreme running. I follow strict routines, ones I have been following for years, and I adopt all the recommended safety precautions, such as leaving a note or making a phone call. I gave my son a map of my route and had a PLB set to send a signal with GPS location to him in case of an emergency, as required. I can fully plan and engage in these events. But thank you, Doctor, I'm happy to hear that this unexpected accident has not caused too many consequences for my health. So, Doctor, when can I leave? Conditional of putting in place an interim care arrangement in my home, as I'm sure you'll suggest.

Dr Eagan flashes me a look. Our first eye-to-eye contact. Is this her way to put me in my place, staring me down to impress upon me I've no idea what I'm talking about? Have I done my usual, stepped too far? Or does she have more to add to her findings? There's an odd taste in my mouth, acid rising perhaps, the one I get when anxiety is building. She opens my file, shuffles papers around and closes it again. She dumps it into one of the trays on her desk with a rather definite thud. In-tray or out-? Eye contact has been lost. Dr Eagan is looking toward the office window.

After consultation with your son, I am recommending an Aged Care Assessment Test, which we call an ACAT. Confusion puts you at risk. Meanwhile, as your hip heals, we have arranged a nice place to take care of you.

With her back towards me, she begins packing her briefcase.

I'm dismissed.

I see you have an orderly waiting. Good.

At that, she takes her briefcase and walks out the door.

I nod my head, telling myself it's not only men who misuse the power of their position. You would think the nature of her profession might have reminded her that even when she may be correct, there are kinder ways to deliver harsh conclusions.

My spark of resistance has flickered and faded. I may need to concede I am out of weapons and strategies. My enemy is Brandon, his strong presence, and his accepted credibility as a caring son. My voice is mute; my opinions blocked.

In my mind, I hear rumbling in the streets and someone calling, 'Bring out your dead.'

16

Dr Eagan leaves the door open as she leaves. My eyes burn into her back like laser beams fuelled by my anger. If only I could use them to punish her. I can't sustain the glare but continue to watch her until she disappears. That's when I notice Neil. Cool and casual, as if he's all the time in the world and no worries whatsoever. He's supporting his slightly skewed body by pressing his shoulders against the frame of a door opposite the doctor's room. He looks very James Dean with one booted foot jammed about twenty centimetres from the floor against the wall and the other solidly planted on the floor. A hint of mischievousness flickers around the lower part of his face, and he's rolling a pencil around and over his forefinger and thumb, like it's a cigarette.

Gave up smoking years ago. Not lit. Hard habit to shake.

His laugh is warm and hearty. I like the way it sounds. It tells me more about Neil than anything that could be spoken.

In a flick, Neil transforms to the professional orderly. He pushes himself off the wall, instantly energised. In seconds, he's standing in front of me. He bends down and, as you might do for a child, his face is level with mine.

Come on, missus. Let's go for a burn.

We trail-blaze the long way back and, as we fly through the many passages between the doctor's room and the ward, I fill Neil in on my disappointing progress, discharging some of my anger in the process of sharing. He nods, but says little, and I am burrowing down into my depressive state, a mood that continues back into the ward where a nurse is quietly checking a patient in the bed next to mine. I notice some beds are vacant or occupied by different women than when I left. I have only been away less than an hour and it's off-putting, as if the world has shifted on its axis. When do I get to move? When's my turn?

The nurse looks up from her patient to watch as Neil and I approach. This staff member is new. There must have been a staff changeover while we were away. On her face, I read that she's got questions, though she says nothing. Maybe she wasn't informed Neil was taking me to the canteen. Or maybe the doctor has spread the word of the troublesome Mrs Corass.

My patience is spread thin, and I'm beginning not to care what any of them think.

Neil puts the wheelchair's brakes on, and I stand, then Neil moves the chair out of the way, and gives me a hand up onto the bed.

Come on, missus. Back into bed. Our joy ride is over.

Thanks again, Neil.

Cheer up. Don't let that old misery-guts of a doctor take you down. You'll sort this.

I nod, but I avoid looking him in the eye for fear I'll blubber. He gently pats my knee, and I am compelled to look up. He's winking and nodding.

You'll be okay. Chin up.

I can't take my eyes off Neil as he and his wheelchair disappear into the central corridor. It's as if they are carrying away my last hopes. I am abandoned.

Every action demonstrated, every person encountered, is undeniable proof that my life is disintegrating. The evidence is clear that I have lost the tools I once had: my ability to stand up for myself, to debate, to show authority over my future. I'm unable to change my life's trajectory.

I settle back in bed, and once again I curl myself into a foetal position, burying my head. I want the world to disappear. I'm drowning in my sadness. It's possible I may bawl my eyes out at any second, but I want no one to hear. The pain inside me is unbearable.

Mrs Corass, are you okay? Are you in pain?

I pull my head from under the blankets and fix the nurse with a steely look I should have used earlier on Dr Eagan when she threatened me with the ACAT test. I know it's unfair to blame the ward nurse. My malaise is not her doing. Her job is to check on me. And she's doing just that.

I don't dare answer her. I can feel a flood of angry words queuing ready to escape and I'm not so far gone that I can't realise the throwing a tantrum will be counted against me, maybe confirming the consensus of my state. The logic of maintaining control is being overtaken by my anger at the world. I need to give myself a serious talking-to. Get a grip, Missie. Breathe in, hold, out, hold. One foot down, then the other. One foot down, lift the other. Forget the pain. Forget the distance. See the bush. Run to the bush. See the rise. Run to the rise. My running mantra has taken over. Habits of a lifetime. I'm in control.

Without looking or speaking, I shake my head in dissension roughly in the nurse's direction before burying back into the pillow and shutting my eyes.

Soon after, my son returns. I'm not accustomed to this degree of attention. I've seen Brandon more times in the last few days than I have over the past several years. My pool of potential positives is low but sticking to my promise to focus on only positives, this is one I can take from today.

He scrapes the visitor's chair on the floor as he pulls it closer. There are furrows across his forehead. I have difficulty in seeing anything good coming out of this, because it is clear this will be another son-to-mother lecture.

Dr Eagan ...

Ah, there it is. The bitch has dobbed. I work hard to not let a little snicker leak out. It wouldn't be appreciated. But, let's say, I should have expected this result.

Dr Eagan, the ED specialist, tells me you went to see her. Are you satisfied with what she told you – that you need support to live for the time your hip needs to settle back into position? Otherwise, Mum – and I need you to listen to me about this – otherwise, because of your age – you, know, something that comes with ageing, well, the state of your bones, they aren't as strong as they used to be. You know, don't you, that you need to take care of yourself. You've already done something to your hip joint, and if you aggravate that injury by trying to be your usual independent self, you may cause yourself to need a hip operation. And again, at your age, that is something you should try to avoid.

He fixes me with his determined stare. Maybe there is a little flicker of uncertainty in them, like telling off your mum doesn't feel right. Inside my head I make a humorous observation, trying to keep my spirits up. I'd say, if I didn't know better, I could confuse him with a Headmaster and I should wait for the rap over the knuckles from the old bamboo cane. I know I'm over-exaggerating, because bamboo canes are from an era long before mine, but it's my little protest to the ageing references. So, boy, do you think I'm older than I really am, from an era before mine?

Mum, are you listening? This is important.

I don't answer. What's the point?

Someone will take you to a nice place. I'll pack your usual stuff from home and give it to them to take with you. I think you'll like it, Mum. It's fancy. Like a plush hotel.

I don't want to listen. It's apparent this is what's happening. At least I will be out of hospital. I've no doubt this other place will be yet another prison despite its luxuries and yet another restriction on my ability to live my life as

I choose. I vow that moving will not be the end of my quest. Once I'm there, and Brandon's satisfied he's won, I'll resolve this issue.

Brandon gives me a hug that can barely be called that, and stands up, ready to move. I can tell either he isn't comfortable with his decision and is feeling guilt, or he expected more of a reaction from me. Maybe my lack of resistance makes him nervous.

Enjoy your trip, and I'll drop in to see you in your new home soon.

A wave of his hand and he's gone back to his life, one in which he's free to make his own choices, and I'm left here, powerless.

It's as well he didn't turn back. I'm not handling this well, and should he have taken another glance my way, or shown more emotion, I would have unravelled.

His use of the word 'home' was the last straw.

I'm confused. I can't say if my sadness is outweighed by the degree of my anger. But a distinct knot in my gut is tightening by the minute.

Who am I? How am I seen? What is my place in the world now? Has my life been declared redundant? I'm no longer me.

17

When my father died, Graeme was too distraught to care for our frail mother or to make the arrangements. He was separated from his wife, and she was disinclined to be involved except provide casual courtesies of helping with the catering and flowers, and reluctantly helping to greet the many who went to Dad's funeral. Dad had a large funeral, as he was well remembered by his business associates. That was me doing everything, from the legal to the day-to-day. Mum's death was a much quieter affair, but again it was me.

When my brother died, I was destroyed, but that didn't serve as an excuse to get out of doing what was needed to be done. Anyway, there was no one else. Grae's ex-wife was already into another marriage with other children, and Grae's kids were adults, busy in their own lives. Again, it was me.

When Brandon needed his Company incorporated and his systems set in place, again it was me.

Where have those abilities and that authority gone? Is this all in the past, now?

18

Yesterday, Brandon brought in some clothes he considers appropriate for my journey. I didn't look at them or him as they passed from his hands to mine. I'm sure he rolled his eyes. Now I've showered, dressed, and taken a position on the visitor's chair awaiting my transport. I've tried meditating but I'm failing. There are too many conflicting and confusing thoughts running riot in my head.

A man arrives at my bedside. He's in the controlling position of yet another wheelchair. I feel sad it's not Neil. Although Neil and I had only one adventure together, I miss him. This man has a kind face. He's dressed in a slightly casual uniform, and he delivers his name via a firm handshake before introducing me to his up-market wheelchair. Charlie, he says. A good, solid name. He looks like he could have once been employed as the doorman of a plush hotel, with an external appearance of someone who can absorb all manner of mistreatment while remaining calm. Not that I'm interested in his disposition or his appearance, but this hint of kindness seems a good starting point to counter my fear of what Charlie represents. Charlie needn't fear. The wind has been knocked out of my sails. I vow it's only temporary, but I did promise Brandon I'll do as he requests until my hip has healed. He promises that it's my hip that will decide when I'll be free to live my own life. But, he added, there will be changes, and I must accept them. I'm not completely convinced that this is all I have ahead, certain as I am there's more to this. Two can play this game of cat and mouse.

Charlie takes my elbow and guides me into the chair, then waits for me to wriggle into a comfortable position before checking that each foot sits as it should on its individual pedal (don't want these old feet to get caught beneath the chair, I privately snipe at him). When all is how he needs it to be, he pats me on the shoulder and moves around behind me to do the main part of his job, which is to guide me and the wheelchair to wherever it is we are going.

Together we pass through the ward, and into the long corridor. We pass other wards. Charlie knows everyone. I hope I'll see Neil again.

Hi Zara. How are you today? John. Looking good there, John.

We reach the lift. My guardian smiles at me as he reaches over to press the button, then returns to his place behind me. As a couple we roll out of the lift and into the foyer. He waves to the young woman at Reception, and she calls out, 'Hi Charlie' then in a flash we pass through the automatic glass doors and leave the hospital. The day is clear, bright, and the air is fresh. Fresh air. I throw my head back and breathe deeply. The non-sterilized air of the outdoors sweeps into my nostrils and my mouth. I swear I can analyse every part: Nitrogen, Oxygen, Argon, Carbon Dioxide ... The change is like winter turning to spring. This is how it should be. My body is back in the memory of a run, breathing in oxygen. As always, I appreciate its availability, something we all take for granted. It can be particularly hard-come-by at certain stages of the enduring effort of the distance. Out there, pounding the course, the air full of dust and dryness, hinting of the dangers of isolation and wildness never far away, battles its way into lungs pleading for the life-giving oxygen necessary to finish the task ahead.

Men and women of all ages and some children are flowing past us, divided into queues by my wheelchair and its driver. Everyone's in a hurry, as though entering this building is essential to survival. Each arrival displays the same urgency to enter as I do to leave. Fleeting glimpses of faces and bodies hint at the stories they carry with them and that bring them to this place. Maybe the smiling ones are visitors; the frowning ones with heads bent, like the couple with a small child wrapped in lemon and blue blanket, are needing attention for a rapid onset illness. There's the grey-haired couple sauntering along in a way that suggest a sureness of both direction and outcome, displaying small ownership or a rite of passage, as if they have been here before not so long ago and expect to be back here again soon.

Charlie has pushed his way past the wheelchair, moving to the front to face me, while crouching down with his knees bent. He smiles at me, a similar false grin that strangers paint across their mug when talking to the mother of a cute baby in its pram. If he starts goo-goo-gah-ing I'll kick him in the teeth. Does he think I'm senile, suffering from dementia? Does he see me as a woman confused by what's happening? Oh, I wish I had a way to prove him wrong. I'm not sure my way is the best one, but I chose to wilfully move my feet off the footrests (supposed to be keeping this old lady's feet safe) and thump them firmly onto the carpark concrete. It's a wordless shout, a soundless 'There! I can do this!' bellow. Before Charlie has time to respond, I follow through, pressing my palms onto the armrests to take my weight and then I heave myself upright. 'Heave' is the appropriate verb, here, because it's startling how disabling a few days in a hospital can be. My years of hard work to maintain strength in my legs seem to have been wasted

Charlie's smile doesn't change. There's a hint of performance about it. Well, it's his job, and the truth be known he probably doesn't care that much about his passengers, only that he gets them from point A to point B without a heart attack or a fall. He rises from his knees, and once standing, turns to support me with a look that says two can play this game, and places one hand under my elbow.

I'm surprised how repulsed I am, but I'm able to talk myself down from pulling away. Charlie bends his head over.

Slowly does it, Mrs Corass.

My skin crawls. I can't deny I need help, but receiving it is belittling. It underscores a helpless or limited state no one wants to admit for themselves.

Charlie turns and clicks the car keys he's holding in his hand. The vehicle responds with a golden blink and a canary chirp and, with the vehicle's permission to enter now granted, Charlie takes a firm grip of the passenger's door handle to haul the door open. The action surprises me. The small gesture of letting me take the passenger's seat feels large, as if, rightly or not, Charlie is acknowledging my show of resistance. I'm probably reading more in it than is intended, but for me it's the difference between being treated as a nameless passenger in the backseat, and being elevated into a companion, sharing the drive, a fellow human worthy of that front seat view.

He bows and ushers me into the passenger seat, simultaneously supporting my elbow. Have I misread him? Is he mocking my attempt at independence? He waits while I shuffle into the seat and then he bends into the car to grab the seat belt and stretch it out. To clasp it, his head needs to move further inside, and my body automatically retracts to maintain my private space. His grin is broader as he withdraws. Is he playing with me, knowing I would feel offended by his action to clasp the seat belt? Or is he doing his job, making sure his passenger is safe? Or is that grin a smugness over my instinctive response to his proximity? Whatever it is, intentional or misread by me, I don't like how it makes me feel.

Charlie is the ultimate driver, continuously engaging in small talk. Current affairs. I could protest that I haven't the faintest, because I've been in solitary confinement, but I don't bother. The weather. Again, I must restrain myself. I would like to say, 'How would I know? Been in an artificial environment for days, mate. Rain or sun doesn't play havoc in a hospital ward.' Instead, I keep my eyes averted as if I am examining in fine detail the cyclist riding parallel. The grim-faced man is donned in disgusting Lycra, acting as if he's on the Tour de France, trying to keep pace with the lanes of traffic. Got some bad news for you, mate. You are growing older each day, my friend, like us all, no matter how hard you pedal and how tight the gear. Ask me. See me. It's how people see you that counts these days. Not how you feel inside. Inside, you are forever young. But if that's your passion, good on you. Don't let them take it from you. For God's sake, don't let Charlie hit you with his car, but otherwise, well, what can I say? Look at me if you dare. No, on second thoughts, don't. Keep your eye on the road ahead, watch for potholes, and for the bloody pedestrians who think they own the road and will step out of nowhere. And never forget your body breaks. When that happens ...

I drag my eyes forward. Where are we heading? Earlier I was too angry at being moved without warning to seek answers. No. I'm not being truthful. I didn't ask because I was certain I wouldn't like the answer and asking for enlightenment would be me conceding my powerlessness, admitting to myself my inability to change the outcome. I examine the dashboard. Tidy. No good luck charms hanging off the rear-view mirror, no unpaid bills spilling out of the glove box, no discarded take-away disposable coffee cups on the console. Not Charlie's car. Company car. So, who is paying?

The vehicle slows. Charlie turns the steering wheel and together we sweep along a circular driveway. Except I know it can't be, but it would be easy to convince me this is the entrance to a luxury hotel. The stable of motorised chairs parked at one side of the entrance tell me it's unlikely that living here will be anywhere near like living in a hotel. My chest is filled with clay. I can't feel the beat of my heart. Breathe in, hold, breathe out, hold. This is it. Until my hip is better. That's what Brandon said. But I don't trust his promises. More like, until I get you there, and you get used to it and stop fighting the inevitable.

Charlie is back with the wheelchair. I can't remember him going through the motions of putting it in the car boot, probably too angry about the implied helplessness after the seatbelt event. But there it is again, the wheelchair once more awaiting its unwilling passenger. The seatbelt gives me one last moment of independence. I snap it open before Charlie can stick his head in and, as the physio had taught me in the last few days in hospital, I swivel my buttocks around so I'm facing out of the door, enabling me to place my feet firmly on the driveway and stand if I choose. For once I draw from common sense. Better to swallow a little pride and wait. If in my stubbornness I stand and my hip can't support me, I'd look a bigger fool than a lady waiting patiently for some help. Besides, there's no way Charlie is taking me into that building in any other way than in this wheelchair. That would be against the rules.

As my feet land on the driveway, I notice a small shake of Charlie's head. Yes, Charlie sees me as a 'done dinner.' He doesn't believe I'll be leaving here, either. He takes a firm grip of my elbow again, obviously to help lower me into the chair, and once again, as he did at the beginning of our journey, he kneels to place my feet in the stirrups. My meanness fills me with a desire to thump him on the chest to force some distance between us, but it would be a futile gesture. As benign and insincere as he seemed earlier, now, as he places a firm hand on my shoulder, as if to reassure me, before taking up his position behind, he lets out a deep, almost sad sigh. Maybe I misjudged him. Maybe he too is frightened by a similar future awaiting him. It's now a uniformed, on-duty, straight-back Charlie who is striding it out and propelling me and the wheelchair along the tidy path leading to huge glass doors, where he pauses momentarily to pad in an entry code. OMG. So that's how it is. At once I realise. This is a secured place. Why didn't I pay attention when Charlie keyed in that code? It might be useful.

The glass doors open in a smooth, silent action and the wheelchair, its stunned passenger and driver sweep into a large lobby.

19

Charlie leaves me. A moment ago, I couldn't stand him near me, but right now I am feeling so alone I wish him back beside me, taking care of me, and yet, there he goes, striding across the foyer with a sense of purpose. He's been here before. He disappears around a corner, and I feel abandoned. More than ever, I wish I had memorised the entry code. I might have escaped, been able to find enough strength and will-power to get up out of this wheelchair and move to the keypad, key in the code and go. But then, where would I go?

I'm not alone. To my left, there's a large sofa on which a woman sits, her blue floral dress covered by a hand-knitted over-large cardigan. She has one hand raised to chest height and her gaze is fixed into one unblinking position, as if she's frozen in a permanent pose of greeting. Should I wave back? Next to her is a woman in all black, sitting straight-backed and with her hands daintily clasped together in her lap. There's a cup and saucer and a slice of cake on a serviette on the coffee table in front of her. Her eyes move to these, her back bends as her hands unfold and her right hand reaches for the handle of the cup. This could end with spillage. Opposite, on another sofa, a frail pigeon-pair, both with wild grey hair spilling over bowed heads and blank eyes turned down, grasp each other with rigid arms over each other's rib cages. On the table in front two slices of cake on serviettes await their attention. There aren't any teacups. A uniformed woman with a broad smile moves towards these two and sits beside them. Her complexion is dark, suggesting perhaps she's someone who has come from the African continent. In each hand she holds a closed mug with a straw and her words, almost musical, English with an accent, are a plea to the pair to 'have some tea and cake'. She receives no response.

I can't watch. It's both sad and disgusting, that an individual can be reduced to this dependence. I turn away. From the other direction, a flock of people using walking frames temporarily fill the large space before passing through and disappearing down a corridor, leaving behind an echo of laughter and chatter which is as equally off-putting and startling as the pair taking tea through a straw. Surely not. Not in here. What is there to laugh at?

There's a rush of fresh air as the entrance doors slide open and, once more as in my departure from the hospital, a river of humanity is temporarily disrupted by me, the stalled woman in a wheelchair. Some brush my shoulder lightly, another pats my arm as they pass, and I can't stop myself from scowling. Why can't they be more careful? An adult female has a small dog in her arms, around which children take turns to stop and rub its head or belly, with cries of 'ooh' or 'aah' and 'good girl', to which the dog replies in tiny yaps. One child squeals the words, 'Gran's going to be so happy. She loves Tiki.' The yapping dog and the children's enthusiasm have garnered attention. Even the pigeon-pair look up, their eyes attentive, smiles growing and, as a group, the other foyer's occupants watch until the lift doors close tight, stifling the sounds of children and dog. The pigeon-pair and their companions return to their former postures, their eyes downcast once more. The aide is still looking toward the elevator as if she's wishing for the unattainable. She takes a deep breath and begins again her melodic pleading to 'enjoy your tea' as she lifts one mug and places it within the grasp of one of her charges' hands, and then the other.

Charlie's back. There's that vanilla smile once more before he takes his pusher's position behind me and propels me forward, no word about our destination. I suppress a powerful urge to scream. He leaves me parked near a reception desk. His farewell speech is short and sweet.

Don't get out of the chair, Mrs Corass, until staff come. They won't be long. Lotto win for you, Mrs Corass. Welcome to the luxury of Fairview.

The Fairview circuit

1

I'VE BEEN HERE A few days, lost count of the actual number. Long enough, apparently, for my bail period to be over. No more hiding in my suite, I've been told. Those in charge, the people in uniforms, the ones of which I'm most suspicious, have issued instructions. I must move around and get to know this place and my fellow 'prisoners'. My word, not theirs. The labels the soft-spoken staff members use are phrases such as 'your companions', 'the other residents', 'your neighbours' or 'your new friends'.

Though others might debate this view, I've always been a 'good' girl where, according to my father, that means an obedient girl, even when I resented the unfairness of many expectations placed on me. Yet again, despite my fear of this place, I agree to do what they have asked of me. I accept the challenge of moving around the facility. What else is there for me to do? Sitting in my room is opposite to how I would normally spend my days.

I start off with a few short excursions along the nearby corridor and around the block of apartments on the same floor as mine. I see mostly only staff members, because I choose to take my hikes in the early morning or in the evening. Because of the times I have chosen I assume the other residents are still in their beds or recently retired to television watching. My hip is still healing, so I need to sit and rest regularly, a necessity that fires up my resentment at the limitations the injury brings. As a motivation to move past the discomfort I'm feeling, I remind myself an uncooperative hip does not a corpse make, a declaration stressed by the disciplines of a lifetime of training, which tell me if I'm getting out of here, then walking and moving past the pain of grinding and grating bones is what I need to do to rebuild my muscle strength. The logic of this, however, does not reduce my anger.

I'm becoming stronger and braver. This latest journey takes me to a large room so far unvisited. It's rather grand, and the only words I can find in my vocabulary to match its appearance are 'lobby' or 'foyer', except it's neither of those, as the room with the great glass doors, through which Charlie propelled me on my first day, has been called both of those titles. I heard one carer referring to 'the great room', and if it is this room, it's indeed 'great' in size, although I can't use that word to describe to the standard of its occupants.

I pause at the entrance and scan for life among the many individuals seated on sofas or armchairs. A wave of repulsion and maybe even of terror hits me, quickly followed by guilt. My ill-disciplined mind throws up words like zombies and gargoyles. I've been to Notre-Dame Cathedral. I learnt about the fifty-four grotesques and their purpose, both practical and symbolic. They protect the great walls from rain, by spouting water a distance away. Artistically they are the fantastic universe of the Middle Ages. The Fairview variety are beyond middle age. My fear of them may be more about me than it is about the sofa-dwellers. Is this how I am seen?

I have ventured further than normal and my hip hurts, but despite the pain or how tired I feel, I vow I will not sit in this space. Never. I'll not become another carcass filling the sofas and armchairs. No. That's definite. For this girl, Wilhemena Rose Corass, that's an absolute 'No.'

There they are, like crows on the fence, but instead, perched on couches and recliners.

I force myself to keep going, to find another route back to my apartment, despite the pain in my hip. I pass by a large rectangular mirror and glimpse myself. I'm shocked. My usually tanned face has grown pale. Is it an illusion or is my face also looking gaunt? My eyes have dark marks beneath them, and my nose seems bulbous. And look at my hair. I haven't been to the hairdressers for some time. I usually organise a visit after an event, but that's not been possible this time. Do I look any different to those seated in 'the great room'? In an instant I see myself devalued, decrepit and disintegrating. I am repulsed. I'm monstrous. I look towards the crowd that fills sofas and armchairs in the great room. They are monstrous. What's our value to society? We take up space, waiting until our number's up, lacking any ability to contribute, so no wonder we're invisible. No one wants to see us because we are everyone's future. Monstrous. Monstrous. Monstrous.

My hip adds to my self-loathing. When sharp pain shoots down my leg, I know it needs to be relieved of holding me upright. When I spot a vacant space on a sofa, I can't ignore it. It doesn't matter anymore. I'm monstrous, we are all monstrous, we can wait out the hours together, all continuing to be monstrous, all waiting for the end. Completely at the will of my body, me and my darkness are carried by my legs towards the unfilled space on one sofa. On automatic, my bottom backs in and carefully lowers the rest of my body onto the seat. I hear myself let out a whoosh of relief. I'm determined not to make eye contact, so I sit there, head straight, eyes looking ahead.

I can't maintain the position. My curiosity betrays me, directing my eyes to slide across each side of me and, much to my surprise, there are distinct signs of life on display. Multiple grey or white heads are bobbing up and down, reminding me of a mob of meerkat. On each face a set of eyes is focused on me, the invader of their private space. There are low murmurs and signs of anxiety, especially by one. This person is openly aggressive, nodding her head vigorously so that it indicates I should look to the right. To ensure I take notice she hisses at me. This is followed by a soft chorus of 'Oh no' from others. Eyes are flickering, mouths clamping or gaping, and tongues protruding. I hear a mumbled chorus and more clearly, I hear the head-nodder's warning, though I don't understand why she's anxious.

Mama Maria.

I look from one to the other, not comprehending, but no one enlightens me. There's only silence, although each pair of eyes is turned toward me.

The tension is palpable.

What should I do? Can I persuade my legs to lift me up?

There's a mass movement backward of seated bodies and one slow, cautiously leaning forward. This co-operative action enables the eyes of a silver-haired woman seated at the far end of one of the large sofas to see past the others so we can make eye contact. Her bright eyes are matched with an equally bright smile, softening my anticipation of negativity. Perhaps it's not me that is the problem.

Hello, there, newcomer. I'm Joan.

Life. Spark. Sense.

Hi Joan. Wilhemena. Or Billy.

Welcome.

Well, thank you, Joan.

If you are wondering why everyone reacted when you sat down where you did, it's because one of our fellow residents is possessive about that seat. She's yet to come, and none of us wish to hear one of her tirades. Would you care to move down here and take this seat near me?

Joan gently pats the cushion of a high-back chair positioned beside the arm of the sofa in which she's primly seated.

For a moment, resistance to enforced rules builds inside me, but better sense forces its way through the rebellion. I push down on the arm of the sofa and struggle to rise upward. I need a few minutes for my feet to steady and my hip to co-operate. I'm ready to move forward when a woman using a walking stick enters the room. Her dark complexion is contrasted by patches of dark hair blended wildly with her greys. There's a wild look about her, and I figure a smile might be good but the flash in those dark eyes warns me this might be the infamous Maria, and she's already in fighting mode.

Proibito. Il mio.

I have a smattering of Italian, enough to get the message. Those two phrases are telling me that seat is not mine to sit on, as it's hers. I respond with a smile, but with my fingers crossed. It's apparent Maria is highly strung.

Nessun problema.

I point to the vacant seat next to Joan and as added reassurance I say something in English, 'Just moving,' and make a gesture of ushering Maria to her own seat, something I instantly regret as clearly Maria is not impressed with me offering her a seat that she already owns.

Some reactions don't need words.

The Italian's pace has quickened, a rhythm emphasized by the click of her walking stick on the tiled floor. I'm still stalled, mesmerised. Her Italian has devolved into a chain of indistinguishable sounds that stop suddenly. She pushes past me and in one last defiant action, she throws her body into the armchair.

I can't help myself. I am filled with a need to react somehow, and I do so by rolling my eyes, although doing so with considerable restraint. At least I say nothing, a remarkable achievement for me, before I hobble towards the seat that Joan has offered me. Once I settle, Joan leans over and whispers.

We call her Mama Maria. Away with the fairies.

She taps her head and smiles.

That's the moment a woman in uniform marches into the room. Perfect timing, I mentally note. Joan whispers 'Ngalia. The Bitch.'

It's not the language that surprises me. It's Joan's eagerness to share this insult with a 'newcomer.' I have a strong urge to giggle, but I'm smart enough to save it for later.

Ngalia's hard, expressionless face does not intimidate me. I have come across her authoritarian types before, ones that if pressed will back down. Ngalia's unblinking glare goes with the personality. It'll be her tool to ensure coercion, and a sign she's yet another individual who perhaps is in the wrong profession.

The many eyes, the ones that had watched me as I had lowered myself into the forbidden chair, now turn to stare at this person of authority, like kindly children, waiting to be told what to do, how to live their lives. Obedient. As if something has stripped them of their power to display their individuality. My fingers claw into the arm of the sofa. Not me. That's not going to be me. Is this a military camp? Yes, sir. Or rather, yes, mam. Don't salute. That'd be too energetic. Lap dogs. Where's your spirit, people? Don't let them turn you into robots.

Afterwards, I struggle in the journey back to my suite, wobbling my way along the corridor, all the while my usual sarcastic observations are rolling through me. I've been observing, judging, and commenting to myself, in an ever-expanding negative audit of my new home. The accumulation of soul-sapping perspectives is weighing heavily on me.

How many years am I realistically likely to live? Are all those years going to be like this? Oh God, help me. Kill me now.

2

I'm determined not to allow myself to sink into depression. I continue my daily excursions, trying to uncover as many of the hidden spaces that my limited ability will allow. One of my passing observations is that, so far, I have not noticed a male presence. The occasional staff member is male, but so far not a resident. Maybe I can mark this as at least one positive point. Men are off my list of preferences. As if destiny is teasing me, barely had this thought flitted through my mind when I hear male voices. I turn a corner into yet another corridor, and there they are, a gaggle of ganders seated around a large outdoor table, with newspapers, and iPads scattered around. One is reading aloud in a strong and yet not unappealing voice. From his words, I can discern he's reading from the Editorial page of a newspaper. The men seem to find his comments hilarious. I'm guessing he's enriching the newspaper pieces. How else could he possibly make the Editorials comedic?

As I draw closer, I try to read the faces of the reader's audience. They are, like most residents, pale in colour, wrinkled and generally lacking expression, unless whatever the reader says causes them to laugh. His comments are what makes their faces briefly light up and fade again. I must give credit to this reader. What a marvellous performer he must be to lift these zombies out of their graves. As I near the group, the reader turns towards me, barely missing a word of his monologue. Amazing hazel eyes. No, they are green. Wrinkles that form flattering patterns around his eyes and lips. Spikey, lively silver hair that moves with his head, like the wave of a breeze through fields of grass. His eyes meet mine. I feel their pull and can't help but warn myself away from him. I instinctively measure his type. A nice guy, friendly, easy to get on with, and good looking. Even a casual acquaintance with someone like him can be dangerous for me. I know it's not the fault of these types but, rather, it's me, and my tendency, after childhood training via my smooth brother and adult training by the other men in my life, including my ex-, to believe anything that such an agreeable face might tell me. I drag my eyes away from his gaze, nod to the gaggle, and head towards my suite. I am determined not to look back, not to confirm if my senses have it right, that each gander is watching me, and the minute I turn the corner, they'll be having a joke amongst themselves. A roar of laughter suggests if they aren't watching, then there has been a joke made at my expense. I surprise myself when I feel my cheeks twitching and my lips turning up in a smile at the possibility.

Turning another corner, I find myself back at the large entrance room, as if the main corridors of the many wings of the building each lead to this central hub. I brave myself to return to this room, but before I reach the entrance, I am blocked by something extraordinary. When I see what is happening, I realise that as I have been lumbering my way around, the traffic in the corridors has been minimal, and now there's a great gathering of uniformed staff and residents in various attire from dressing gowns to Sunday bests. It's as unexpected as coming across another person in a desert location, a place where it's normal never to see another soul.

Staff members form rows each side of the corridor. Beyond them, residents are gathered in small groups. Down the centre of the guard of staff members, several ambulance officers are guiding a gurney on which it's apparent a body lies, respectfully covered by a sheet. There's a wreath of flowers resting at one end. The procession is heading towards the large glass entry doors where there's a vehicle waiting.

I am transfixed. I'm both sickened and moved, appalled at the recognition of the potential frequency of death to these halls, and stirred by the display of respect that counters my presumption that this place functions as an emotionless departure lounge, lacking human care. I had imagined in this limited view that the only way anyone is getting out of here is in this manner, like this poor soul today, via a trolley but that each departure went unnoticed and unacknowledged. As the dearly departed exits the front door in the care of the ambulance crew, staff and residents are going through rituals not dissimilar to those observed at funerals, as if this is about loss of a family member, not about mindless dispatch of an anonymous ageing being by its warders. Today, here, I'm listening to words being spoken about moments recalled and seeing tears shed, all so very personal and far from mechanical.

I need to review my harsh take on Fairview.

I'm curious, and I study the expressions on display on the faces of the audience beyond the funereal parade through the lobby. Did I have expectations that this is an audience who might see itself as only a few steps behind the person now leaving Fairview, and such a sight might strike terror, as this event forms a reminder of their own looming fate, as it does for me? I hear an 'Oh', as the gurney's passing has taken someone by surprise. A woman makes the sign of the cross; other residents wipe tears from eyes.

I'm overwhelmed. I'm terrified. I'm uplifted. There's too much to unravel, not only about Fairview and those who live here, but also about myself and the reality of my own impermanence.

3

My spirits are sinking to the bottom of a deep, dark well. There's no water in the bottom. I can't see the sky. There are no desert hawks hovering. The oxygen is thin. I'm struggling. Oh, Brandon, why did you do this? It doesn't matter if I can't do what I used to be able to do. This place is demoralising.

I don't cry easily but I can feel tears rolling down my cheeks. This is embarrassing, I need to move, to get out of sight, but I can't make it back to my apartment right now. I pivot, head down the first corridor I come to, hoping it's one that takes me away from this space. I don't care where I end up. I ignore the discomfort in my hip and force myself to walk as fast as I'm able.

Deep breaths and an energy-sapping fast pace carry me to where the corridor ends in an unexpected smaller lounge room, somewhere I've not encountered so far in my explorations. It's furnished in small, not large, sofas and armchairs, a more private space, encouraging less people, something for which I'm thankful, especially as at this moment there's no one here except me. I drop into the first armchair I come to and bury my face in my hands, my tears flowing freely. I wish to be anywhere provided it's not in this place, yet leaving seems impossible. My larger concern is the unacceptable way I'm dealing with all of this. I can't find distance from the topic that's overwhelming me, and that's what I need to do if I am to find a solution for myself. More devastating is the realisation I don't recognise this stranger I have become.

I'm stalled, both mentally and physically. I'm avoiding thinking, because it feels as if any contemplation will swamp me. I hide behind the artificial darkness formed by my hands shielding my face. Time passes, whether it's minutes or hours, I can't say, but gradually a sense of calmness is growing. I desperately want to cling to the serenity offered. I remove my hands and compel myself to study the intricate pattern on the floor rug, as though there are answers to be found somewhere in the weft and warp of its weave. Again, time stretches out unmeasured until I'm broken out of my spell by a timid touch on my left shoulder. Behind me stands a woman with a broad smile stretching her face. There's something familiar about the woman. Have I met this person and can't remember? Was it in the dining room? Or the lobby? Then it comes to me. Her facial expressions are remarkable. How could I have forgotten? In my first few days at Fairview, she had caught my attention. I'd labelled her the 'Deer Lady' because of her quiet, graceful manner, quick movements and her wide-eyed expression, features that made her stand out among the many expressionless faces of the lobby.

The Deer Lady bows her head toward me and says, 'Excuse me.' Once our eyes have acknowledged each other, she continues.

You're new, aren't you?

I nod, while trying to blink away my tears. I'm ashamed of my weakness.

You look sad.

I don't answer. The Deer Lady tilts her head to one side and adds to her observation.

You need a little time to adjust, but you'll get there.

What do you mean, 'I'll get there'? Where am I getting to?

I know my response has too sharp an edge to it, but she doesn't seem put off. Even if she is, that doesn't stop me from continuing.

Are we compelled to sit here and watch those around us die, while waiting for our turn?

The Deer Lady's facial expressions change only slightly, as her smile becomes a little sadder.

Are you referring to the Guard of Honour? Maybe you need to think a little differently, my dear. This is a big place. There are those like us who need a little help to live a good life. And those well beyond that. Dementia, sickness and so on. Yes, they might seem to wait for death. But while they are doing so, they are being cared for with dignity. And they have us for company.

The woman's face breaks back into her beaming smile, as though this place is everything anyone would wish for. If this was intended to reassure me, it has achieved the opposite. A grip of fear squeezes my heart. This Deer Lady seems to drink the good stuff. Is this it? Is this what life must be from now on? Close to tears again, I point down the hallway towards the great room, to that place and that event where the prominence of death hit me.

How often do you see that?

Not as often as you might convince yourself you would, but I don't count the number. All over the world, people are dying every second of the day. Only last week I had news of my cousin's death. He was in full swing of life and nowhere near my age, only fifty-five, and he had a stroke. Now that's sad. We live in a place where the chances of knowing a person who has died, or being friends with someone who will soon die, and seeing the respectful procession out of the building, will occur more often. That doesn't mean we come here to die. I'd say for many, we come here to live, but in saying that, you will need to accept some of our current residents were already dying before they came here. They have come here to receive the care they need. So, you are certain to see evidence of Death more than you might in your old home. Of course, if you choose to burrow away from the realities, well, I guess that's where you'll stay, back home, possibly alone, although I don't know your circumstances. However, I can tell you there's a mob of us who plan to be living this glorious life of being served beautiful meals, enjoying the company of people of our own age, and being kept safe so we don't injure ourselves. We plan a long life of positive and stimulating ageing. Mind you, that's a certainty for which there's no guarantee. I'll bet you didn't think about dying before you came in here, and now that word is being displayed in large font on a neon sign flashing in front of you.

She's right. Only recently did I face the idea that my death might come sooner than expected. That was in the time I spent on the ultra-run track believing no rescue was possible. I didn't die. But how quickly I have pushed that threat, that possibility, and thoughts of my own vulnerability aside. I have receded into denial of my own limited life span. No one wants to think about their own death, or the death of anyone they care about. I stare at the Deer Lady, trying to take it in. When I remove my fear of dying and of a diminished life out of the equation, I can't deny the truth in what she says. But there's still the elephant in the room: Death. No one wants reminders of Death's nearness. As I scavenge through Deer Lady's wisdom, I glimpse what may be behind my own fear and revulsion of Fairview. Out there, before my fall and before my transfer to this place, in the world as I was for me before now, I could deny the realities of the future until the cows came home, but here, it's right there in my face, and it's as distasteful as falling face first into a sloppy cow pat. The Deer Lady's face looks apologetic.

Let's start again. Hi. My name is Coral. And you are?

Wilhemena.

Even to my ears 'Wilhemena' doesn't sound as if it's my name, well, not the name I should use here. I let go of my stuffy attitude, no doubt inherited from my father and put my hand out. Somehow, I find it in me to offer Coral a half-smile.

How about we go with Billy, Coral?

Come on, Billy. Let's go to the back lobby and have ourselves a latte and some creamy cake. The world always looks much brighter after consuming those treats.

Coral holds out her hands to help me rise and waits until I'm steady. I look at Coral's open palms and then to Coral's calm face, and back again. Coral's confidence doesn't waver. Coral releases my hand, steps back and waits, then turns and waves her hand to show the direction we should take. Side by side, the two of us hobble towards the promise of lattes and cake.

My mind can't switch off. The Deer Lady's words have a ring of truth to them. Yes, I concede, it's undeniable: the inevitability of human mortality. But why is it now that this has landed on me? Oh, that damn accident. And damn, damn, damn, you Brandon.

4

I don't know where to put myself. When I hide away in my suite, it's lonely. The lobby, despite its large, glassed areas and inviting furniture intended to make the area a pleasing space, is full. Contrary to Coral's inspirational oration, I need more time to find my own understanding of residential care, ageing, and dying. Daily the space intended for contemplation and relaxation, the great room, is full of individuals with thinning grey hair atop of heads that seem unable to hold themselves upright, and scrawny hands folded in depleted laps, each offering a challenge to my theories. Surprisingly, what this space offers are distractions. It becomes the perfect spot for me and my misery. Most of the sofa sitters are non-responsive, happy to sit and think about the past or contemplate their limited future or think of nothing, if it so pleases them. This means I'm free to allow myself a similar luxury. I can sit and stare into space as my private and internal rebellion rages. I'm angry. I can't say there's any person or event at which I can level my anger, but it's likely to be everything and everyone. It's humiliating to be bundled in what seems to be an anonymous group of aged individuals.

About my fellow residents, I am simultaneously condescending and sympathetic, the latter because I am one of them. Like them I am in this place, wondering, waiting for whatever is ahead, and probably wanting the life I once had to exist once more. Telling myself I'm not like them, I'm 'with it', isn't working. It's derogatory and discriminatory, and I know I should be above that low behaviour. And yet it is how I measure the unfairness of being here. I'm now part of the invisible mob. And judging by my own classification of my fellow inmates, shouldn't it be assumed that we are each not only invisible to the world outside but to each other? Does anyone care why I'm here? Have I bothered to show interest in why the individuals I have encountered need to be here? Have I enquired about their life story?

A carer pushes a wheelchair into the lobby, a common occurrence on a daily, even hourly, basis. For some reason, maybe something about the way she is steering this wheelchair, the carer and the wheelchair's passenger catch my attention. I sense they are searching for a suitable spot in which to park the wheelchair, one of which her patient might approve, rather than just park her anywhere. The wheelchair is the vehicle for a woman who is struggling to lift her head and hold it upright, a limitation that doesn't deter the woman's eyes from busily scanning the room. For a fleeting moment I recognise she and I are not dissimilar. I follow the same routine whenever I enter this room. I identify which spots are more, or less, risky than others in terms of the already seated to measure the potential for conversations or, to be honest, more often for lack of, depending on my mood.

The wheelchair-bound woman waves her hand, and the chair pusher bends down to listen. It's clear they are heading to a spot near where I'm seated. My nasty side encourages me to turn aside so I'm less accessible. My tactics fail, because at the last moment, an accidental eye-to-eye contact with the wheelchair-bound woman stalls me from committing entirely to the evasive action. The second of fragile connection between us convinces me the wheelchair-bound woman has appraised and formed an opinion about this petulant, antisocial person near whom she will soon be parked. There's a hint in her eyes she's up for the challenge, an intelligent spark that contrasts an inert body and the trembling and twitching hands that seek refuge in a malnourished lap. She exudes an air of defiance, a suggestion she might see it appealing to be seated close to an obviously discriminatory person like me.

From her first word, wheelchair-woman's attitude challenges her external signs of disability. Her voice is strong and lucid. As if she's already decided I won't respond, she turns her head towards me and allows her bright eyes to offer me a cheeky challenge.

Ah ha. An emigre. Crossing the border into dystopian territory. Welcome, stranger. Don't concern yourself. You will soon find this alien place less confusing. When we so called normal beings enter this place, we don't expect to find an almost normal world inside those large glass doors. Soon it's clear that inside, despite its infamy as a home for the aged, isn't that different to the world we left behind except – and I don't expect you'll believe me, because you are in the early stages of adapting – you will find this place presents far fewer conflicts and contradictions than the outside world. I'm Gwendolyn, by the way.

Billy. Short for Wilhemena.

Well, that makes me Gwen, short for Gwendolyn.

Gwen extends her trembling and skeletal right hand towards me, and to my horror I momentarily experience fear. Will this hand snap and break if I grip it too tightly to give it a good handshake? Gwen's grip is almost as firm as mine despite her arm's constant movement, and her eyes are laughing at me. She has read my mind.

Sorry for my strange language earlier, but I want to use my words before I can no longer speak. The dreaded moment is coming far quicker than I want. Along with the loss of everything else. Would you believe in my previous life I was a high-flying lawyer? Words are my tools of trade.

Gwen makes a valiant effort to disguise her grief for her future losses by waving her shaking arms and screwing up her face to form a grotesque smile, but she fails. Her tearless emotions are visibly scrolling down her ruined face. Despite my determination to remain emotionally aloof, I register the pain of empathy somewhere inside my chest and unexpectedly, out of character for me, a sob builds inside, an empathetic requiem for what has passed and yet is still ahead for Gwen. I struggle to not let it show as I sense it might be taken as an insult rather than empathy. It surprises me. I'm not one who usually would let my empathetic moments overtake me and, so far in this place, empathy from me has been absent, a flaw in myself I don't like admitting. Like a long pause of an audio recording, neither of us speak, until Gwen breaks the moment. Her still-bright gaze turns towards me. Her aged-destroyed slash of a mouth widens. Despite its grossness, I can recognise this as yet another attempt to smile. In return for her generosity, I offer one of my own. Without thinking, I bend my face until it's level with Gwen's drooping one, and surprise myself with my proposal to Gwen.

Let's go over for a latte and get to know each other better.

And there, once more, is the marvellous ice-breaking line at work. Let's go for a latte and get to know each other better. Fairview planners knew what they were doing when they set up these little self-serve cafes around the complex.

Recently educated with the workings of wheelchair propulsion, I stand and move to Gwen's wheelchair, then I unlock the brakes, check Gwen's feet are safely on the pedals, step in the driver's position, and we are off, on our way toward the rewards of caffeine. Afterwards, back in my suite, I give myself a going-over. What kind of person are you, Billy Corass? You haven't been displaying your best side of late. I had not given the wizen, chair-bound woman a chance to make her true self visible until it was forced on me, this the crime of which I had accused Sam and Chris, my rescuers back in the desert, of perpetrating.

5

In my induction to Fairview, a twice weekly shopping bus was mentioned. Residents are taken to and picked up from the local mall. The staff member carrying out the introduction smiled a little when she added, 'Mostly the shoppers are women.' Today, I'm sitting in the lobby and watching the likely shoppers gathering near the front entry, many of them dressed up in styles not normally seen inside Fairview, or anywhere else for a decade or two, according to my cynical appraisal. In a nod to my mother, I think 'Sunday Best', though I can't help but smile at some of the choices. One must have resuscitated her 'sixties wardrobe to find her sparkly t-shirt and jeans, a seventy-plus but beautiful piece of mutton dressed in lamb's clothing, to misquote the cliché, but the wearer has a smile as wide as the sky. She's happy, and in the end that's all that matters. Does she care about my internal commentary? I think not. Another woman looks like a daytime version of a

Las Vegas showgirl in red that contrasts violently with her pal, who's teamed a 1980s-style straight skirt with a contrasting prim jacket.

Schoolgirls.

I've done it again. I have let my internal thoughts out into the world, and proof comes by way of puffs of soft laughter from somewhere behind me. It's lawyer Gwen in her wheelchair sharing coffees with Mr Newsreader. Caught out, fair and square. I know Gwen's humour is like mine, but is that the same for the Newsreader? I'm embarrassed and, once recognising my critics, I emulate my father by adopting a stiff back, a head turned away, thus displaying no acknowledgement of the pair's presence. I know I haven't escaped unscathed when I hear the tyres of Gwen's wheelchair squelching closer.

Oh, we agree, Billy. Just proof this is a diverse community. Take a sample of any population and you will uncover the thinkers, the schoolgirls, the performers, the stuck ups, the risk-takers, the loathsome, the princesses and princes, and then there will be us, ordinary people.

Gwen is laughing at me.

There's those like me who need to be here because we need help and among our specific group there are some who would not care if this place merely comprised of four walls in which there's a bed, a shower, and a toilet, if there's also someone there to bathe and feed them. That's the extent of what they can handle. For them, these luxury hotel-style interiors with the lovely furniture like these comfy sofas, the facilities, the shopping buses and cafes are merely trimmings with only small benefits. If I was cynical ...

At this Gwen looks over to Newsreader and laughs, as she struggles to support her glance with a shrug of her shoulders, 'Me? Cynical?' at which the Newsreader has a hearty laugh at her self-appraisal, then she turns back to me and continues putting forward her case, picking up where she left off, her speech punctuated by glances toward the Newsreader.

If I was cynical, I'd say that fancy trimmings are essentially here to provide reassurance for the families and loved ones of residents, as those caring individuals go through the process of making big decision around what's the right thing to do. Maybe the façade of luxury will ease them into making the decision they must make, provide them the excuse needed to convince them they will no longer be perceived as uncaring for choosing home care. In truth, in the act of making these kinds of decisions, they show they are indeed caring people. But there's nothing like softening the hard choice by an appearance of homeliness. And it's not a lie. Except for a percentage of our residents, space is set aside in a way that it mostly feels like 'home' once you get used to it, a home shared by many members of a large family. For me, it's like living in a hotel. I have companionship, plenty to watch like the girls on their shopping excursion and the petty fights that occur over seating or invasions of privacy and so on, none of which I would have if I did what my family wanted, which was to apply for home care and stay in the home I love and have lived in for many long years. Knowing I feel this way about my home, my family drew on those emotions to form the core of their argument towards me remaining in my home. My family didn't, or couldn't, understand why I decided Fairview was the path I wanted to follow. That's because they don't live my life. They don't have my body to deal with.'

She has more to say.

You know, I can't always get to the toilet promptly, so someone needs to clean me up. Humiliating for me, and difficult for whoever that someone might be. It's degrading to need someone to help you dress and undress and bathe. If I did what my family wanted, well, it's beyond consideration. The distance between receiving professional help and having a loving family member do the same is vast. Family members aren't trained. They can't do the job, as much as they might want to show their willingness. And besides, this way when they visit, I can maintain my dignity because my badly behaving body is less on show, and they are comforted by my appearance, because in those moments I look as good as can be expected for a person who has lost control of much of her body, and who needs a wheelchair to get around. Never underestimate dignity.

Gwen emits a nervous giggle, encouraging me to wonder if she has gone further with her lecture than she had intended, thus revealing more than she should. Gwen has a big finish, it seems, as she uses her good arm to point.

And then we come to people like you and the shoppers, free to come and go whenever you wish. You can enjoy the full benefits of being here, like going for walks in the garden, shopping, dining in or out, going to the movies or the theatre, or going on holidays. There's no one-rule in here. You need only to find your way through the maze. You'll get there, Billy. Go shopping next week, just to see. Those girls, despite their differences, enjoy themselves, or so I hear.

There again is the promise that 'Ill get there.' I repay Gwen with a smile that I had intended to show came from my heart, though these days I can't tell if I express my emotions appropriately. Gwen's lecture delivers more food for thought, as disconcerting as it may be to have it delivered almost from the woman's lap as her crippled body struggles to hold her head upright. Gwen has the last word, served with a wicked laugh.

I warned you, didn't I? I like to talk, and because it is a dying commodity in my case, I refuse to hold back. I don't mean to offend but I never tire of hearing myself. I'm making the most of it while I have it.

The Newsreader moves to take control of Gwen's wheelchair. Their departure from the lobby is marked by the echo of Gwen's gurgling laughter.

6

When the next shopping day rolls around, one of the carers knocks on the door of my suite and, once I open it, pokes her head in.

Hi there. Billy, isn't it?

She doesn't wait for me to answer.

Well, as you can see by what I am wearing, I am a staff member. My name is Maude.

Maude pinches her thumb and forefinger of both hands and pulls out the skirt of her uniform as she makes a courtesy. Maude's face is soft. Her large brown eyes overwhelm any impression made upon her viewers. Her smile is warm and easy, convincing all who see it of its genuineness. My immediate reaction is to make a mental note this one is good.

I am wondering, Billy, if you might like to join the bus crowd today. Most do little shopping, but they enjoy being in a different surrounding, and from what they tell me there's a coffee shop in the mall that offers the most divine coffee and pastries. Your hip is coming along nicely, and I reckon a walk around the mall might be the exercise it needs. What do you think?

Maude doesn't give me time to think. She places a firm hand on my right shoulder, twirls me around and gives me the once over up and down.

You look just fine, there, Billy. Grab your handbag and off you go. Joan will guide you. She's waiting for you downstairs.

With one gentle but firm push toward the door, Maude follows me as I walk along the corridor. As we reach the elevator door, Maude turns and gives me her largest smile.

Oh, and Joan has a borrowed walking stick for you to use. To give you confidence.

This terrifies me. How will I manage a walking stick? And then an even more depressing thought comes into my head. Will needing to use one mark me as 'one of those?' This is punishment for my criticism of the shoppers last week. My pride forces me to accept the challenge and by the time I am reaching the group waiting in the lobby, I have convinced myself I can handle this. I won't let it get the better of me.

A bright face is lighting the way for me. It's Joan, the lady I met during my encounter with the possessive Italian. Joan's hand stretches out and grips mine, as if she's still welcoming me to Fairview.

Let me introduce you, Billy. This is Lily Grey.

Lily is tall and broad shouldered, and her booming voice matches her build.

Good to have you join us, Billy. It's a ball.

Joan moves over to another, a curly-headed, short and round woman.

This is Barb. Barbara Phillips. Billy.

Barb gives me a small royal style wave and a smile, then moves onto the bus. I notice the driver is already seated in the bus with his hands on steering wheel. The expression on his face tells me he wants to be gone, so he may be willing we bunch of blathering women to do our introductions later.

Once the bus comes to a standstill in the mall car park, one by one each elderly passenger makes slow progress down the steps of the bus, each hesitating before taking that one final, deeper than normal, step down onto the car park bitumen. Only after a successful landing does each lift their head from their feet and share a triumphant smile, a celebration of making it through a precarious passage to arrive safe and unharmed. I question my sanity for letting Maude railroad me.

Like a herd of nervous animals, our group makes its way across to the entrance and trudges along the first corridor as if this is the set path. Shoulders are bent as if the bodies to which they are attached are resenting the need to move forward, and yet everyone's eyes are alert, glancing this way and that. There's constant chattering and finger-pointing. The further into the shopping complex our group traverses, as it works its way through a maze of corridors, the fewer remain. Pairs or threesomes peel off to explore a newsagency, or a boutique, or a pharmacy, each group calling out as they disappear, 'see you, you know where,' a secret that is accompanied by a tinkle of giggles, like schoolkids on an illicit outing.

Shopping has never been something for which I hanker, always only ever engaged in to meet practical needs and rarely for the pleasure, unlike many others for whom it's a great day out. Today, it's being out here, doing something among a 'normal' population that's satisfying me, even if I know that's not PC. My senses are sharp. I'm acutely aware of the sounds of voices echoing down corridors, footsteps on the flooring, and rubber wheels of prams and trolleys squealing across the tiles. The blended aromas seeping out from the cafes and food stores we pass assail my nostrils. I'm alive. I'm experiencing life. In my previous life, before my fall and Fairview, I would rarely spend enough time anywhere like this, not even somewhere else than a shopping mall. Today, for a reason beyond my understanding I feel as if I have led a deprived existence, and I know this has nothing to do with being in Fairview. Truthfully, in my previous life, any of my non-working time would have been spent on preparing for, out on, cleaning up after, or reviewing the outcome of a competitive event. Today, because I'm limited by a clicking hip and a cane, both of which keep my pace regular and slow, I have the luxury to take in every experience this complex has on offer.

I follow Joan and Lily as they explore, with me tapping along the solid mall floor behind them, reluctantly allowing myself to concede gratitude for the support of the stick. The aid, as demoralising as I was sure it would be, provides reassurance, something solid to hold me steady. However, it also forces an unnatural gait, which is wearying. I'm about ready to beg for respite when I see familiar faces and hands waving. Though many of these women are still nameless, they have included me as if they have known me over a lifetime. Our group has taken over a large table in a cafe dressed as if it belongs in some European country. Faces glow in triumph, as if they have won an event and wish to be congratulated. It's clear this is 'you know where.' Joan and Lily lead me along a bypass to the glass display cabinet, confident the table has been secured. Like children in the lolly shop, these so-called mature individuals are excitedly pointing to items under the glistening glass.

Joan checks to see if I'm still with them, a mother checking on her errant child.

Come on, Billy. What'll be your poison?

I tap my way across to where Joan and the others have gathered, and gaze into the display cabinet with less enthusiasm than my companions. The shelves are loaded with a broad range of pastries and cakes. Ah, here they are, the treats promised in return for venturing out on the bus.

7

Another week passes, and despite my persistent negative take on Fairview, my new residency seems less foreign. Every day fresh sights and more information continue to both surprise and shock me. I have tried to cling to Deer Lady Coral's logic, handed on the day of the sombre Honour Guard, but it's incontrovertible that I'm not yet ready for this extraordinary change in my life. I'm still clinging to the hope that once my hip has healed, Brandon will keep his promise. That I haven't had a visit from my son since I've been in Fairview nags at me. Has he met his goal? Does it mean I'm here now, and he's not in a hurry to change that?

The rest of it, like Coral's philosophy, is worthy of deeper exploration, if not for now but for a future that's not so far down the track, all worth considering if I want to stay in control of my life. This requires me to be brave and face that some hard-to-digest realities will be unavoidable. For now, there's too much to work through, as my entry into this alien existence has been too sudden, too unexpected, and I have had no time to prepare myself for the transition from my life as it was – Oh, how long ago has it been? Oh yes – only a month ago.

A month? That short? That long? And where's my son been since I've been in Fairview? Is he checking on my hip's progress so he can fulfil his promise? I suspect not. I'm turning back towards my previous prediction, that he probably thinks he's won this battle. He has promised to get me here, assuming once I'm here, there would be no going back. This way he has me under control, and he need not be worrying about my next unpredictable action or, as he calls it, my risk-taking.

I'm not going down without a fight. This is my life. If I choose to stay here, that's one matter, but if I choose to leave, that's another. I have trusted my son to allow me the dignity of deciding my own path, but I've an inkling he might be avoiding me. Without more thought I reach for the residential directory in my bedside table. I scan it for the number of Fairview's Manager. Her name is Ms Polina. I dial the number and speak to her receptionist.

This is Billy Corass of apartment 624. I wish to have a conversation with Ms Polina. Can you give me a day and time for me to do so, please.

The receptionist sounds a little surprised by my request, and I figure it's likely to be because of the unusualness of a resident asking for an appointment. Discussions about residents' situations might usually be conducted with sons or daughters or other family members. But I could be wrong in my assumption. I am on high alert for signs of discrimination, supercharged by my failed challenge to authority via Dr Eagan at the hospital still sharp in my memory. I'm determined this will go better.

8

Today's the day. I enter Ms Polina's office with as much dignity as permitted by a still healing dislocated hip. I drill into my mindset to adopt the demeanour ideal for a job interview, that is, show good posture to promote a perception of confidence while displaying an air of competence and the ability to think rationally and clearly. I smile broadly, hoping to display an air of co-operation rather than one of resistance.

Nice to meet you, Ms Polina. I believe my son has spoken to you on my behalf.

The Manager nods with her head slightly bent to one side and a tiny smile playing across the lower section of her face.

Mrs Corass. Yes. Your son has done the hard work for you. You are a lucky mother.

He's a caring boy, Brandon. But he has his own ideas about what my needs are so, Ms Polina, I'd like to clarify and repeat those Brandon has set in place for me to see how they fit my requirements.

Is the change of expression on Mariella Polina's face one of surprise, or anger or disbelief, or amusement? Or, maybe, Ms Polina is merely acknowledging my interest in my own affairs. I'm suspicious of anything and everything, especially when it hasn't been run past me first.

I believe, Ms Polina ...

Please, Mrs Corass. Call me Mariella.

Ms Polina, or Mariella as I now have the privilege of calling her, points to the chair in front of her desk. This is the moment my hip chooses to catch, bad timing as far as me keeping up appearance. I do my best to disguise my reactions to its grab and any limitations it places on me. It's difficult to tell if Mariella has noticed. On the other side of the desk, she sinks back into her oversized leather office chair, her face closed to any interpretation.

Thank you, Ms Polina. Mariella. I'd like to state up front I don't wish to cause you any problems. That's why I want to speak on my own behalf at the beginning of our relationship. I know you are a busy woman, and you won't want me returning to your office every five minutes to sort out any misunderstandings, so may I ask, Ms Polina, Mariella, if you will note my list of requirements for my stay at your lovely establishment.

Even to my own ears my words sound forced and unnatural, more like the authoritarian clip by father often used, and it will possibly not be helpful to my cause. I'm a little put off that no pen or notepad has seemed to record my wish list. Mariella's eyes drop to the paperwork spread in front of her and then roll over the top of her spectacles. Now there's an action that demonstrates authority. Her gaze, displaying a calm sense of professionalism, locks into mine, and I immediately feel myself shrinking. I need to regroup and assert myself once more.

May I state my requirements, please? I want privacy. I'm not a pack animal, and it's my human right to live in the privacy of my space the way I wish to do, especially as my son is paying for my accommodation, not the government through any pension.

Mariella's lips twitch. Is she amused? Or merely waiting to hear the rest of my list?

Of course, Mrs Corass.

I feel I've had a tiny win and continue.

Yes, I still have some bruising and a healing hip, but I am far from dependent on help. I need to do as much for myself as I can, so I am ready for when it comes, soon I hope, where I'm independent and can leave Fairview.

I try to lighten the mood with a joke.

You know how it goes: use it or lose it.

Mariella's face is almost expressionless, if that's possible. I can feel my patience slipping, and know I've behaving a little bit childish. As she's not made any comment, I slip into rebellion again. I read her silence as indicating total power because I did think at least she'd come out with those smooth PR phrases, making empty promises, offering words to placate but not to be put into practice. I'm certain Mariella has heard similar demands before. If not by a resident, then by sons and daughters acting on behalf of their parents. If I look closer, I can convince myself I can see a hint of impatience, but that might also be me being suspicious, that if it is impatience it's possibly because she sees this as a futile exercise and wants to move from this phase to the next, one I expect that might be her 'selling the dream' spiel, or maybe she's focused on whatever is written on the sheet of paper beneath her index finger. It's only my perception.

I am mesmerised by the tip of Mariella's finger tracing around and around on the paperwork in front of her. She doesn't look down, even when she sees my eyes watching. My eyes follow her finger as it maintains a regular pattern, until finally she draws a miniature triangle by moving across the horizontal, upwards to the apex, and down again. Then all motion stops. Is the tracing finger her way of getting through a conversation that she knows can go nowhere? Does the ceasing of movement mean Mariella senses her moment is almost upon her, the time is right to spring? That's how I read it, rightly or wrongly, and I feel as if I'm a naive deer waiting for my inevitable annihilation when the stalking leopard pounces.

My eyes move back to Mariella's face, searching for clues. Her half-smile has returned. I'd love to say, 'It's wasted on me, mam,' but I doubt my ability to hold my ground. I'm beginning to sense this isn't going my way. Mariella's eyes don't even blink. I feel edgy. Our one-sided conversation is not showing progress, and I can't read Mariella's facial expressions, except that it's saying she has all the answers and is toying with me. I try boldness. Last resort. Same approach as the one I used with Dr Eagan.

I haven't seen you write anything yet, Mariella.

Oh, no need to record, Mrs Corass. I am with you all the way. I agree with everything you have to say.

Smarmy bitch, I say to myself, but I won't utter those words, and I hope my face doesn't betray me. Mariella's sense of total power is apparent, and why shouldn't it be. She's a corporate manager with a vast number of people under her umbrella of responsibility. And that does me in. I'm back reliving every moment of my life in which I have been put down by someone in power, often unjustly. The hairs on my neck bristles with stored up anger. If I must live in this place because they have taken the choice of residence from me, I'll resist being held under someone else's authority with no means to speak for myself. As this is the last phase of my life, there's nothing to lose by standing up for my own rights. Not Mariella. Nor Brandon. No one is frustrating me, ever again.

Even as I declare my resistance, there's a dank odour of the inevitable, an inky black sadness that begins down low and works its way up through my gut into my chest, gagging my throat. Is this where my CV ends? Taking the literal meaning of curriculum vitae, or the course of one's life, to succinctly measure my present dismal situation. Whatever of life that is left to me seems to only be on a downhill run, collecting speed as my body and then my mind eventually disintegrates. No longer of value, and with nothing to contribute, I am a dead woman walking.

Mariella hasn't made her final punch yet. I can sense the crescendo is approaching. Her attention returns to the paperwork in front of her, and she picks up the bundle, bangs it down on her desk again and again to bring the individual pages into alignment with the others, and once in a tidy stack, she places them inside a blue folder, which she closes with a dull thud. As in Dr Eagan's office, I notice it's labelled, 'Wilhemena Rose Corass.'

I am glad you came to chat today, Billy. You have made yourself clearly understood. Please come again if there's anything troubling you.

Business has been concluded; there's nothing more to be said. And a mountain of reality avalanches down on me. I can only conclude Brandon and Ms Polina have had their conversation. Brandon has signed off on his mother's future. The powerless individual, the aged and redundant person, uninvited to contribute. Done like a dinner, as Charlie had forecast.

9

There's a buzz from my intercom. It's Reception.

Morning Mrs C. Your son is here, and he's asked if you would meet him in the café.

Trust big-shot Brandon to get the receptionist to do his job. Would it have broken him to come up a floor or two and knock on my door? Oh, that's right, he probably doesn't know where my suite is. It would be nice to walk down to the café with him. I reprimand myself. I should be grateful that he has finally found time to visit. I feel somewhat nervous, wondering if he's come to say I'm permitted to leave, or is he aware that Mariella has done his job for him, and made it clear this is my forever home. Not that Mariella did, not really. She said only that if I wanted to discuss anything with her, I was most welcome. There was nothing said about plans for my future or the permanency of my stay. I recognise this is mainly about my fears, and as usual I take my cheapskate way out and resort to sarcasm. Maybe Brandon's worried 'oldness' might rub off on him. Couldn't have that, could we?

Hold in your bitterness, Missie, or this might be your last visit from your son. I can make excuses for him. One might be that Brandon might have seen going through Reception as the way he should conduct himself when visiting the offices of his colleagues, or out of respect for my privacy. There might have been no malice intended.

Despite my good intentions, I don't seem able to control myself. The anger is still there, fuelled by loss of control and a sense of helplessness. I am a ball of fury without a way to put out the fire, and as I scramble for control of my emotions, I hear laughter in the corridor, almost as if someone is mocking me. I open my door a crack, ready to blast the wise arse, and see two women passing When they see me, their faces light up in recognition and together they flutter their hands over their shoulders, still hunched in laughter.

Billy, remind me to tell you Clare's joke at lunch. It's a beauty. We are on our way to Bingo right now and running late. See you later.

With a flick of a hand, the pair move rapidly along the passageway, still chatting and laughing as they hurry on.

This, like other tiny moments of friendship, reminds me of the positives of living within a community of peers. My life experiences, my career, my choice of sport, have promoted detachment from others, in the main making me a loner. This includes extreme running, that by its nature makes it difficult to mix with other passionate participants except before and after events and, more often, those competitors come from other places to which they must return often promptly after the events. I've never seen it as an issue but contrasting that way of life with the experiences of Fairview has brought home the loneliness of those choices. Work pals are just that, someone with whom you dine out, complain about the boss, talk about footy or cricket or the weather, but rarely do individual lives entwine.

I bring myself back to the present by reminding myself Brandon's waiting. I need to swallow my nervousness. I scramble to find my comfortable walkers rather than my dressier pumps, because I don't want my limp to be noticeable. I puff up and flatten down my hair without looking at how it appears, and run my tongue over my lips, hoping that will replace lipstick. I take a deep breath and stride in a determined way, neither slow nor fast, toward the elevator, mentally counselling myself to let go of my anger. As the elevator door opens on the ground floor, my eyes locate Brandon seated at a table, and with that sight, I'm surprised by a rush of maternal love that fills my chest. My boy. The way his head is bowed reminds me of a younger lad, waiting to be scolded for some small mistake. Maybe that is how he feels. A reel of micro-flashes of his life from baby to adult, too quickly scrolled to acknowledge any specific event, and I can feel a softening of my face, and the anger dissolving. My pace increases, and I surprise him with my arrival, and probably as well with my smile, which hasn't been offered to him much of late.

Good to see you, my boy. I'd hoped you hadn't forgotten where you left me, like you used to lose your sneakers.

My attempt at being jovial falls flat because my touch of sarcasm is too close to an already contentious, if unspoken, subject.

And you too, Mum.

Brandon's smile is soft, as he offers me the smallest nod, as though it's his body's response but not his heart. Brandon drops his head and studies his shoes, then gazes into my faces.

It's suits you, being here.

Now Brandon is doing what I did earlier. His comment, though probably innocent, feels loaded. Is this an instinctive response from Brandon? Or is it a soft form of manipulations, an attempt to see if being here has turned me around? Is he so out of tune with how I'm feeling he doesn't realise this comment could be read by me as insensitive? So fragile is my emotional state, I'm close to tears, and noting this, a question comes into mind about how emotional I've become of late. Inwardly I feel as if I'm teetering on the edge of an abyss. Tears in front of Brandon are the last thing I want. I won't show hurt.

If I'm to hide my feelings I can't look my son in the eye, so I attempt to distract myself by undergoing a thorough examination of the tabletop.

Afterwards, he and I, a son and his mother, sit at the table, coffee cold, and with nothing to say to each other. For me, it's because I'm not sure I can hold back what's thundering around inside me. Is his, by chance, a consequence of guilt? That's if he even recognises that some damage has been done between us, especially if he sees himself as the good, caring son, who's doing what he should do and I'm the uncooperative mother.

I find some courage and look over at Brandon, who in turn is looking across to the entrance door. My boy looks sad. Bugger. Attack is not the way to go, old lady. I need strategies, tactics, cleverness and negotiation, and this is neither the time nor the place.

I want to say something that will break this stalemate, and I open my mouth to try and find words, but before any thing comes out of my mouth, Brandon shakes his head and stands.

Don't start again, Mum. I'm trying to do what's best for you.

By doing what? And what do you mean, by 'start again'?

I have heard your protests. You are like a child. This is the right thing for you at this moment, given your condition, and you need to come to grips with your situation and settle down. Stop fighting and listen to reason. See things as they are, not how you think they are.

Once it might have been me, his mother, putting him in order, bringing him to a better way of thinking, or aiding him to see a reasonable way forward by using the same tone as he is using, the one an adult uses when speaking to a child. When did this change? Did it only take my accident to revert me to the powerless infant? To him, did this momentary weakness offer an opportunity he knew would come at some time? Why, suddenly, does it seem so cruel and hurtful to be spoken to as if your life has taught you nothing, as if you are an imbecile? Do I deserve to be spoken to in this way? Have I done something, anything, that has justified this attitude from my son? Even if he thinks he's doing the right thing by me, can't he show enough respect to try and explain his thinking, and not just make it happen without consultation? I will protest, but so far protesting is not doing me much good. At least if he tells me what he has in mind, I could prepare myself, but it seems the only way Brandon can handle this is for me to accept and not question.

A silent sob echoes in my chest, its epicentre is my heart. It's breaking.

So great is my pain, flight is my only option. I want to be the child now. I need to fly around a corner, to find any niche in which I can hide. Instead, I squint my eyes as if I'm trying to read the menu, even though we have already had our coffee. My upper and lower teeth are grinding against each other to control my desire to cry. I am blotting out Brandon's words, but I can only sustain this plan for the shortest period. I pray my face does not give me away. I focus hard on containing the anger that is boiling over. No good can come from letting it seep out. Inside, I'm screaming.

I.

Am.

Human.

I'm capable.

Why can't I make...

My own decisions?

What has changed?

I'm lost.

I've lost me.

Lost any signs of dignity.

Where's any respect for me?

Inside, I feel my resistance forming a core of steel. In a desperate gesture to show I am in control of my external appearance, I hope with all my heart that, by internally chanting my running mantra, I will present a calm face. At least, I might keep silent and find the courage to look at my son and smile. In my mind, the chant begins. 'One foot down, lift the other. One foot down, lift the other. Hear the rhythm. Like a heartbeat. Bouncing off the ground. One foot then another.'

I've done it. I've gained control. I smile in Brandon's direction without making eye contact. He'll know, but it's the best I can do. I review the short menu once more, and I surprise myself with the ordinariness of my voice.

I might indulge myself in a cream horn today, Brandon, and another latte. Hope you are feeling generous.

I'm aware residents and their guests need not pay. If he thinks I am stupid, I will be, my stubborn mind affirms. I haven't fooled Brandon. He tilts his head toward me and gives me a half-smile.

Playing games, are we?

I meet his challenge with a return stare, this time my gaze into his eyes is as challenging as his into mine. Mine is a silent response: two can play. Years of discipline tell me this is about the long game, not the skirmishes.

Only after Brandon waves goodbye, and as I watch his rigid back passing through the glass doors of the lobby without turning to wave good-bye, do I notice the Newspaper Reader sitting in the corner, those intelligent eyes taking in everything that has transacted between Brandon and me. His face doesn't hide an expression I have noticed at other times. Mr Fix-it wants to fix things for everyone, and now it's me he sees as needing fixing. I avoid eye contact and prematurely congratulate myself for the growth in my ability to control my responses. Working at seeming indifferent, I rise, turn without looking at the man, then as steadily as I am able, I walk towards the elevator as if nothing is amiss. My anger is directed on Brandon but also at Mr Fix-it whose only misdemeanour is to show concern on his face. This is the rocket fuel that enables me to exit the lobby, aware this is what's necessary if I'm to reach the sanctuary of my suite before I dissolve into nothingness. My self-control is verging on reaching its limits.

Yet, I still haven't challenged Brandon. I'm still in limbo.

10

Somehow, I make it back to my suite without encountering a soul. I snatch open my door and slam it shut with the force I wish I had used to repel my son's disdain. Except I never would hit him, and I know I'm more shattered than ordinarily I might be only because my son is the one who is challenging me. At least the physical exertion of door slamming absorbs some of my frustration. The temporary satisfaction it provides is immediately overtaken by shame. The sound of the slamming door has reverberated along the corridor, and I imagine my frail companions receding deep into their recliners, trembling at a potential threat to their normally quiet and protected sanctuaries. Inside my suite, I throw myself onto the sofa like a petulant teenager. Rather than drape myself lengthwise as a tantrum thrower might, I take my usual position of misery, as I did when things were against me in the hospital. I roll into a ball, back bent and shoulders hunched. I seek a cloak of anonymity.

The regular time for the evening meal in the dining room comes and goes. Food has no appeal. I'm too invested in my mood to move. Neither asleep nor in the real world, with time passing without measure, I indulge in self-pity and remorse. Inevitably, my body demands a change of posture, and despite a growing discomfort, my unleashed anger makes that bodily request another something to fight against. Cramping muscles and a stiff neck override my resistance, and giving no thought to where I'm heading, I stand and stumble my way through to my bedroom, stopping only when forced by my shins colliding with the edge of my bed. I should shower. I'm aware I would feel better if I did, but instead, I let my body drop diagonally across my bed, face-down, fully dressed, and shoes still on my feet, a practice that would have been perceived as a definite no-no during my growing up years. This minor rule-breaking is me making a whimpering form of protest. Is it minutes or hours later, when I make a stand and remove my dress, kick off my shoes, and crawl under the doona. I'm flotsam, lost in a sea of doubt, and it's such a foreign and lonely place for me. Even in the direst of situation, I find a way through, always able to pick myself up off the floor and tough it out while my mind works on finding solutions.

Brandon's visit was mid-afternoon. When I awake next, it's time for breakfast. I'm an automaton, acting out of habit. I throw on the handiest casual dress and strap on some sandals. I trudge to the elevator, enter, and leave it, and slouch into the dining room for breakfast. The event of choosing breakfast, taking it back to a table, sitting and eating it happens without a word of greeting or of farewell to my dining companions. I ignore their curious glances by keeping my eyes set directly ahead. I return to my suite, locking my door behind me, and enter once more the oblivion provided by my position on my sofa. Weighed down with grief, as if someone dear has passed, I've stopped functioning in the way I have always done. My mind is blank. I am not reviewing or teasing out the complexities of yesterday's fiasco, as I normally would. Nor am I stepping up to take control of my future, whatever it may be.

I skip lunch and dinner and satisfy my slight hunger in the early evening with some cheese snacks found in my fridge and a weak black tea, after which I persuade myself to shower and don fresh night wear. I'm empty of incentives. What's the point? Even television, the perfect medium for mindlessness, is unappealing. My only option is to crawl back into my hidey-hole under the doona. An unintentional glimpse at the clock tells me it's only 6.30 pm, and this scares me. What am I doing to myself?

I doze and wake, and soon I'm once again wallowing in my misery, this only interrupted by the sound of what I think is soft scratching on the door to my suite. I pretend I've not heard anything, but the scratching is persistent, and is soon followed by a voice, calling.

Billy. Billy. May I come in?

It's Maude.

I grunt, hoping that is enough to put Maude off, but there's no mistaking the noise of a key being pushed into a lock and turning, and the sound of my front door opening. I can hear Maude tip-toe-ing through my living area as if there's a baby asleep that she doesn't want to wake, and she doesn't stop until her kind face peeks cautiously into my bedroom.

Used my master key, sorry for the intrusion, but are you okay, Billy? Your friends said you weren't yourself at breakfast and didn't turn up for lunch or dinner. Doesn't seem like you.

I try grunting again to dissuade Maude from the need for further conversation.

Maude shifts my small bedside chair until it's sufficiently close for her to stroke my hair and look closely into my face. She carefully picks up strands of my hair and lifts them away from my eyes. She leans closer, and whispers. I'm a child again, being cared for.

Was this anything to do with your visitor yesterday? Joe thought you seemed upset.

Joe? Who is Joe?

Oh Billy, you know Joe, don't you? He reads to the men and runs the Men's Shed.

Damn. The Newspaper Reader. I was right. He is a Mr Fix-it, and my inkling he'd want to interfere was correct.

Without warning my eyes fill and tears stream down my face. Soon I'm crying so wretchedly I'm surprising myself. I tell myself it's not because of Mr Fix-it's neighbourly concerns, or that my friends know me well enough to recognise there's something wrong, but that it's merely Maude's kind enquiry. I know in truth it's every one of these factors combined. This is not my usual experience of life. I live for myself and by myself, and mostly no one knows whether I am happy or sad, or struggling or on top. And this generosity is yet another something that adds to my bewilderment.

Maude reaches over and whisks out a couple of tissues from the box on the bedside table.

Billy, dear, I have made a note for the doctor to drop in. You seem low, and we can't have that.

No, please no, Maude.

We all want our old Billy back, and maybe you are coming down with something. I won't countenance objections, Billy dearest. Would you like one of your friends to come in for a chat?

This is the final straw. I want to bury my face into the pillow.

Sure, Maude. Send the doctor along. In case. But I will be all right, I am sure. Thanks for checking in. Tell the ladies, oh yes, and Joe, thanks. I will see them tomorrow. For sure. I'll be right tomorrow.

Maude gives one last gentle shoulder massage, and stares into my eyes for what seems a lifetime, then rises and heads to the door.

We never know when the doctor is available, but I'll let you know beforehand when he's likely to visit. You rest, Billy.

Thanks, Maude.

As the door clicks closed, I try to bury my tears into the pillow.

11

New day, new perspective and a new start

I begin by seeking facts and making assessments as well as I'm able to do so. The threatened ACAT test hasn't happened. Rightly so. ACAT testing measures an individual's ability to live independently. A dislocated hip is not enough to deem me needing 24/7 care. Assistance, yes, but that could be obtained in my own home.

Back in the hospital, during my non-productive meeting with Dr Eagan, the doctor referred to a file that noted on its cover that Brandon was my guardian. At the time in my confused state. I convinced myself this was not so. But, clearer in mind now, I remember I'd given in to Brandon on this. No. 'Giving in' is not the proper turn of phrase. It had been my decision, part of my plan to take care of my future. It's common sense. If I am no longer capable, he should be granted the ability to step in. The problem is, when you sign these powerful authorities, you have no foresight. Your imagination does not let you think of the likely scenarios in which they will come into play. However, I am certain that when I entered this arrangement, I'd been told that guardianship can only come into play under certain circumstances. I need to refresh myself on this. I turn on my computer and search.

And there it is, on my computer screen. 'A person puts in place an Enduring Power of Attorney (EPoA) while he or she knows what they are signing, assigning the authority to a trusted person to make financial and legal decisions on their behalf at some future time when the authoriser ...' (me) '... is no longer capable of decision-making. This form covers only finance and legal decision so, when planning for future impairment and health care, you need to name an agent within another document, an Enduring Power of Guardianship (EPoG).' Furthermore, there's also 'a General Power of Attorney (PoA)' which 'is restricted by only being valid for a certain period or transaction.' In short, an EPOG extends to hold authority after one loses their mental capacity whereas the PoA is done for a specific event or period and once that is achieved, it's no longer valid. Providing you are mentally capable, you can revoke the authority. Of course, you would need a doctor to support the claim of your mental capability. So that's the financial side

Then there's the EPoG, in which you appoint someone to make personal, lifestyle, and treatment decisions on your behalf if you become unable to make these decisions yourself. This role is fulfilled by an individual known as your guardian. 'An agent who has the powers to represent someone must presume a person possesses the mental capacity and must know that mental capacity is decision specific whereby a person continues to make their own decisions, for as long as they can do so. Any substitute decision-making is the last resort. An agent must assess a person's decision-making ability only and not by the decisions they make.'

Yes, please everyone, such as Dr Eagan and especially you, Brandon. The last point is enormous. Don't assume that a person lacks capacity because of age, appearance, disability, or behaviour, just because you disagree with her choices. I can't count the number of discriminatory actions I have suffered. What I need is an answer to how I can challenge this?

There's a list of medical professionals to consult if there's doubt about a person's capacity to decide, but this list is for the other side of the arrangement, in my case, Brandon's perspective. I need more detail on my rights and how, if needed, I could challenge any assessment. Nowhere does it say anything about a consultant being an emergency ward resident doctor such as the one who may have decided my fate.

The Principal – that's me – can override the Powers.

The small task (not so small) ahead of me is to clear my head and stop panicking about having control taken from me. Until the moment when I need to depend on others, which will hopefully coincide with where that being so will be beyond my caring, I need to put effort into imagining my best life, the one I choose to live while I can still do so, whether it be back in my own house, or here, or somewhere different, and make it happen. My choice, my plan, and in my control, all the while remembering what's important. To do this, I need to find a way through the complexities that doesn't destroy my relationship with my son who, although he may show his love differently, I love with all my heart. Meanwhile I must remember the absolutes. You're young until you aren't, you're able until you aren't, and you're alive until you aren't. In the meantime, you're free to live however you choose.

Neither the start nor the finish

1

Yesterday, I joined the ladies for morning tea, an irregular event for me. My companion was Meghan. Meghan wasn't her usual perky self. If I'm truthful, Meghan and I aren't always on the same page conversation-wise, and yesterday she was deep into her own thoughts, which she relayed in a way that didn't require responses.

Do you know Missy and Sid, Billy? They live in Apartment 625, near you. Missy is my best friend. I have known Missy from before we both came into Fairview. Missy and Sid used to be social. They'd never miss Bingo or Quiz nights.

That's marvellous, Meghan. Nice they do these things together.

Meghan flashed me a quick smile that disappeared as fast as it arrived. After this announcement, her spirits fell again. I looked around. Missy wasn't there. Maybe, I thought, this offered a reason for Meghan being a little down. I was ready to question her, but Meghan had only the subject of Missy and Sid on her mind. She continued her rhetoric.

Oh, Missy and Sid are the regular Romeo and Juliet. Fastened at the hip. Fairview was supposed to be special for them.

Briefly, I considered questioning why Meghan had chosen to use the words, 'supposed to' but to be blunt, I was bored, and this was nothing more than chit-chat for me. I was struggling to maintain interest. I thought perhaps I might have changed the topic by introducing discussion about some current television show I know a lot of the ladies were involved in, but my attempt to do so failed, too. Meghan continued to look glum. For her, it was talk about Missy and Sid or nothing. When she left, her shoulders were slouched, and her head hung low. I had a flick of guilt that I might have tried harder.

Today, the subject of Missy and Sid is forced to prominence, and consequently my guilt over my dismissal of Meghan has been given considerable air. This morning, as I pass by Missy and Sid's apartment on my way down to the lobby, I see Ngalia, the duty manager, knocking on Missy and Sid's door, and she's not alone. There are three uniformed officers with her. It's not a big leap to realise this doesn't bode well for Meghan's two friends.

My instincts, or maybe my sense of guilt, urges me to warn Meghan. Of what? God only knows. Whatever the issue may be, it must be serious to involve the police. I follow my instincts and take a detour on my way back from breakfast via Meghan's apartment.

Meghan, you should come. Something's not right with Missy and Sid.

Already Meghan's face is crumbling, as if she has an insight into what that problem might be. She snatches up her cardigan and keys, loudly slams her apartment door shut, and is pushing herself to walk with speed despite her uneven gait caused by severely arthritic knees. She achieves enough speed for my abilities to be pushed if I hope to keep pace with her. Meghan's only wish is to rush to Missy's aid, but I'm certain she won't be able to, given the police presence, and I've a strong desire to shield her in any small way I'm able.

No, Meghan, not that way. Let's go to my apartment. You'll be able to see from there without getting in anyone's way and you'll be able to tell when it is right to be there for your friend.

We furtively take the back corridor and rather than go inside my apartment, we sit on a bench in the open area, from which we are provided a view down the corridor to Missy and Sid's door where activity has increased dramatically. Someone has erected poles with yellow tape marking off the area. It can only be bad news, and I can't look at Meghan, not wishing my fear to amplify hers. Or because I'm a coward. The latter is more likely the truth.

As we watch, Ngalia comes around the corner pushing a wheelchair and waits just outside the taped-off area. A bowed and stumbling Sid comes out of the apartment with a policewoman on either side to support him as they guide him into the wheelchair. Meghan's mouth opens. I hear a sound that begins as a soft scream, which sharpens to a squawk, followed by a great gulping intake of air. Like me, she can't take her eyes away from the scene ahead, and like me, no doubt her thoughts are flying through endless possibilities and hoping for some reasonable result.

One policewoman bends down to Sid. There's nothing in her actions that suggest anything but benevolence for the passive man seated in the wheelchair. She tucks a blanket around him, pulling it up to his chin and patting his shoulder. Sid doesn't respond. We, the spectators, see the policewoman nod to the duty manager, while another policewoman, her countenance stern and perhaps deliberately blank, bends forward and lifts the tape. Once on the other side, the tape-lifter takes control of both the chair and Sid, and steers the chair and its passenger towards the elevator. On either side, Ngalia and the first policewoman take up support positions as if guarding the wheelchair's occupant. As the elevator door closes behind them, another group of police personnel spill out of the second elevator. Outside of the apartment, they pull on the white plastic all-in-ones.

This is too much like a scene from one of the crime-shows I love, and it reinforces in me the seriousness of the event in Apartment 625. I'm filled with regret for my impulsive decision to inform Meghan of signs of trouble at 625. But it's too late now.

Meghan is sobbing loudly. It's clear Meghan will not be able to comfort Missy, as others are already doing what is necessary. No longer does our act of voyeurism feel right, but Meghan is refusing to move. We can't stay here.

With one arm over Meghan's shoulder and the other under her elbow, I slowly encourage her to rise. We stand, side by side, paralysed by the shock of the scene. I'm filled with a sense of guilt, that I have made this event so much worse for Meghan,

The first to move is me. I turn to face Meghan, hugging her, and as I do, I rotate her, so her back is facing down the corridor and her face no longer able to witness the drama being enacted there.

Come on Megs, Let's have a cuppa? We can check on Missy and Sid later.

Instead of accepting the offer of the magic elixir, distraught Meghan mumbles sentences that might have made sense in the right context but at this moment sound like confessions of guilt, as if Meghan blames herself for this outcome, whatever it may be. I stick to the plan of trying to lead Meghan into my apartment, but it's difficult. Once inside, I ease her onto the sofa. Shock requires tea and lots of sugar, my head informs me. Before I rise, I wrap my arms around Meghan's shoulders and kiss her on her forehead. Meghan doesn't seem to notice, so I continue with the plan of making tea, constantly checking on my grieving companion as I do. Meghan's demeanour has changed in a strange way from the earlier hysterical form, and I'm becoming increasingly worried. Her body is stiff and tight, and she's staring straight ahead, mumbling words that are becoming increasingly indistinguishable. I should seek help, but under the present circumstances I'm certain I'd be burdening the staff when they already have enough to handle.

The kettle has boiled, I have made the tea and laced it with several teaspoons of sugar and now I only need to persuade Meghan to drink. Stiffly, Meghan accepts the mug without looking. Her tear-filled eyes are making a plea as if I have for an explanation to offer her. Messy words fall from her mouth, fat with grief.

Oooo Missy. I tried to get Missy to seek help.

Help? What do you mean, Meghan. What kind of help?

Missy needed Sid. Afraid he couldn't come with her.

What do you mean Meghan? He was here.

Missy said he had mood swings, bad ones, before they moved.

Don't we all?

My attempt at levity sounds hollow. I reprimand myself for my insensitivity. Meghan's too deep in her hole to notice.

No. Terrible mood swings. He needed psychiatric help. Missy knew. She was convinced he was doing better here. She never even told his family. You know how Missy is. All bright and bubbly. She could convince.

And as that thought overtakes her, she jumps up. Tea splashes out of her mug.

I should ask the police officers if I can be with Missy. Missy's my friend.

I haven't the heart to say, 'Didn't you see the white cover-alls?' From my perspective, there are no good signs of Missy's safe keeping, no appearance of ambulance staff, no scurrying away of any survivor, but only Sid's escape in a wheelchair. The situation offers me one terrible explanation for Missy's non-appearance, and my dark appraisal is supported by the external signs we have seen. I pray I'm wrong. Until I know more, it won't help to share my forebodings. I hope with all my heart Missy is elsewhere, and whatever had occurred in the apartment only involved Sid, but I think the likelihood is not high. Whatever may be the reality, at this moment, I must focus on caring for Meghan.

I'm sure this lot will take good care of Missy. You know how caring they are. Missy is likely to be cosseted away enjoying a cuppa like you. If she needs you, someone will come and find you. Drink your tea and we'll see what happens next.

Through the still-open apartment door, over Meghan's shoulder, I have a full view of the lift and there's no mistaking the uniforms of grim-faced ambulance lads and lasses heading to Missy and Sid's apartment. My grip on Meghan's shoulders tightens, and I keep her close until the troops have disappeared.

Meghan has grown restless and now is insisting she should return to her room. I suspect she sees me as an obstacle to finding Missy, because the reasons she offers for returning to her apartment aren't logical under the circumstances. She wants to shower, change clothes, and go to the toilet. I am running out of stalling tactics. The next best option is to go along with Meghan to her apartment by taking the back route to keep her away from Apartment 625. We make it to the lift, to the lobby, and are ready to head to Meghan's room when the lift doors open, and filling Meghan's view is the gurney carrying its usual cargo of a covered human body and two custodial ambulance officers controlling its movement. A man in white coverall takes up the rear. Meghan need not be Einstein to reach a bleak conclusion.

Instinct had kept me silent, but here we are, barely fifteen minutes later, and I wonder if I made the right choice. Might a hint of what is about to be revealed have meant Meghan could have been better prepared? Meghan drops to the floor in the centre of a rapidly enlarging pool of pale-yellow. Staff run from every direction. I hadn't noticed them before, not their presence nor their absence, and I was equally oblivious to the fact the lobby is abnormally empty of residents.

What are you two doing here?

Rose, the Occupational therapist, gasps, her face a mess of shock and worry.

Aniya, the nurse on duty, bends over Meghan, feels her pulse, nods, and whispers to Rose.

Grab a wheelchair.

By the time Rose has returned, Meghan's eyes are fluttering. The two staffers help her into the chair.

Come on, young lady. We are calling your doctor for a check-up. And you too, Wilhemena.

They need to fold Meghan's unresponsive body into the wheelchair and now, there she remains as they placed her, curled in a foetal position, head almost touching her lap, arms wrapped around her midriff, and the only sign of life being her soft pleading to hear the fate of her friend.

But what about Missy? What's happened to Missy?

Behind us, in the space we have left, the yellow pool of Meghan's wee is a sight I can't ignore. I'm overtaken by a powerful urge to salvage some dignity for my friend, and I pause, turn back, ready to undertake cleaning chores to remove the sad sight of Meghan's shocked response, when Rose applies gentle pressure to my back that ensures my forward movement. One last look, hoping for some minor sign of restored normality to the lobby, and I see one of the other staff members doing the job for me. It's Maude. Maude winks at me, as if to say, 'She'll be right, Billy. I'm taking care of it. Off you go.'

And here I go again, being overtaken with emotion, as tears are building up behind my eyes. I feel frail and perplexed, not my usual self when facing a crisis. Why? Suddenly, tiredness weighs on me, and I wish myself in bed, with sleep blocking out this catastrophe. Ahead, from her crumbled pose within the wheelchair, Meghan is whispering.

Missy. What about Missy?

I'm filled with remorse. Never did I expect this outcome, but what damage has my naivete brought upon my friend?

2

With so many people living in one complex, 'flu and the dreaded gastroenteritis can cause havoc, so the staff is quick to isolate infected individuals. This is what is called lockdown where management limit residents to their apartments, arrange for the delivery of meals, and assign individual staff members to a block of apartments or rooms to assist those allotted to their care. These individual care givers become the only conduit to the rest of the world for each resident. I hate lock down. Early in my residency, I suffered from severe hay fever, the symptoms of which could have been seen as forerunners for one of several contagious illnesses. I learnt how limiting lockdown could be. My body is accustomed to engaging in the rigors of exercising and walking. Lockdown is physically the opposite. Mentally, it's agonising. As if merely because they have ordered a body to stay in a room, the desire to move out and go elsewhere becomes an absolute necessity.

Today we have been restricted to our rooms for mental health reasons. Everyone is having a few days 'holiday' in their suites or rooms. I'm too weary to fight the limitation of movement, but what I am resisting is the keenness of Katherine, my assigned staff member, to shower me before settling me into my bed. The bed part is appealing, but the showering is too much for me to handle. Nor do I eat my dinner, despite Katherine's coaxing.

Oh, come on, Billy, at least try to eat the desert.

This morning, still weary from a night filled with dark and foreboding dreams, I awake to find Katherine is back. This time while there's no doubt where I want to be is in the shower, I'm less keen on supervision. I try to assure Katherine I can manage without her, but I fail. Katherine isn't swayed. If I am truthful, I might admit my legs are shaky and my hip hurts like hell, brought on no doubt by the long day of standing and the traumatic experience, or maybe an outcome of my disturbed night. I should concede being washed and massaged feels like an indulgence. One certainty is the relaxing sensation of warm water on tense muscles. Clean clothes, too, feel like absolute luxury. I emerge as almost a new person. If only ...

One day of restrictions is sufficient, apparently and today Katherine is checking if I'm ready to move on.

Will it be breakfast in the room this morning, or with company?

I can only think of one thing. Meghan?

Meghan needs to rest today. Maybe she'll be ready to join her friends by tonight. The doctor has been. She's had a shock. As have you. So, now, the same question, Miss Wilhemena. Breakfast here or in the dining room?

Not here.

Then, on one condition. Should you feel off, please come back to your apartment right away, and call me. Promise?

I nod my head, but there's a tiny rebellion going on inside, a thought that if spoken would be, 'not likely.' Yet I'm not as certain as I'm trying to persuade myself I am. Can I handle it, out there, with the gossip? News will have spread like wildfire. Maybe out there, I'll get an inkling of what happened rather than the one I have invented, something straight off the television series 'Thirteenth Street'.

My legs are reluctant to do their job, making me feel as if I'm walking through mud. The walk to the dining room seems longer than usual. Once there, being amidst familiar faces lifts my spirits, especially when many display gestures or expressions that convey their concerns, or maybe it's more about their curiosities, or that collectively they have something to say. I behave as if this is yet another normal day, as difficult as this may be, choosing my usual seat and following normal routines. I convince myself I have a handle on it, but for some reason I can't move myself. I'm stalled. I'm beginning to panic when I feel the light weight of a hand on my upper arm. When I turn, there's Joe, Mr Fix-it/Newsreader, his grey/green piercing eyes displaying only kindness, and he's holding a latte. I always begin my breakfast with a latte. How does he know? I'm struck dumb and meekly take the mug, blindly reaching around to place it in front of me, as I keep my eyes locked into his.

Think you need this, Billy. Can I place your order for you, just for this morning? You need respite.

Hand in hand, two opposing emotions saturate me. There's relief not to have to do what's he offering to do, and there's suspicion of the intentions of men, even ones who have shown me only politeness. I haven't the energy to either resist or to be grateful. Did I nod my head or say thanks? When I look back, I can only remember gazing into his eyes and, who knows for how long after, his hand places something like my usual breakfast in front of me.

It's later that I hear the external report, the official one that makes the tragedy real. 'An 88-year-old man has beaten to death his wife of fifty years in a residential care home,' Joan reads from the news headlines.

Sid beat Missy to death.

And later still, maybe a week or more after the event, Meghan shows some improvement, though external appearances prove sometimes to be deceiving. Back in the community, Meghan has taken to targeting anyone who will listen to her and the 'trapped' listeners become Meghan's substitute for a priest in a Confessional. In these outpourings, Meghan repeatedly utters one sentence.

I wasn't the friend I could have been to Missy. I should have insisted she get help for Sid.

There are no words of comfort able to reach someone who has become deaf. I can only offer her hugs, as I continue to work through my contribution to Meghan's instability. The staff decide her individual seclusion should be extended.

3

Meghan's recovery is slow. Will she ever be the same? I hear myself using the phrase 'at her age' when I think about the massive trauma she has undergone, and afterwards I cringe. It's so easy to fall into thinking that all hope ends when you are 'at that age.' One thing is sure. My prejudice against men has come back stronger than ever, thanks to Sid. I know it's unfair. Missy's contribution to this disaster provides an undeniable twist to my anti-men narrative. Women who seem unable to take a stronger stand are both a mystery to me and yet understandable. I blame social mores from a past era, where women were drilled into believing their essential need for men, beyond their obvious roles as fathers to future children, to manage their lives, for without them how could a woman stand for herself? To be single was unholy. In making this judgement, I've made invisible my own weaknesses in this realm. And it's not my place to measure others' needs and wishes. Belonging, being loved and loving in return is part of human existence. If we mess up, well, that's being human, too. Plus, there are always anomalies, such as Joe's kind eyes and pre-empted latte in hand when it's most needed that challenge my biased view. And, anyway, who am I to say that dependency on Sid was why Missy ignored his failing mental health? Maybe she was looking after her own needs, wherein life without her sweetheart would be unbearable.

I regularly pass by Meghan's suite, hoping for an opportunity evade the scrutiny of the ever-changing member of staff, each of whom have offered me a little shake of the head or the brief phrase, 'Not yet, Billy' when I attempted a breach.

Today, on my usual round I see the door is open to permit the green-eyed Newsreader entry.

Darn. How did he get in when it's been so difficult for me?

My hackles are up. For what reason? What does the man want? What does mister-dragon-eyes think he can do for Meghan that a friend can't?

There's a bench seat not too far away, a perfect position to observe any comings and goings. I can see Meghan's door. I plan to take Joe's place when he exits the apartment. The minutes tick by, dragging, though in reality, probably less than three-quarters of an hour has passed, when the door opens and out comes the Newsreader. His head lifts when he notices me, and he heads in my direction. My stomach churns. There's a stream of emotions running through me, among them one of panic.

Hi. I'm Joe. We kind of know each other but not formally so I will ask, are you Billy?

Yes. Wilhemena Corass. Mrs Wilhemena Corass.

There I go ahead, being my stuffy father's daughter. What's the matter with me. Why does this Joe guy get under my skin? I extend my hand in a formal handshake, but the smoothness and warmth of his reciprocal grasp rattles me. He seems keen to meet me, but why would he be? That's what the small voice in my head is telling me. My eyes explore his face and see only kindness and generosity, and yet, there's that weirdly off-putting, slightly crooked smile of his that continuously flickers across his face. Is he laughing at my attitude? I can't read him. This is confusing me. I pride myself on my ability to pick up a genuine sense of the real self of anyone I meet but he's got me beat. He's doesn't seem phased by my coolness.

Well, Mrs Corass, Wilhemena, Billy, I am Joe. Now you have a name for the face you see now and then. As you might guess, I have outsmarted the guards and snuck in to see Meghan. In my opinion, and hers, she's ready to face the world. I suspect the staff are being over-cautious. Meghan would like to see you. How about we go in together? If the carers interrupt, I can fend them off. What Meghan needs is her family, meaning her residential family, around her, supporting her, getting her back onto an even keel.

Joe sounds like an evangelical faith healer. This makes me cautious. But if this is a way for me to get into Meghan's suite, then I'll take it.

Together we enter Meghan's suite. Joe closes the door behind us. I'm relieved to see the way Meghan's face lights up when she sees me, yet even that doesn't stop me from continuing to thrash myself for my part in the horrible day.

Oh Billy, it's so sad, isn't it? I so wanted to talk to you about Missy and Sid, but everyone seems to think I am a fragile flower. Guess they are only trying to do the right thing, but I needed to talk with you because we were there, together, were we not? And we saw it all. You know how I felt about Missy, and only you can understand how I am feeling.

I rush to close the distance between us and wrap my arms around my friend. At that moment, the door behind us opens.

Oooo, what's going on here? Billy, you were told to allow Meghan time. And Joe, what's this? You, too?

My fault, Maudie. I encouraged Billy to come in. It was me who broke your rules, and Meghan begged me to find Billy. She wanted to talk with her friend.

Joe's friendly smile is already working on Maude. I can see acquiescence written over Maude's face, as she struggles to maintain a professional seriousness. Gradually it softens into a knowing smile.

I guess Meghan might be ready to face the world again. I will have to explain this to the Boss, but ...

I rethink my appraisal of Joe. He's a charmer, that's for sure. Warning, warning, Will Robertson. Danger, danger. I keep those thoughts inside and broaden my smile, looking from Maude to Joe, agreeing with the decision to let Meghan out into the world. Joe the bedeviller holds the door open for sweet Maude and follows her out, turning at the last moment to wave and smile at Meghan and me. I walk over and firmly close the door behind him, and I turn to Meghan trying not to show how much Joe has rattled me.

Wow. He's a smoothie.

Billy. Don't let Joe's ways trick you into seeing him as something he's not. That man has had a tragedy in his life, and he acts the way he does because he wants to keep people far away. The smile is all a front. But he genuinely cares and is always doing things for anyone who needs help. It's his thing.

Meghan's great reference does not sway me. Charmer. That's what he is. Too smooth.

4

Early in the morning, I read a notice someone has posted in the main lobby.:

> Please gather at 11 am today to form a Guard of Honour for
> Mrs Melissa Palmer (Missy). Please assemble in usual location,
> appropriately dressed for this sombre occasion

Every resident is aware that Missy's body was taken away weeks ago, so in general conversation the question being asked between individuals is how a Guard of Honour can happen. Some say Meghan has organised this, but when she's questioned, Meghan shakes her head and shrugs her shoulders. The consensus is that it won't have been Mariella, the manager. No one can recall witnessing from her a show of any emotion or attachment to specific residents, though in less emotional terms they have agreed Mariella's impartial and unemotional approach may be appropriate to maintain equilibrium. As many staff members are caring and invest in individual residents, this opens the possibility of one or some of them instigating this action. Or the family, perhaps. But to Meghan's knowledge, there's no one close enough to either Missy or Sid who might organise this kind of event.

At 10.45 am, a solid crowd of residents gathers, most in their Sunday best, some women wearing hats and gloves. The noise level is high, many still teasing through clues about who might have organised this Guard of Honour and what form the event might take, given the absence of the usual focal point of the trolley and its escort of ambulance officers.

At 11 a.m. comes the sound of music. from the PA system

It's modern, a female vocalist, Demi Lovato, a song about overcoming adversity, asserting that even when everything has been smashed, it is possible to arise from the wreckage.

Joe has moved up to stand beside me, the move stunning me and setting my mind afire with questions not only about why he has chosen to do so but also about my own confusion. I say nothing and hold my head steady, looking in front, rather than acknowledge his presence.

The next piece of music is 'Shallows' by Lady Gaga. Something about this song moves me, whether it's Gaga's vocal range, or the contrast of male and female perspectives, or the raw emotion it captures. Lady Gaga introduces the entry of a flower-laden trolley escorted by four staff members. I'm drowning in the volume of tears I'm holding inside me, and I'm certain I'm not alone. Meghan's hand and mine are intertwined, blending her emotions with mine. She turns away, her eyes widen momentarily and as she does, she withdraws her hand from mine. I feel as if I've done something wrong but, soon, I can see she only wanted to free her hands so she might bury her face in them.

I recognise the next piece, which turns out to be the last one. It's James Blunt's 'Goodbye My Lover.' In this context, its title is poignant. Unexpected choices, but weirdly appropriate. I have a warped and perhaps slightly snob-bish pride in my own eclectic tastes in all things arty, and when I look around at those with whom I share this home, no one stands out as likely to be of similar ilk, as these choices might hint. Again, I am slipping into framing my friends as stereotypically preferring 'old' tunes. It's an embedded habit I am finding difficult to rid despite knowing how angry I have been at time when I have found myself to be a victim of such classifications. I am ashamed of my weakness.

Another flaw in my character is becoming annoyingly apparent to me. It's my curiosity in the one person from whom I'd agreed with myself to keep far away. Where's Joe? What's his role in this? I can't imagine Meghan pulling this off on her own. Is the choice of music something from Missy's life? What stories have I missed here? What layers might explain the tragic final chorus, why James Blunt uses the word 'hollow'? Are these songs Joe's choice? If so, I would have to add them as another part of Joe's history that intrigues me, even though I constantly need to remind myself I do not want to know any-thing about him. I mean, he doesn't seem to have any physical disabilities, not a repairing hip as I do, or lack of strength as Meghan suffers, or progressive deterioration like Gwen, so why is he here? Is he the insider, the staff member you have without his being a staff member? Overtaking all other thoughts are my contemplations about the many untold stories inside Fairview, all of which must represent unrecognised and rapidly disappearing successes and failures that each ageing individual must learn to live with or without. No wonder, as I have heard on the Fairview grapevine, the pharmacy often runs low on antidepressants.

Maude and the other staff members have distributed the floral arrange-ments around the lobby, and those gathered are slowly recognising the extent of this event, which, once the posters went up, had only been conjecture. The laughter and chatter sound less guarded. The cloak of abject sadness and confusion over Missy's death and Sid's departure for elsewhere has been lifted. Gradually, one by one, individuals are realising it's time to remember

Missy as she has been to them, and not the murdered Missy, about which any thought drew horrible connotations. As always, the women are hugging each other and the men, as is their habit, are standing back. However, I can't ignore that their faces say far more than any words might. Whoever organised this did a good thing.

I look around for Meghan and see her with Joe at one side of the main group, heads bowed towards each other. Joe is doing the talking and Meghan is nodding her head. Then Joe turns toward the congregation and makes an announcement his voice clear and calm.

Thanks everyone for joining in this farewell to Missy, who we all know did not deserve to enter the next life the way she did, and to Sid, who sadly has gone to another place because of his actions. We would be harsh not to concede he was not himself when he carried out this terrible deed. Sid and Missy were not my friends, but they were good friends of Meghan, here, who asks for your patience so she can say a few words on her friends' behalf.

Some clap, but the sound quickly fades. Somehow it doesn't seem appropriate to be applauding. Within seconds, the room becomes eerily quiet. I notice a few residents are diverting their gaze from Meghan as she steps forward to the centre of the room. Maybe they can't trust their emotions and, instead, their eyes drift to the windows and corners of the room or into their laps, with only a minority lifting their faces. Meghan clears her throat, looks down to the floor and then up to the ceiling. At first, her words falter, but soon they become strong and sure.

I have known Missy and Sid for a long time … A long time.

Meghan stalls, the pause that follows is suspended, almost to the point where it feels uncomfortable. Should I or someone else step in? Joe stands beside her, calm and patient, as though this silence is intentional. Meghan clears her throat and continues.

Missy and Sid have always been the romantics. Sid adored Missy, and Missy believed the sun rose and set in Sid. Until the horrible blight Dementia took away the old Sid and created a new person, one that sometimes showed himself to still be his former self, but increasingly became a confused and violent new person. Missy, however, never gave up hope old Sid would one day come home again. She delayed action about his illness, hoping he'd recover and become once more the man he had been. Even then, she made light of his deterioration. And I guess you might say ...

Meghan crumbles and gulps down her tears. Joe whispers to her as his arm wraps around her back. She shakes her head and straightens. Joe drops his arm to hang by his side, and patiently awaits Meghan to garner composure.

You might say Missy paid a heavier than normal price for growing old. The lesson we might all learn from this is don't just blame things on growing old. Speak to your doctor, your family, your friends and find support. Don't hide the issue and hope it goes away. Had Missy spoken out, Sid would ... might ... could ... have received the proper care he needed. And Missy could see him as often as she wanted to, instead of being ...

Again, Joe lifts his arm and wraps it around Meghan's shoulder, pulling her close and holding her tight. His face appears over Meghan's shoulder, letting me scan it centimetre by centimetre. Is it my imagination? Are they tears rolling from the corner of Joe's eyes? If they are, he's ignoring them because, from over Meghan's shoulder and without reducing his hold of his friend, he speaks to the group.

Farewell Missy. Be safe and well cared-for, Sid, wherever you live the rest of your life.

With perfect timing, the tea trolleys trundle their way into the lobby. Several members of the staff had lingered on the periphery of Missy and Sid's Guard of Honour, and have entered the room, encouraging everyone to have a cuppa. A cuppa can fix everything at Fairview.

With a cuppa comes contemplation, offering a time to reflect on Death, its presence so visible in this place now, but no less so also lurking everywhere through all times, ready to make its appearance when least expected. From birth there are no guarantees, nor does it present in the same shape on each of its appearances. A person can't plan for it. Nor can anyone foresee how its impact will strike the survivors.

I'm reminded of an apt example in the death of my ex-husband Mitch's young wife. This woman's association with me was mostly as the target of many hours of jealousy and resentment rather than as a friend. After too often erasing Mitch's wife's name from my conversations, I have almost forgotten it—but yes, her name was Bianca. Bianca died suddenly. She hadn't been ill for weeks or months beforehand. There was no preparation for the event. After a long drought of communication between my ex- and I, out of the blue, that one stop-the-world phone call in which Mitch's words were saturated in grief, his sentences fragmented by his inability to announce Bianca's departure. Mitch's grief removed any doubt about whether he still loved me despite his second marriage, and the fiction I'd created that his marriage to Bianca may have been only an escape from me, not because of his love for another woman.

The unexpectedness of Bianca's death left me in shock. I couldn't explain to myself why I felt this way, especially as I'd always internally claimed no friendship, probably only a resentment of her for taking over my role. Yet, there was I, becoming overly emotional, overwhelmed, and distracted, as if Bianca was a dear and intimate friend rather than my not so well-known competitor for Mitch's love. I couldn't come to grips with the contrast of my expression of grief over her to the numbed, silent bereavement I had felt years earlier at the loss of my, Mitch's and my, second child. Brandon's sister. Grace. I gave her a name, though her life only happened inside me. Is it a truth that even the death of a woman whose name is evasive, and whose hopes and dreams, disappointments and disillusionments had been of little concern, can evoke the heart-wrenching grief experience of another death at another time? This question lingers for me. Did my expressed grief for Bianca reflect the resurrection of my earlier and overwhelming but unexpressed grief for Grace, a grief I had suppressed and repressed? Or was my grief for Bianca for my own future passing? This huge existential dilemma is something I'm still unravelling, knowing full well we are all the least truthful to ourselves about ourselves and our emotional responses.

And now, here at Fairview the tragic departure of a stranger evokes another equally emotional mourning. In my mind, a question begs an answer: are our moments of grieving a dual event, an overlapping of a current event involving a loss in our lives, and a private and instinctive lamentation of what we deny but is unavoidable, our own future death? There's an end to everything. Each of us will die. Most of us behave as though we are the exception who will live forever, remaining forever young throughout the duration. Maybe the dead, now pain and trouble free, are peacefully on their way to a better life, as many will argue. But we, the living, cannot deny the inevitability of our own death, peaceful, tortuous, or otherwise. Are we weeping for others, near and far, out of fear for ourselves? Should we not be conceding that life has a beginning and an end; should we not be stopping our crying and get over our fearfulness by living what remains to its full extent? Carpe diem, as John Keating, Robin Williams's character in "Dead Poet Society", whispers to his rapt audience, thus connecting his present-day students, for whom death would seem remote, to a group of young men, like themselves, who are no longer living. Yes. Carpe diem.

Private lecture over, I compact my reflections and pack them away as too hard to unravel.

5

Fairview adopts forward-thinking in residential living by introducing mul-
ti-generational ideals into their facilities. They offer many configurations
such as apartments, like mine, for less needy care provision, that is, for the
still mostly independent 'seniors' who can afford the higher cost not covered
by governments. These include two- or three-bedrooms and two bathrooms,
encouraging family members to come and stay. There are also single bedsits,
and a range of packages that cover the varying extent of help needed by each
individual resident, labelled as 'home care packages.'

Beyond the small courtyard-style gardens attached to various lounge-
rooms, there's also a park-like garden incorporating a playground and bar-
becues with tables and benches, as well as miscellaneous seating scattered
around. Residents interested in horticulture are encouraged to join the gar-
dening staff whenever they feel inclined. In the centre of this area, there's
an Early Childhood Community Centre. I've heard of one resident whose
grandchildren go to this centre. If I could be more generous in spirit, I might
concede Brandon has made a good choice. But I haven't found that generosity. It took some time for me to learn about this extension of Fairview's
facilities, primarily because I was too angry to be open.

6

Despite the formal farewell, it's apparent the events surrounding Sid and
Missy hang over everyone like a heavy blanket. It's as if everyone is measuring
themselves and their own situation against that of the tragic couple, and as a
result they are weighing the potential for similar sad outcomes in their own
lives.

To clear my mind, I find a quiet spot in the courtyard recently discovered,
a hidden gem I stumbled across in one of my wanderings.

A penny for them.

Darn. An interruption, and worse, I know it's Joe.

Why hadn't I heard him arrive? Had I done so, I might have prepared myself. Truth is, I know I'm incapable of doing so. I feel vulnerable with anything that involves Joe. I need to steel myself, shore up my guard. I'm being ridiculous. Joe has done nothing. It's only my stupid notion about men through years of negative interactions. Get over it.

Mr Fix-it obviously has something he wishes to say. I search his face for clues but see only a calm deliberateness. He has a purpose. I cannot escape, so I dig out my nice side and pour it on thick.

Oh, hello Joe. My thoughts aren't worth even a penny.

Pennies these days can be worth a fortune.

His face shows no sign of the humour normally embedded in his words, yet I laugh as if he has told a marvellous joke, and then judge my response as embarrassing.

Good to see you smiling.

There hasn't been a lot to smile about around here lately.

I don't think about my reply but, when I hear my own voice, I realise it echoes a thought that has lingered of late, a passing observation about myself. Unlike him, who seems to perpetually wear a smile, I'm not naturally a smiley person, but every interaction I've had with Joe ends with the twitching of my cheek muscles and in a rare lapse, even a quiet giggle.

Joe settles down on the bench a proper distance from me, neither too close nor too distant.

It's a strange state we are in, don't you think, Billy?

What do you mean? The state we are in as an aftermath of Sid and Missy? The state we are in by finding ourselves in a location and way of living we never included in our long-term plans when we made them five years ago? Or the state we two are in, sitting here, in this calm, sunny courtyard, discussing such matters with each other, two almost strangers digging into personal and private thoughts?

All the above.

Well, Joe, only a couple of months ago, I would have been planning and preparing for a solitary long-distance run out into the desert. Fairview is as alien an environment for me, as my deserts might be for others, not only in here but out there in the normal world. What about you?

Yes. I'd say you and I share that in common, the alien-ness I mean. Others in here have possibly been heading to the security of a place like this for the past few decades, with no need to consider any other future. To them, there is security in this future, one that assures them professionals will care for them, as well as feed and comfort them. Despite the limitation of body and mind, they can be socially active, if only for observing the activities of fellow residents, all the while living in lovely, modern accommodation. Especially those who don't have families or who don't have families nearby. But for you and I and others, fate and circumstances have brought us here, and that makes it more difficult to adjust to accepting we need care. Until the event that changed our circumstances, we had been confident in our ability to take care of ourselves.

The phrase 'you and I' has halted my ability to listen. What does Joe mean? Does he know something about me or is he surmising? And what's his story? Instead of asking, I do my usual and blast double barrels back at him.

Mind if I ask? Are you the community counsellor?

Joe throws back his head and laughs, not a roar, as many men do, but one that displays genuine amusement, rather than mocking me. I can't stop myself from mentally noting its warmth, surprising myself when I admit I like Joe's laugh. This flusters me and I'm pretty sure it is showing on my face. Joe's watching me with those eyes that don't seem to miss anything, and that's the moment my mind decides it's time to resolve the issue about the colour of Joe's eyes. Are they Green or Grey? Grey green with gold streaks through them. Not cat-like but opal-ish. They spark with intelligence. I need to get myself back into the game. Joe is smiling and nodding his head, and again my mind wanders off to focus on his mannerism, the way his silver spikey hair moves when he does this.

Billy, you miss nothing.

I've forgotten what I said. What don't I miss? Oh, yes, about him being the counsellor. I feel my face grow warm, because for an instant I was sure Joe had read my thoughts, the ones that focused on his eyes and hair.

Well, whenever I see you, you have your head down, and that smile of yours swiped across your face, and you look like Yoda dishing out wisdom and comfort.

You are funny. I guess it comes down to I like to listen, and the price for that privilege is to engage in a conversation. I like to listen to people talking about their lives and their interests. Reminds me of what life is all about.

So, is that what you are trying to do here? Get involved in something you think I am struggling with or need to share?

No. Just want to talk. You look like someone who might have plenty of interesting things happening in your life and with strong opinions about them, and I enjoy those conversations.

Well, thanks Joe. But no thanks. Should I find myself with something I would like to share, on the rare chance I see a need, I will seek you out.

I may have intended my words to sound like a light-hearted flip-off of his offer. I've no clues to measure how he heard them. He laughs again and carefully stands while patting me gently on one shoulder. I find it difficult to ignore the expanding spread of warmth radiating from the smallest of human touches. As he moves away from me, I'm conscious of his absence. Had I not been watching him leave, his departure might have been as indistinctive as his arrival. I feel a little shame that I may have been unnecessarily rude with my tendency to bluntness. I sense a regret inside me as I watch the receding view of Joe's back, noting the sway of his hips and shoulders that imitate a much younger man, and see no evidence that might show Joe agrees with me about any inappropriate behaviour. He's reached the entry to the courtyard, after which he will move out of my sight. He turns and waves back with that too-cool-for-school smile plastered across his dial and his spikey silver mane flopping a similar farewell, as if he had no doubt at all I would watch him leave.

7

Beverly James's entrance into Fairview is grand, though probably not intended to be so. I witness her arrival from my place in an armchair. I watch, along with many other occupants of the foyer, as the glass doors slide open and note a short lively brunette, a smile spread wide, bouncing in. The persona of this woman, who in my estimate might be in her late sixties, reminds me of the cute Tarsiers I had seen in a David Attenborough documentary. According to Mr Attenborough, Tarsiers are one of those animals close to the top of the cute list because of their velvety smooth fur, small size and very large eyes. However, a point that Mr Attenborough made is they are the only venomous primate, and while that may make them sound vicious, they are bashful. They become very stressed if touched or caged. I doubt this lady is a native of Malaysia or Indonesia as are Tarsiers.

This new arrival's big brown eyes dart from one face to another; I imagine her ears twitching in their keenness to catch every phrase, every hint, as if she only has seconds to take in all she needs to know about her new life. This perspective is far from the way others might have been perceived me when I was delivered in my wheelchair on my first day. For me, Fairview and the occupants of the entrance lobby had been a shocking revelation and I'm certain my brutal assessment of them would have been visible to anyone who had bothered to look at me in my miserable state in the wheelchair. This lady convincingly displays her convictions this is the right place, and everything is exactly how she believes it should be.

Each day, people come and go through these large doors. There'll be servicemen, suppliers, relatives, professionals like doctors, and newcomers.

Those seated in the lobby may lift their heads and give a visitor a look-over before returning their attention to whatever held it before the interruption. Beverly's arrival comes with teeth-gritting audio. It cannot fail to catch the eye of every soul within hearing distance. What each of us see, once our attention has been grabbed, is a lively older woman followed by a morose middle-aged one dragging a reluctant grey suitcase, the source of the irritating noise. As Beverly explains later, their only suitcase had a problem with one wheel. Given the chance, Bev knew her daughter would use this as a reason to delay her mother's entry into Fairview, and no way was Bev having that.

From my place in one of the armchairs, I watch the performance as it plays out in front of me, internally commenting on human behaviour not-unlike David Attenborough might of the animals in his documentaries. It's apparent one of these two would soon join us. I notice the diversity of body language between the two arrivals and the responses of the regular occupants of the lobby. This is supplemented by a visible deterioration of goodwill on the face of the younger one, highlighted by the aggressiveness she applies to the yanking and tugging of the uncooperative suitcase. There's an air of martyrdom about the suitcase-puller, no sign of joy or positiveness about her body language, allowing me minutes to contemplate the underlying issues. Surmising it is the older woman who would be the new resident, then maybe it's fear for her companion that the younger woman is displaying, the reverse of Brandon's attitude to having me admitted. Maybe the younger of the two sees this place as the last stop, or maybe she does not like the frightening future being brought to the fore by the older woman's placement in Fairview. If so, was the older woman's projection of the opposite mood a measure of her lack of hold on reality? There's so much to keep my mind occupied. But fair point, I concede. The younger one's doubts must be given some credit. It's not the building, not the people, but having to face the implication and consequences of choices being made. There's no escaping the great myth of 'The Retirement Home' as a dark, miserable place where families abandon their elderly family members, nor is there anything being spoken or written to shatter that bleak impression.

The entrance hall adopts multiple personalities. It's the day-to-day gathering point of residents as well as an intersection between those from inside and those from outside. It's where the residents entertain their friends and relatives, and it's the service entrance to the corporate business related to the management of the home. My residential companions and I have a legitimate right to be sitting in this room, filling in time, so why did watching Beverly's transition from the outside world to becoming a resident and the apparent pain of her daughter feel like voyeurism? Perhaps it's because fully on display is the theatre of personal conflict between these two women. Blending the memory of the shock of my own first impressions with my detached observations of Beverly's entrance, I come to a point of view that herein lies an oversight by management. If they are focused on ensuring their clients feel secure and welcomed, they should consider a way to provide a softer, less overwhelming, method of entry. From another perspective, I wonder if the designers were possibly very wise. Recognising the likelihood of Dementia sufferers filling the armchairs and sofas of the lobby, what better way to provide simple stimulation than the constant flow of inward- and outward-bound humans.

This insight motivates me to step forward.

Hi there. I'm Billy. Can I help? Do you know where you need to go?

The younger of the two gives me a steely glare that would silence a lesser person. I ignore her and reach out to the older one.

Hi, I'm Billy. Welcome to Fairview.

My hand is eagerly grasped.

Beverly James. Bev. My daughter, Kristy. And yes, looking forward to getting settled.

Welcome, Bev.

Some others have followed my lead, ready to introduce themselves, when Ngalia, the staff member whose task it is to meet and greet, takes control.

She's called 'The Bitch' by many, part humour and part fear. Many claim they 'are going to' write to the Management to suggest they have the wrong person doing the induction into Fairview. To date, no one has found the courage. I choose that moment to be bold by ignoring Ngalia and offer my best smile to Beverley James.

Once you're settled, Beverley, find your way back here, and we'll have a coffee together.

It's Bev, Billy, and I'll be happy to join you.

The sharing of coffee, again, a useful tool, and my reward is the brightest and broadest of smiles.

8

Apparently the latest Fairview intrigue has been building to a slow crescendo over a couple of hours.

Often my regular walks through the complex are unremarkable, but today, I've noticed little sparks and flashes here and there. In a corner of the back lobby, I notice a group of ladies engaged in an intense conversation, rarely noteworthy a common occurrence as the smallest of subjects can often bring about a coming-together but, as I pass a Nurses Station further along that corridor, there's a watch of nurses (I mentally apologise to all nurses for using the collective noun for nightingales), less commonly gathered in one place. Something is amiss. As I pass the Newsreader's corner, I notice the men displaying nervous traits and fidgeting. It's disturbing to see that, far from usual, Joe's calm conversations are doing little to quell.

Joe flashes me a grimace as he turns quickly back to settle one man more agitated than others. Once the man is calm, Joe lifts his eyebrows, as if to wordlessly say, 'Well, this is how it is.'

Lost one guy.

Lost?

Well, according to Roy here, not lost but Tim's gone AWOL.

The Newsreader settles his hand on the agitated man's shoulder, serving two purposes, one to point out to me which man is Roy and the other to calm Roy.

Roy, here, claims our missing man is in love and has climbed on board his battery-dependent chariot otherwise called a Go-For and headed out to locate a florist. He wishes to buy a bunch of flowers for his one true love. Let's hope the flowers don't end up with another purpose, if you get my drift, because our lover does not know the road rules as they apply to an electric wheelchair.

Should we do something? Should I tell the staff?

They know. You haven't passed through the foyer? The cops. They're here already. I only hope this is not a senior version of Nicolas Cage and Laura Dern in 'Wild at Heart.' Love can bring out the best and the worst in everyone, even in the over seventy-fives.

I tear myself away from the beguiling tones of the Newsreader's voice and it's intoxicating down-play of comedy reinforced by his controlled smile and the way he glances from me to the men in his care. It's impossible not to giggle, though clearly this may be a serious situation.

My curiosity leads me to the lobby. What greets me is a sight that reminds me of a sci-fi movie I saw some time ago, where a crowd of humans are standing on a shoreline gazing towards something unseen but imagined to be a spaceship represented as a bright light beaming down from the sky. In the lobby, the many that have gather to act as spectators to what is an unusual event have created a pathway from the front door to the reception desk, not dissimilar to those shoreline humans of the movie. Each set of eyes are vigilant for whatever might arrive. At the moment I enter the lobby, so does a contingent of police officers enacting an irregular parade. One female police officer is gently leading the 'criminal' by his hand. There's a smile playing around her mouth. Closer to the entry, a male officer is dithering around with the getaway vehicle. I've concluded, rightly or wrongly, that the cop is not sure if he should treat this as 'evidence' or ensure he stores it in a place where it won't risk injury to the residents. Or maybe he's befuddled by finding himself surrounded by a geriatric mob.

Tim. Tim. What's the do here, Tim?

The carer Maude, the one who introduced me to the shopping excursion, has her arm around the stunned Tim, as she leads him to a sofa.

Now Tim, you sit here while I see to these guys, and then we will sort you out. Okay?

The faces of the cops have disintegrated. They'll have stories to laugh over in the lunchroom and at home with their families tonight. No one seems put out by the escape.

He tells us he wanted flowers for his lady, so we called in to the florist on our way home to calm him down. They're in the vehicle. Isn't it reassuring to know romance is alive and kicking?

Maude's head bends to minimise the sight of her laughter, as another officer arrives with an enormous bunch of flowers in his hands. Maude can no longer contain her laughter. The officer looks ill-at-ease, as if he's uncertain whether Tim or his residential carer has primary rights to the bouquet. With a flourish, he makes his decision and hands them to Maude, who then places them in Tim's hands. Tim looks up at Maude then down at the gloriousness in his hands, an expression of satisfaction on his face, the blooms recognition of his success at an act of freewill.

You got your flowers, mate. Next time, talk first, will you?

9

Una O'Reilly had been a regular member of the lobby group from Day One. On that first day in this place, the brilliant gleam of Una's eyes and her wide smile had buoyed me. Not that I knew this cheerful woman's name was Una. Since then, her brilliance has been the one bright light that gave me hope of something other than that which seemed so obvious: the bleakness, the near-death-ness, and the no-longer-living beings that were to be my companions. It took several weeks of asking for a repeat of the name before the name Una took a hold in my brain.

'Why, it's Oo-nah,' the tiny lady always answers. Not grasping the name is not because my hearing is not up to scratch, but Una's Irish lilt had me so charmed I did not listen properly.

Una is one of those individuals who miss nothing. On Una's CV, perception would rate high. Una notices if someone is a little down, she remembers birthdays, and she even remembers, for those in her close circle of associations, the names of husbands, partners, children or grandchildren.

Una's attentiveness makes me feel guilty, particularly in moments like when Una is the only one who has remembered Eileen's grandson's birthday.

And, Grandma Eileen, may I ask how little Evan's birthday party went on Sunday? Was their laughter and sounds of joy filling every corner of the garden? Oh, if we could only stay at five years of age for the rest of our lives.

Another example is earlier today, when at breakfast, Una whispers to Mary-Jane.

Are we allowed to make a fuss of you today?

It's Mary-Jane's birthday, but Mary-Jane is normally shy and never pushes herself to the fore. And yet, there for all of us to witness, Una's words have pushed the magic buttons and instantaneously Mary-Jane's face is one of a seventy-five-year-old whose expression resembles that most likely exhibited by Eileen's grandchild Evan seventy years her junior. Someone has remembered; someone is paying her attention. At that moment it became apparent that age is irrelevant. Everyone longs for recognition. Being loved for the uniqueness of who we are is what each of us hunger for. That need begins at birth, or maybe before then, at conception, and remains until one's last breath. A resident celebrated her one-hundredth last week and there was much hullabaloo with letters from everyone from the King down. Never mind, she wasn't as bright as some other Centurions have been, but everyone agreed it was an impressive achievement making it to that grand age. She seemed to enjoy the fuss despite not hearing anything anyone said and looking a trifle confused at the speechmaking and the hugs and kisses, but throughout her face was that of her inner child lapping up the gifts of recognition.

Seeing this generosity from Una encourages a deep sigh from within me, an expression of my own sense of unfulfilled need, a lifetime of want that rises inside me, and memories of all those years of being loved—oh each of those who loved me said the words, didn't they—but never seeing that love displayed in actions. Even people who love or have loved me took my demand for independence in both hands and let me go ahead, no one particularly invested in what my feelings might have been, rarely congratulating me on my achievements in running or in my career. While that could be taken as them showing confidence in my abilities to achieve, the oversights usually reinforce a sense of aloneness. Meanwhile, I see Una's actions precipitating a viral spread of smiles and nods across any space she enters.

Even Una's laughter has an Irishness to it, like birds twittering in the Camellia bush, and it sounds as fragile as the woman looks, as if each note is a crystal droplet left hanging for a brief time. In my estimation Una is the ultimate feminine woman, the complete opposite to the woman that I see myself as being. Too often my directness has invited criticism or brought suggestions I am too 'masculine', not ladylike, especially from my father who once scolded me, 'You are a grown woman, Wilhemena. Act like one. It's not flattering, nor is it dignified to hear your strident voice. There's nothing you can contribute, here.' When his words struck me, wounding me, I'd work hard to hide the hurt inside, but that's a wound that has never healed. For my father, Una might have measured to be the perfect daughter, one who might complement the perfect son he already had. But no daughter might match a son.

As I ponder this, a never considered idea has popped into my thinking. My father might have preferred another son. Ah, does it matter? Just as me trying to please my father has always been futile. The more my father tried to suppress his strong-minded daughter, the stronger I became. Here I am, 'old' as I'm classified these days, and, still, it seems impossible for me to shake free of the sadness of being such a terrible disappointment to him. And perversely, though I feel guilty in admitting it, even to myself, I know a tiny amount of jealousy accounts for my occasional annoyance over Una's bright-ness and sweetness. This jealousy or resentfulness may have contributed to my inability to retain Una's name. I am ashamed of myself. It has taken some considerable soul searching and honesty to analyse this flaw in my character, but despite my guilt, I seem unable to halt those little, if unfair, resentments from sneaking in. Being older does not guarantee wisdom. These stupid responses are of no credit, possibly something my father might label as yet more signs of my imperfections. Despite my mixed feelings, Una proves to be a wonderful friend many times over.

Una uncovers the issue between Bev James and her daughter Kristy, about which she only hints and never reveals. Kristy's visits to her mother are moments of curiosity for many spectators in the lobby, as the inquisitive ones try to understand why Bev is so cheerful while her daughter is so miserable. No one is sufficiently brave to question Bev.

Margaret Ferguson arrived a day or two before Bev. Margaret sneaked into Fairview, unnoticed by the welcoming committee or the gossipmongers, and this is an astounding achievement, as she is a woman who is hard to miss. You can hear Margaret's conversations with others or her voice in song or in laughter echoing down corridors. Equally loud is her choice of bright red hair and a garish choice of style, all befitting her showgirl persona. She's easily recognised and identified as 'that' Margaret, but not an easy person with whom to connect. Everyone knows her name, and that name comes into many conversations because of something she's done or said. Everything about her is so unmissable. I am a little more charitable to Margaret than most as I am convinced her loud and over-stated presence may be a mask for underlying insecurities, but like everyone else, I'm only willing to offer a trickle of empathy and little time with Margaret.

10

The sounds that greet me this morning as I enter the lobby for morning tea are louder and more excited than usual. Predominantly female faces fill the space, each aglow with mischief. There's a hint that today's conversations are more than the normal day-to-day vanilla variety I only half listen to as I pass, only acknowledging with a nod of my head. Mostly those are grumblings about family members, the inefficiencies of a doctor, the (constant) failures of the cleaning staff, or are centred on the Royal family gossip, especially about the Sussexes, none of which pique my interest. But today there's a sense of something different, a lottery-draw of intrigue suggesting something sufficiently meaty that moves my feet quickly to what seems to be the centre of chit-chat.

The first phrase I hear is 'Bev James.' Then 'Margaret Ferguson.'

This makes sense. Those two have become great pals, as unusual as the pairing seems to people who know both. They hang out with a few other similarly giggly women. Whatever involves one, will involve the other.

Next, I hear a word, uttered sharply, 'hospital'. A joint gasp rushes out of the mouths of the listeners. Whatever I have missed must hold the key to the scandal. Too many individuals are talking at the same time. I have a strong desire to whistle and shout 'Shush', but that wouldn't go down well. I rein in my impatience and await the moment that will come when I hear a more comprehensive version of events.

Finally, a lull.

What's this all about?

Silence. A virile spread of smirks contaminates each face of the gathered gossipers, with Miriam at the epicentre. Miriam's eyes are locked into Bec's. Then Bec's eyes break away from Miriam's and dart from one member of the major group to another. First, there's giggling, a few pairs of hands rush to close off mouths, eyes grow wide as if in shock, and then there's a unified gasp when Bec makes her announcement.

Bev and Marg are being treated for a sexually transmitted disease.

The pieces of the jigsaw can now fall into place. The word 'hospital' is the key. But there's obviously a much larger story behind this surface one. The tightness of Bev and Marg, added to the evidence of my own eyes of the presence of one guy hovering on the periphery of the giggling group, but because I have been disinterested in this minor drama, I've never concerned myself with his identity. He seemed benign, mostly only fluttering around, helping anyone who needed aid, but he seemed to focus his attention on Bev and Marg.

I reconsider this assessment. Looking back, maybe his attention was more on Bev than Marg. At this moment, with my thoughts taken up by the gossip, I wonder if I have misjudged his good intentions. Maybe he's a bee in a honey pot, pollinating buttercups who can't stay away from this anonymous male. I hope someone's checking him out, too, for STDs. And no wonder those ladies are so giggly. Slowly a small recall pops out of my memory. Was it the first week after I moved in? I'd overheard a whisper of a slight scandal, of a man found in a female's apartment in the morning, but I was too new to access the full story. Was this the same bloke? Maybe not. There are so few men here, you'd think I'd remember. But at the time I didn't want to know anyone, neither men nor women. Even had someone mentioned a name, I wouldn't have remembered it. I might not have even registered the scandal of it all, as I do now. It's like being in a convent. Not with a religious bent but closeted all the same, and a place where every small detail looms large.

The thought of sex happening within the walls of this institution shocks Lilian, apparently. Her face is showing her disapproval.

Absolutely depraved.

Marcella offers a suggestion.

Well, aren't we all wishing for companionship?

Cristabel hoarsely whispers her question.

But at their age?

And now I have heard enough, my guilt over my own tendency to use that phrase making me sound aggressive in my response.

Why are you saying, 'at their age'? Being old does not mean we turn into another person. Some of us have lived conservative lives, others haven't. Why would any of us become someone different now, just because we share a home? We need to display the person we are, who we have always been, not be forced to be someone else. Don't you feel the loss of being touched?

I've put the question to others but in my own mind I can't stop remembering my own surprising response to a gentle touch on my shoulder, intended to be nothing more than offering reassurance. Inwardly, I feel the warmth of a blush.

Some smiles sneak out onto a few faces, and one brave person from the back of the group claps. Another turns away, as if this is all too much, but doesn't go far before she does a double take. It's difficult to read what she's thinking, but some memory or insight must have brought her back. Her mouth is partly open as if there's words there ready to be released and yet she says nothing. Another scowls. I'm guessing when I deduce the silence suggests that everyone might be sifting through the changes that might have or are still to come between them and their companions because of small or large revelations within these conversations. This brings memories of school-yard antics, of teenagers giggling and gossiping over exploits that mostly were pubescent explorations. The air is thick with the politics of whether to express an opinion or remain silent, an edge-y hint that any response might invite judgement or affect external perceptions of oneself. However, as always, both expressing an opinion or choosing to remain silent also is loaded with conceptions. A quick visual scan tells me there's only women here. Have the male residents their own scandal through which to sift? The lack of men allows freedom of expression. I watch as one woman glances at another, as if to measure a response, and then another notices a hint of humour in someone else's eyes, and soon a giggle builds into into raucous laughter that reverberates around the lobby.

It's a surprise that shouldn't be one, that the sheer delight of this scandal has found a means of expression. Women are contacting others, gripping the others by the shoulders or hands and laughing into others' faces. One hides her cheeks with her hands in a display of mock modesty, laughing all the while. Another is bent over from the waist, arms out like a child pretending to be flying, and her companion is leaning back with hands supporting her lower abdomen. To my ears, it's a beautiful noise, embedded with individual life stories. The laughter is a sign that one woman after another is feeling sufficiently uninhibited, thus able to share their perspectives and stories, some tellings hesitant or encrypted, some partial or revealing, and each one so very human, filled with wants and needs and frailties and celebrations. I let my mind slip temporarily away from this amazing female gathering and sharing to wonder if the Newsreader has convened his own forum of men. This female one is gaining momentum. From the most prudish women private stories are being revealed.

My prim and proper mother was floored when she found out I had several men friends, none of which I planned to marry. Our so-called best girl friends' weekends were the times I enjoyed most in my life. Out from under, we could be who we wished, and, boy, did we do outrageous things. Oh dear, the good old days.

Oh, to be young enough to invite a whistle or two. Forget this MeToo business. Nothing like male appreciation to lift one's spirits.

Hubby and I had date nights once a month. The kids would have a stay at either of their grandparent's homes and we'd experiment. The rest of the month we'd research. Nothing weird, but not missionary style. Until the body did not co-operate, then we turned conventional. He's gone, and those days are, too.

Maybe we should suggest to the management they should set in place a clinic for STDs or arrange conjugal visits like they do for prisoners in the US. How would old Po like that?

Offering this suggestion to the manager, Mariella Polina, brings a flood of laughter. Po is the name they have given her. To be fair, it must be a tough job that Po holds. She must manage staff, many of whom seem to last only for a few months while others are almost a fixture. There must be a mountain of legal requirements to juggle. Not to mentioned her need to deal with her clientele who are the many bossy residents and their families. Each will have their own views on how to do things, or what's wrong with this or that, or have grievances from the tiny to the mammoth. All will require kid-glove handling. Just as infantrymen need to slap a nickname on the person handing down orders, so it is in a care facility. Ms Polina won't be able to shake the tag of Po. It's hers, forever.

The laughter ends when the boys' brigade infiltrates the women. Bob is the leader of the pack and like a sniffer dog, his eyes fly from one woman to another. The others pick up on the atmosphere and Bob's alertness. With half-smiles on many a male face, they stop mid-room and wait, hoping for a scrap, a clue to what they sense has recently taken place in this space. I check their faces to see if there are any give-away smirks. It's possible they heard something.

A cuppa and coconut slice bring the room back to normal. There have been things recalled with spirit, things half-heard and only guessed at, and yet together they have left a sense of something more important and invigorating than the usual conversations.

The elevated atmosphere continues until residents move on to prepare for lunch. I'm on my way back to my suite, when something blinks on in my brain. Was this mystery male Tim and is this a follow-on to the flower scandal less than a month ago? I can't suppress the smile that escapes, recalling the stories told afterwards, how they had found this man calmly riding along on the side of a road. Out to buy flowers for his lady friend, he'd proudly told everyone. If it was Tim, then my only judgement could be to see him as a romantic. No wonder Bev and Marg are head over heels for the guy. That fuzzy, warm thought was as good as a glass of fine red. My smile lingers all the way into my suite, into my bathroom, while I'm putting a comb through my hair and some lippy on, and all the way back to the dining room where, if the noise level is an indicator, Bev, Tim and Marg are providing great material for discussion.

11

The Bev/Tim/Marg situation has me checking my prejudices once more. I will admit a faint sense of unease when my imagination forces upon me a vision of aged bodies enjoying a sexual relationship. Others' ageing bodies, that is, making me aware that inwardly I see myself as younger than what the mirror reveals about my external body. Even as I denigrate the appeal of an ageing physicality, it is apparent whatever may have occurred within this trio has less to do with physical attraction, maybe something about sexual desires or loneliness, but is it something more? Am I denying the possibility of love in this so-called final phase of living? A topic I rarely need to explore is being forced into my thoughts, based on my philosophical views around human love.

De Beauvoir believed in two kinds of love, which she labelled either as inauthentic or authentic. To De Beauvoir, the inauthentic variety is an existential threat. By believing love will complete us, we erase ourselves as independent beings because of the differing needs of partners. But authentic love must be based on 'reciprocal recognition of two freedoms', where neither partner is subordinate and each is an independent whole, freely choosing the other each day without trying to possess the other entirely. This is the love I desire.

Contrasting this, Plato was less about sex. He saw love as something that could inspire us to appreciate all that is divine and beautiful in the universe, both physical and spiritual, inviting us to try to produce beauty in the world.

Schopenhauer believed romantic love to be the greatest force in human life, strong enough to drive people to death or madness. Yet, to Schopenhauer, love boils down to the instinct of sex and the perpetuation of the species.

Albert Camus recognised only one duty for humankind, and that is love. He considered love as an act of rebellion. His theory was that even the best of lives will end in death, with no shortage of suffering beforehand, and for the worst of lives, there was even greater suffering. Camus considered how we should deal with the weight of recognising that for every one of us there's only suffering that ends in death. His answer was we do so through rebelling against that misery in art, in beauty, and in love.

All versions tell me age has little to do with the who, or the how, of love, nor about sex. Adopting Camus's theory, might I remind myself that by demanding the best life possible for me within my capabilities is an act of rebellion, a resistance to the suffering that is life. Back in the real world, the advice might be to make the most of what's available.

12

My experience of love is rather tatty. I have had only one official husband, and that was Mitch. After losing him to another, I stumbled into two other major relationships, men who were once dearly loved and the memories of whose relationships still privately provide some warmth, yet, as in Camus's view, the paths of all three partnerships were in their own way tortured.

Mitch Corass was The One. Well, I thought he was. I fell head over heels for him. He gave me a son (and almost a daughter) and he gave me his name. But deep down, there seemed a lack of depth to our feelings for each other, despite both of us working to convince each other it was there. Marriage requires hard work, but maybe ours was too much hard work to sustain. I have no idea; too close to the engine to properly examine. I wanted our marriage to work, and I honestly believe so did Mitch, but the marriage failed, love failed, and that was it. Love and marriage are mysteries always in need of solving. Mitch has gone, dying early, a death that stunned me, so completely unexpected as its timing was. Mitch was only 58. At the time of his death, and earlier, he was no longer my husband as far as the paperwork said. He was Bianca's husband after me, and then Zee's. Bianca had beaten him to the Pearly Gates, and Zee was left to mourn him as his widow.

In my heart, I had never divorced Mitch, nor had my heart acknowledged he had found someone else. Yet, he had, twice, and so had I, twice. At his funeral, I struggled to remain in the background, the right place for a former wife who was not the wife of the time. However, I hungered for someone to acknowledge my loss, which I felt almost equalled the loss of Zee. Instead, it was me who dispensed sympathies to the younger Mrs Corass. As I saw it, she was the polar-opposite person to me, Mitch's former wife, though not too dissimilar to Bianca, his second. And that being so, these two younger wives, so alike, one living and one not, came as the personification of my inability to meet Mitch's requirements, and the symbols of my regret over a loss never fully expressed. Was that why he needed to look elsewhere? Because I just didn't hack it? Too ...? Not enough ...? Not right ...?

Divorce, whatever path it follows in its achievement, must bring loss of identity, a self-doubt, though not always likely to be valid. Mitch's funeral ceremony, in an absence of any acknowledgement that Mitch had played a large part in my life, resuscitated that sense of blame or failure in me. In the service, our son became Mitch's son, not Mitch's and mine, and I could not understand why that son, my son, had not seen I might have been shattered by his father's death. Brandon was included in the funeral program, and I was excluded, thus extending my grief. I had been Mitch's wife. He had been my husband. We had shared a life, we created a son and a daughter, before our union ended. Someone should have said so.

And what might I say about Christian and Morgan? Well, both had their lovable side, each different to the other, and together we had our highs and lows. I may have stymied both relationships through my caution fuelled by my battered heart after losing Mitch and my young experiences with my father and brother. At the end, after Morgan, my confidence in my ability to retain affection had hit rock bottom, nothing to do with age. And for whatever the reasons, I concluded that not one of these men – sibling, parent, or partners – made me feel fully and irrevocably loved. I don't count my son in this. Brandon might love me, and even if I should persuade myself to doubt this is so, I know I would be wrong. He's my son, and the rest is only noise. Should he find a partner, should he move on, at the core, how I feel about him, the love I have for him, will not change. I love him, and he's my baby, my pre-teen, my young adult and my mature son, whether I make any visible claim or merely hold this irrevocable knowledge inside me. My measure, as with most things in my life that relate to the external assessment of others, is an acceptance of a truth that I'm one of those people who cannot hold attention. There's a small sad voice inside me that suggests a brutal question: if I can't find myself lovable, how can anyone else?

I mentally apologise to all those unknown men I have clumped into my small collection of bad relationships. Maybe it's not men as a collective that bring me this disappointment, but me, and my inability to make good choices.

Christian de Belis, my Italian Argentinian partner, was the showman, until he was not, and then he was lost. When he reached the point where he could no longer generate the energy to be the life and soul, he rapidly gave up on everything, including me who, I guess, reminded him of his glory days. Morgan Leigh was a manipulator, someone who presented as a kind listener and then used what he'd learnt to get his own way. I was the one to call quits with Morgan. In each relationship, the good times were good, but the bad, as all such decays are, were heartbreaking. Each partner first were great friends and, for some time, great lovers. Sadly, however, there are no Nicholas Sparks' movies or books coming out of my life, no love-of-my-life companions for which I'm someone's only love and soul mate, despite catastrophes faced. For me, no enduring love despite troubled beginning as experienced by Noah and Allie in 'The Notebook'. Or the futile love between Jamie, who is dying of Leukaemia, and Langdon in 'A Walk to Remember', a love that Langdon would describe as being like the wind, not visible but felt. My body and my spirit ache for that ultimate expression of love, the one where there is no doubt of a shared intertwining of love and knowledge of each other. As has been most events and decisions in my life, choosing a husband may have been in a small part an outcome of a shared chemistry but inevitably they were not earth-moving or transformative but practical or circumstantial. My partners spoke of love but were easily dissuaded in the display of it, reinforcing the undemonstrative practice of my parents and a sense of me not having what it takes to move others in extraordinary ways. As I heard often throughout my childhood, you can't have what is not there. Compromise has given me a salve for my disappointments: move forward and make the best of what comes your way. Fate has other plans for me. If only ... but, time's running out for such miracles, so the only course for me is to concede.

After Morgan, I closed the door firmly. But bodies and memories and emotions hold strange powers over lives.

13

Has revisiting my past relationships stirred up my emotions? Over the past few nights, I've been having weird dreams. In them, I sense fingertips, rough in texture but with a gentle touch, that trace their way along a sensitive curve from the outer edge of my breast near my armpit and then down underneath, ending in the centre of my chest, a marvellous sensation tinged with awkwardness and a sense of rule breaking. My waking self draws on logic. What are the rules being broken? Only the rules of childhood promoted within my prudish upbringing. My logical analysis counters arguments against the sense of shamefulness I detect in myself. I don't cringe from the display of sexuality in movies or novels, but I would rarely have discussions with others on the topic, nor do I allow myself to explore my own sexual responses. My conclusion: childhood imprinting is hard to override, but how ridiculous for an adult, an aged adult, to respond in this way, especially one who has been wedded three times.

Although I'm dreaming, when I awake my skin still tingles with the recall of this imagined connection. This is beyond my understanding, suggesting something is wrong, like, maybe a warning sign of psychosis. At my age, what else can it be? In my dream, I feel my body tensing in a pleasurable way, the memory of which can only have been hidden within my psyche. Last night, I dreamt the fingers, full length digits, were rubbing across my pubic mound, stroking my labia major, then softly invading the space between my legs. I felt my legs instinctively move apart. In my morning review of my dream, I'm left with a sense of my desire for my dream lover to go one step more, and a recall of my body quivering in anticipation of potential fulfilment. The dream evaporates. For the rest of the day, I can't keep my mind from 'down below'. How can this be? Why can't these emotions be ignored? Somewhere 'down there', my 'private parts' are misbehaving. Nerve ends are a-tingle. I waver between guilt and pleasure. I fight the urge for somewhere private so I can touch myself, but when I'm back in the privacy of my apartment, my attempts at masturbation fail and my disappointment is huge. Nothing there but a wet, floppy pad of tissue.

Each morning, when I awake, my body is aching to retain the tension of the dream. Awake and resisting my inhibitions, I allow my fingertips explore my body, something that oddly I have never done before. Under my breast, my fingers identify a smooth band, as if flesh has pushed through my ribcage and moulded my breasts. Am I fooling myself, or does this area feel as firm and sexy as it always has? The changes ageing has wrought upon my body are undeniable. Wrinkles wreck my once smooth face and neck, my arms – especially between shoulders and elbows – are misshapen ugly flaps, and there's definitely no Marilyn Monroe-ish chest and legs. All these areas have suffered damage from exposure to sun and wind over the years of my life, an unavoidable cost of my obsession with my chosen of sport, and, despite my dedication to training, there's loss of muscle mass, which I might blame on the natural post-menopausal depletion of Oestrogen. I allow myself a minor concession: my body is not too bad compared to others of the same age, thanks to my years of hard training and running.

My self-assessment takes me to the bathroom mirror. I cringe at my lack that it reveals. My deficiencies are unavoidable as I push my face closer toward its vision of reality. No lies or avoidance on offer in there. Apparent in the reflection is the monstrous me, still there, only temporarily less visible because of late I've kept my mind away from the topic. Monstrous. Vanity knocked to its lowest level, in a world where beauty is packaged in youthfulness. This view is the one I present to the world, the one from which new acquaintances draw their first conclusions. I flick my hair. Wiry, greying, with a tendency to be untameable, it frames my colourless and age-blemished face. Lips that are no longer plump, eyes veiled by sagging eyelids that are capped by almost invisible faded eyebrows. Under my chin, folds of excess flesh. Once, in novels and movies, the older woman was portrayed as wise, calm, serene and beautifully grey. That's a leftover from the era where the label of 'old age' was applied, say at sixty or younger, and life spans were shorter. In our modern world, at sixty we see ourselves as still taking part in our great adventure of living, not conceding to the nearness of the next phase. The only issue is that our external appearance hasn't received the email, and is persistently progressing on towards the final phase, when all padding has disintegrated and it's only tissue stretched over a skeleton. I could spend my dollars and artificially reclaim some of the external indicators of youth, like dye my hair and eyebrows, have Botox, and use a pile of make-up, but the self I see within my own mind will always remain the monstrous version. I'm still monstrous, despite my attempts to push that view behind me, and I swallow its distastefulness like a dose of castor oil. Ultimately, ageing can't be held back. That's how it is. Bleating about it will not change things. I need to learn to love myself for the inner me, not the external one, and live life to the fullest. I need only to convince myself this must be my goal. It's a hard sell.

Despite my affirmation of accepting my ageing self, I can't deny my latest explorations might be measured as veiled attempts to recapture a past version. Weeks have passed, and I continue to suppress both my rekindled desire and curiosity about its return, all the while being plagued by my internal questioning and a conclusion that won't be suppressed: is this a sign perhaps that my libido is not as dead as I'd supposed? My Google research reveals statements such as expressing opposition to the harshness of the word masturbation, suggesting other perspectives such as it's natural to self-pleasure, to love your own body, and to feel a need to release sexual tension. This is a foreign language to me, especially the instruction to love my own body. I have never felt that way. It's been a tool, and nothing more, and certainly never seen by me as something that might attract admiration. Is my curiosity a sign it's time to act boldly? Particularly as there's one certainty: time is running out for any form of experimentation. Can a body heading for failure, as I no longer can deny mine is, and which perceives itself as monstrous, be willing and able to extend and twist itself into the positions required for any self-pleasuring like this? Who knows if I am, or no longer, capable of exploring things not yet considered. And who would care? I have no one to whom I must answer except myself. But if this is so, why am I resisting these thoughts; why are they filling me with guilt and shame?

I've convinced myself.

Time to be bold. Nothing ventured, nothing gained. I've seen the ads on television. Others must do it. You read about it all the time. Can I be brave enough to buy a dildo? Or a vibrator? What's the difference? But how? Incoming mail crosses the receptionist's desk. I'll die of humiliation should I cause the imagined snickers from the young chick that sits there. Next, what kind? I google-d and there's a variety available. 'Use your imagination and there will be an object or device that suits.' How disgusting are these thoughts? I can't believe my mind is stooping so low. How shamed I'll feel if someone finds out. They'll think I'm bonkers. They'll put a night watch on me in case I take to roaming the corridors in search of a willing male. I'm priming myself to become the next subject of lobby gossip, if I keep this up. But it's my own body that's doing the prompting. And it isn't asking for a male. Besides, there's not a man sufficiently appealing that comes to mind, I remind myself, as I ignore the faint poke from somewhere inside that recalls opal eyes, a head of shivery grey hair, and the memory of a light touch to my shoulder. I tell myself my only desire is for touch, sensation, and a sense of life. I'm testing myself with a warning of a vision of my future: a need for a straitjacket for the stupid old woman in room 624. She's off cue, that biddy.

Awakened to this unsettling sensation, as I have been recently, causes me to do some pondering. Have I ever heard anyone talk about sexual urges in the elderly, beyond the Bev, Tim, and Margie scandal? Of course not. This subject is taboo. Too distasteful, too shocking, too out of the box. My own reactions are proof of the prohibition of such thoughts within the general population, although I have no proof, and only a view that is limited by my own moralistic mind.

The more I consider this question, the more often the dream comes. Its tantalising tentacles are overtaking me. Time to take this matter seriously. What's the worst that can happen? I'll die of embarrassment and, being realistic, death is the only significant challenge ahead of me. No great stretch of years ahead for me to concern myself with how others might view me and, let's be brutal, if I can't live on the edge now, there's never going to be another opportunity.

I've charged myself to press forward. Each morning, I take another step. First one is to research via Google about older women's sexual drive, the likely spots of her body that might generate arousal. I note the oddity I have never done this before, and I've learnt things I might have found useful about female anatomy as it relates to being engaged in the act of competitive running. Dare I admit it? This might have provided my younger self more pleasure. Did I ever think that I deserved pleasure? Was I too busy trying to fight for my visibility rather than fight for myself? Did I never consider other ways beyond my sport that I might have grabbed control of my own life and chosen another way to live it? Never. I had no doubts whatsoever that the path I was on was the only one I was offered. As I review my path to this point, I'll concede the only obstacle may have been myself, only me suppressing my own potential as much as I've accused men of doing. And why am I feeling so awkward? It's ridiculous. My long life has been lived in schoolgirl naivete. From everything I've read, now that I have allowed myself to venture into this realm, tells me the desire for fulfilment is natural, maybe instinctive as part of the primary drive for reproduction that is not bound by age. What was once taboo, providing the shock in movies such as 'Peyton Place' and 'From Here to Eternity', are now common viewing in so-called 'soft porn' such as 'Bridgerton' on Netflix or 'Fifty Shades of Grey'.

Determined to no longer hold back, with the mantra 'What's to Lose' resounding through my thoughts, I attack the situation, keeping my eye on the goal posts. Focus on the rise, focus on the bush ahead, focus on the rock. One foot down and then the other. Breathe. Keep moving ahead.

On the next shopping bus trip, I'll visit the local post office and buy a postal box. One step forward.

Google 'dildo'. Oh, for goodness' sake. Who would have ever thought there are so many possibilities?

I close Google and clear my history. But realistically, who will care?

14

Fantasy sex is never far from my thoughts in any still moments that show themselves briefly and spontaneously throughout the day or night. Have I opened Pandora's Box? I'm back at the Google website, scanning through the many options. My face is burning with what I interpret as shame for my weakness of giving in to a desire. Or is it guilt after years of conditioning?

Having so many choices is not helping. There is an array of lifelike, weirdly shaped devices in bright colours. Mind blowing, almost shocking me off the website again, but a little pep-talk pushes me to decide. This is it. I pay my money and immediately receive confirmation of the order, and now it's only a matter of waiting. In the marketing blurb, discretion is a word repeated often, its frequency of use no comfort.

If only that's where it ended. Now I must face the dilemmas that come via the day-to-day realities of practicalities. I find that attaching to this device the label of dildo or vibrator is off-putting, so I convince myself the way around is to give this thing a name. Working through a list of male names is not working for me. Not Graeme or Mitch, Christopher or Morgan and not Brandon. Not my favourite doctor's name, or that guy at the library I used to pant over. Finally, I settle on Anton, merely because it sounds slightly foreign thus exotic, but also retains a touch of conservatism. A male character not quite fitting within my world of acquaintances and yet not too far beyond the boundaries. Anton. Anton's delivery should happen in a week. And that will be another challenge. Even though the supplier promises discretion, many hands will pass this package along its journey from supplier to purchaser.

Already I'm blushing.

And now the day has come. Anton is in my post box. The Post Office is sending me email reminders of deadlines for collection. I feel as if I'm wearing a hi-vis shirt with the word 'Weirdo' across the front and back, so I refuse to make a special journey. Anton must wait until the next shopping bus in two days.

The two days drag out. I am becoming more and more uncomfortable. Finally, the girls and I are climbing on board the shopping bus and on our way to the mall and to Anton.

What's up your nose today, Billy? You not feeling well?

What am I going to say? For one of my friends to notice means my discomfort must be obvious. I need an answer that will satisfy them. A lie.

Didn't sleep so well last night.

That's not totally a lie. My body is teasing me more than ever, especially now Anton's waiting. And I can't stop worrying about being found out by a chance slip, or maybe something on the packaging. My friends aren't dumb. They might recognise the trademark and put two and two together.

There's no avoiding the look that passes from one friend to another. They'll each have come to explanations which are hopefully far off the truth. Part of me wants to share this adventure, but the other part, the conservative side, is not willing to do so until I can measure my own responses. I imagine some future moment when I feel free to share a giggle with the ladies over my whim, and I feel my cheek wrinkle in a smile.

As is our new habit, we have morning tea together before breaking into pairs or trios to explore the stores of the mall. Minutes drag out as my companions sip their lattes and teas and press the last crumbs of muffins onto fingertips to lift to mouths. The practice is not to hurry. It's not the luxury of morning tea that the group enjoys, for delightful morning and afternoon teas, and even suppers, are served by the Fairview. It's a sense of being 'normal'. Today the nerves on my bottom are trembling with impatience. I don't want to be the one who hurries the others along. That's guilt speaking. Instead, I wish another might do the job for me, but, no, this is not that day, apparently. I need to be creative with an excuse to ensure my visit to the Post Office is solitary. The others rise, and I take my time until I'm given a look that says a silent, 'What now, Billy?'

Betty is after a birthday present and heads to Target. Lily follows. Barbara wants a new bra and heads to the department store. Maggie can't decide. Will she stay with me or go with Barbara? I hope my supernatural willpower will head Maggie in Barbara's direction. I dither around in my handbag, controlling my body from displaying any indication I'm about to stand and move, hoping that's enough to persuade Maggie that the department store will be more appealing. The indecision drags. Finally, Maggie gives me a cock-eyed look, before waddling off a few paces behind Barbara.

What a relief. I wait a few more seconds to allow some distance before heading towards the Post Office at as fast a pace as my still slightly stiff body will permit. The box key resists being turned. Once opened its disappointing content is a card. My lack of ability to escape my friends has been replaced with a fear of other disclosures, like to the woman behind the counter to whom I need to present this card to claim the package containing Anton. A deep breath gives me courage to step into the Post Office, as if preparing for the start of a race. Breathe in, breathe out, breathe in, breathe out, with the card extended in front of me.

'Morning,' the young blonde behind the counter says. Her customer service smile is like the morning sun, though her eyes don't lift from the form she is filling. Her peripheral vision must be excellent as, somehow, she's able to foresee my needs. 'A parcel, eh?' Only as she snaps the card from my fingers does her eyes meet mine, then she swivels around and reaches out. Behind her is a honeycomb of shelves.

Ah ha. Doesn't need a signature. All ready. There you are.

My whispered 'thanks' sounds foreign, but I take hold of the parcel with both hands and quickly turn and head out the door. Once outside, I scan all sides of the parcels for any give-away clue. The only information available is my address and some anonymous sender details, so nothing to draw suspicion. Unless someone knew. Unless someone has made a guilty purchase off the internet. Now I can focus on following my plan by buying something with a bag large enough to hold the postal package as well as the purchased items. The drapery store is to be my savour, and the purchase is a throw for my bed in Turquoise. I'll show the girls my new throw without pulling it out of the bag, and my criminal package can sit safely beneath.

15

Anton has been transported in a plain cardboard container of about 50 cm x 15 cm x 13 cm. Sizeable. Are you that brazen, Anton? The length of the box makes it difficult to hide. These girls are curious types. Hope they've something else to keep their minds busy.

Back at Fairview, not wishing to show my eagerness to hunker down in my own apartment, I only half-listen to conversations over lunch, willing myself throughout not to fidget. At last I'm home in my suite and my apartment door is firmly closed, locked and I'm blocking out any thought that should one of my friends come by and find this so, they would suspect something is 'going on' and would not give up until they found out what that might be. My ears are pricked, and my breath rapid.

I take a deep breath and stand there, mid-living area, with Anton's container in my hands, as if suspending time, gathering courage to take the next, bold step of using Anton for the purpose for which he was designed. I need scissors to cut open the Sellotape that seals Anton inside, and once that's done, I lift the tabs of the cardboard to reveal an inner box, shiny and colourful. Anton. Eight inches. Lifelike. Pink and veined. According to the image on the smaller container. With balls. Ten functions. Oh, what have I done? One part of me sees the humorous side and wishes to share this with my friends, the other struggles with the shame.

From inside his personal container Anton beckons. A bright pink tip breaches the protective wedge of clear plastic in which he rests. Below that, double wrapped in clear plastic is the full mount, silky to the touch. Underneath, there's the vibrating mechanism. I'm on a high, like a rebel leading a challenge to the Presidency of some foreign third-world country. I'm pumped, as if I'm making a stand against the grand afternoon-tea primness that is the public space of the Home, too 'public' to reveal individualisms, which is duplicitous of me, considering my earlier hesitancy and doubts. In this moment of minor triumph, I've almost convinced myself that one small stand such as this might spark a return to 'normal' for us many institutionalised beings. And yet my logical mind tells me it's only more denial. It's not the big bad institutions set on suppressing its residents, more that the many needs within a facility such as Fairview are diverse, and it's easy to confuse the protocols for the nearly able with those of the dependent.

Back to my breakout of institutionalisation via Anton, a grin is spreading across my face. I can't believe my audacity. Smugness. The courage to buy was a big step. Whatever else comes, well, that'll be like me breaking into a long-distance run and (again) giving a finger-gesture at the disapproving men of the sideline.

Anton is calling.

His container has no instructions on his use, apart from boasting about the 'satisfaction,' although whatever the phrase 'all-encompassing' is intended to mean makes it sound enticingly promising. There are a few pointers on his 'care.' About any method of use, little. I guess the suppliers assume this will be instinctual. The promise of ten functions written in English is encouraging. However, when reinforced by the words written in French—Good vibrant realist avec testicules 20 cm—they become more exotic. A tremor runs through me. Will this meet expectations? Will I be able to overcome my guilt?

After my first experiment, the only conclusion is that Anton requires a lot of effort for the reward of little pleasure. Later, I rethink. Maybe Anton has done his job. Maybe it's I who hasn't given the experience my best effort.

The second excursion into wildness and erotica is mildly better, but my sense of shame shortens it. I clean Anton and carefully place him into the box he arrived in and write the word 'Anton' on the outside. I find him a suitable place at the back of the top shelf of my wardrobe.

Sorry, Anton. Not your fault.

He might not adequately service me, but he's there as a reminder I have a back-up plan, if I find the courage at some other time to try again. Already keeping such a secret makes me feel more in control.

I gaze up toward the top shelf where Anton's cardboard box sits, barely visible.

You did your best. I'm the failure. Thanks for being here.

Anton expands beyond the prick and balls in the carton. He may be faceless, but he assumes a personality of no specific age, one who has a gentle soul and who is a good listener. I scroll through the men in my life and can find no one on which this description might fit to take over the role of a real-life Anton. Anton can symbolise for me that elusive but ideal man I have not yet found, if only because I can assume with a little practice, he may satisfy me for his primary purpose of pleasure, but his most important quality is that I can be reassured he will always listen but never reject me.

It becomes a habit to share a whispered conversation with Anton about the social activities and gossip of my temporary home and new friends. Am I 'losing my marbles'? I laugh at my own suggestion. This is not the first time I have had an imaginary friend. Loneliness invites such opportunity, and sadly I have experienced more than my share of that, not just in childhood, but also within my marriages, no doubt a result of souls not meeting and being in relationships that work at a pragmatic level but do not fully encase the heart. So be it. That's my lot in life.

16

Another day of buzzing and chatting. The grapevine is in full fruit. Beverly James's daughter, Kristy, who everyone remembers for her nervousness on Beverly's first day, is in Mariella's office. She blew in like a southerly squall, changing the temperature along the way. Her face shows her displeasure. Like flashes of lightning, the gaze of her eyes hit earth via the bodies of those she passes, as if everyone who falls into her vision has conspired against her and her mother, that all are a party to the corruption of the perfect mother she has left in care. No one doubts the reasons behind both her visit and her anger. Bev has returned from hospital and is back in her suite. Everyone is certain Kristy will go straight to see if her mother has settled back in Fairview, but instead, it's to Po's office that Kristy heads.

As for Bev and her co-conspirators, the hospital has completed their tests and prescribed antibiotics for all three. Bev, from all accounts, acts as if nothing out of the ordinary has happened. A part of life, she says, with a flip of her hand. Marg is bouncing around like she has won a gold medal. Only Tim, befuddled by the ruckus, has volunteered any information. What has ruffled his feathers is broadcast to anyone he encounters, since his return from hospital. He's being 'treated like a criminal and been questioned about his life's sexual history.' He says they (meaning anyone of authority) are telling him that one of the three is guilty of contaminating the other two, and that they seem to believe it must be him, when it's not. Tim may have a good point, as no one seems to suspect the women, and Tim is giving a good impression of someone surprised by the outcome, an unexpected response from a sexual fiend, and most would say Tim's nature makes him seem more than likely the victim. In which case, the question is, was it Bev or Marg?

Residents have opened a pool, betting on the likely promiscuous character in a novel being written into the imaginations of their fellow inhabitants. Beverly, the arguments concede, is friendly and social, and these qualities tilt the case for her as the likely one. However, Margaret has the distinction of being seen as mysterious. No one can recall seeing family visit and there's been no chatter about her former life. No clear culprit leads to speculation of pre-residency history. One of them must have brought the disease in with them. Bev has a daughter, and they all know she lived with Kristy. This reduces the opportunity for sexual excursions. Marg's anonymity tilts many bets her way.

As the arguments are put forward by the speculating crowd, I make a comment to a couple of women chatting away near me that listening to them is more stimulating than reading an exotic novel, and this causes a shock wave among other listeners. By their reaction it seems the thought there is even such a thing as an exotic novel exists is new to them and furthermore, as if to admit their awareness of such a genre would be beyond them.

Earlier today I shared breakfast with Beverly. Despite her notoriety, Bev seemed very happy with her situation, a broader than usual smile brightening her face as she told me she hasn't had so much fun since the nineteen-sixties and the fun she refers to is not about sex but the infamy and attention. She whispers to me over her bowl of cereal.

You know, Billy, Tim is gentle, and he's the most romantic man I have ever known. But sex? Well, let's face it, as a society we grossly overrate sex. There's nothing like having an enormous bed to yourself, one in which you can spread out. Sharing is over-valued. None of this putting up with someone else's body heat and weight. It took sex with Tim to remind me of that. But we are good pals, Tim and me.

I heard this as suggesting Margaret is the spreader. I could be wrong.

After breakfast, and the arrival of Kristy brings all focus to Mariella's office and Kristy. The curious have taken up sofas and armchairs in the lobby waiting to see what unfolds. Suddenly, Kristy bursts out of Mariella's office with a bang, flinging the door wide, enabling a flurry of loud and angry words to burst into the public space. Mariella follows Kristy out. Those in the lobby lift their heads to pay attention. Mariella is her usual calm, unruffled self, or as the residents describe her, her cold, dispassionate self. Kristy is shouting.

I advised against Mum coming in here. I knew nothing good could come from it. Oh, but she insisted. You are the manager. What are you doing, here? The idea was to place Mum in a safe space, and now I hear this. It's disgusting. The idea ... actually, it's revolting. Why didn't you ask for a Police investigation? Rape. It must be rape.

Without a word, Mariella ushers the irate woman towards the elevator. Kristy is still frothing at the mouth when the doors slide close.

A universal snicker rolls through the audience. Many settle-in, waiting for the sequel. Once the amusement dissolves, conversations spark up to discuss the likely outcome.

Does this mean Beverly will leave?

Oh, I hope not. She's such lovely person.

Well, that daughter didn't want to bring her here. We all saw the performance on the first day.

The daughter'll get her way. Wait and see.

I don't agree but keep my opinion to myself. Behind Bev's smile is a smart, independent woman. If pushed, she'll dig her heels in. She's not going.

But what word did that the daughter utter? Rape? What does she mean?

It means she thinks Bev came about catching an STD because someone forced her to have sex. No doubt she believes that to be Tim.

The daughter doesn't know her mother. Nor does she know Tim.

But a Police investigation? That's harsh.

Won't do this place any good. We'll all be under question.

The voyeurism on display amuses but also disgusts me, and yet there I am, joining in. One part of me wants to stand on a chair and shout, this is not your business, me included, but I choose instead to retire to my suite.

It's the next morning, and once again Bev joins me for breakfast. There seems no change in her. She's smiling and cheerful, and yet a hint of sorrow takes the edge off the bonhomie that time with Bev usually offers.

Bev takes the last sip of her coffee and slides her cup to one side. She monitors her fingers as they lightly linger on the edge of her empty coffee cup.

My daughter thinks I am a slut. She thinks this place is a Ho House.

Bev's statement sounds like a joke, but this isn't the moment to laugh. I remain silent, and so does Bev.

After what seems like hours but is probably only seconds, my eyes catch Bev's and neither of us can keep a straight face. Together we break the normally quiet consumption of breakfast with our full-hearted laughter.

A Ho House? Fairview?

And that starts us off again, laughing until tears rolls down our cheeks. I need to hold my tummy. I might wet myself. That could be the biggest scandal of the year. And we are off again, until Bev's laughter suddenly stops, and she holds her gaze directly toward me, her eyes glinting with a fire.

My daughter needs to get a life of her own. How ridiculous. But it only proves how little she knows me. To her, I am not a person. Only Mum. A two-dimensional figure. It's my fault. She is immature for her age because I have indulged her. Now I will pay the price.

What are you talking about? What price?

Kristy wants me to go back home, but I don't want to. There are several reasons. First, I do not want to be Kristy's fetch-all. I don't want to be a pawn to puff up Kristy's life. It's time for Kristy to work on her own dreams and leave me to have a life of my own. I am running out of time to live for myself. So far, throughout my life, I have lived for someone else, as a daughter to my parents, a wife to my husband and a mother to my daughter. I want to be me. Beverly. I want my own friends. I want to make my own choices, and here within reason I can do that. I need freedom.

You can tell your daughter this is what you want?

I can tell her, but she won't listen, and I am so used to obeying her I can't fight her on this issue.

Oh dear, the problems between parents and their adult children, like Brandon and me, adults treating their parents as if they are children, the power play, the dancing around for positions.

This display of honesty, as if it's her failure, causes Bev to drop her head low. So accustomed to Bev's good spirits, when I see this other side of Bev my heart goes out to her. Although I can't see Bev's face or hear any sounds of crying, I have little doubt she's feeling devastated through her lack of choice, a position that resonates with me. I stand and move around to enable me to wrap my arm around Bev's shoulder. Bev looks up at me and now there are tears.

Oh, you are breaking my heart, Bev. There's got to be something we can do to put this right. We need a committee meeting to throw notions around.

Bev looks doubtful, as if she thinks this can't be helpful, but she doesn't argue.

Come on, Bev. No time like the present. Let's gather the smart ones.

I hold out my hand to Bev, and then scan the dining room for Gwen. Because the behaviour of Bev and I is out of the ordinary, Gwen, like most occupants of the dining room, is watching us so I need not catch her attention, only to make a finger gesture that points to the space beyond the dining room. I then crook my finger in Una's direction, and Una looks slightly surprised, as if she's aware of my reserves in her regard. Regardless, she stands, speaks to her companion, then flutters over in her fairy way to join Bev and me.

A united pack

1

I'M STANDING, WITH MY arm around the shoulders of my friend Bev, in a small seating space not far from the dining room. In my mind, I'm looking back at myself fifteen minutes earlier also standing with my arm around Bev's shoulder after arising from the table at which Bev and I had shared our meal. I watch the replay of my actions. I see the confidence I display when I stand, when I embrace Bev, and then as I gesture to my select group of friends. Even to my usual self-critical mind, it is easy to discern in my actions – first gesturing, then nodding my head in a general direction, and moving out of the dining room without looking back – that I am assured of the support that will be following me. Was it only months ago that I was the solitary runner with very few close friends? And not so long ago was I not the angry new resident who saw nothing human in those with whom I shared my residency? I can't explain the changes within me. Nor am I any the less confused. If I look inward and am honest, maybe seeing myself again through the eyes of the person I was, the runner who saw no fragility within herself and yet somehow landed in this place – that could only represent an oncoming rush, or a slow evolution toward the end of life – I know I'm still terrified. I push that inner conflict aside. I broaden my grin to reassure my friends, and I internally count the blessings of being part of something much larger, something that reminds me I have not yet lost my ability to contribute through my actions, especially as I'm still living my life, still a worthy person.

I watch my budgerigars gather. On my runs I've often seen the gathering of the feathered kind on stretches of water such as billabongs. The sounds of their constant calling to each other, and the visual constancy of rainbow movement are signs of their joy in community, of being with others of their kind. Each time I have seen this, I've been filled with a sense of happiness, of being part of a vibrant, constantly changing, spirited world. Today, my budgies, my fellow travellers, are slower in pace. Their gathering point is this small lounge area a short distance from the communal dining room. In their diversity, they – we – are as colourful as those of nature. I see Gwen being wheeled by Maude, the carer. She waves her wildly disobedient hand at me to indicate she's making a toilet stop on the way. Una, her flowery fairylike disposition, daintily dances directly toward us and is the first to reach Bev and me. Like a bright, curious budgie, she bends her head to one side, and her sparkling eyes gaze first at Bev then me. She has a question requiring an answer.

Oh, ladies, are we the privileged gals getting an advance copy of the authentic story?

I love Una's tinkling, lyrical voice, and I love Una's ability to always be empathetic and insightful. I've seen in practice her ability to actively use her sensitivity to social cues. Am I mistaken? Have I misheard the less than Una-like tone in her question, a sarcastic sharp edge to it? Am I imagining this? What has brought about this unusual response? Maybe I missed that she's one of those who believe Bev has indulged in what many thought of as scandalous behaviour, and disapproves. I hadn't tagged Una as a prude.

I feel the automatic change in my facial expression, certain I am frowning and displaying my puzzlement. Una glances from me to Bev and I can see she's replaying her question, searching for what has encouraged my slight display of disapproval. I can see from her face she's mulling through the possibilities, when Bev interrupts the process.

Okay Una. I get it. You are suspicious.

Una looks very uncomfortable, a sight I have never seen before, and her mouth opens slightly, still trying to find the words to put right. Bev pats her on the shoulder.

Don't worry yourself. I'm good about this. Don't apologise, Una. Not much to tell. It's all there for everyone to see, anyway. I'll explain when the others get here.

I stroke Bev's shoulder to reassure her, but I know I haven't reassured Una. The tension is eased somewhat by the time Gwen's wheelchair draws near. Gwen's chair has been rolled between the armchairs that Una and Bev have taken. I take a seat on a three-seater opposite them. The other three chat with Maude about some topic that fails to gain my attention. Again, the memory of the waterhole budgies flash through my head. Perhaps there's a truth embedded coming together. All living creature – even lone runners, wilderness budgies and ageing females in residential care – are social beings who need to be reassured by sharing with and hearing from others.

Maude seems reluctant to leave. Possibly the unusualness of this get-together has roused her curiosity. Now my instincts are on alert. I'm concerned our impromptu gathering might draw attention, and sense this might be disadvantageous to our choices of approaching the issue at hand on Bev's behalf. Gwen might have had a similar thought, recognising the necessity of finding a polite way to give Maude the hint there's nothing to see here. To convey her gratitude, Gwen gives Maude the largest smile her unwilling and uncooperating facial muscles will allow.

Thanks, Maude. We appreciate your help. The ladies will see to my needs from now on. You've been a great help. I appreciate it. What would I do without you?

Maude looks disappointed, and gives everyone one last, lingering glance. No one speaks until Maude is out of hearing, and then it's Gwen who opens the conversation.

Right then, what's this about?

Bev shrugs her shoulders, suggesting lack of knowledge, and looks at me, her eyes asking the same question. I lean forward but turn to reassure myself Bev is okay by lifting my brows and nodding my head to ask her permission. Then I plunge in.

Bev tells me she fears Kristy will force her to leave. I figure we have sharp minds here that can figure a way to avoid that.

Gwen winks at Una. Those two scallywags must have been sharing their inquisitiveness. No wonder Una charged in with her question earlier.

Well, maybe we first need to hear the circumstances. We need to know what we are up against here.

Una's smile widens.

I scowl at the mischievous two.

Come on girls, don't be bitches. And Una, you are always the one with the empathy. What's turned you around here?

Well, Bev, I have empathy for your situation, but it's my opinion this is making a mountain out of a molehill. Except the moral issue of the STD. That means someone in here is promiscuous or worse, a predator. But if it's all about 'lerv' then I am a romantic through and through.

Bev's laugh breaks the tension.

Oh, I'll tell you. My version first, then what Tim told me.

Una holds one hand out, palm facing Bev.

Bev, wait a mo. I think if we will seriously take on the management and a prudish daughter, then we need another person on our committee, a negotiator. Please hold off your story until I come back.

Right away, without awaiting approval, Una leaps up in aged style, which is to stand, wait a minute or two, then stride off leaving the rest of us to look from one to the other with furrows on our brows trying to comprehend who it is that Una has in mind.

Who...?

There's shoulder shrugging and head tipping as if no one can think of anyone in this establishment that Una might consider as a necessary addition to our group.

As a long silence becomes uncomfortable, Gwen decides it is time to tell a joke. She clears her throat and checks everyone is looking at her.

After the death of his wife, an elderly man gets himself a pet to keep him company. He goes to the pet shop and explains his situation to the manager who recommends a hamster as an ideal companion. The man buys a hamster, and all the equipment needed and returns home. A couple of days later, he brings the hamster back to the shop, citing dissatisfaction. The manager gives him some advice. 'Go home,' he says. 'And place the hamster in a blender, turn it on, and then spread the contents on your back garden before bed. In the morning, you'll be the happiest man in the world.'

Gwen's audience responds with screwed up faces and groans of disgust, but Gwen is not put off.

The man follows the instructions to the tee. Next morning when he wakes up and looks out his window at the garden, he sees nothing has changed. He returns to the pet shop and once there, the manager asks him: 'Well, what happened with the garden?' The man replies, 'Nothing.' 'That's strange,' says the manager. 'You usually get tulips from hamster jam.'

There's a delay in the responses. One by one, her audience comes back with their responses. 'Oh, I get it', an unconvincing 'Hilarious' or an unembellished giggle. Someone says, 'I can't get past the blended hamster, sorry.' This brings a round of laughter and nodding of heads. I'm trying to find a postscript to offer when I see the person Una is bringing with her into the lobby. I'm not discrete with my reaction.

Shit.

Gwen and Bev turn to see what I've seen.

Una is her usual froth and lightness, as she ushers the last committee member into a spare chair.

Joe is a calm head. His experience in negotiation might be helpful. I hope you are all okay with me inviting him to join in.

What could anyone say? My gaze briefly catches Joe's. By the way he is looking at me, I know he expects my objection, and as always, I refuse to take the expected route.

Welcome Joe to the Don Quixote brigade.

I drag my eyes from his face and turn to Bev. Might as well get on with the story, now, Bev.

Bev turns to Joe.

Ah Joe, as I was telling the others, I am starting with my story and then I will tell you what Tim told me. I believe his story but then, I would, wouldn't I? Tim and I have over the past few weeks, well, months, become close friends. We talk a lot; we are interested in the same things; and Tim's considerate and vulnerable. And yes, we had sex.

Bev hides her face from Joe, an unexpected show of modesty, something she doesn't display when talking to her female friends.

But both of us think sex is over-rated. Nice, comforting, but, well, not as essential in a relationship as some would make it seem.

Una is twitching. She wants answers to that one big question, so she butts in.

Then how come the STD?

Well, I have told you. We made love.

Bev blushes and she sneaks a peak at Joe. Her head hangs low. Gwen reaches over and grabs Bev's hand.

Oh, never mind Bev. We're just jealous.

I can't believe my own response, which is to wag my finger at Una as if I have the right to censure her when all I want is for us to maintain focus. To get the conversation back on track, I add my two-cents worth.

Without doubt, Bev, we're all curious. But Una has a point that's important to know. How come you both tested for STDs, Bev? Which of you came in here with the disease?

I'm not naïve. I know about STDS, and I can tell you until now, I haven't had sex since my husband passed, a long, long time ago. Here's what Tim told me. And I believe him. You all know Margaret. She is an extrovert.

The women giggle. Joe smiles and adds, 'Extrovert? That's a "nice" description.'

Each face hints of personal impressions of Margaret. Bev continues.

When Margaret arrived here, she was all a-flap. She came here against her will after being unfairly judged in her other Home. She never told me for what she had been unfairly judged. And Tim says she latched onto to him. He was crying when he told me she attacked him.

Una is aghast.

Attacked?

Bev nods.

Sexually, that is. When I questioned why he did nothing about it, he said, no one would believe him. Everyone always assumes men are the attackers.

Gwen is nodding. It's clear her lawyer brain is working.

Tim's right. Statistics speak to his argument. No one talks about female perpetrators. Tim's right on the mark. We immediately think it's a man, but unless I have lost my marbles, the numbers aren't that much different between men and women predators.

No one has a solution. All five stare down at the floor or their hands or feet, until Bev decides it's time to bring her case to Joe's attention.

Joe, the issue here is my daughter Kristy never wanted me to come in here. She wants me to stay with her. On the surface, that makes her sound like she's a caring daughter. She is, but she also is a very indulged daughter. When I was at home, I liked to go to writers' talks at the library or meet with friends. She would question me, making me feel guilty if I went anywhere. Part of the quizzing was out of care. She worried about me and my safety. But some of it was to preserve her own life. I know I was a willing yet unpaid servant, doing everything I could to make my daughter's life easy. It was me who worked hard to come in here. I have no medical reason to be here, so I pay the full residential fee. But I'm scared this STD issue is exactly the excuse Kristy can, no, will use to get me home again. I need a strategy because, honestly, it's hard to fight your own family. You don't want to ...

Bev buries her face in her hands, not holding back her distress, noisily crying and sobbing. None of us has anything to add. We all know the powerlessness of being old.

Una is the first to offer a suggestion.

If you are paying your residential fees, unless there's some clause in the contract you signed, then your daughter has no say, nor does the government. This suggests they have not assessed you as needing help. This means you are a voluntary resident. Wouldn't that be right?

Maybe so, but I can't stand up to Kristy.

You can appoint a representative. Joe. What do you think?

Joe shakes his head, puts a thumb across his mouth and looks down at the floor. Everyone waits.

This will be a rare event, someone fighting to stay. It's usually someone fighting to not need to come into care. We have a few things going our way, well, Bev's way. We can have her abilities assessed somewhere away from here. If, as I am sure this will prove, she's capable of making her own decisions and she can get a stat dec to say so, then the only argument the management might have would be if she hasn't paid her fees. And that's not the case, is it Bev?

Kristy manages my financial affairs.

Joe sucks in his breath.

Do you believe she is doing a good job? What authority does she have? An Enduring Power of Attorney?

Bev's face drops once more.

Yes. I gave her an EPoA. That's it then, isn't it?

Gwen's wearing what she calls her thinking face, which translates into a furrowed brow.

No. Bev. Not the end. If they consider you capable of independent living, you can revoke the EPoA. You need to complete a Revocation document and inform the attorney – that means the person to whom you handed over power – and that will be Kristy – that she's fired.

Oh, should I?

Joe takes Bev's hand.

What's say we do this, as Gwen says, have you assessed and prepare a Revocation document, and before we issue it, we speak to Kristy and see if we can negotiate a resolution. Then we have these documents as Plan B. Kristy loves you. She might put up a fight to get you home again, but she'll see sense. And you won't need to attack your daughter and cause a rift between the two of you.

Bev looks at me for reassurance. I nod my head.

Joe has a good plan, Bev, let's go that way to reinforce your case to persuade Kristy to see it your way. But on the other matter, what Tim said, maybe we can find out about Margaret's eviction from her other home? In case, you know, we need other ammunition.

I glance to see how Bev responds to the implications of my suggestion. But she has another point to make and continues.

Poor Tim. How traumatic for him if what he says is true.

Una leans in.

How can we find this out? Maybe we can do it in steps. First, find out where she was before. Then we can try to see if someone at that place will squeal.

The grin on her face suggests Una is looking forward to volunteering for this challenge. Right up her alley.

When next I lift my head to look around, I see the main population is moving back into the dining room. It's lunch already. Where did those hours go?

Okay, everyone. Give this some thought, and next time we get together we need to come up with a possible, if not a definite, plan. On Bev's behalf, thank you.

Yes, thanks everyone. I feel a lot calmer now.

There's a shuffling of feet and the squish of rubber tyres. We are ready to move on. Stage one completed. To reassure myself of the others' commitment, my gaze moves from Gwen to Una, and from Una to Joe. The mystery of this man, and my nervous resistance to connecting to him, is disturbing. My eyes cautiously track towards his face, and then I recognise this is a mistake, because his eyes are fixed on me with an intensity that's unsettling. For what seems a lifetime, Joe and I stare at each other, as if we cannot drag our gazes elsewhere. For me, it's as if I have no will of my own. There's just Mr Fix-It and me, peering into each other's souls. Afterwards, when I try to explore why this happened, I feel as if for a nanosecond I had stopped breathing. Why does it bother me? For this I have no answer. This Joe guy is virtually a stranger who pops in and out. Primarily, our paths cross because we are both trapped in this place. Yet, why did that moment feel surreal, as if Joe and I had been floating around in space like debris, until serendipitously we connected with each other?

2

Una is the first to report in. Her news comes to individual's ears, those of us she encounters somewhere within the complex. Una's whisper loses some of her spoken conversations' melodious qualities, seeming more serious despite the mischievous content.

Maude knows a Carer at Crystal Waters, which is Margaret's last home. There was a scandal over there. Crystal Waters' management asked for Margaret's family to move their mother on to somewhere else for the other residents' sake.

With curiosities aroused, the committee re-convenes to hear the full version. Una is fully-wired as she introduces the subject.

Oh, oh, that Margaret did a bad, bad thing.

In this situation, the details still unknown, at least Chris Isaak's lyric makes me smile. My wandering mind then takes me to Warren Ellis's theme for the movie of 'Bad, Bad Girl' but there's no time to ponder on any connections because Una doesn't pause. She isn't thinking about who she sounds like or what picture her choice of words is painting.

According to Maude's friend, Margaret had attacked several men over there. She traumatised them. At first, the management thought these incidents were the acts of an overfriendly person, but Maude says her friend described Margaret as an elderly showgirl, prancing around in her gaudy clothes and flirting constantly. Like here, Crystal Waters hasn't many men, so Margaret had to focus on the few. At first everyone thought her behaviour amusing. Some had argued maybe it was a sign of dementia, but when one man and then another complained they had found her in their suite or she had paid them a visit and forced herself on them, they strongly suggested she respect others' privacy. It wasn't until Margaret went one step too far and they realised it wasn't only privacy that was being abused. Crystal Waters suggested the family to follow through by arranging for Margaret to have a medical examination. Maude has nothing to confirm if this examination happened before Margaret entered Fairview.

Bev chips in.

Tim won't come out of his room. He's mortified. He believes everyone is blaming him.

Una envelopes Bev in her tiny arms and kisses her on the ear.

Tim should go to the police so he can talk to them about charging Margaret with rape.

Bev's hands fly to cover her face. Gwen turns her head, as if deep in thought. I give in and let my instincts direct my eyes to Joe. Is this because he's the only male, or something else? I'm not willing to question the reason. Joe nods.

If Tim is willing this might be something he should do for himself. I'm not sure if he will be. But nor can I gauge how distressing it is for him. Maybe I should have a chat, man-to-man.

No one speaks. Joe takes this as signifying everyone agrees. He stands, and my eyes watch as his long thin legs carry him with a determined stride across the lobby towards the corridor that leads to Tim's suite. I'm not the only one with eyes on Joe. Bev watches, too, a frown clouding her face. She makes her announcement as if speaking to thin air.

Kristy has a meeting with Mariella on Thursday.

Gwen pats Bev's knee.

If they request to see you, Bev, tell them you want someone to represent you. I will go with you and together we can see what they are conspiring, see if that's what you want or not.

Una chips in, wringing her hands.

I did my bit about discovering any gossip on Margaret, but maybe I should have suggested to Maude she could have looked at Bev's files to confirm her residency status. Although I don't feel so good about that. The evidence lies in what we know is missing. We know Bev did not do an ACAT. We know it's Bev's bank paying her fees. That's evidence she's here of her own free will and we can use that same free will to demand she should stay if she can afford to. The only part we haven't had time to gain is a person of authority declaring Bev capable of making her own decisions. That we probably can do if we meet resistance. It would have helped our case if the police had investigated Margaret's involvement, but maybe that too can be the backup if all else fails. What do you reckon, ladies?

Without thinking how it sounds, I release a deep sigh, that almost sounds as if I'm thinking it's all too difficult.

That's the hand we have. We must not let bullies knock us around.

Here, here.

3

I'm sitting, reading, in the Big Room when the usual gaggle of ganders with Tim at the centre begins to disrupt the peacefulness with honking. Una and Gwen come to join me.

What the...?

Tim, a normally soft speaker, raises his voice above the others.

I am doing it. It's not fair.

Yeah, good on you, mate.

Go get 'em.

Are you sure, Tim? Let sleeping dogs lie, pal.

Tim shakes his head at this last piece of advice and heads at his usual snail's pace, feet barely lifting from the tiled floor, towards Po's office. He knocks, and through the glass wall, the audience of men and women in the Big Room watch as Po's head lifts, and her eyes scan the watching crowd, then her finger crooks to invite Tim in. We all watch Tim slide across and stand in front of Po's desk, and we note that Po makes a gesture that invites Tim to take a seat. After that, it's like watching a silent movie, the only evidence of the shared conversation between the two is a deepening frown on Po's face and agitated hand waving by Tim. They guess Po wants to persuade Tim to take another path, but Tim seems adamant. After half an hour, Po picks up her telephone and Tim's body relaxes into the back of Po's visitor's chair. There's no sign of Tim returning to his suite, and as we the audience have afternoon tea delivered to us, so does Po and Tim. Its apparent their conversation is ongoing, with Po seeming to do most of the talking and Tim nodding or shaking his head.

In the big room a considerable crowd settles down to see what happens or maybe to grill Tim when he's released. It's a long wait. Dinner time is fast approaching. There' no evidence of action until a police vehicle pulls into the driveway. The many who had risen ready to head off for their evening meal are stalled by the entry of two police officers, a female and a male. Eyes follow them as they walk to Reception, and from there, the receptionist leads them to Po's office, where Po is standing, holding open the door for them. She ushers in the pair, simultaneously sending out a message via her eyes to all and sundry to mind their own business and move on. We don't move. We watch as Tim stands and shakes hands with both officers. All four of those in Po's office look uncomfortable. It's clear for we the spectators to see they are fidgeting and glancing at others or looking away, as if he or she is unsure of what might be the next step or uncomfortable with what is being said. All the while, there's a suppressed cheering and fist raising from the male contingent on one side of the room that leaves the women with furrows on their brows, wondering what the men know they don't.

Maude and other staff have appeared and are herding everyone into the dining room for dinner. The show is over.

Come on, you lot. Entertainment's over for the day. Dinner is being served.

The following morning, there's reports of Tim going on an excursion. When he returns, he's like a man let out of prison. He tells his story to each person he passes in the corridors or lobbies.

I did the right thing. It wasn't right what happened.

Each one who hears assumes this has something to do with the Chlamydia episode, but the greater detail to which Tim is referring is the fuel for conversations for many days to follow.

4

There's an air of anticipation blanketing the lobby today causing me to re-visualising the movie 'A Tale of Two Cities', and the mad crowd around La Guillotine, hungrily watching the lopped noble heads dropping into the basket. The big day has arrived where Kristy has gathered courage to demand that her mother come home with her. Bev's daughter has been in Po's office for a considerable length of time, and a mass of residents have collected in the

Big Room, watching. A passing thought distracts me. For privacy's sake Po should replace her existing windows with smart glass. There are no secrets. Here, everyone has an opinion about Bev's wishes, and the conflict between Bev and her daughter. Every resident knows that the Chlamydia episode has grown out of all reasonable proportion so a daughter's wish may likely come to fruition. Today's event is like reading the last paragraph of the last chapter of a novel.

Mariella has finally had enough. She comes to the door of her office and in a strong, authoritarian voice, makes her declaration.

Excuse me. Would all of you please mind finding something to do or go back to your rooms or suites? This is a matter for the James family.

I for one feel embarrassed, belatedly I am forced to admit, but I barely have time to explore my actions and emotions when something stalls me. In this place, where subservience and acquiescence are the norm, it's a surprise to everyone present when someone vocalises a universal indignity. Slowly each of us register someone is protesting the prohibition that Mariella has placed on their involvement. As if, for the first time, each has realised that Bev's issue in some small way might be symbolic of their own situation thus this may be a time to recognise there is a need to stand up and ask for a chance to express a view about what is the right thing to do. The someone speaking on every individual's behalf is Joe. Through the babble of many questions about what is going on comes Joe's clear, steady voice.

May I speak on behalf of every resident, including Bev James. Yes, the issue here is a problem for the James family to resolve, but it also involves the rest of this. We consider this place our home, and everyone in it our family. What happens within this facility has implications for each of us. It's belittling when you tell us to withdraw, as if we haven't any input into the behaviours and outcomes of our fellow residents. It's as if we are prisoners with no freewill in the outcome of anything that happens here.

Most of us don't push our opinions and you might read that as saying we are acquiescent, that mostly we agree with policy or practice, and that is probably true in the most part. But now that you have made this request for us to move on, it brings me to put a question to you. When was it we all lost our individual rights? When was it we could no longer question anything? It seems almost as if that loss occurred simultaneously to our entry here. Or was it, earlier, when our bodies became stooped and bent, or when our hair turned grey, or when our thoughts and views could not be as clearly articulated as they once could, or when our families and friends thought we could not make good decisions?

I will suggest that coincidentally with entry into a care facility, it has been assumed we have no desire to speak for ourselves and for each other. It's a shame because this is a lovely and caring home. However, I dispute that the physical act of walking or being wheeled through those huge sliding glass doors renders us as submitting ourselves to the whim and wills of others.

We admit our dependence. What we ask for is respect. Here, the respect comes by acknowledging that no matter what is decided by the James family, there is a consequence for each of us in some way or another. Bev and her daughter will work out their differences, but our routines and lives have been implicated in the events that led to this upheaval and furthermore, the outcome here today offers a marker for any future events that may affect our lives as residents of Fairview.

This is not a prison, but our home of residence. The staff are not our wardens, but our helpers and friends. The management team is not Judge and Jury making judgement about whom we are and about what our wishes and capabilities are. They take advice from people who specialise in making assessments and giving advice. The responsibility of management is to ensure they meet the needs of their clientele while not infringing on individual rights. We are the clientele. Our families are our representatives.

We aren't fighting against authority, nor challenging you, Mariella, nor your staff's authority over us. We aren't claiming our families and others don't love and care for us. And we aren't declaring this place is where we don't want to be. We only want to show our unity to fight against the pandemic disease of Ageism that is rife in the world outside of this place and, as odd as it may seem, also inside. We all indulge in ageism; mostly we are unaware we are doing so.

Today, we are focussing not on us as a group but fighting specifically for Beverly James who has told us she loves it here and wants to stay here, and we all want her to stay with us. Providing care of the aged is a business with a commercial need for maintaining a good reputation. How might this influence decisions made today? Will this bring outcomes that may culminate in jeopardising Bev's chances of staying as she wishes to do? We fear that to protect the good name of Fairview, Bev might without intention be made the culprit, the one despoiling the reputation of this prestigious establishment. But she's the one who pays her bills, she has committed no crimes, she's not violent, nor does she harm others. As you and the James family discuss this issue, please remember that Bev's fellow residents are in her corner.

Tears are streaming down my cheeks, shocking me in my response to Joe's words. I have never been a crier. This man about whom I know so little has moved me, and within his words he has revealed a part of himself that had not been visible. I'm normally proud of my tough exterior, but today I do not even bother to dry these tears. I'm not sure whether it's because I have instinctively rationalised that tears will dry or as subterfuge, realising that by wiping them, I will reveal my vulnerability, my soft side, and more particularly, that Joe has crept into my heart and soul. My face is stiff and sticky. It's not accustomed to this inundation, and I imagine it as a map of a dry creek bed being filled with a recent downpour upstream, small pond of water leaving a salty trail down my jowls. All the while, I haven't taken my gaze from Joe who stands tall surrounded by grey heads and shoulders bowed over walkers. Those in wheelchairs are crowding in to pat his arms or shake his hands or smile up at his face. Voices normally feeble and restrained are chattering, laughing and cheering.

Joe has spoken for everyone. Sure, he may have been carried away in the fervour of his mission, but the expressions on faces as they listen to the man speaking on their behalf display many emotions: dazed, meaning perhaps those haven't heard or understood his words through failing hearing but know something is going down, to wide smiles that shout, 'Wish I'd said that.' An important factor, despite all the give and take around placing family members in aged care, is that Fairview's many residents, regardless of ability, are not living a life alone. Despite their limitations, they each will have a much better chance of surviving the biggest killer of seniors: loneliness.

Mariella is trying to catch Joe's attention by stretching her head and moving it to point to her office. She must be granting Bev's wish for Gwen and Joe be part of discussions about the STD transmission and Bev's wish to remain a resident. Once she sees Joe has noticed, Mariella changes to her hand to beckon him to join her and the others. She has already ushered into her office Bev, who pushes Gwen in her wheelchair in front of her, and Kristy, who is seated with her hands covering her face. I settle myself into an armchair that gives me full view of the office and its occupants. It's like watching television on mute. I can see Gwen roll her eyes at something; I watch as Bev leaves Gwen suitably parked and scurries over to her daughter, around whom she wraps her arms and puts her head close to her daughter's, as if Kristy is a young child, only releasing her daughter to pull up a chair close to her; and then Joe, the last of the group remains standing, tall and straight, behind the others. I concentrate on body language and facial expressions to interpret what may be happening.

The pantomime begins with Kristy lifting her hands away from her face and moving them in front of her, her extended fingers quivering, her open mouth shaped into an O, as if pleading for help, reminding me of Munch's 'The Scream', a horrible way to see Bev's daughter. She may be causing her mother grief, but no doubt she is also suffering for her own reasons. The O might mean Kristy is hysterical. The event viewed through the glass is dramatically enlarged by my imagination in which I create my own dialogue, of Kristy hysterically making her point, 'I have had shame and embarrassment rained down upon me.' It's easy to imagine she may wish to blame her mother and the management for their role in this. Or maybe she doesn't know what's right and what's wrong. Should she be her mother's advocate or accuser?

Mariella is patting down the air, her mouth working as she moves around to sit behind her desk, so that her back now faces me. The group's body language shows a concession that Mariella's in charge. It seems apparent to me Kristy's hysterics have upset Bev. I'm filled with an urge to enter the room and comfort my friend and can only assume Bev is absorbing the blame for causing her daughter's response. On the other side of the room, Gwen from her wheelchair has raised her good arm. Joe, still standing, bends over to Gwen, nods his head, then steps forward. Billy can see his left arm is pointing in Gwen's direction, as if Joe knows Gwen has something to say, and everyone turns to Gwen.

Right at that moment, Mariella's office door flies open. It's Tim. His face is flushed as if he's been running and has consequently been caught short of breath. Not that Tim runs, more shuffles, but clearly, he's put effort in getting to the office as quickly as he can. Bev turns to him, her right hand covers her mouth, and Tim scurries toward her, then without touching her, he stops and turns toward Mariella, his mouth opening and closing. Must be a magnificent speech, as from my external view it seems much more than Tim's usual short bursts of commentary. I examine those of his audience whose faces are visible. Joe has a lopsided smirk on his face, Gwen a broad smile, Bev gives the impression she is suppressing a smile, and Kristy is aghast. Bev's hand reaches out and strokes Tim's arm. Tim turns to Bev, his face transformed. No lip-reading is necessary to understand that something important has happened.

I utter my surprise. "Oh,' and others look up to see what has caught my attention.

Now, Gwen and Joe are taking turns to speak. I decipher this as them putting forth their arguments on Bev's behalf to Kristy and Mariella. Bev and Tim have only eyes for each other. I can't take my eyes from those two, and without explanation again my emotions are overwhelming me. It's unnatural. I can only guess what's occurred in that room, and yet my body is trembling, and tears are rolling from the corners of my eyes and filling my throat until it burst into the public space via a sudden but audible intake of air. I look around. The crowd has thinned and those that remain are back to normal rituals of sitting and staring or reading. No one is taking any notice of the conference in Mariella's office nor the external voyeur making a fool of herself, so I permit myself to weep quietly, but about what I have no idea. While my unbridled emotions shock me, I recognise this comes with a great sense of liberation. This unprecedented loosening of control feels almost luxurious. The absence of a need to protect myself, to no longer feel compelled by my will to have a self-defined image of myself, is wonderful.

Fairview and its residents have moved on to other matters. I don't know what they spoke about in that room. I can only see evidence of outcomes. According to the lobby grapevine, Margaret has undergone several medical tests and is being treated with drugs to 'keep her in her cage'. That's how Una describes the action. I assume this will be libido suppressant medication or an anaphrodisiac. Margaret's red cloud still floats through the public spaces, although not to the same heights as she once floated and at the sight of her, I wonder how Tim feels.

Tim and Bev seem to have moved to another phase. Of late, there's an open display of affection, such as holding hands or one stroking the upper arm of the other, and yesterday, one finger touching a cheek for which the stroker, Tim, received a reward of a beaming smile.

Bev was missing for a few days after the meeting in Mariella's office, which caused concern but, on her return, Bev again shared not only breakfast with me but also her news. Bev's return to her former home had the intention of reassuring her daughter while attempting once more to present her case in a calm familiar environment. She told me she had explained to Kristy why Fairview is where she wants to be, and that her visit home was only temporary. She has told Kristy she'll have holidays with her, but most defi-nitely Fairview is her home. Bev admits she may not have fully convinced her daughter, because Kristy is still angry, but at least she said her piece and acted on it.

Joe and Gwen have melded back into normal routines, which means my encounters with them are irregular and less frequent, unless I deliberately pass the spots where they will be, for example, Joe's reading corner or Gwen's suite because that's where she has mostly been since the meeting with Kristy and Po. Gwen's body takes a demand on her energy levels. Her recent investment and effort into a solution for Bev's situation has taken its toll.

I'm sharply aware of the reduced encounters with my friends, but I'm not willing to explore ways to change my ways to improve this, chiefly because I can't decide which is more worrying: my avoidance of self-reflection over my responses to Joe or my determination to make life hard by going solitary. In running, the ability to analyse why the same mistake or misstep happens repeatedly is beneficial, as is the value of having a support team behind you. I'm achieving neither.

On the day Brandon comes to visit I most regret letting go of my support team.

5

One look at the expression on my son's face and I'm flying into defence mode, mentally retaliating with the question to myself, 'How long since his last visit, Billy?' If I'm honest, I hadn't noticed but now recognising something is afoot, I'm retrospectively noting he has only come to visit when he had a point to make about my continued residency. Every hair on my arms and legs, every nerve throughout my body, is on high alert. What's today going to be about?

I persuade to make an effort, so I reach out and take a firm hold of my son's upper arms and pull him towards me into a hug, and then I stand back so my eyes can gaze into his eyes.

Brandon. I am so pleased you came to visit. Come, let's have something from the cafe.

My lanky son bends towards me and kisses me on both cheeks. There's a smile painted across his lower face, a sign he too is working hard. For the moment, at least. He's little taller than me, so his bending forward at first implies he needs to hold himself far away, but then he shatters that by moving in closer to wrap me in his arms and squeeze me. He takes my hand, and almost child-like swings it back and forth as we walk towards the lobby cafeteria. The atmosphere between us feels artificial, stretched and tight. Is it me making it feel this way?

Brandon uses the honour system to buy lattes and cupcakes and brings them to the table I've selected near an open window. He smiles as he carefully places the tray down and lifts each item off. As he takes the tray back to its spot, I scrutinise his broad back and shoulders, loving the muscular shape of his arms. Motherly love washes down me, filling me with temporary guilt for my caution. However, on his return journey, his knotted facial muscles are twisting, and the unsteadiness of his gaze confirm my fears. Something is coming my way.

How we maintain a conversation about trivia is a miracle. I'm holding my breath, waiting for him to have the courage to say what he came to say, but he's struggling to venture past the casual titbits of everyday. After a lot of crumb-pushing around on his plate with his index finger, he uses his big boy voice to tell me with authority the exact opposite of what Kristy told Beverly. Brandon is brooking no arguments. There is no changing his mind. 'It's in your best interest, Mum, to stay where you are.' The matter of my house, he will put off for a while. Meanwhile, he has stored my belongings and is preparing the house for renting.

I'm wordless and empty of tears, a complete contrast to my recent emotional overload, even though this time and these circumstances justifies both words and tears.

Brandon doesn't wait for my response, and I'm aware of his reasoning. He's a softie and he will guard against his likely inability to handle any opposition. This is something he inherited from his father. He has said what he came to say, and before the situation can deteriorate, before he loses control, he stands, kisses me on the cheek, and leaves without making eye contact.

The anger on display in his body language and the manner of departure registers as a punch in my gut. I guess I'm in shock because it feels to me that time has been suspended. I remain seated, staring at the empty mugs and crumbs of cupcake on the abandoned plates that symbolise my shattered emotions. Tim and Bev pass by on their way for a coffee. Their greeting is their usual cheery 'Hi'. I vaguely recognise that my failure to respond has not gone unnoticed. They turn back with furrowed brows, and yet, while now realising I've caused them to worry, I'm incapable of moving or reassuring them.

Tim and Bev don't return to check on me. Joe is their emissary so it's Joe who receives my angry spray.

Oh, it's Mr Fix It. You think you can make things right here, do you?

Well, thank goodness. Billy is in there and Billy can speak. For a moment, I thought Billy had left the building.

Joe laughs at his own joke, but it's forced. He's uncertain of his grounds, probably weighing up which is more important at this moment. Is it his need to respond to Bev and Tim's request, as I'm sure that is the reason he's here, or to take himself out of the Lion's den into which he's walked?

The lobby is emptying, which means it must be time for a meal, but Joe ignores the exodus and nods to Bev and Tim for them to go too. He follows up with a shrug that indicates he's not sure how long it will take to break through my hard protective armour.

I know I am not your best friend, Billy, but maybe, by being a stranger so to speak, you know, me being situated a little distance from your personal business, might make it easier for you to tell me what's going on here. It's darn easy to see you're not yourself. Has your family been to see you?

Joe's use of the word 'family' reminds me how little of my life's details I've shared with my friends here. It's as if I see myself as two people, the one I was before entering this place and the one I have become. One has a former home and a son, and a former life that revolved around training and running and with no plans for an ageing future, and the other, in a suite of my own with the companionship and support of virtual strangers. It is the second woman who is sitting here in the foyer café with a stranger who wants to fix everything, a Billy who never had bad husbands nor a successful career and a deep investment in a sport of her choice, both of which let her measure her achievements. Brandon is the conduit between these two, polar-opposite characters from worlds and expectations alien to the other.

It's been my mainstay that I can and will always decide my own future. That's been my path of action since barely out of my teens. Why am I failing now? I hear my response to Joe without controlling the tone I use or what I scream at Joe is. What I want to say is, 'You damn well know I have had a visitor.'

Instead, in a voice that sounds as if it's someone else's, a voice of a weak and bewildered soul, I allow three words to slide out, three words that reveals that my emotions are beyond my control.

Brandon. My son.

I hadn't intended to admit this. Not to Joe. It's not his business. But do I stop there? No.

He's the only family I have. A surviving ex-husband or two, neither of whom have time from their otherwise busy lives to worry about me, especially as I have never invited them to do so.

How old's your son, Billy?

Old enough. Adult.

Is he your only child?

Yes. His name is Brandon.

I flinch. Joe already knows this. I told him this only seconds ago. What a fool I'm revealing myself to be, an emotionally dependent wreck.

From my first marriage.

You have had multiple marriages?

I drop my head, and smile with a pretence of a guilty nod. Joe laughs.

Glutton for punishment, some might say.

I manage a grimace, which in truth was intended to be a smile.

Those wise someones would be right. You men.

Yeah, we are a handful. 50% of the world's population has voted in agreement of that statement. Is Brandon a regular visitor?

I let my head shake the negative response, feeling shame about the behaviour of both Brandon and I, for reasons I can't understand.

We aren't seeing eye to eye. He's too scared to visit.

So, still the little boy at heart, then?

I squeeze out another smile, this one manages a better performance.

Guess you might say so. A little boy with a big voice.

Mind if I ask what's the beef?

Well, Joe, it's Bev's problem in reverse. He believes this should be my home from now on.

And you don't?

To be honest, I don't have an opinion. My beef is that he has decided without consulting me. I should have some input. But he acts like my father used to do, just blurts out a command and slams the door. I guess that also upsets me because Brandon is not anything like my father. I am sure his heart is in the right place. He's convinced this needs to happen, and he doesn't want me to sway him. But it's humiliating. It's insulting. And it hurts. Is that how he sees me, just because of one minor accident?

What do you mean, one minor accident?

I stare at Joe. Of course. I have told no one how I landed here, that it may only be temporary and that I'm a reluctant resident. Was my pride too dented? Else why I couldn't I bear to talk about it? There's no doubt in my mind I'm liked by my fellow residents, and they like me not because of my successes and failures. They like me because of who I am, because of how I comes across. I've not admitted this to myself before. I have found this response unexpected and hard to accept, given my life experiences of not-so-good relationships and connections. Perhaps these doubts I feel about how I'm perceived is why I don't trust my companions sufficiently to share my personal stories.

Joe pats my hand, like I'm his grandma. Even so, its removal leaves a warm spot. I want it back, but that would be too forward, too bold.

Are you okay? You look like you have seen a ghost.

Thanks, Joe. No ghosts. But I have had an epiphany.

Is it contagious?

We both laugh at Joe's joke.

You know, Joe. You have woken me from a dream.

Wow. Did I? Is that good or is it bad?

Well, I'd say it's mostly good. You probably know how long I have been here, but me, well, I couldn't say how long. I'd have to look back and figure it out because I haven't been paying attention. Paying attention is what I have always done, so I don't understand this other person I have become. I guess I have been in shock. I should have realised. I mean, even earlier today, when I was talking to my son, it had flashed through my head that I have two personas. One is me as I was before I came here, the person who probably believed once out of here she could just start again where she left off, and the other is me as I am in here. I don't know which is the permanent me; I don't know which me I like. Or rather, I can't figure out which me is the one for whose rights I want to fight.

Sounds darn serious. But why shock? Didn't you plan to come in here?

And before I can stop, I spill out my past to Joe, an almost stranger. I begin with my love of long-distance running, and how it developed, the battle to enter a sport that excluded women and becoming a champion, through to the era where I had no choice but to do solitary runs and how that led ending up in here.

Instead of experiencing regret about sharing, Joe's patient gaze and occasional questions calms and reassures me. There's a weight shifted from me. The two Billys have reconciled. Thus, freed from the blockage of emotions, I'm able to reflect and review.

Joe, two things stand clear. First point is, had I taken that wrong step and landed on my face staring at the desert floor five or ten years earlier, without doubt I would have healed and been right back there, competing again. I guess I'm focussing my anger in the wrong direction, Maybe I should point to Mother Nature who caused my loss of collagen and elastin fibres that gives licence to others to take away my control. Add to that, the visual evidence of sun damage to my skin from the many days spent on those desert runs would not help my cause. The second point is the same as the first, but more hurtful. Those same external physical markers lead strangers to enact belittling and reducing actions, categorising me by appearances of age and associated limitations without assessment. Like my rescuers, Chris and Sam. Like my caring and loving son. A desire to help that overlooks how it feels to be on the other side of the negotiations and in some ways being treated like a child. No wonder old people have a reputation for being cranky.

I'm almost breathless as the words continue to rush out of me.

It's so wrong, Joe. But no one listens.

Maybe, Billy, you need to sit down and think about what you want and then invite your son back and explain to him how it makes you feel when he decides on your behalf without consultation. The responsibilities might terrify him, you know.

Terrified? Of his own mother?

No. Terrified about making an incorrect decision. He has the weight of world opinion pushing him. Read the media. See it for yourself. All those criticisms about not caring for our elderly parents. About our neglect of our most senior citizens. Warehousing is a term I've read. Advice on what everyone else sees as the right or wrong thing to do. Guilt, no matter how they address the issue, might be a contributing factor for families. Put mum and dad in aged care? What bad, unloving children they would feel themselves to be by doing this, even if dad's got dementia and is a handful. Right, so then they convince themselves that the right thing to do is put mum and dad in a granny flat in the backyard but soon after Mum has a fall, and with Dad already incapable of caring for her, those same loving but untrained adult children, while dealing with a mentally disabled Dad, also need to help her shower and lift her on and off the toilet and get her in and out of bed. How can they not cause bruising to Mum's body? And silently won't they be tempted to resent having their lives disrupted? These duties, as onerous as they may be, are what a good son or daughter should do. Then there's the financial implication. It's all so complicated. We oldies are equally negligent. We don't want to face our ageing, so we don't express our desires and wishes. Very few of us set plans for an ageing future, because we just can't handle it. I'm one. I was let off the hook because any choice was taken from me. Come on, you've got to agree, our kids love us. They fear facing the reality of a life without us, and our ageing makes that future highly visible. You need to have a calm and well thought out conversation with your boy, Billy.

Someone else telling me what to do is just too much for me, as sensible as it may be. I channel my frustration on Joe, glaring at him, but some part of me recognises the common sense of his advice and stops me from uttering any words. Instead, I only want to escape, so I push back my chair, its legs squealing on the tiled floor, and rise.

Thanks for your advice. I'm sorry but I need a rest, now.

I hear the tone I use, know it cuts the air and probably cuts into Joe. Am I angry for revealing so much, or with Joe's advice which I find hard to accept, or am I scared? Joe raises his eyebrows and shrugs his shoulders. He doesn't respond. I turn and stride toward the elevator, and instinctively I turn back. Joe's face is turned toward my departing self, displaying his usual half a smile. He hasn't moved from the table. He doesn't wave. Nor do I. I continue toward the elevator and, as I walk, the image of Joe's face remains with me. I regret my nastiness. My dramatic exit has robbed me of a chance to ask for an explanation for one of Joe's statements. He said, 'I was let off the hook.' To what is he referring?

6

This morning, still recovering from my outburst, I'm hoping my regular walk around the corridors will lift my spirits. My usual path would take me near where Joe reads to the male dementia-inflicted residents. I can't face him, and I'm trying to convince myself I'm doing this because I don't want a repeat discussion on yesterday's topic, but there's a doubt niggling away at me, and I feel uncomfortable with my uncharacteristic evasiveness.

I attempt to quietly bypass Joe's corner, but my attempts are futile. Though I'm at a distance, he's seen me and is calling out.

Oh, hi there, Billy. Lovely morning, isn't it? Can I steal a minute or two of your time?

My urge to say no is strong. Why did I come this way? Is there some part of me that wishes for Mr Fix-it to creep in? Please, I beg myself inwardly, don't let him start on the Brandon topic again. Joe is recognisable for his slow saunter, but today, possibly realising his victim is keen to escape, he takes long, rapid strides towards me.

Look, I know this might be asking a lot of you.

I brace myself for the inevitable, the undesirable topic.

But after listening to your life story yesterday, I was wondering...

Look, Joe, I don't ...

No. I understand. Brandon is your thing to solve. No. I am talking about something different. Now that I know a little about you and your life, and given your success as an endurance athlete, I was hoping you might give some thought to how you could adapt your regime and disciplines into a gentle plan, something that residents can do seated on chairs or, if I am being ambitious, in their wheelchairs. At least it would keep all our bodies moving.

Just give it some thought. No obligation. Just say the word and I won't mention it again. Thanks. Catch you later.

Joe turns away without a response from me, and with the same rapid strides, returns to his group. I'm stunned. Paralysed by the unexpectedness of his request, I can't move myself away, stalled in the spot, compelled to watch as Joe picks up a newspaper and begins to read as if there had been no interruptions. I'm still there, in that spot, when Joe pauses his reading and glances over at me, winks with one eye and gives me one of his common smiles. I feel my face flush. What's it with this guy? Isn't he yet another ordinary resident? He's not a staff member or a privileged resident, as far as I can figure. And yet, he's like a man on a mission, and he's getting under my skin.

7

Everything seems out of kilter. Now, Joe has become both more visible even when not within my sight, and more absent. It's as if my radar has tuned into him, even if I can't see him, and I haven't seen him for several days. His absence is worrying me. I'm persuading myself it has nothing to do with me. I tell myself I'm following my usual walk around the facilities. But that's a lie. I'm walking to see if he's in his usual locations, like the newspaper reading corner, or the men's shed, or in the courtyard. He's not there.

His absence is throwing me off-course. A state of denial is an unnatural and unusual path for me to take, but I can feel myself withdrawing from potential realities, as if the questions around his absences are something with which I won't be able to cope. I have tried telling myself that in earlier days of my stay if I had not seen him for long periods, I might have noted the unexpectedness, nothing more. Perhaps, in the early days of being a resident, when I saw him as being yet another charmer I should avoid, I may have even thanked my lucky stars for not coming across him on my rounds. Why should his nonappearance bother me now? It's his life, his privacy, and what part in that do I play? Despite my denials, there's an inexplicable sense of apprehension rising inside my chest, as if Joe's absence invites an unravelling that goes beyond the questions of where Joe might be, or if he's in some trouble, but to the uncertainties of my own life, such as how my next phase of living might shape up, and how might I find a way around having the conversation on the subject with Brandon.

The look on Brandon's face the last time I saw it haunts me. I hold a clear memory of the annoyance distorting his good looks, or the lasting view of his straight and rigid back, as he passed out through the sliding doors from the lobby onto the driveway, not once turning back to wave goodbye from the driveway. I speak to myself, questioning myself continuously. This is my boy, my one love in the world. Why is he treating me this way? Why am I making it so hard for us to negotiate? There are bites of anger arising from Brandon's reluctance to see my point of view, followed by knotty fibres of frustration over my inability to convince him, mainly because I don't know what I want and I can't put in words something I don't comprehend. I'm worried that when I uncover what those wishes might be, will it be too late to change the outcome? Will he listen? Will he see my perspective? The final chili-burn to any self-respect is the embarrassment I feel over letting my inadequate communication cause me to make futile one-liners, childish verbal retaliations, sufficiently hurtful to cause Brandon's sudden departure. I'm supposed to be the wise lady that always has matters under control. I haven't heard from him since. But then, too, I haven't called him. We are two stubborn people, both made of the same stuff, both with personalities that find offering apologies difficult. Having lost so many of those I loved, nothing overrides my fear of losing Brandon. He is the only person left in my life that I love. I must act. But how can I find a compromise?

Flittering around these other concerns is the more palatable incentive Joe offered me, the exciting notion of preparing a suitable exercise regime designed to meet a criterion covering the limitations on and expectations of a community with a full spectrum of individual abilities. This right up my alley, and it offers me a distraction from Brandon.

I only need to adapt what I know to suit the purpose, as I did when I made the shift from studying sprinting, the field in which my brother Grae succeeded. I studied anything I could get on my hands from the moment my brother shared what he was learning each week, long before I was granted permission by my father to participate. When I identified my abilities were taking me towards long distance, needing different skills, I changed my focus. My specialty is keeping a body active and fit, knowledge informed by years of reading, listening, and putting into practice. I know I can help. I know I can translate the fitness training for an active runner to suit the diverse abilities of my fellow residents. I puff with pride that I have this ability, something I'd never considered before, and I'm confident of the benefits simple routines will bring to all levels of ability.

I look back to my learning days. It had been my need to stand up against constant resistance to a woman engaging in a male-dominated sport that fuelled the depth of my research and study. There weren't many male athletes willing to share knowledge, basically because they genuinely felt women weren't suited to their sport. Without the knowledge, understanding, and the physical fitness I would always have been exactly the person they saw me as being, an ambitious female capable neither physically nor intellectually to endure the rigours. The strictness demanded made the term 'sport' never adequate to describe long-distance running. The word 'sport' suggests enjoyment, fun, recreation, but this serious engagement requires discipline, more-than-the-average stamina, and mental strength and, quite frankly, sometimes, to a participating athlete, it might feel the opposite to enjoyment. A sense of achievement comes afterwards, after the adrenal gland has dumped its load of cortisol and adrenaline into the bloodstream to mask agony and pain and weariness, to fool the body's senses into believing it has an immunity to pain. All high-level forms of sport require qualities of excellence, that comes out of proper training, nutrition, rest and attention to form. For example, lack of these in sprints, as I often joked to my brother Grae, only opens an athlete to a strong possibility of losing in competition and a higher risk of injury. However, in my form, in long-distance or endurance running, in which each competitor's abilities can differ vastly, lack of persistence in attending to these areas has killed.

I have completed my circuit for today and am back at the central lobby. Will I sit for a while or head for my suite? Visitors and residents pass in and out. Conversation levels are high today for reasons unknown. This persuades me to head upstairs. As I turn to walk to the elevator, a vehicle is pulling into the circular driveway and by chance its arrival catches my attention. There is no reason for me to notice, but as the rear passenger door opens, I recognise the distinctive and familiar spikey grey hair. It's Joe. The vehicle has the words Patient Transport inscribed in tidy font along one side. Joe waves to the driver, slams the door, and heads toward the entry. He speaks to one man seated on a nearby sofa as he enters. His usual smile shows no hint he's not his usual self, but is it my imagination? He isn't standing as upright as he normally does. A hunched back is not noticeable in this place of many bowed and bent backs, but when a man whose posture is usually perfect, any deviation is obvious. Particularly when someone is acutely aware of the man's presence, as I have recently become. He's walking a lot slower than his usual gait. I'm unable to take my eyes off him, and note as he draws near another resident, he straightens himself, smiles and chats—normal Joe—but when the conversation is over, as he walks away, his shoulders droop heavily again. As my gaze washes over his departing back, I observe his right hand is resting on his lower ribs, as though he has injured that part of his body. I've now another unanswered question about Joe to fill my thoughts.

8

I can't keep my thoughts away from my relationship with Brandon. Should I challenge him? I'm aware I have every right to check myself out of Fairview if I so wish, so why am I hesitating? Why am I using Brandon as an excuse? I pride myself on being self-aware, and I recognise when I'm stalled. My solution is to find a distraction to keep my mind occupied until an answer comes. The obvious activity is to implement Joe's suggestion. I've no doubts I can use my knowledge to design a plan that works for most of my companions, those in wheelchairs with limited movement and those with balance, sight, hip, knees, or back problems. Recognising the range of capabilities within the complex, I settle on the plan to create a routine that meets the lowest level of ability, that might be someone like Gwen, who depends on a wheelchair to get around but is further limited by the lack of flexibility and movement in both her arms and legs.

There's a notebook on my bedside table and a pen, so I fetch it and settle into a chair at my dining table. First things first, I record the obvious and essential way group exercise sessions should begin.

Point 1. Everyone needs a clearance both from their doctor and Fairview. That means I need to converse with the Po sooner rather than later. Po won't go for anything she can't control.

Moving on from there, the ideas flow easily. While my own exercises may be more demanding than these, at the core there is a base point that all routines must meet.

Exercise 1. Please ensure your chair is placed so it's level and firm. If in a wheelchair, please ensure the brakes are engaged and foot pedals folded up. Sit up tall, back straight, chin not too high and hands resting on your thighs Take a deep breath in through your nose and exhale through your mouth. Repeat, breathe in and breathe out.

Exercise 2. Lift your head to look up at the ceiling and keep it there for about three seconds, then look down to your toes. Look up to the ceiling and down to your toes once more.

Exercise 3. Turn your head to look over your right shoulder. Bring it back to look straight ahead. Turn your head to look over your left shoulder, then bring it back to look straight ahead. Repeat, looking over right shoulder and back to the front, then again turn to your turn to your left and back to the front.

I record four more phases to add to the three, a perfect foundation for whatever follows. At this point I can visualise my goal on behalf of the residents, whether wheelchair bound or limited in other ways, and a plan accordingly. I take the page of notes and screw it into a ball, then begin anew, the ideas coming almost too fast for my hand to keep up.

I spend the entire morning writing and editing and running through the routine in my mind. I re-write them in a form presentable to Mariella in the form of a proposition that addresses risks, evaluation of capabilities, and so forth. In the early afternoon, I'm at Mariella's office door, filled with uncertainty about Po's likely response to a resident offering to conduct exercise classes, despite benefit to other residents. I am a representation of confidence as I take a seat to face Mariella, reminding myself nothing ventured, nothing gained.

Mariella, you probably know I have spent most of my life training as an elite athlete for long-distancing running. I know the importance of exercise and I am missing my regime. As I look to how I might adapt to suit this environment, I realise most people in here would benefit from some gentle chair-based exercises, those designed to suit even those with limited movement. After giving this notion careful thought, I ask for your permission to conduct regular gentle and safe exercises for anyone who wishes to join in. Here is a plan. From this you can measure the minimalistic and safe nature of the exercises.

I push my carefully written exercise program over to Mariella's side of the desk along with my broadest smile intending to broadcast this is my forte.

Can you scrutinise this yourself and have the medical staff examine it, and I look forward to receiving your permission to arrange a suitable day for a regular session.

I examine the flow and ebb of Mariella's facial expressions, like shadows of clouds rolling across the stubble of desert grass on a windy day. Is Mariella searching for reasons to oppose? Surely not. Or maybe this is something she hadn't expected. Within mere minutes, Mariella dons a strong, non-negotiable expression and finds the words she has been searching for.

Oh Billy, very nice of you to put this effort in, but I am not sure how Occupational Health and Safety guys will view a resident, no matter how qualified, conducting this event.

That's why I am presenting you with this proposal, Mariella. Please garner all the professional comments you need, and I will return to listen and respond to them appropriately. I am confident there will be no health and safety issues as I have given every foreseeable risk considerable thought and consideration.

I'm Billy of old, sure in her knowledge, capable of making appropriate decisions and able to present her case well, but I'm sensing Mariella has put me back in my place, only able to see me as a feeble resident, another of her responsibilities, and someone who dropped all her life knowledge and experience the minute she walked in the glass doors of the foyer. Billy the athlete, Billy the corporate analyst, is once again invisible. There is a heavy weight in my heart because despite the professional way I've presented my proposal, I fear the invisible, incapable and monstrous me is the only one on display and therefore, for Mariella, my proposal is already doomed. How quickly I lose confidence. Only months ago, this wouldn't have been me.

I leave the manager's office, and with no clear intention, my self-doubts take me towards Joe's door as I fight vainly to hold my despondency inside. As the door opens, I rush in and throw my body at Joe's. My mind registers his shock alongside my own, as I instantaneously recognise that I'm acting on instinct. I'm on automatic, taking actions without thought. I've wrapped my arms over Joe's shoulders and buried my face into his neck. I feel Joe's body tense and then relax, and his arms wrap around me, making me feel secure, safe, and assured.

Oh damn it Joe, I don't think Mariella's going to let me conduct exercise classes. I presented a written plan, covering all contingencies such as needing a doctor's and medical clearance, and the impact of each exercise on body and muscles for appraisal. She will ignore my request to have it evaluated.

Internally I register a potpourri of emotions, ones related to a faint recognition of my uncharacteristic behaviour in respect of Joe as well as those that come through my expectation of a rejection of my project in the near future. Beyond the hurt and disappointment that will come if my idea is pushed aside, there's a deeper sense of loss I can't comprehend. Slowly a possibility dawns on me. It's loss of hope; a sense that the remaining phase of my life will be devoid of uplifting moments; that there will be nothing that my mind can imagine and give birth to, nor anything that will remain within my own periphery of control. From now on, someone else will direct what happens. Convinced as I am, as I have always been, that living in the day, making the most of every minute, is the right way to live, this is soul-destroying. Even if a person is limited, as Gwen is, there should be no reason for not squeezing every great drop out of each day by remaining curious, constantly finding ways to learn new things and to make new friends is the essence of life. The vision I had landed upon is to live, not wait to die; to live, and not expect nor focus upon inevitable illness and eventual end. Those moments will come, for that's the way the end of life arrives. Instead, the emphasis must be on the now by waking each morning with a goal to continue life and possible by laughing, exploring, and sharing with other travellers through the ageing process. What I am experiencing is grief.

As I prepared my proposal, I'd once again felt worthy. I vowed not to let any sense of worthlessness a rejection might cause to overtake me; to resist any sense that my almost-seventy years of life and accumulated knowledge and experience have been erased. Yet already I'm failing.

Out of Joe comes that strange grunt people make when the words they need aren't available, or when they have been unexpectedly overtaken with emotion. His arms are still wrapped around me, but I have no idea whether this is voluntarily or by compulsion because of the way I charged into him. His hands are patting my back as if to comfort me, as is often instinctive, possibly nothing more, but the action brings me to sudden awareness of my position within our pose. Everything from Mariella's office is blurred, but a ridiculous question does pop into my head. How did I find myself inside Joe's hug? Now alert and embarrassed, my body becomes rigid, my back straightens, and I push myself away from Joe by peeling my arms off from where their full weight rests on his shoulders. When they fall back, they hang despondently by my sides. Joe's face reveals nothing, neither his reaction to my spontaneity, nor to my equally sudden withdrawal. He merely tilts his head to one side and gazes at me with his unreadable eyes.

We'll give the Po a chance to reconsider, but in the meantime, your visit comes at a most opportune time. I need you. Can you help me organise this equipment.

As if nothing untoward has occurred, he points to one side of his living room, where there is a mound of cardboard cartons in various size. Joe strides over and opens one of the top ones, pulling out a tambourine in bright red.

Rose the Occupational Therapist has offered to hold a once-a-week percussion group after I offered to buy simple instruments. I have Egg Shakers, Chiquitas, Bells, Finger Castanets, some Mini-Cabanas and so on. I need to organise them somehow so they can be pulled out and packed away easily. The first session is tomorrow. I have a problem bending over, to pick them up off the floor. The delivery man wouldn't put them on the table for me.

Oh yes. I recall seeing Joe in the foyer, noting how he clutched his ribs, and the way he had tried but failed to hide the flinch of pain he clearly felt. Having my fears for him confirmed is unsettling and weirdly stifles me from continuing the conversation further, as I might. Instead, I bend and lift each box onto his dining table as if there's no issue.

It's like Christmas. Joe opens the first package and places each item on the table with a jingle. He nods.

Bells.

I choose one and shake it. It's a soft sound, perfect choice for a gentle group. Then Joe picks up another and together, smiling at each other, we tinkle out a spontaneous little tune. By the time all the instruments are carefully arranged on Joe's table, our smiles have turned to laughter.

I shake my head at Joe.

It's been a long time since I have had so much fun, all because of a few bells and whistles.

Joe's grin is from ear to ear.

9

After two weeks of no response, I'm at Mariella's door with point-by-point arguments for what I've assumed might be objections to my case. Joe has helped me prepare this. I knock, enter and take a deep breath. Mariella cuts off any chance for words.

Oh, Billy. I was hoping to see you. Given the success of the Percussion group under the Occupational Therapy department's oversight, we should give your Exercise sessions a trial. What do you think?

As seems my tendency of late, I find myself short of words, but I know my face is beaming if the tweaking muscles around my mouth and cheeks are any indication. I keep some professionalism by extending my right hand, inviting a handshake without uttering a word.

Check with Occupational Therapists about regularity and suitable days and equipment required. The OT's will help you can get under way.

Overtaking my pleasure of receiving approved is the surprise of Po's brilliant smile, an image that lingers for some time.

The first day has arrived, and many apprehensive faces mill around for the first session. Rose and other OT staff have brought in chairs and checked wheelchairs for brakes and pedals. The number of interested people may be attributed to Joe, Gwen and Una who have spent the past week canvassing, but I suspect the success of Joe's Percussion group has encouraged attendance. During those sessions, the building was filled with the raucous laughter, nervous giggles and conversations mixed with tinkles, chimes, thuds and clackety-clacks. There seemed less concern about making music than the joy of making noise and participating. It's as if there's a little magic in those bells and whistles. As soon as they are out and into people's hands, even people who have never ventured into music making, there was rattling, shaking, tapping, or pounding, regardless. I hope but don't expect a similar positive response to my session. Music is one thing, exercise is another. For some, the word is off-putting.

To offset, I choose a perky choice of tunes which I set at a comparatively low volume. I try to reassure the nervous novices that it's to get in the mood. There are a lot of fiddling and fussing as I settle individuals onto chairs, showing them a good starting posture, and check the safety of wheelchairs, brakes on, and pedals raised. Then I begin by making an announcement.

Some of you already know that before I came to live at Fairview, I was an endurance athlete. What this means is I have spent most of my life exercising to keep fit and stay healthy. Today I will share my knowledge with you, not only to improve our fitness and health but to have fun. I know you will enjoy this. This is not my program, so no credit to me. I learnt most of this from my friend. In this first week, we will mainly do some warm-up exercises. Next week, when you decide it's as much fun as I say, we will add to the warm-ups using my friend's program. There's no pressure. Do as much as you can, and I'll bet you will surprise yourself by how easy this is and how good you feel afterwards. Let's see if I am right.

I've dug out my professional skills for today, directing my eyes to scan the group, here and there catching someone's gaze, smiling, and all the while conveying a confidence I'm not fully feeling. Can this motley crew follow my lead? Will this be the first and last gathering? I clear my throat.

First, we need to get some oxygen into our lungs so, everyone, breathe in through the nose until you feel your ribcage expand, gently, hold for a count of three, and then softly exhale, blowing out through your mouth – a long cool breath. Don't strain. Again, in – hold – out. Keep breathing in this way, while I acknowledge my friend's wisdom. Gil is my Tai Chi Sifu, and she says, 'Tai Chi is a good all-round exercise that is gentle. It uses the breath and mental focus to exercise safely without undue wear and tear on the body. Physical and cognitive training are essential for the mind/body connection. While both are beneficial, each form is usually separate from the other. Scientific studies have proven that Tai Chi provides both physical and cognitive training through its focus on fluid physical movements, which bring a positive effect on both the immune and nervous systems. This lets the body's natural intelligence kick in and start a self-healing process within, using gentle breathing, mind focus or mindfulness, and soft fluid physical movements. When energy is circulating, always returning, always collecting, then exercise is revitalising not draining.'

Sounds logical, doesn't it, so let's have a go. Now we have drawn oxygen into our lungs, let us do some warm-up exercises. They are easy to do. These are to warm-up your body, and next week, as I said earlier, we will add to these.

I know my intro is a little bit too serious for most of my students to take in, but it feels right to ground my instructions to establish their authenticity. Everyone's too nervous and not listening. They're all waiting to see if they will be tested. I've met my goal, to state the necessary, and now I can move on.

I work through the first seven exercises of breathing and shoulder-rolling from a position seated in front and facing the group, carefully watching and waiting for individuals to understand or copy others or attempt to act as instructed. Time isn't important. Although the exercises aren't difficult, for anyone who isn't used to this action, it might seem complex. I realise that it's not only physical limitations I must factor in, but also mental. For some, the ability to take in information or instructions doesn't happen at a normal pace so I change my delivery, then slowly and carefully show what the action is and wait for each person to find their own way. Next time, I hope some will remember, but on reflection, I know I should downgrade that hope. Probably no one will remember. One outcome for me has been a success in testing my patience. This is not a trait normally associated with me. My normal style is to identify the challenge, find solutions, and plunge head in. No dilly-dallying. No procrastination. Get in and do it. This will not happen in the delivery of this program, that's a certainty.

Participants seem comforted by the gentleness of the moves as well as coming to grips with the slightly repetitive nature of each.

Okay, everyone, maintain your upright body posture, and now instead of lifting right or left shoulders separately, this time we will lift both shoulders together. Both shoulders up, both shoulders down. That's once, now lift again and down again, so that's twice, up and down again, up and down again and up and down again.

Next, we will do a little shimmy. Sitting tall.

There's a twitter around the room.

Now, drop your right shoulder down and lift your left, then drop your left shoulder down and lift your right, and keep going for five, four, three two, one times.

Someone at the back begins giggling over her own confusion and slowness to 'shimmy', and like a pandemic it flies through the group.

What? Forgotten your Disco days, ladies? You'll remember next time, won't you? You'll love this next one. Lift your arms out either side like wings and give your shoulders a shake up and down. Now, let's fill our lungs with oxygen again. Breathe in through your nose, and exhale out through your mouth, and same again.

I'm moved by the trusting expressions facing me. They are keen for more. Now they are comfortable with what is expected, more assured they can manage this, they can recognise there aren't any repercussions for failure. I take this as positive feedback.

Now please put your hands on your thighs and turn your hands, palms up. Raise your hands to touch your shoulders then drop them back palms up to your thighs. That's once, twice, three-times, four and five. Lift your right hand and reach straight out to the front of you with your fingers stretched, then clenched your fist as you bring it to your chest with hand still clenched. Five times. Five, four, three, two, one. We'll repeat this with your left hand five times. Left hand out with fingers stretched out in front, clench your fist, and bring to your chest. Out, stretch, clench, and back.

Faces grimace as they thump their chests. Then they share congratulatory smiles with each other for achieving the task.

This time, I want you to reach straight up to the sky with your right hand and look up at it, then bring your hand back down to your waist, five times, then repeat with your left. Reach up, look up, down, four, three two, one. Left up, look, down five four three two one. Great work.

We will now flex our wrists. Hold both your arms out in front of you and at the wrist turn both your hands five times in a clockwise direction, then five times in an anticlockwise direction. Rest your hands on your thigh. Let's take in more oxygen. Breathe in through your nose, exhale out through your mouth.

How are we going? Not as hard as you thought, is it?

Let's keep on. Lift your elbows and bring your arms up to chest height so the fingertips of both hands touch together in front of you. From your waist, swing your arms and your torso to the right, back to centre, then to the left and back to centre do this five times. Now, back out to the right to the centre and back to the left then centre, that's four, back to right and so on, that's three ... two ... one.

Now it's time to move the lower part of your body. March your feet on the floor, as long and as fast or as slow as you wish or are able. After you have stopped then march your feet and swing your arms too, ten times, as if you are marching in a parade except your bum is glued to your seat.

That causes a ripple of loud laughter. I know now my students are relaxed and happy in their workout. I am relieved, too.

Okay, time for more oxygen, breathe in through nose, out through mouth twice.

Lift your right leg straight out, as far as you can, in front of you and bring it down to the floor five times. Good, good. It doesn't matter how small your movement or if you can only lift your leg a little, it's still achieving movement and I'm proud of you. Next, do the same with your left leg, out in front and drop it down five times.

Now let's do some dancing. Using both feet, press and hold your heels on the floor and tap your toes, five times. Both feet again, but this time hold your toes on the floor and tap your heels five times. Still using both feet, rock your feet from heel to toe and back five times

Let's get those ankles moving. Raise your right leg in front of you and roll your ankle in a clockwise direction five times, then roll it anticlockwise five times, then put your right leg back down onto floor and raise your left leg and do the same with your left ankle. And that's it. Place both feet on the ground, sit with body tall and breathe in through the nose and out through the mouth twice.

Great work. I hope you enjoyed this. I can assure you. Your body will benefit from the movement. Congratulations. Next week and if you come back – there are a few giggles – we will move from merely warming up, and I will have a surprise for you.

Grins of achievement and applause for their instructor fill the room.

Rose, the OT who's the care manager for the day, places a hand on my shoulder.

Billy, you can safely say that was a success. Great work and congratulations to you too.

To the rest of the group, she says 'Make sure you drink some water, and make plans for next week's session. Let's all thank Billy for her work.'

More applause, and as I turn, there's Joe with the biggest smile of the lot. From inside me a warm flush is spreading. It's not just Joe's smile, but of feeling appreciated and contributing and a whole large package of emotions I'll unwrap in the privacy and quietness of my suite.

10

Today Joe's face is alight with some mysterious energy.

I am so blown away that you are an endurance runner. This is so impressive. You must be so disciplined and regimented because, well, as an outsider, it seems to me to be about being ultra-fit and there are so many little things that can go wrong through no fault of yours. I mean, the weather is a good example. We all know the forecasters get it right most of the time but it's common for unexpected sudden changes to catch us out, like the hailstorms that they apologise for later. Or you are caught in lightning storms, explained in hindsight as unpredictable intersections of two weather systems they never saw coming. If you are out there, out in the never-never, you need to know what to do if things don't go to plan. My mind can't stop thinking about the millions of possibilities. Like stub a toe. How do you manage?

If Joe feels 'blown away' by my sport, I'm certain it's nothing on how I'm feeling. Someone is vocalising acknowledgement of my skills and qualities. My recent rescuers' sharp cuts of disrespect are still open wounds, but there's been so many other incidents. Joe hasn't finished.

What's it like to be out there? What's it feels like the wind and rain and sun blasting you and the sensation of the impact when your feet pound the earth thousands of times repeatedly?

Joe, you surprise me. No one is usually interested, not even the guys I compete with again and again. For me, the desert is marvellous. It's demanding, sure. But the solitude is amazing. Even on that last disastrous run, when I ended up face down in the dirt and unable to move, etched into my memory was the view of the sun rising across the desert. The light is so different. On that day, I could only see out of one eye, but I could watch the dawn as the first streams of clear light of the rising sun kissed the red earth in front of me. I had no choice because of my position but to watch the subtle changes in its hue and the withdrawing of the shadows as the night disappeared into the west. Had they not rescued me, had I lain there for an entire day, those same sun rays might have been deadly. It would have been like sleeping in a baker's oven. Oh, dear. Now, when I think about that, there was also the risk of hypothermia, because desert nights are freezing. Now look what you have done, Joe. You are scaring the pants off me. I might never run again.

My head drops at my intended pretence of a joke, but I recognise down deep that this is a fear I have held in denial since my fall, the fear I might never return to the desert.

Joe gives my shoulders a squeeze.

I have an idea. Might be dangerous. You know me. I don't have a brain. But do you drive, Billy?

His question takes me by surprise, and yet automatically I nod.

Are your deserts far away, measured by driving there, not running?

Nooo. I guess there are places within a couple of hours driving distance that are desert-like. What are you asking, Joe?

Well, I can't drive. So, if I hire a car, will you drive me and you there for a picnic? I have a hankering to see the places where you would have trodden to see if they match the picture I have painted in my head. That's if the Boss will let us out. Oh, I am assuming you have a driver's licence, don't you?

Such a strange question I struggle to find a proper answer. I'm still taking in his statements about 'can't drive' that at another time would have surely prompted questions. I know so little about this man.

11

We decide on an early start. As far as Mariella and the staff know, this will be about six-thirty a.m. and, as, apparently, Joe needs regular meals, we have promised to stop for breakfast on the road. We have ticked off all the safety precautions, including agreeing to drop into the nearest police station' to inform the cops of our plans, so someone can come looking if we don't return within the agreed time frame. However, Joe is keen to see the dawn as I described it to be on the day of my accident, so the actual plan is to load the vehicle in the evening and illegally leave around four a.m. Joe's need for regular meals is covered by stocking up enough food for several days, which he plans to place in an Esky he has bought. This will serve also to keep his meds cool of which, again, apparently, he has many.'If we decide not to return.' Joe says as he winks at me.'In case.'

We have agreed to meet in the underground carpark at four. I have warned Joe he will need a warm jacket because while the day might be warm, the pre-dawn hours in the desert won't be.

My alarm wakes me at 3.30. Electricity is running through my body, as it remembers the many early mornings of my life, where I must subdue any excitement of participation to prepare. Concentration and thoroughness might make the difference between life or death, success, or failure. The time before the event always takes me into a zone of complete focus. It is potentially disastrous if in that last hour or two I should overlook something important. My mind and body have forgotten nothing after years of practice. Entrenched habits of readiness mean I'm efficient and methodical. Today is no exception, despite the presumed safety of this event within the environs of a motor vehicle fuelled by petrol and following well-known roads, rather than depending on legs fuelled by stamina and via unreliable pathways.

My backpack holds the essentials, collected as part of my habitual thoroughness. I stealthily move from my suite to the elevator, press the 'B' for

Basement button, and cringe at the loudness of the electronic ding of the doors closing. I imagine the dreams of occupants of nearby units being interrupted by this sound, and smile at the distorted possibilities of those dreams. The connection of dreams and the subconscious has always intrigued me, and in the strange stillness of the early morning darkness, such thoughts seem relevant when the quietness suggests dark bedrooms and sleeping humans.

In the carpark, only the security lights are still on, adding to the eeriness of the venture. But there, standing by an open boot, is Joe, his smile lighting the space. I can feel my own smile stretching. Joe salutes a welcome and whispers.

I feel like I am fifteen again and sneaking out to some illicit gig. It's invigorating, isn't it?

I can only manage a soft, almost teenager-like giggle, an unfamiliar sound. Joe takes my backpack and deposits it in the boot, which he tries to close quietly but fails. The basement carpark amplifies the noise, rolling it around the dark corners like thunder, causing Joe to chuckle, as if he's also endorsing his persona of a pre-teen who knows he has broken the house rules. He scurries to the driver's door and holds it open for me, taking care to wait until I'm settled before closing the door. I watch as he takes his big bouncy steps around to the passenger's side, opens the door and throws his tall body into the passenger's seat. He fiddles with the seat belt. There's something about the way he is moving and the tautness of his facial muscles that hints he's trying too hard. Is he nervous about my driving skills?

I have excellent driving skills, Joe, if you are worrying.

Nah. Just me. Me and cars aren't a fit. Ignore me. I'll settle.

I'm not reassured but decide now is not the time or place to grill him. I start the vehicle. The hire car looks new. The quietness of the engine supports this. I turn on the headlights and nod to Joe.

Ready? Here we go.

The car tyres squeal on the rubberised surface of the carpark, then become noiseless as the vehicle moves up the concrete ramp and onto the bitumen of the dark suburban street. There's a Christmas card feel about the houses we pass where soft light filters from a window here and there, break-ing through the early morning darkness. Controlled excitement charges through my bones, reminding me of other early morning starts. The only unusual part, a standout from the others in my memory, is my companion or, to be more specific, having a companion. My previous early morning ventures were solitary ones. I glance over to an abnormally silent Joe.

Joe, are you okay? You don't seem your usual self.

I'll be okay when we get out of the city.

Joe's voice has an unexpected timbre to it, like he's speaking through clenched teeth. I'm nervous now, unconvinced he'll settle. Is this too much for either or both of us, this minor event of a drive into the country? We have been incarcerated and not felt the freedom to do this thing before, although, as it appears, there was no reason we couldn't, neither of us being impaired to a degree that we might be at risk to ourselves or others. I imagine this is what being released from prison might feel like, suddenly granted the liberty to go wherever and whenever we choose and yet strangely cautious of finding oneself unrestrained. It's not that I see our life as imprisonment, but lack of choice through degrees of dependence is subtly limiting. Whatever the reason for Joe's reticence, it seems awkward to press him further. Then he surprises me.

Billy, can you talk while you drive?

I can. Why?

How about you imagining this is you, and today you are off on one of your runs. Paint the picture for me. Talk me through your preparations. I want to imagine I am you.

What a funny thing to want to be, Joe. Are you prepared for an aching body, sore or torn muscles, blistered feet, parched and sunburnt skin, and complete exhaustion at the end?

Are you trying to put me off?

Preparing you.

My mind is working overtime, needing to concentrate on negotiating the traffic as I work our way to the north-eastern highway but, somehow, I indulge Joe's whim.

Months before the planned event, I would eat a specific diet to build up my muscle mass, measuring both intake and output. Oh yeah, great stuff. I would engage daily in both gym workouts and long runs. Closer to the day, I would research the route, read all the information prepared by the event organisers and, beyond that, I would research further, so I might be as well-prepared as possible, so all that is left to cover are the specific circumstances and conditions of the actual day. Weather plays a big part in planning for an event, even down to the sustenance required for the heat or the cold. I have identified all the items as essential and collected them in the preceding weeks. I pack these early the night before when I also run through my checklist, revise the data and check for any likely changes in weather or other conditions. I go to bed as early as I can. Once I wake, I follow my routine of dressing for the event, and make one final check I have everything I need by trying to visualise the likely challenges along the way.

I am in awe, Billy. What's it like, pushing on through the pain for all those hours.

I don't think I have the words to explain, Joe. Hypnotic? Maybe. Or ritualistic? My brother was a sprinter. Sprinters gather all their energy and spend it in one burst. Long-distance runners must learn how to spread their energy and keep some in reserve so they can sprint the last phase if needed. It's all about pace, rhythm, and breathing. My mantra helps me concentrate and gets me through the inevitable moments when my body is shouting it can't take another step.

Oh, what's the mantra?

You are pulling my leg, aren't you?

No. I want to hear. You are just so amazing.

Well, it goes something like this.

I fight my resistance to sharing something that has always been private.

One foot down. Lift the other. One foot down. Lift the other. Forget the pain. Forget the distance. See the bush. Run to the bush. See the rise. Run to the rise.

I quickly glance over at Joe to check his facial expressions. I feel foolish. But he nods his nead in encouragement to continue.

One foot down, lift the other. One foot down, lift the other. Hear the rhythm. Like a heartbeat. Back straight. Chin high. Free the airways. Take a breath. See the pole. Run to the pole. Trick your body. It won't betray you. Keep the rhythm. Pace it out. And so on. I make it up as I go, to keep me focused.

I feel sheepish, exposed, regretting being lulled into sharing. But Joe's response is convincing. His eyes are wide. He repeats certain phrases a second or so after I say them, and when I finish, he looks across at me, like a school boy awaiting approval.

Wow.

I have never shared this with anyone, Joe. So, if I hear this from elsewhere, you are dead meat.

I'm honoured you have shared it with me. This is a demonstration of absolute motivation and focus. How did you learn this?

Without a moment's hesitation, my life story spills out of me, something I rarely tell anyone. I doubt even Brandon knows the full story. I tell Joe about my early life, in more depth than the summarised version I shared when he had tried to fix me after Brandon's last visit. I talk about Grae, about listening and learning from him long before I could participate, and as an adult, how I had to continue my fight, first to compete, because the male members of most clubs were constantly telling me and other women we don't belong in this sport.

When I competed, I then had to struggle to have my successes or achievements acknowledged. It's a male sport, Joe. Women are in it now, but the men who control it consider women as lacking in stamina and persistence to measure up. They overlook an important factor: women learn early the value of persistence. Life teaches us we need to fight for what we want. And we do.

Joe doesn't respond. I worry I've gone too far.

Have I frightened you off with my feminist/'MeToo' passion? Sorry. It's something I can't hold back. Having to fight my father's authority, and my husband's, and that of other males in my sport and in my workplace, I'm constantly angry and totally over the unfairness.

Joe turns toward me, his gaze lingering until I become self-conscious. My face feels as if it's flushed.

No. I quite understand. You might think I'm making this up to appease you but I'm not. I'm genuine when I say I understand the way you feel, especially if I look back into my past. I have not the slightest doubt I have been guilty of that sin on several fronts. I can see it's how we men take for granted our positions of power, we as the holders of all knowledge thus superior to women and children and, also, dare I say, anyone over a certain age. I really do understand as now I'm a victim of discrimination, too, for being a resident in aged care. Anyway, I apologise.

Why are you apologising?

Well, not to you per se, but to every woman. Life gave me a slap in the face and since then, I have had a lot of time to revisit mistakes I've made in my life. It's only right I apologise. Hey, look, Billy, a roadhouse and it's open. Time to give the driver a rest and get some brekkie.

Yeah, well, we promised, didn't we, but if we want to be out in the desert country before daybreak, we can't waste too much time. Maybe we make it a toilet break and get take away coffee and toasties.

Sounds good.

We leave the car and head in different directions to the toilets left and right of the main spotlighted building. I'm the first to enter the roadhouse proper, and after the darkness of the early morning outside, the over-bright fluorescent-lit space inside requires time to adjust. A young woman, un-missable because of her iridescent purple hair, stands behind the counter.

She makes it clear she appreciates no delays from her clientele. Her eyes drill into me and an expression of irritability floods across her face. There's only one other customer, an unshaven middle-aged man in 'flannies.' He's reading a newspaper at a pretend marble table. In front of him must be the well-advertised Big Breakfast and a cup, probably containing black coffee. A driver, I decide. He has been serviced, so the young woman's impatience is hard to understand unless she has a low attention span and needs to serve every new arrival immediately as a reprieve from boredom. In this minute, I'm the one and only. She seems anxious I have not already decided, glaring at me as I scan the list of what's on offer, unable to decide. Joe enters, his lop-sided smile as bright as the morning sun we are yet to see, and Purple-hair turns her full attention and charm to Joe, discarding me. Joe waves his hand in my direction, as if to say, 'this customer was before me', and the woman shrugs her shoulders and says, 'Grandma can't decide.'

Joe leans over to me and, with his mouth near my left ear, offers his own quiet observation.

Now there's a demonstration of ageism if ever I saw one. Should her employers be holding more appropriate in-service courses, do you think?

His breath on my ear frazzles me. I've lost some control over my response. The consequence is that I snort with laughter, unselfconscious of how it sounds. I'm reassured Joe and I are aligned. Joe is reacting to the discriminatory, probably thoughtless throw-away line. Some speakers possibly don't even intend harm, often only throwing out old well-used phrases for something to say, but I like to take opportunities to remind irresponsible speakers that I'm listening, and they need to keep on their toes. I do this often. Probably no one takes a lot of notice. Joe's inclination to do the same makes me feel as if I've known Joe a lifetime. Why did I ever feel uncomfortable in Joe's presence? Was it my own prejudices that kept me wary? Labelling him as a charmer didn't help.

With our coffees and toasties in hand, we head back to the car. Joe suggests maybe we should take a few minutes to eat and drink, if only for the driver's safety, and not wishing for a scalded lap. And that's what we do. We watch in silence the approaching full beam headlights of the monster road train rushing at us along the highway. As it draws closer, we absorb the roar of an engine in full throttle and then ride out the turbulent aftermath of its tailwinds that shake the hire car.

Whoa. Scary to meet in the night.

I nod. Realising Joe can't see me, because the roadhouse lights fall short of the interior of our vehicle, I add a comment.

Dangerous, sometimes.

Once the rubbish is deposited in the roadhouse's trash bins, and seat belts back on, I start the car, ease my foot off the brake, move it onto the accelerator, and we're on our way again. The thrum of the bitumen is mesmerising, but I know it's short-lived. Soon we'll turn onto a gravel road that follows the fence line of what daylight would reveal to be wheat fields. In this season, there would probably be only dry pale-yellow straw poking out of the soil. In another half hour, we'll turn onto a two-wheel track and head into an area that is as desert-like as we can manage in the limited parole time Fairview has granted us.

The sky is turning from black to deep blue by the time we reach the clearing. Joe takes from the boot two camping chairs.

Where's the best location, Billy? Which way is east? My sense of direction is crap.

I point to our right.

Over there, Joe, away from these bushes. Then you will see the sunbeams moving along the ground.

Joe ensures the chairs are steady on the somewhat uneven surface, and returns to the car, to once again bury his head in the boot. He emerges with two aluminium mugs.

Cuppa?

The air still holds its night chill. I pull my jacket a little tighter, take the mug from Joe and thank him, and then watch as he lowers himself carefully into the other chair. The silence between us is comforting. The only sound is the easterly breeze teasing through the wild grass and the occasional sound of hot drinks being sipped. It's after we have both set down the mugs under the camp chairs I detect the faintest glint of pale light on the horizon.

Joe, see there. It's beginning.

As I've seen many times before, I share with Joe the changing hue from cool white to warm yellow, and the gradual going down of the long shadows of the boulders, the stunted bushes and the spiked grass, until the sun is sufficiently high above the horizon to flood the whole scene with its brilliance. It's an hour before either speaks or moves, until Joe lifts his left arm up to read his watch. He sucks in a breath, jumps to his feet, and strides towards the car.

After a few minutes, he returns with a flask of water, two plastic glasses and a lidless square Tupperware container in which I can see several sandwiches neatly cut and stored away.

I need food to take my meds. I am late, and that's not good, but you might as well benefit from my needs. Here, hold the glasses, will you please, while I pour.

I examine Joe's face as he fills both glasses. He re-caps the flask and, with hands free, takes one glass from me and then holds out a container of sandwiches. I choose one and challenge him with a question as I look into his eyes.

What's wrong with you, Joe? Why the strict routine for medications?

I have DIC. Or in grown-up words: Disseminated Intravascular Coagulation. I need to take blood thinners to stop my blood forming clots and some other medications to guard against infections and so forth. No big-y.

I'm sorry, Joe, but I don't believe you that it's no big-y. I will understand if you don't want to tell me the full story, well, that's your right. Just tell me what I need to look out for, please. As you can see, and I can vouch, we are a long way from medical aid here.

Joe holds out the container again, but I shake my head, waiting to see if he will tell me more. He sits down, extracts a sandwich and balances it on his thigh just above his knee, then takes the lid he's been holding underneath the container and slips it back on. He carefully places the sandwich container near his right foot, and chomps on the sandwich. When it's all gone, he reaches into his shirt pocket and pulls out a tiny, sealed plastic bag.

Can you hold this, please?

He hands me his glass of water and tips the pills onto the palm of his hand, then throws them all as one into his mouth. I experience an involuntary gag, imaging the fight to swallow all those pills, and as Joe reaches to take back the glass of water, I'm acutely aware of the electrifying touch of his fingers on mine. He gulps a huge mouthful of the water, swallows hard, then finishes the remaining water.

Well, Miss Sticky-beak, I had a terrible accident a few years ago. No one else survived.

This is followed by a long and awkward silence, which Joe breaks by sucking in air. I wonder if that's all I'll hear, but soon after, as if he's garnered courage, Joe drops his head and continues in a barely recognisable voice.

They didn't think I would live either.

Another pause.

Maybe I only survived because I needed to suffer for what I had caused.

Another silence.

Anyway, the damage to my insides was horrendous. I lived, but I pay a price, and there's no cure. I need to watch for the complications that come with it.

Like what, Joe? What are the complications?

Bleeding from anywhere. Bruising, which, after all said and done, is bleeding under the skin. Heart attack. Thrombosis. I am a joy to be with.

The others, the ones who didn't survive, were they people you knew?

Yes.

I'm so sorry, Joe. That's ... I don't know ... sad, I guess, or torturous. Yes, that word fits.

Joe turns his head away from me, as if he's gazing due north, but I can see the ripples of his jaw muscles and from the stillness of his chest it's easy to recognise he's holding his breath. I reach across to place my hand on his forearm, and he looks down at it, then puts his left hand over the top and lifts his eyes to meet my gaze. Joe's eyes are tiger green watery pools, but they somehow hold steady with mine for what seems a lifetime before he relaxes and returns his left arm to rest on the chair., and I take back mine.

How long have you been at Fairview, Joe?

About three years. I need constant surveillance. I had to put myself into somewhere like Fairview, and the truth is being in the Home probably stops me going mad. Keeps me busy and stops me from thinking too much about things I can do nothing about.

You do a superb job there, Mr Fix-it.

He turns and manages a smile and says 'Tah'.

12

I expect only silence for the rest of our excursion, believing Joe's pain will not permit him to talk, but once started, he doesn't stop. It's as if talking about other things is better than lingering on the cause of the accident. The words are coursing out of him, in the same voice he uses when he's reading the editorials to the dementia-sufferers, almost as if he has rehearsed and repeated this story, but I'm certain this is not so. I'm confident I'm a privileged listener.

I became friends with Una and Gwen soon after I took up this new residency. Was it fate, or did I recognise their intelligence? They're smart women, those two, aren't they?

I nod. I realise Joe doesn't want an answer. He only needed a place to start his story.

Una hides her smarts behind adopting what I call her 'fairy' persona. I like to tease her about the way she flits around the residents, checking they are doing okay, and she chitter-chatters in her Irish lilt, so she presents as a lovely and loving woman, all brightness and spark. But if things are sufficiently bad to have a need to see the real Una, man, what's there to say? The real Una only shows up for people who are knee deep in mud and sinking. Then the clinical, cut-to-the-chase logic comes to the fore. I've seen it a few times but, thank goodness, not too often. No one wants anyone to be hurting so much they need Una to rescue them, but when you see her with that serious expressionless mask, only her deep penetrating eyes and unsmiling mouth apparent, there's no doubt of the situation. No lyrical Irish blarney then. A succinct phrase, right on target. I'll be honest with you Billy, if I was at all open to love, then I might have fallen in love with Una. But nah, I have had my time with love, and I am done with that, so Una has become my advisor, counsellor, advocate, mate and on occasions my adversary. She keeps me on my intellectual toes.

I laugh and add my own observations.

Oh yes, I reckon my dad would have fallen in love with Una. She's the perfect woman. Feminine, articulate, but knows when to be quiet and just listen. The opposite to the daughter he had.

Oh, come on, Billy, your dad must have loved you for your own special qualities. Dads do, you know.

I don't acknowledge his viewpoint. I don't doubt this was true. My dad loved me because I was his, and for him possession brings love. He expected nothing from me except loyalty and respect. He didn't think I was lacking, no matter how much I convince myself he might have done; my only short-coming as far as my father was concerned was that I was a woman. How can Joe know what that feels like? Nice of him to say so, to try to make me feel better about my father, but his words do nothing. And now, Joe's off again.

And then there's Gwen. Gwen is observant, intuitive, clear-headed and logical. People are put off from seeking her opinion on any subject, because they can't see past her physicality. Being limited to a wheelchair and being unable to keep your head erect and control your limbs with any apparent finesse can be off-putting. But nothing escapes her.

Joe's head drops. He looks sad, but then picks up with his rhetoric.

I don't know where I would be without these two.

This statement makes me feel a little out of sorts, like I'm feeling a tiny niggle of jealousy. Stupid of me, with no legitimate claim of possession. Joe is unaware. At least I hope he's unaware. He doesn't pause his story, so I take that as a reassuring sign he's oblivious to my pettiness.

I took a little time to realise the gift I had received in their friendship. I'd hit rock bottom by the time I signed into Fairview. Knowing them as I do now, I can see how I might have appeared to them in those early days. Morose. Miserable. Lost. Unapproachable to boot. But they put up with me and pulled me out of my self-pity. As clear as a bell, I can remember the first time I met Gwen. After a few days' grace, I'd been ordered out of my room by the staff.

I laugh, for my own memory of a similar event is sharp.

You too? They are good at the 'get out of your room' edict.

My words are not needed. He's back into his Fairview story.

Well, there wasn't an actual order given, but in hindsight I can see the staff had worked hard to make it difficult for me to stay inside. Somehow, they kept me moving. Eventually, I found myself in a small courtyard, silent and empty. I immersed myself into its peacefulness and almost forgot what had brought me there. I wanted to stay there forever. I prayed no one found me. Moving meant thinking. I remember sitting there, mesmerised by the creeping shadow along the blank brick wall opposite. To show you how long I'd been there, when I first sat, shade covered one-third of the wall, and when I came to my senses, or life broke me out of my numbness, there was only a small triangle of sunlight left. I gave myself a fright. Oh, let's be honest, I was still damn sorry for myself, and I didn't care if I followed the routine or not, plus I had a strong conviction I should be dead, so I had no purpose for living. But clearly my will wanted me to live, no matter what my miserable self might have thought it wanted. I knew sitting there all day, not doing what I should, was not good for me. But I didn't care.

I didn't just snap out of it. Something had brought me back to the life, and I took a while to realise it was that weird sound the rubber tyres of Gwen's wheelchair make. I heard someone clearing their throat. And there she was, this wizened woman hunched over in her wheelchair, whose presence raised many questions for which I wanted answers, like, how did she get herself here, in the courtyard? Did she have the strength to move that chair? Was it also a habit of hers to watch the sun's journey across the wall? I might have asked her for the answers except I had a dummy spit and reminded myself that I was no longer willing to socialise nor interested in other's lives or issues. I remember how it seemed as if someone had switched off the light because the courtyard went from twilight to darkness in an instance. The last tiny triangle of sunlight had slipped away, and there was I and this woman in a wheelchair, staring into blackness. I couldn't say if she was still there, or I was alone again. I hadn't heard the wheelchair go, but my head was in such a confused state in those days, I just wasn't paying attention. I squinted to try and make out in the darkness if she was still there. The minute she saw me look, she smiled. I could see her teeth and later I wondered how I might have because her head never seemed to be high enough to give me the opportunity. It surprised me when I heard her perky voice. You don't expect it, do you? And there's ageism in full bloom. If not ageism, then some other form of discrimination. Maybe I only saw the hunched shoulders, or the wheelchair. Anyway, I didn't expect her to speak. She said, 'Hi there, new fella. I'm Gwen. Been here for a long while. How are you handling it all? It's overwhelming at first, isn't it?'

I was deep down in the well of self-pity and anger. I recall being filled with a strong desire to shout back at her something like 'what's it to you. Just fuck off, will you?', but I just couldn't. It was a dangerous place. Guess the brake goes on via a sympathy vote after seeing a person so crippled and stuck in a wheelchair; someone who at the time needed more sympathy than me was talking to me like she'd recognised I was the one needing help. For that restraint, for not blurting out that insult, I can only thank my parents for raising me to be polite. My parents, or maybe... let's not go into that.

Just someone else. Whoever it was, it was their voice I heard speaking quietly 'That's not like you, Joe. What's going on here? You need to pull yourself together.' So, I gave myself a talking to and turned and faced this woman called Gwen. I couldn't quite make eye contact. You know how it is. You need to bend down a bit. But I looked in her general direction and hoped I was displaying enough respect to quieten the voice in my head. I tried my darndest to be on my best behaviour and rather formally answered her. When I think about it, what a prat I was. Anyway, I said something like this. 'Thanks for asking, Gwen. I am Jerome Vella. People call me Joe. I don't mind either. And, yes, you are right. I require some transition.' She came straight back with, 'Well, Joe or Jerome, or Mr Vella or mate. If you need someone to show you around, I am your girl. Don't let my limited mobility fool you, Joe. Yes, I can't walk but you can push me and I am darn good at both talking and listening. You seem lost, and we can't have that. But then we need our own space, don't we? So, your call. See you around, Joe.'

You know, Billy, I struggled to reconcile the words, the voice and the body/wheelchair situation, but over time and after many, many subsequent conversations, I know the voice reflects the mind. Gwen's wits are sharp, and her mind is on the ball. It's only her body let her down.

I nod, again knowing the chances of Joe seeing my response is low. He's in his own world, remembering the past. Joe is on a roll and listening to him, being privileged with his honesty, is a gift. Joe has more to say.

I am ashamed to tell you, Billy, for a long while in my mind I used the word 'wasted' regarding the external appearance of the incompatibility of Gwen's mind and body. That usage was a big mistake on many levels. I have confessed to Gwen about my disgusting habit of labelling her, she laughed and swept that one good arm of hers from as high and as low as it would reach, emphasising her point. 'Well, Joe,' she said. 'The disguise I use is rather handy. People take me for a fool and, boy, do I hear some interesting gossip.'

I wait for Joe to continue. He's paused but I'm sure there's more to come. Until now, I've had my eyes on the landscape, but now I badly want to see why he has paused, and when I turn towards him, I see he's looking toward me, as if waiting for me to react. His green and brown eyes are clouded.

Sorry. I rarely ramble on like this. Maybe it's the DIC, clotting my social reserves.

His effort to smile slashes through me. Again, I need answers to more questions about DIC, but he's off again, on his oration, slower, more cautious this time.

Truth is, when I say 'wasted', it's how I feel about myself. I wasted people's lives. I wasted my life. I was driving when we had the accident. I wasted the life of my wife Mina and my son's and his wife's lives, and their unborn baby. I killed them. The cops might call it an accident, but it wasn't. I had been heading for a disaster and this was it. I wasn't high on alcohol or drugs, but on ego. Jerome Vella, the big businessperson riding high, and there beside him, his accoutrements, a gorgeous wife and a brilliant son with a beautiful wife and a grandchild on the way. I was hardly ever at home. Business first, floating around at events, soaking in the glory of my 'great' achievements, when all the time my most valuable gifts were waiting at home. That night, I was boasting and bloated, so full of myself my mind was not on my driving. Now they are dead, and I am dying. Not today, but eventually, because this ... this patch up, all the missing bits and pieces in here, will only linger my death. And this is how it ought to be. That gives me time to see the error of my ways. To repent the damage my self-centredness has caused. Too late for my family. That's why the word 'wasted' pops so readily into my head. 'Wasted' is my word. I wasted my gifts. I wasted the lives of my family. I guess you might be wondering about who it was I was referring to when I mentioned earlier about keeping me in line and making me a better person. Aside from my parents, that's my beautiful wife Mina. Mina was perfect. She accepted my faults and loved me anyway. And what do I do? I end her life.

I'm waterlogged from the inside, drenched with sorrow and empathy. My heart is commenting and wants me to offer comfort, but I can say nothing. I can't interrupt Joe's remorse. What can I say? Part of me would say to him, there's no doubt she would love you, Joe. How could she not? Another part is filled with sorrow and pain for Joe and his burden. For a while Joe retreats, and I'm convinced that's the end of his story, but it's not.

I told Gwen all this and you know what she told me? She said, 'Joe, my lad. You may be right about time to repent and time to forgive yourself. But some things are out of our hands. You need to dig into yourself to understand or else you will drive yourself bananas. Are you a religious man? Some might say that's the way to go. I have seen it work. Me? Well, I haven't decided yet. The facts are still being examined. To each his own. But I know talking helps. And as I keep telling you, I am a superb listener. That's what we lawyers do best. Listen. Next best thing we do is present an argument for the best-case scenario. I'd be happy to help you find that, if that's what you need. This is too heavy, my friend. We should lighten up here, so come on, let's get a latte.'

I laugh.

Good old Fairview lattes.

Joe laughs too, as if the offer of a latte is happening and Gwen's forthrightness is pushing through the morning air on this isolated stretch of desert.

And Billy my girl, that brings me back to Una, who offered me serious advice. 'Time. These matters need time. You can't hurry them, Joe. You might never feel the way you did before. Things happen that change us. But time helps us to find a way through the mist. You'll be right, boy-oh.' Her last point was a bit of the impish Una one, now I think about it, and she said 'A pity your name's not Danny. Then I could sing "Oh Danny Boy" to you, and that'd fix you, right as rain.' She kissed me on the forehead, as though she was my mother instead of a woman about my age. Did you know it was only a decade ago when she stopped being a highflying surgical research doctor? How quickly life can change. We all know we will die, but we don't know how we will get there. I'll bet the Centurions in Fairview didn't think they'd still go this long. You can plan, like big-flyer Jerome Vella did, and end up as the destructive, surviving-by-the seat-of-his-pant Joe, in the time required to smash your car and kill your passengers.

Again, there's nothing I can say, no assurance, no advice. I'm drained of an adequate response, and yet I'm overflowing with emotions. Side by side we stare ahead into the vast emptiness, together as we bake under a blazing mid-morning sun. Strangers and yet not, both skirting around an unexpected friendship, one I cannot deny is intensifying by the minute. Neither of us are sufficiently brave to drag our eyes from the scenery ahead to look to the other, for that might be admitting the evidence of our instinctual pull to each other, as well as our unwillingness to resist.

Hey. Sorry, Billy. Too much. Wipe it from your mind. Let's get back to the present. What else can we do out here?

I won't permit myself to let him dismiss what is more like a verbal flagellation than narration.

Joe, thanks for allowing me the privilege of hearing your story. I am overwhelmed with your honesty. I truly am. And my words, now, are so understating how I feel. You'll never know how you moved me, because I can't put it into words like you have.

He gives me a small smile and pats my arm.

I've put you through torture by burdening you. I thank you for listening. You can never undervalue the act of conversing, especially when blessed with your choice of companion.

He gives me a weak smile.

Come on. Too serious. Let's shake it off and decide. What are we doing?

Let's drive the long way home. Do we need more food and pills before we head off? How's the schedule?

13

The week has flown by and it's the day of my second exercise class. When I arrive in the Big Room lugging a cardboard container on my hip, the size of the waiting crowd surprises me. I help the staff members to check that the brakes on wheelchairs are on, that chairs for the rest of the group are well-placed, and that there's water at hand for hydrating. A sea of smiling, expectant faces are in front of me. The success of the first lesson have banished the fear of failure, inability or pain. I hope these individuals feel the same after actual exercises come into play. So far, all they have done has been warm-ups.

I begin the class by reminding everyone of my Tai Chi Sifu's overview through a summarised version and then move into the warm-ups. My goal is to keep the group moving, so as the warm-ups end, I reach into the cardboard container and pull out a handful of resistance bands, which I pass to the staff members to distribute.

Please give these out to everyone. I hope I have enough.

More and more come out of the carton and are handed around, continuing until everyone has a resistance band in hand. There's some frivolity happening around suggested alternative usages, but this is good. It means the introduction of equipment and the assumptions of a change of routine are not being perceived as a threat.

Right, everyone. Are you ready?

One or two look around at others and lift their shoulders, but they are smiling. Others are testing the bands, stretching and testing the feel of them.

First, we will do some upper back stretches. Use your hands to hold each end of the band, then raise the band up and over your head so the band sits across both shoulders on the upper back.

I show the exercise and wait as the group experiment with the actions required.

Contract your core muscles, those of your abdomen, and stretch out as far as you can until your arms are almost straight.

Some struggle. Some find it difficult to position the bands, but the staff or the person next to them help.

Breathe in and hold, exhale and relax your arms. We will do this today for five times. One. Tighten. Stretch. Breathe in and hold. Exhale. Relax.

The group work through the five repeats, and then I move to the next.

Bring your bands to your laps and this time clasp one end of your band on your left thigh and take the other end in your right hand, then extend the right arm up and out until you feel a resistance. Relax your right arm and then extend again five times: one, two, three, four, and five. Now change to your left hands and right thigh and repeat the same: one, two, three, four, and five.

Some members of the group seem uncertain about how they went. This might be foreign for many.

You all did great. So, let's move on to the next. Place your band under one foot if you are able. Some of you will need help. Hold the handles then bring your arms up into a bicep curl, you know, the crunch up of arms you see those muscley men on TV do. If you can't manage the band under your foot, then let's see some curl ups of biceps holding tight the muscles, then a release down without the resistance of the band.

Smirks and giggles relieve the worry of lack of ability.

Okay, five times, please.

I continue through the set of exercises, five each time, and then when the bands need to be placed under feet, the staff help. There's grunts and giggles over awkwardness. When everyone had completed their extension, the bands collected, I move to the front of the group once more.

Now we will do some Tai Chi exercise. First, for your lungs. Make two gentle fists like this.

I demonstrate.

Hold your arms straight out in front, then move your arms out on each side and breathe in, expanding your lungs and hold. Spread your fingers, breathe out through your mouth and bring arms in until hands meet. Again, we will repeat this five times, so now gentle fists, stretch out arms to the side, breathe in, spread fingers breathe out through mouth, and bring arms in until hands meet, then gentle fist and that's one, two, three, four and five.

Next it is a spinal twist. Pull your core in and your hold arms out in front. Let your right hand grasp your left elbow and your left hand grasp your right elbow, then swing as far as you can to the right, and swing through as far as you can to the left. Again, one - two - three - four - five.

Next week, I will add a few more Tai Chi exercises but today let us finish with some breathing. Sit quietly, belly soft, close your eyes and bring your vision to your diaphragm. If you are like me and aren't too sure where that is, it's this place between abdomen and chest. Imagine that space in your mind. Place your hands on either side of your ribs and breathe in through the nose, feel the ribs expand, hold your breath for a count of three, then breathe out through your mouth, like blowing out a candle. You can now feel your ribs relax, and your belly goes soft as these actions follow the rhythm of the breath. Keep your breathing gentle. Do not over-breathe. Follow your natural capacity for breathing. Do not strain. Let us continue to do this, focussing only on our breathing.

After some minutes, I call an end.

I hope you'll be back. We might extend our Tai Chi and will attempt some meditation. Thanks, everyone.

I'm relieved the atmosphere remained positive, despite a few struggling, which is normal, and it was reassuring that they didn't give up, and were helped and supported by the staff. It's difficult to explain how I feel. This knowledge I have held and used on my own, and now I'm sharing and receiving a positive reaction from others. It's uplifting.

14

Since our visit to the desert, Joe and I are never far apart, somehow one of us radiates towards the location of the other. Residents' participation in volunteered activities has grown. Gwen's love of words and her awareness of her potential loss of voice in her future has chosen an easy one. She's taken up the role of reading classic novels to a small group of listeners. I suspect that more pleasure comes to the reader than the listeners, some of whom may only find in the readings a sense of belonging and being comforted by the sound of someone's voice than in an ability to comprehend and gain understanding from such heavy tomes. Does it matter? Any benefit gained is valuable. Una has taken on recording in writing remembered and long-loved recipes. She has ambitions of persuading the chef to give some a try out, though Cook, as we call him, keeps a tight ship regarding the quality and balance of the food available to his clientele. Una suspects some family recipes may not fit modern assessments, such as the one she recorded last week with one ingredient being dripping 'that makes it so tasteful', so obviously a dish that circulated around the era of the Great Depression, or so Una jokes to Gwen and me, when making her decision whether to erase recipes that might fail close inspection.

Aware as I am that Joe doesn't wish to have a fuss made over his health issues, I can only observe from afar his comings and goings via the patient transfer vehicle. I worry over the consequences to Joe of what my newly educated self observes as his apparent if somewhat violent upward and downward swings. I'm unbalanced by the change in my own perspective. When I was unaware, the only curiosity I could raise was a question about why Joe needed patient transfer and what had caused him to double over as if someone has injured his rib cage during whatever treatment he had received. Informed as I now am, after searching online for DIC, every one of Joe's actions, every response, means something different.

I recall in my early days of living in Fairview how I'd appraised Joe, as he read the newspaper to the male dementia sufferers, as possibly a member of staff. Later, I'd wondered why a man, with no visible limitations, lived in this place. Now I know he's here to die and these blood transfusions must occur to extend his life. Only through our excursion am I aware of quantity of pills he consumes and his strict routine for food, water, and medications. The most damning piece of information that emerges from my research is that less than half of those with DIC survive, and those that do may live with organ dysfunction and threat of blood clotting that can lead to amputation or heart attack. I struggle to disguise my fear for his health, and despite a thorough self-lecture, I continuously hold my breath to prepare for the inevitable moment.

These days I spend long hours of sleeplessness trying to untangle my emotions around Joe. There's my empathy for him, my concern for him, my fear of losing him, but also the one I most struggle with, an awareness of my need for him. I see Joe and me like pieces of a jigsaw that fit neatly into and against one another. This goes beyond chemistry and sexual attraction. But there's that too. He comes into a room and a change comes over my body and if he comes near to me, without touching him or him touching me, I feel a magnetic pull to be closer, and sometimes I swear invisible threads run from me to him and from him to me, as though we are one and the same person in two bodies. If I see him talking to others and he glances in my direction, I feel a flush run through me, like a teenager, uncontrollable even if I'm fully aware that glance and my response leaves me exposed to Joe and to everyone within sight. When he returns via the patient transfer vehicle, I fight my desire to hurry over and hug him, and follow his bent, wretched body into his suite to provide comfort for him. That's the one threshold yet to be crossed.

Those sleepless hours convince me I may have a gift I could offer him, if only I can be sufficiently emotionally strong to survive my generosity. The brave exterior he uses to mask his frailty makes me wonder what it might be for him in those moment, when he can no longer deny his fate. I imagine his tortured dreams filled with the demons of approaching death, emotions he may be reluctant to expose to others. Does he wonder how his death will arrive? Does he contemplate if it will come as a heart attack, or clotting, or an embolism? The gift I can offer him is to help him carry the burden of that certainty, not to reassure or deny but to accept his reality, to be a listener and not a fixer. Primarily, my commitment to this gift would need me to be strong enough to control my own fears, so he doesn't feel the need to protect me but rather be able to express his own. Can I? And will an opportunity to volunteer this treacherous service arrive in time?

Today I am seeing Joe's struggle to alight from the patient transfer vehicle. The driver is helping him. Joe tries to straighten his body but needs to place his hand on the driver's shoulder for support. I notice him looking around, as if he's checking to see who is nearby. The lobby is full. The driver's head is bent to one side, nodding, as if he's pointing, and his hand is under Joe's elbow. I imagine a conversation wherein the driver is suggesting, maybe a wheelchair, which Joe is rejecting. With effort that is writ in every muscle and every limb, Joe's body at last is perpendicular, and he turns to the door. The driver looks unhappy. Instead of closing the rear door and moving around, he stands and watches as Joe heads toward the automatic doors. If it wasn't for the grimace Joe is vainly trying to mask and the scrunching to one side of his torso, it might fool someone into thinking this was just Joe, as always, coming back from shopping or doing personal business. The driver isn't moving. He remains standing and, like me, is watching Joe. There's a frown wrinkling the driver's forehead. We are stalled witnesses, longing to go to Joe's aid but respecting his desire to show independence. I watch until I can bear it no longer, until the pain inside me on Joe's behalf overwhelms me. I work hard to adopt a casual demeanour as I scurry to intercept Joe's entry, as if by accident.

Hi there, Mr Fix-It. Let me do some fixing for you today.

My forced smile should display brightness. It probably doesn't fool Joe or anyone else. I tuck my arm around Joe's. Our eyes meet in silent agreement.

By granting me permission to support some of his weight, I'm left with no doubt about his condition. Together we slowly stroll through the Big Room and down the corridor into Joe's suite. He hands me his keys, and I open the door. He stumbles quickly past me to the sofa and collapses.

What can I do for you, Joe? Need a cuppa? Or water? Need to get those clothes off and into something more comfortable? Please let me help you.

Water would be great, thanks Billy.

I hand him a glass of water, which he gulps down and hands back empty. He bends to remove his shoes. I shake my head and lift his feet onto the sofa. I locate cushions and stuff them behind his head, before unlacing his shoes and dropping them to the floor. I take the throw off his bed and cover him.

Sleep will do you good, Joe. I will check on you later.

Don't go Billy. Please. Even if I go to sleep. Can you do that for me?

I nod, not trusting myself to speak. My heart is shattering, torn into many pieces. He has asked me to stay. That's the greatest gift he can give me. But the reason he needs me to do so is shredding me.

I drag an armchair over nearer the sofa but before I sit, I fill the electric kettle and turn it on.

I will have a cuppa, Joe. Are you sure you wouldn't like one?

He shakes his head. He's already drifting into sleep.

Tea is made, and with cup in hand, I make myself comfortable in the armchair. Sipping the hot brew is meditative, the slow sip, sip, sipping, the mellow warmth, and my brain slowly calms itself. I'm on automatic. Sipping and allowing myself the luxury of taking in everything there is to see about Joe. His spiked silver hair suggesting a tendency for cheekiness, to be a rogue. His long lashes are usually invisible because I can never see past his amazing green and gold eyes. There's a small scar on his chin, and I picture a daredevil boy jumping over obstacles on his push-bike and coming to a nasty end. But the truth might probably be this is a scar from the car accident he told me about, the consequence of which is losing his family and causing an injury that resulted in DIC. Or he might have cut himself shaving with a blade. So much about him is unknown. My fingers long to trace his forehead, cheeks and chin, but I'm afraid of disturbing him. Instead, my gaze turns to his hands.

He has his hands folded across his chest. His fingers are long and slender, not lumberjack's or farmer's fingers. He described himself as 'high on ego' so that implies he had succeeded at something. I know so little about him. Normally I would question everything about anyone I meet for their back story. I can't explain why Joe's presence has silenced this side of me. It's not a matter of rationalising that at some point I'll learn about Joe's former life, or that I'll be told when Joe's ready to share, or the withholding of this personal information declares our relationship as casual, but strangely it's through being able to be in Joe's presence that quenches my thirst. I'm in the present, and happy that the gift of Joe's friendship, despite its uncertain level or depth, has come my way.

I can't measure how much later it is when there's a light tap on Joe's door. Maude is there with a trolley and two trays.

I noticed him come back and you helping him. Thought you might like some dinner.

I lean over and hug Maude, wishing I could hang there and cry my heart out but instead I whisper in her ear.

Oh, Maude, you are a genuinely caring person. Thank you.

Took it hard this time, didn't the poor love.

Sure did, Maude. Tries to be strong, as always, but failed this time.

He's had other times like this, but they are becoming too frequent.

I can't hold down a wall of water swelling up inside me, so I cover the threatening flood by bending over and lifting the trays off the trolley and placing them inside. By the time I'd finished that chore, my eyes are back under control.

Thanks again, Maudie sweetheart.

As I carefully latch the door, I hear Joe move.

Want a hand up, old soldier?

I reach out and he takes hold but doesn't use my hand to pull himself up. There's a weak smile playing around his mouth, wriggling its way around the bottom of his face, as if he knows something I don't. All the while, the fingers of his other hand choose the particularly disorientating option to trace around my cheeks and down my neck. What good is giving him a hand right now? He has weakened me by this simple action. His grip abruptly tightens, and I feel his full weight as he comes to a sitting position. His feet drop to the floor.

That dinner smells good. Do you mind if I have a quick shower first? I feel like shit.

Are you okay on your own?

Are you offering to join me? Now that's enough to revive a guy.

There's Joe, trying to be Joe, his words fading into a half-laugh and a wicked smile that isn't fully convincing. He's probably joking, but I would need only one small clue that he's not and I wouldn't be able to stop myself from taking up his invitation. He doesn't wait for an answer, as he drops his feet off the sofa and onto the floor and manages, with a few grunts and grimaces, to stand upright. After a second or two, he takes his first steps towards the door of his bedroom.

Chill the wine while I am gone. Oh, wait. No. No wine allowed.

He doesn't fully close the door. Coming out of the bathroom are the disconcerting sounds of undressing, the click of the glass shower door being closed followed by the spash of the shower, then a deep Joe sigh, the clunk of the tap being tightened, more grunting and groaning, all indicators he's moving, followed by the intimate soft scrapings of drawers being opened and closed. A few minutes of muffled silence then Joe re-appears in navy track suit. This goes against Joe's tendency towards casual but more formal style, slacks and long-sleeved shirts with arms rolled up to his elbows.

Excuse the gear. More comfortable on the gut.

I surprise myself by laughing.

Boy, Joe, all you can worry about is your casual form of dressing. Makes sense to me. Looks good,.

I give him a thumbs up, and there's a tiny smile on his face when he says, 'Come on, let's eat.'

Joe crosses to the kitchenette and opens a cupboard to take down two glasses, which he fills with water. He places them on the dining table and struggles over to pick up the trays of food.

His activities shock me out of my stall mode.

Hey Joe, how about you sit down there, and I will set this up.

I transfer the meals from the tray to the table, set up the cutlery and put to one side the desserts and fruit.

Do you need meds with this meal?

Yeah, thanks for reminding me. In the plastic bag in the fridge door tray.

There is a line of zip-lock bags. I had evidenced the quantity of tablets he takes when we were on our driving trip, but it's sobering to see the number of little bags lined up on full display.

It's my weekend job. Sorting them into little piles. In case. I might lose my marbles and get confused.

I can't join in on Joe's humour. Invading his privacy has a price. I have no option than to face the reality of his existence.

We eat our meals sharing conversations about the daily trivia of our surroundings such as Una's latest addition of a weird recipe, and her dilemma about inclusion or otherwise in the booklet she is compiling.

I clear up from the meal and turn to Joe.

Time for me to go.

Must you, Billy? If you would care to, I'd like you to stay. I need company.

Well, how about we make you more comfortable than sitting on this dining chair?

Okay, but only if you join me on the sofa, Billy.

Joe takes a seat and pats the space next to him. I am hypnotised by his hand patting the cushions, the gesture and its implications fill me with a mix of emotions. This is a place I've never been before, being invited in a gentle and appealing manner to sit next to a man I feel I know but who, when weighing up everything, is still a stranger. But the pull of my connection to Joe makes that place now the most desirable and appealing spot in the entire world. Once there, side by side, it seems we have nothing to say to each other. More out of instinct than careful planning, I allow myself the liberty of speaking on a taboo subject – Joe.

Joe too is breaking the silence. His first word blends with my word, 'Joe.'

Can ...

I turn to look at Joe.

You go first.

Joe shakes his head and ushers his hand towards me.

You, first.

Joe, I don't quite know how to put this. There's no simple way. I researched your illness. I'm aware the outcomes might not be so good, hell, most definitely not good at all.

That prognosis almost chokes me. My words lose their clarity. I need to say them.

Isn't it lonely keeping all this to yourself? Could you trust me and let me listen to what's going through your head as you deal with this, like, be your sounding board? If you'd let me, I could be the person to whom you can let fly with your anger or whatever you need to do. I can't promise I will always remain brave, but I will try. I'd like to be that kind of friend for you, if you will honour me with that level of trust.

I can't look at him as I say these words. I'm afraid to see his disapproval or rejection because of my invasion of his privacy, so I close my eyes. They fly open with the sensation of a touch on the opposite side of my face to where he's sitting. He's bent in front of me, and his index finger is tracing my cheek. His face is near mine. I can feel his breath.

Billy, oh Billy. You are my damnation.

What?

I decided when I lost my wife that I didn't deserve love. I would not put myself in a position to be close to anyone, let alone love anyone. I don't deserve that gift.

Joe swallows once, twice.

Billy, you have broken my resolve. I can't go a day without seeing you. Until I met you, I had coped with being a solitary being, and now all I can think about is telling you about something I have seen, or discussing a subject with you, any excuse to be sharing time with you. It isn't fair to you. I'm doomed to a short life. But I'm also addicted to you, and that's the stronger demand. Equally, though, with time so precious, I'm selfish enough to want to devour you, to get as much of you as you'll give me.

When it comes, his kiss blows away my recall of any other kisses I've ever experienced. It's flesh tenderly pressing flesh; a burst of oxytocin; senses igniting, body tingling, and a demand for more I can't believe I'm feeling. Instinctively, I respond. My kiss extends to the sensory area, just beyond the lips and onto the part of Joe's face where his dimples live. He replies with more pressure, and the cycle begins again. I marvel at the sensation. Soft, erotic and responsive. Not a smash and grab. Not a one-sided raid.

I've waited all these years to feel the emotions that are flooding through me. This is my Nicholas Sparks moment.

15

The ladies gather, ready for their shopping-day outing. Like runners lining up for a slow start. And yet there's someone missing.

Where's Una?

Three of the ladies are having a lovely chat on the side, giggling and patting another's shoulder or arm in glee, heads thrown back, eyes alight with humour. Something is amusing them, but they aren't sharing.

I call to them.

Have you old hens seen Una yet?

Maude is passing by. She would normally call out and wish them fun during their shopping, challenging the group with her standard gee-up, like, 'Do nothing I wouldn't do out there, ladies.' Or 'Have one on me. Make mine double strength.' Today there's no sparkle to her demeanour., no jokes or toss-away comments She notices only the floor in front of her. Her shoulders are rounded, her head bent. Must be a bad day for Maude. Very unusual. I call to Maude before she has left the lobby.

Hey Maude, have you seen Una on your rounds?

Maude's sharp lift of her head should have warned me. Maude's brow wrinkles and she shakes her head. She's almost out of the lobby when she turns back.

Go without Una today. Her family is visiting.

Rarely if never has Una had family come to visit. It's off-putting to hear that the mostly absent family is here. These kinds of visits usually indicate something abnormal is happening. Before I can question her, Maude has disappeared around the corner.

I sense the serious nature of Maude's suggestion and search the faces of the other soon-to-be shoppers for their reactions. Rhonda Barnes turns to go, as if impatient to be out there, in the mall.

Let's do as Maude suggests, just get on our way. We can bring back a cupcake for Una when we check in on her later.

The others take reluctant steps to follow Rhonda towards the Home's bus, waiting for them on the driveway.

I'm not going shopping today, I haven't been going for some time, reluctant to be too far from Joe. I had chores awaiting my attention, so it's not the delay to departure that keeps me in the lobby, yet my feet are reluctant to move. Una is in some trouble. We all know what it means to have everyone in the family visit. There's nothing I can do, not at this moment. I wave goodbye to the shoppers and go in search of Joe. He's likely to know what might be happening if it involves Una. What is confusing me is that Una is a spritely woman, a fairy, as Joe calls her. She doesn't talk about any serious health issues except her arthritis that eventually ended her career. More recently the disease has caused her pain and slowed her down, not that most of us would notice. She still buzzes around. The seriousness of a family gathering does not fit with the Una we all know. I need to talk to Joe, who would right now be reading to his dementia crew.

As I turn the corner, there he is. Those first few months when he was only a stranger reading to other strangers, he had caught my attention by the way he'd move continuously around the men in front of him to show them picture appearing in the newspaper, continually walking backward and forward while reading, always on the move. Lately, Joe reads while seated.

Excuse me Joe, have you heard Una may be in trouble? Maude says they have called in her family.

Joe doesn't answer. His only response is to suck in his lips and frown, then he rubs his spiked hair, so that stands even taller. I can see I've rattled him with my query.

You have heard nothing, Joe?

No. But I agree. This is worrying. Her family isn't close.

Joe turns to his listeners, who as always are taking in every word Joe speaks. He pats the air, settling them down.

Sorry fellas, news reading will be brief today. No. Let me say it as it is. It's over for the day. I have some important stuff to do.

Some men rise and scuffle away, but others look confused, like puppies waiting for their supper. Joe moves closer to each man and takes the time to explain to each man in simple terms there's no more reading today, sorry, guys. He doesn't wait to see if the remaining ones stay or go but turns and takes my hand.

Privacy regulations. We won't be able to find out anything because we aren't family. I can't see how this can be anything good.

We hover in the lobby, the space where all action in Fairview eventually passes through. Others have picked up the vibe of concern for Una and are hanging around with troubled expressions clouding their faces. It's almost time for dinner when an ambulance arrives. At first, no one moves into the dining room, but chaos will rule if they delay meals, so staff are cajoling and persuading, some even applying firm pressure on shoulders, to herd the majority to where they should be. Joe and I remain. We want to be in the lobby when the ambulance people come back through. The staff form a guard of honour. Joe looks over at Maude for confirmation. We've still had no official word. Maude nods, her face awash with grief. Any lingering hopes Joe and I might have held have disintegrated by Maude's acknowledgement. Joe and I join in the staff's guard, both weeping as if we've never cried before, tears running freely down our cheeks, our hands interlocked, both loudly suck in each wet breath. I hear Joe whisper. His words going straight to my heart.

Bye my friend, bye my little Irish fairy.

There has been no information or explanation. Una is a friend. And we are not family. It feels like a betrayal, but no one can report a departure except to so-called family. No one knew she had any family. Had they visited, we'd have known, so we are left feeling these unknown individuals were family in name only.

Over time, the events of that fatal day slowly emerge from various sources. In simple form, Una had a fall, after which she had difficulty in remaining conscious. It was clear she was in pain, so a doctor was called. Una was beyond saving. Later tests proved she'd had a massive heart attack. The family, called because of the seriousness of Una's situation, were two third- or fourth-cousins, people whose names Una had recorded as the ones to contact only because naming someone was a requirement. Una had never married. As an independent single, she must have seen no need to depend on almost strangers, maybe a reason she had invested so much into those she called 'family', her fellow residents at Fairview. Joe was, she often joked, the son she never had, and that almost-son is shattered in his grief.

The reality of knowing so little about someone who was so loved is an absolute crime. This omission brings me to make a declaration on this subject to Joe.

We should begin a folio of remarkable things we would like to share with our fellow residents. I will buy a good quality leather-covered journal that will last through time, and make the first entry about Una, in which I will write: 'Irish, tiny, perceptive, with an intelligent mind. She is everyone's perfect friend. Una lived a successful and independent life as a surgical specialist researcher. Limits to her agility care of arthritis and a minor eye condition brought her to Fairview where she became a specialist in making the lives of individual residents happier by way of her 'live life to the fullest' attitude. I may even write in it that Una was the protector of Jerome Vella, and wise advisor of Wilhemena Corass. What shall I write about you, Joe?

That he met his match late in life. And don't forget: 'Wilhemena Rose Corass, Daughter, Wife, Mother, Athlete, Management Analyst and very much loved and adored; Gwendolyn O'Shaunessy, Lawyer, Intellect, Mother, and a wheelchair bound pro-activist.'

16

The shock of losing Una is being registered. For some, it is a reminder of our own individual vulnerabilities. For others, the gap left after Una's departure is being rapidly filled by other distractions, as if that bright lady had never lived in Fairview or shared the lounges. Una's passing has been seen by Tim as a sign to make the most of each day. At morning tea, Tim makes an announcement.

Hey, everyone. Bev and I have some news. We are marrying. And you are all invited.

The first surprise is that it is Tim who goes against his nature to act as the broadcaster. Bev would have been the one expected to do that job. The next is the unexpectedness of the planned event. A wedding? Here? In Fairview?

Where everyone believes their life is over? And soon, says the happy couple. This proclamation turns minds away from a loss, toward teasing their way through the many possibilities of two residents uniting. Discussions rage from the public perspective of this event, the ceremony, to the private topics such as how did Bev negotiate with her daughter? The dispute between Bev and Kristy has been well-reported. Bev's a chatterbox and her many conversations with individuals or small groups adequately answer the Kristy conundrum. The evidence that mother and daughter have come to a reconciliation is that Kristy is helping with the preparations. The ceremony will be in the garden with a small group of their closest friends as witnesses. After this, there will be an extra special afternoon tea.

Secret plans are underway among those in the craft group to create decorations such as buntings and streamers and signs for various doors. The singing group are practicing an a cappella rendition of 'Here Comes the Bride', with some difficulty because of the limited timeframe.

Another reconciliation is under consideration. I have returned to my previous acknowledgement I can easily challenge Brandon's insistence that I should make Fairview my home for the long-term. The question is, why have I taken so long to act? Am I trying to win an intellectual or power battle with my son over this matter, or am I genuinely conflicted about what decision gives me the best future? I have overcome my prejudices about living in a place like this, conceding I could only see this place through the prism of my own ageism. How ridiculous that a woman who herself falls into the category of 'aged' could not deal with a concentration of aged individuals. I've faced my fear that living in a facility such as this assigns its residents to a seat in the Departure Lounge. I have been compelled to recognise that death comes in many shapes and forms and at many ages, like Mitch's beautiful, perfect, and young second wife, or my own newborn daughter, or in an instant, my friend Una, and not necessarily only among a gathering of ageing beings. Living here does not make death more common as living 'out there', nor can occupying my former home guard me from it. What's the cliché? When your number's up ...

Since my accident, my big take-home from my experiences has been that I realise the right choice is to live to its fullest every second that ticks over across the unknown span of time we are granted between birth to death. No matter how short or long our lives are, we can live every day of them, by not sitting and waiting for the man in the black hooded outfit and the crook to come a-knocking. Wherever we choose to sleep at night—in our home or in a Home—does not determine our ability to maintain that quality of living, whether like Gwen wheelchair-bound or like Joe, seeming able, but internally treading a definite path to his own death.

I've softened my view of my son's actions. I know that between my anger and his fear there's a huge gap I need to find a way across.

Decision made. Time to make it official. I like this person I have become in the companionship of others. While I may still fear the end, well, yes, truthfully, I do, but by recognising that by choosing my own path, in the main, it remains within my control. What I can't control – most of us can't – is, for example, my health and clear thinking, but being fearful won't hold them at bay or save me from them.

I make the call, to tell Brandon he's right. This is the place for me. At least that's my call at this moment. I ask him if he can find the time to come and talk it through. I know he will.

17

There's a celebratory air around the place because of Tim and Bev's upcoming wedding. In myself, I feel lighter. I feel as if I may have decided on my future, needing only to square things up with Brandon to make it definite. But I cannot overwrite the bleak loss of Una. Each day little reminders of who is missing pop up. In all the days I've been in this place, I can't recall one in which Una hasn't featured, and now the missing music of her voice and the sight of her flitting around is ominous and bleak. It feels like a prelude to the certain future loss of Joe, who is struggling to find energy, as if the weight of his grief over Una is the straw that has disarmed him.

The 'Big Day' is here. The staff are contributing by bringing in a husband or son to help fix the buntings and streamers. Being given a task to prepare and participate in an event such as a wedding has erased decades from the ages of many residents. Maybe this reminds each one they are part of a dynamic community.

A group of men mull around Tim when he turns up dressed in his new suit, a grin spread across his face. There's a lot of back-slapping, guffawing and chortling, and Billy imagines there's a few ribald jokes being made at Tim's expense.

Coral Fuller is Bev's bridesmaid. Coral enters the big room dressed in pale blue. Barely six paces in, she stops and claps her hands.

The bride is anon.

In floats Bev, a vision in a silver gown with a matching silver camber fascinator tipped to partly cover her face, yet permitting Bev's sparkling eyes to be seen through the netting. Bev's audience applauds, and there's a chorus of oohs and aahs. The group of men step back, leaving Tim alone. Tears are coursing down his face.

Joan Hooper, the person I spoke to first after arriving here, moves closer.

Doesn't matter what your age, we all love ceremony, and we love to be loved. Isn't it a marvellous day?

The excitement about the wedding and the energy required to participate means many weary individuals have skipped the evening meal and retired to their rooms and suites early. Joe and I decide to share a snack and tea in Joe's suite. I'm keen to tell Joe of my decision.

Joe, I have given thought to my stand-off with Brandon, and I have worked hard to stop behaving like this is a competition. I can recognise my son is trying to do the right thing, and for him, me making this my home is what's best for me. It's not a matter of him putting me in a corner, out of sight, and out of mind, or him wanting to get his hands on the money raised from the sale of my house. Putting that aside for the moment, I question myself. What do I see as my best outcome? And I have decided. I may come and go, as I would if I lived in my home. I know at some future time I will need more help but, meanwhile, here I am assured of balanced meals, companionship with little effort, and care if I need it. In my home, I would have to work hard to maintain friends and keep myself socially active. Inevitably I must hire someone to maintain my house and, well, I guess there would also be a solution for meals like Meals-on-Wheels, though to be honest, you can't beat the beautiful food they serve us here. If I go home, there will come a time when eventually I must find a place in a facility like this, at a time when I would be less able to do so without help, because of whatever brought me, be it sickness, dementia, frailty or some other debilitating condition. I would then have to re-establish friendships, and likely to be less open to doing so. Yet, here, I can handle the catastrophes in life, like losing Una and... other things... because I have support. From my home, I only have Brandon.

As I utter the phrase 'other things' a fist clenches my heart. I must concede that for some of those 'other things' there is no way to prepare.

Well, what's the decision, Billy? And what are you doing about it?

Joe, I have called Brandon. I want him to come and chat.

Someone is knocking on Joe's door.

Maude. You are making a habit of interrupting us. Are you our chaper-one?

No Joe. I need to speak to Billy.

Maude's face warns that what she has to say is not good.

Your son has been in an accident, Billy. He's in hospital.

An urgently called taxi takes me to the hospital. Once there, I need to wait for authority to enter the ICU. I gaze through the observation window and with no one saying so, I can see Brandon is in a bad way. Seeing my son attached to machines and tubes and looking vulnerable in the ICU shocks me to the point of disorientation. For a few minutes, my ability to think dissolves. Only my grip on a support bar is keeping me upright. I wish I had let Joe accompany me. I need his strength and clear thinking.

Someone wearing a surgical gown, with their head appropriately covered in shower-cap style gear and feet slipped into brightly colored Crocs, approaches me. I've no idea if this person is a doctor.

Mrs Corass. Your son is doing as well as can be expected. He needs to be stabilised but possibly later tonight he will be moved into a step-down unit where he will be closely monitored for a day or two, and then possibly, with no setbacks, he will need a few days in the Wards. In the step-down unit, tests will be done to check there are no underlying affects. He is a lucky man. The other driver has not been so blessed. If you wish to spend some time with your son, you can. But remember, what he needs most is rest.

I concentrate on getting my feet working properly so I don't stumble on my way into the ICU. I'm ushered to a chair set beside Brandon's bed. He looks to be unconscious, but I can't find the words to ask if this is so. My throat is tight and blubbery. The truth is I'm too afraid to hear what the medical staff might have to say, in case it's something intolerable. I'm not able to say the usual words someone might say to a loved one, awake or asleep, like 'I'm here, now,' 'It's going to be okay,' or even 'I love you.' I can only place one of my hands over the one of his that's free from tubing, and sit there crying. I've experienced nothing like this before. It's hurting.

Brandon's eyes flutter open.

Mum.

Hush, Brandon, my love. Mum's here.

I thought I would die, Mum.

They tell me you have been lucky.

The car came straight at me. I couldn't do a thing.

Don't think about that. Just rest. You need to rest.

I don't miss the irony that now it's me using the same phrase of reassurance Brandon used when I was in the ED after my accident, the one that made me angry. I can hear it now for what it is, nothing more or less than what you can say when you don't have the answers. I lift his hand to my lips and kiss it.

You would not die Brandon. A son doesn't die before his mother.

I can see Brandon has slipped back into sleep, and I'm hoping that means he didn't hear what I said. As I run it through my head, I recognise it to be a rather morbid pronouncement of a forthcoming death, not that's how I meant it to be. I stay there, holding his hand, until someone tells me I must go.

Outside, in the foyer, as I wait for the taxi, I weigh up my words, about a mother and a son. There is no guarantee. Death doesn't do what's expected. Once more I vow to live each day as if it's my last with the ones I loves.

A high of a wedding, and the scariest fright of an accident, these arriving in one day, are stark reminds of the insecurities and unpredictability of living.

18

Joe and I visit Brandon several times during his stay in hospital. Today Brandon is visiting Fairview. We've booked one of the private rooms to share a lunch.

By the time Brandon is limping back to his car, between us we have come loser to settling the matter of my future home. There's an agreement to visit a solicitor to sort out a plan for organising my financial situation, one that considers all the complex issues of Governmental requirements, asset means test, and so forth so my financial future gives me the best options with what monies I have available.

Joe and I stand side by side to wave goodbye to Brandon, but barely is Brandon out of sight when our hands fall instinctively into each other's and we turn to walk towards Joe's suite, our usual haven. We've barely taken a step when Joe stops in his path and turns to me with a big grin on his face,.

It's time you become the 'hostess with the most-est.' How about we head to Billy's suite today, and let's invite others, such as Gwen?

I see the appeal. My suite is larger, a group of friends, and laughter, but in my head and overtaking all priorities is a clock ticking off Joe's life. I'm greedy. I want every part of Joe I can gobble up while I am able. My need can't be ignored. It's overtaking my whole living existence, and my constant wish is to be touching Joe or standing beside him every second, taking in his every word, every mood, and if I can, his every thought.

When I see Joe's keenness, I force a smile and counsel myself. He's aware as I am of his time running out and he has wishes, too. They might be to spend time with our friends. By the time we reach my suite, a giggling group is waiting at the door, each bringing contributions such as a bag of potato chips, chocolate biscuits, a bottle of wine, some juice and sparkling mineral water, and the key part, a Monopoly board. I reprimand myself for my selfishness. These friends love Joe too. But my selfish heart is unconvinced. I want Joe to myself. Despite this, I know it will be a great way to spend the afternoon.

Only once, soon after we had settled ourselves, did someone say what everyone was thinking.

Una would have loved this.

Heads lower, nod, and a hand or two rubs at the corners of eyes. After some seconds of silence, the challenges begin: who believes they will win, who will buy what property, who must sell, who has the tactics, and who will earn a bundle of Monopoly money.

I'm finding it difficult to concentrate on the game. Hard work is needed for me to stay in the moment and enjoy what I know is precious. My responses to the teasing and joking around the board is hollow. As I go about my job as hostess, I'm on rote. My eyes look past others' heads, from the distance of the kitchen or across the room, so they can lock themselves onto Joe's face. I feel a twang inside me when almost every time his gaze and mine catch and linger. This is only broken by the social needs and distractions of our companions. I'm aware of, but am ignoring, the evidence of shared smiles and nods that show our friends are not oblivious. How could they not be aware? It's apparent they can feel the highly charged atmosphere in this room. They must sense it. Inevitably, one by one, they find excuses to leave. Their generosity is apparent, but I've pushed my thanks to a place where it can be dug up at some other time, and not used today. I haven't room for these acts of politeness. Building inside me is an urgency making it difficult for me to act normal. As the moment comes for one to leave, I usher them out, neither showing my eagerness nor pretending regret. I'm hoping another will soon do the same. I'm on automatic, engaging in only the social habits expected when there's guests in your home, but I'm barely achieving the norm. I want them to be gone but as true as that is, my focus is too specific to acknowledge my wish. I'm trying to downplay a sense of urgency because of what it says about my frantic awareness of limited time. My senses are overloaded, like I've overdosed on a tranquilliser and doubled up on stimulants. Part of me is running slow, and the other revving high. I have one focus and that is my need to have only one person in my suite with me.

When that's how it is, time slows for me. I'm in a psychedelic dream in which Joe and I are entering a spiralling dance without touching each other. We are staring into each other's eyes. I'm certain I haven't blinked. I may not be breathing. We don't need words. Our two existences are locked into a rare atmosphere of high intensity.

We've made love before, often. This isn't entirely sexual. Something larger, greater, more demanding is happening here. We are both in this heightened state. Perhaps, for me, the experience of Brandon with the tubes hanging out of him and the beeping machines has highlighted that every second with Joe is precious, that at any moment he could be taken from me. Stumbling so recently across this miracle of Joe, of being loved as much as I love, and knowing it can be only temporary, is soul destroying. The pain is extreme. I need release.

I want to devour Joe. I want every part of him inside me, both physically and mentally. In this way I can hold him forever. I will remember every touch, every sound, every response, even the sense of his drawing breath in and out.

I want it all. I need it all. My hold on Joe is tenuous, and there's nothing either of us can do about that. I desperately want to pack its fire into my heart and carry it until my own last breath, so I can take Joe with me when I go. My urgency goes beyond my awareness of the likely brevity of our time together. It's coming from inside me, a need to give love and be loved. I've waited a lifetime for a love like this and my hunger is like that of a starving refugee waiting to be fed. In them and in me there's a space left open borne out of the habit of being without, a need that will never be fully satisfied, despite any future surpluses we might be granted.

The seconds of Joe's life are ticking away. It's brutally unfair we have only so recently found each other. I want his chest on mine. I want to arch my back and feel my body melding with his. I want his breath to be my breath. I want to smell his unique aroma. This will be all I will have, only Joe's essence and a memory of his presence imprinted into my soul.

I absorb the sight of his twinkling dimples, the tightening and releasing of his jaw muscles, the pulse of blood in his throat, and the delicate reach of his long thin fingers. I want it all.

Afterwards, we laugh and cry, as we use our fingers, lips even our noses and faces to trace the other's body. Wrecked of energy, we collapse and remain side by side, eventually sleeping. I wake first. My eyes scan every millimetre of Joe's face, painting a memory portrait of the man I love. I close my eyes, willing it to be indelibly imprinted inside me, fearing that in some near future, dementia or some other consequences of the ageing process might rob me of this precious image of Joe. Then, like a lightning striking earth, I register something about myself. How long has it been since I stopped seeing myself as monstrous? Has loving Joe and being loved in return made me kinder to myself? Or do I now see myself as the Billy Joe loves? He sees and loves the inner Billy, the real Billy, not the wrinkled, grey, slower version, in the same way as I see the inner intelligent, perceptive Gwen, not the wizen, chair-bound, trembling outer version.

19

Activities are returning to normal. Singing, Percussion, Karaoke, and Exercise sessions are beginning again. Life is settling into its usual rhythms.

Meanwhile, Joe and I explore the complexities of each other's lives, loves, fears, successes and failures, as the bonds between our residential friends are expanding. Serendipitous and accidental connections between strangers have been combined and developed into solid physical and emotional relationships of a residential family. A few new residents have found their way into our group, bringing with them fresh stories and experiences, and my Folio is rapidly being filled with details of lives lived before entering Fairview. Another group is taking shape. This is where individuals tell their stories of interesting events or insights they have experienced. It's Fairview's Human Library, and an often-appearing cast member is Gwen with some marvellous stories to tell about twists in the application of law. Joan is revealed as a writer of short fiction. Coral is a traveller.

Another death has occurred. This time it's Maria del Bosca, or Mama Maria, whose dive into dementia was apparent from my first encounter in a battle of wills over possession of the sofa, but which has remarkably remained at a manageable level for a long time. Maria died peacefully in her sleep. Her fellow residents and the staff, as always, assembled for a Guard of Honour to show Maria respect and love as she made her last journey away from the place she had called her home. Ciao Maria.

And, so, life and death continue in Fairview.

The final run

1

WHEREVER JOE IS, I am there, too. We are both smiling, immersed in the satisfaction of our love for each other. And everyone knows that's how it is. I feel like a teenager. Never have I felt the pull of one person so extremely. Even though our bodies might not be touching as we sit side by side on a sofa or across a table from each other, I feel a charge in the space between us. I'm certain I glow, that every cell in my body is electrified by the reciprocation of my own burgeoning emotions. I can't explain why but I know it's there, a hunger in me to learn everything I can about Joe, to uncover the Joe that existed before he came into my life. I'm on an exploration for every detail of his life, from childhood until now, locking every detail into my heart, a beggar for whatever he offers me. If I was sufficiently brave, I would encourage him to tell other stories, such as how he met his wife, how he felt, and about the birth of his son, and even, as cruel as it seems, to hear again Joe's rendition of the events that led to his loss of those most important. There's an urgency to my need, a sense of compensating for meeting him so late in life and, deep down, it continues to feed my fear that I'll lose him too soon.

Despite his irregular but frequent and increasing need for transfusions and tests, on the surface, there's an illusion that the joy of being together has lulled both of us into believing the risks to Joe are less. For Joe, this is par for the course. For me, it's easier not to dwell on those medical journeys, but rather to only concentrate on making Joe as comfortable as is possible on his return.

I know I've slipped into convincing myself that these attentions are keeping at bay the risk of death, but in the quietness of night, the fear that today, or tomorrow, might be the last moments I will share with Joe overtakes all other thoughts.

When that day comes, I hear the sirens, but I do not connect the dots to recognise an ambulance has arrived at the front door of Fairview. I'm in the lobby when the ambulance officers enter, but as I'm in a funk, reviewing the miracle of Joe. I observe the activity that goes along with an ambulance, such as the lifting of the gurney out of the vehicle and organising the equipment, but I'm not fully registering the associated consequences, such as another death or someone seriously ill. I fail to notice the flurry happening among the staff and it's only when Gwen's wheelchair scoots in front of me, turns and retraces its path that I snap out of my reverie. Gwen says one word.

Billy.

With the utterance of my name and the tone of delivery, I know.

I run towards Joe's suite, Gwen trailing after me like a wonky wooden car held by a long piece of string. Gwen is trying to say something, but she can manage only a word or two, as she gasps for breath, working as hard as she can with her one good arm to keep her wheelchair moving.

Not ... good.

At the door to Joe's suite, Gwen gasps two more words.

Massive ... bleeding.

Behind Gwen and me, rapid footsteps grow closer, no doubt the ambulance team right on our tail. I open the suite door and enter. Joe and too much of his blood and several nursing staff are filling the space. Joe sees me. His dragon eyes lock into mine, and there's no escaping his loss of hope and his fear.

The nursing staff move away for the ambulance officers' entry. Someone is tugging at my shoulder, urging me to move. I need to be beside Joe. He lifts his head.

Billy, Billy. It turns out I want to live. One foot down. Lift the other. One foot down.

I hear the strange noise I know has come from me, a half sob and a half snort in response to Joe's affirmations. Maude is there, and she takes a firm grip of my upper arms to move me out of the way. The paramedics do their job, crowding around Joe, blocking my attempts to be nearer. I can't see his face, nor hold his hand, and its agony for me. There's a quiet urgency to the attention Joe's receiving, and this is a warning that I'm working hard to deny. The home's nursing staff are conferring with the paramedics, their words low and serious. I hear 'risk of exsanguination', and an icy chill crawls up my spine. One authoritative voice is heard.

Time to go.

Joe's hand flops out from under the covering and I can hear him say my name. 'Come on, come on,' one officer mutters, but I reach past him to Joe's hand and squeeze. Joe's grip is equally firm and only broken by the movement of the gurney towards the door. I'm gifted a brief glimpse of Joe's face, his eyes seeking me out, before someone steps in to do what must be done and blocks my view.

As the procession moves out through the lobby towards the waiting ambulance, Maude strokes my tears away from eyes with no choice but to follow Joe's path towards the waiting ambulance. The group of professionals continue to work on him as the gurney moves toward the door. I watch as those gathered around Joe stay in their positions until the gurney is inside the ambulance. The vehicle drives away, sirens blaring, leaving behind a depleted team. Their body language does not offer hope for the spectator searching for reassurance.

I continue to gaze at the now empty space where the ambulance had parked. Maude is still there, stroking my shoulder.

It would always be one thing or another, Billy. He was fighting a battle he could never win. I'd say he's done marvellously well to not have had a crisis before now. I am so sorry. Come now, come. You need some quiet. We'll bring you any news that comes. Come on, let's rest.

I remove Maude's comforting hands. On automatic I stumbled back to Joe's suite and drop my sagging body into Joe's armchair.

Maude must have followed, because I learn of her presence when she makes a weak attempt to persuade me to move, her way of acknowledging she's uncertain of any way to help me. I'm unmovable. Maude sighs, nods her head, and attends to the bloody mess left behind by Joe's departure. She bundles the blood sodden linen and takes it out of sight, then picks up Joe's quilt and spreads it over my legs.

You stay here, Billy. I'll come and check on you later. I'll keep you informed of progress, honey.

2

Maude is true to her word. She returns to Joe's apartment with news.

Billy, I have permission for both of us to go to the hospital. Do you wish to tidy up or are you ready to go as you are?

A taxi is waiting at the front door.

Maude gives the driver the directions and helps me into the rear seat before wriggling in next to me. She takes my hand and strokes it. The silence between us is deafening. I'm thankful. There's nothing Maude can say I would want to hear. I'm in a fog. My head feels as if it's swollen with tears, and I feel sick.

At the hospital, Maude needs to push me out of the taxi, and once out, I stand, unable to move, waiting to be directed. I dread what I know is ahead. The signs are there, clear and undeniable.

Maude pays the driver and leads me towards the hospital foyer with a gentle but firm hold of my upper arm. She leaves me for a moment to move to the desk, and after a lot of head nodding and pointing, she returns and moves me toward a lift. Maude presses buttons, the elevator moves upward and there's an electronic ding when we arrive at the floor level.

So normal, so every day, I note. And yet it's not.

Now Maude breaks the silence.

Come and sit over here, Billy. I must speak to the staff and then I will come and get you.

I read the actions and reactions and recognise this is far out of the ordinary. Discussions happen, and someone leaves and returns, and more talking, pointing, head nodding. I wonder if it's because I'm not family, thus I have no authority to see Joe. Merely his friend in official terms. A snag of anger is building inside me, until I see Maude nod, turn and gesture to me to come.

She whispers to Billy, 'Joe's unconscious. The bleeding is widespread. Mariella thought I should bring you to see him. I am sorry Billy.'

My gut shouts, 'Sorry? Why sorry?' I know the answer. But I don't want to hear it.

At the side of Joe's bed Maude pulls up a chair for me. She withdraws to a respectful distance beyond us.

There's Joe, the scary cables and tubes leading away from him, as he lies there, surrounded by the constantly beeping and flashing indicators that measure his fragile hold on life. But his face is at peace, his dimples stilled, his dragon eyes closed and his silver spikey hair standing proud, unchanged by the drama that has brought him here. I bend and kiss his forehead, run a finger over his cheeks and down to his mouth, and then I kiss that spot near his dimples.

I whisper, 'Oh, Joe. There were no guarantees, but please don't leave.'

Sitting on the chair Maude has provided, I take Joe's hand and hold it, imagining he is responding and gripping mine. There's nothing. This is the body of Joe, but has Joe already left? Did the bleeding reach his brain? Contemplating Joe's peaceful expression invites thoughts of the lost possibility of a life with Joe under different circumstances, and many questions. Is this how it should be, how it must be? No more pain, no longer torturing himself with his guilt, no more waiting for the inevitable deadly moment to arrive. Should I let go of my own emotions, my anger at his loss, my wish for more time, and gift him with my blessing? I'm certain I'm only permitted to be here because the medical opinion is he will not recover. I review the equipment attached to him, looking for signs. I try to shut out the reality that he's only alive because of these. There are questions I desperately need answers to, such as have they given him a CT scan to see if there's damage to his brain – because, if there's no damage, then there's hope for me to speak to him again. I glance over at Maude, hoping she has something to tell me, but Maude is crying and shaking her head. Maude has read my mind.

Maude pulls up another chair and nods as if to say, 'We're here for the long haul.' I return to stroking Joe's hand and whispering to him.

'Thank you, Joe, for coming into my life, for showing me I'm a person who now feels loveable and who's loved, and thank you for being who you are, my soulmate. Thank you, my love. I should be generous and say it's the right time. You can let go now, Joe. But I'm selfish. I want you back with me.'

I bury my head on his hand, reminding myself of his gentle touches of love, when he'd stroke my cheek and I'd see those beautiful eyes fill with a glow, and know it was for me. It's nearly dawn, and Maude is dozing on her chair when the alarms shatter the peace of the ICU. The medical staff, who have regularly checked on Joe throughout the night, are rushing in, doing what they do in emergencies, and I half-rise, reluctant to leave, but realising I've no choice. How long the flurry continues I can't say because I'm withdrawing from the reality, trying to deny what is apparent, but failing. Maude grabs me from behind and moves me backwards, away from their medical activity. I stay where Maude has placed me, my eyes not moving off Joe's face. Tears are streaming down my face and my body is shuddering, There's no relief.

Nothing feels real. The frantic medical attention, the noise, and Joe there on the bed, his face as calm and peaceful as it has been throughout.

Then silence.

Someone speaks softly to Maude, and the machines are turned off. Maude whispers, 'Say your goodbyes, Billy. He's no longer in pain.'

3

I know I'm a mess. I'm trying but nothing is working. I know a funeral is being arranged. But by whom? Joe has no family. In fragments, and slowly, it becomes apparent that Brandon has stepped in, already conceding Joe as his mother's love, and the importance of Joe. He has told me, though I hardly hear him he recognises how important Joe is to most residents, so he's volunteered to help Mariella organise a wake.

The day arrives. As awareness of the event dawns on me, I doubt I'll survive it. I know I must. It's my last chance to say goodbye. More than ever, I need my mantra. It's rolling around in my head constantly as I respond to the words and actions of those around me, the good intentions and sympathising words that only reinforce the fact of Joe's absence. One foot down. Lift the other. One foot down. Lift the other. One foot down. Lift the other. One foot down. Lift.

Joe's last words were, 'One foot down …Lift …'

In my head, I'll continue the rest of my chant.

Forget the pain. Forget the distance.

See the bush. Run to the bush. See the rise. Run to the rise.

One foot down, lift the other. One foot down, lift the other.

Hear the rhythm. Like a heartbeat. Bounce off the ground.

One foot, then another.

Back straight. Chin high. A runner's posture.

Erect. Perpendicular. Let gravity do its job.

Free the airways. Breathe.

See the pole. Run to the pole.

Trick your body. Don't let it betray you.

Keep the rhythm

Pace your footfall. Co-ordinate arms with legs.

Habits of a lifetime.

The last words I heard from Joe was his affirmation not only that he understood me, but also the words that preceded those came straight from his heart, 'Billy, Billy. It turns out I want to live.' He, like me, recognised that what we have shared was exceptional; that he too knew that we had compacted into our short time together, only months, an intense relationship. But it also shouted at me his awareness of his inability to survive. Instinctively, he knew those words would be his goodbye. If ever I disbelieved I would find someone to love and be loved by, his shortened time with me shattered those doubts. Joe was my soulmate. I felt everything he felt. He and I saw the world in the same way. As if our hearts were beating to the same rhythm. That's how it felt, and that's what I believe. Those last words told me irrevocably he didn't want to give up what we shared; he did not want our connection broken. Nor did I. But it's gone. All that lingers are the vivid and pain-inviting memories alongside my regrets over the time I wasted, those months I fought against giving in to my intuition, as I kept him far away by damning him as an untouchable.

Maude and Brandon are knocking at my door.

Time to get ready, Billy. Your son has asked me to help you get ready.

Maude turns to Brandon and nods.

She'll be okay, Brandon. We'll be down soon.

Maude closes the suite door behind Brandon and moves to the wardrobe, throwing open both doors.

What are we wearing today, Miss Billy? Which of your gowns will say what your heart wants to say to celebrate a special life? This one? Or this?

I decide, and tell Maude my decision. I don't want to be doing this. No gown will change the outcome. My heart is crying, 'Too much, too much.'

Maude is persistent. She flips through my wardrobe, pondering each item, then shaking her head. Many beautiful dresses hang on their hangers but for today's event, they cannot meet Maude's measure. Finally, she comes to a pant suit of pale blue.

This is the one. Sufficiently conservative to show respect, but equally important on this occasion, the silvery shade compliments your complexion. You need to look your best for Joe, Billy.

I don't care what Maude has chosen. I move through the habits of dressing, tidy my hair rather than do it, poke my feet into my shoes and trudge toward the apartment door.

What about some make-up, young lady? For Joe.

As if dragging an unbearable weight, I return to my dresser and do what I have habitually done, goodness knows how many times throughout my life, absent-mindedly picking up my foundation, then my lipstick, and applying it to my deadpan face. Maude scrutinises the result, adds a little colour to my cheeks and nods.

I'm a robot, on automatic, walking obediently beside Maude to the elevator. We emerge in the lobby, and I can't ignore the size of the crowd, the bouquets of flowers on coffee tables and stands, the sudden silence of conversations and yet I feel nothing. Brandon appears beside me and takes my elbow. He says something to me, but I can make no sense of his words. Faces, those of my close friends, who are also Joe's close friends, bend towards me and speak, but I'm deaf and mute. Some cell in my brain recognises the service is beautiful, that many speakers heap praise on Joe's generosity of spirit, and that there's an ocean of shared grief within the group. The only words I can offer, in a voice that doesn't sound like mine, is 'Goodbye Jerome Vella. It's my privilege and pleasure to have known you.' These two short sentences are barely indiscernible among the many words I might have drawn from to describe the emotions I have packed inside, but I'm certain Joe would understand. Not everything must be articulated. There's always room to lock in and store the most precious of feelings and memories, especially the ultra-precious private and personal ones.

4

Shopping days come and go. The regular group board the bus and often bring back pastries to share as they wait for me to find my way back to some normal routine. Exercise Group is postponed, also waiting for the instructor. One of the OTs has taken up Joe's percussion mob, though the decision to do so was heavily debated. New residents have entered, some behaving as if Fairview is a STAYZ resort and while others wear faces that shout of fear and confusion. The Welcoming Committee has worked hard to find a less threatening ritual for these newcomers, one that acknowledges for some people change is difficult. Some individuals need to find their own way through the maze, especially those who have left situations or locations where their social connections were few and now they are faced with several hundreds of strangers. The irregular occurrence of Guards of Honour continues, as will always be the case, and staff changes are always too frequent for those who like to see familiar faces bringing them their morning or afternoon tea or administering their heat pads before bed or their pain killers and other medications as they are needed. The aged do like to feel in control. It's through an assuredness of those around them and their surroundings that this certainty in their daily lives is affirmed.

Brandon has been to visit me regularly since Joe's funeral. Since we reached our compromise, he's been waiting to hear what I want to do once I'm ready to decide on my future. It's apparent to everyone who knows me, I'm not yet ready to face anything but waking up, getting dressed, eating breakfast, returning to my suite and doing who knows what as time passes before the next scheduled meal, and so forth, until the day ends, and I fall back into bed. My friends regularly call in, but conversations linger around light subjects and are cautiously carried out.

For some inexplicable reason, on one day, I choose not return to my suite after a meal but indulge in an excursion, ending in the small loungeroom at the rear, the place where I'd conversed with Coral, the woman I'd labelled

'The Deer Lady' because of her quiet, graceful manner. As if it was yesterday, I remember what had driven me to this space on that day: my first encounter with a Guard of Honour, a confirmation for me that Fairview could only be a death factory, that everyone was merely waiting for their turn to be carried through the Guard of Honour by gurney to the waiting ambulance, no matter how seemingly respectful the gathering of staff and some residents intended the departure to be.

A weight has lifted off me, encouraging me to remain in this space and allowing me once again to enjoy time spent outside of my room, though I pray for the rare privilege of spending that time without conversation. Everywhere and anywhere in Fairview there are people willing to chat. Away from my suite, I'm able to expand my reflection on recent events. By lunchtime, I'm ready to eat and go back to the suite. It's tiring, this constant sense of being emotionally shredded. This time, my afternoon nap is natural, a nice change from my sleep patterns of late.

Another week has passed before I venture out again to other parts of Fairview. This time it's the courtyard. I've been working hard not to enter the corridor that passes by the corner where Joe would read to his group of dementia suffering men. Now, in the courtyard, an even larger recognition comes. In this courtyard I had my first conversation with Joe. He'd said on that occasion, 'It's a strange state we are in, don't you think, Billy?' I can see the flash of his dragon eyes, the movement of his silver spikes as if he's here, now, waiting for me to answer. I hadn't known to which state he was referring. Did he mean the one that involved Sid and Missy and their tragedy, or, generally, the realisation of finding oneself in a location that had not been part of any forward planning, or specifically the two of us, strangers in the main, who were there discussing the 'state of things.' I'd identified him as the community counsellor, and he'd laughed at the suggestion. Now I know he was telling the truth when he had responded. He'd told me he likes to listen, and listening needs a return conversation. He was always listening and paying attention to the important things. I permit myself a few tears for his absence. I'll never recover.

In the courtyard, the sun moves along the far wall, and with its movement I can hear Joe telling me about his first encounter with Gwen, who had somehow propelled herself in her wheelchair to this space, arriving as the last rays of sunlight were capitulating to the darkness of night. He'd told me this on our day into the desert. Then, his fixation of the word 'wasted' had troubled me, but it was through that word he told me about his accident and his condition, the DIC diagnosis. As special as that day had been, as moving as it had been for me to hear his story and share a part of myself, particularly my love of running and the desert, never had I expected how much more Joe would come to mean. So much more, so quickly.

Joe, Joe, Joe. I must remind myself of the blessing I received when you came into my life. But I am greedy. I wanted more. I want more. I need more. I never fully realised on what a razor-edge you were treading, and with you, me too. If I had, would I have done things differently? Oh, it's difficult to say. Our moments together are the trail left by a comet flashing through the night sky: a burst of brilliance and then gone. But thank you, my love. Thank you.

Gradually I'm able to compact my memories of Joe, even his death, so I can carry them with me and pull them out when the moment's right, bring Joe back into my life by carrying him with me into my future experiences. He'll always be alive.

I recognise my friends are treading on eggshells, watching and waiting, as I find my way back. Shopping is still not on the agenda, but starting up the Exercise Sessions has been beneficial. I can't bear to hear the tinkling and clanging of the Percussion Group, but maybe some time there will be less pain.

My doctor has given me the all-clear around my hip, and it's time to decide. No longer am I fighting the battle for my rights. They had never been taken from me, but that I hadn't realised my own power. Looking back, I wonder if much of my anger came from the shock of an unforeseen chain of events that had me bound and weighed down so suddenly, because of my fall, as though it was waiting to pounce on me. Had I been more pro-active, I might have set in place arrangements to cover such potential adverse happenings, much like the contingency planning I've done for my extreme sport events. But, possibly like most ageing individuals, it seems we can't do that. Rather, it's as if to admit that there is a time ahead where there's a need for help is like giving up on life. I realise what a flawed view that is, one that inevitably results in the control of your life being taken out of your hands.

This stupidness almost cost me my son. The wedge between us was the point Joe made about a need for reconciliation. Those who care about us carry a heavy burden to make right and responsible decisions on our behalf. Wise Joe. After we calmed down, I could see that Joe was right, and Brandon backed off his need to dictate, letting us find a way together to work on solutions. In deciding about on my future, I've put in the same effort as I did for running. I've researched, read many books, consulted with those whose job it is to find solutions for this time of life. I learnt in the fight against dementia of the importance of social engagement and having something to look forward to, even if its Exercise Sessions on certain days, or shopping excursions on others. Without doubt, however, the biggest risk to ageing individuals is loneliness. In my home, would I have been lulled back into becoming the lone wolf I'd spent my earlier life being? Probably. It's easier sometimes to just stay put and not move out of your comfort zone. I remind myself of the responses of Joe's dementia-sufferers, to his reading and conversations, And the lifted heads of previously lifeless individuals when, on my first day, as I waited in Charlie's wheelchair, a family of children brought in a yapping dog to show grandma. And what better example than the smiles and response of similarly afflicted residents as they celebrated Bev and Tim's wedding. Sometimes it requires only the smallest moment of normal life to spark a remembrance. For a moment, faces too-often vacant of expression, become animated, eyes widen, mouths stretch, providing a flickering affirmation that hidden within each mostly unresponsive soul, there are personalities, memories, thoughts, and intelligence. Physically limited by failing muscles and tissue as they may be, they are still living. I remember something I heard or read once: we are alive until we aren't.

I've made my decision.

Brandon is coming to help me fill in the forms for long term residency and then he can do what he needs to do with my home. I can live out my life with the knowledge there's contingency plans in place for whatever struggle I might need to face. I can enjoy whatever I can do confident that I've taken care of my final lap.

Joe, I only wish you were here to share this life with me. Thank you, my darling, for the gift of you. Meeting you, knowing you, loving you, none of this ever expected or even hoped for, has given me is a sense of self hidden throughout my previous life. Being loved by you, brief as our time together has been, has formed me into someone new. Recognising through you and your love, the way love expressed can bring change is the gift I plan to share with everyone I encounter from now and through the rest of my life, as long or short as that may be. My race is not over yet.

It is clear now, in hindsight, had I not been blinded by my fear of ageing and dying, I may have put the same effort as I have always put into planning ultra-runs to consider the shape my future life should take. Though, any future I may have painted for myself would not have forecast me as frail and dependent, like Gwen, as I may have been, or foretold the delightfully unpre-dictable, like Joe, or prepared me, a lone wolf, for fitting into a community. By looking ahead and recognising the possible challenges, I may have found the path to this future life less fraught. We aren't forever young, as much as we might wish to be, but life does go on even when we are grey, wrinkled, and less able (or even severely disabled like Gwen) and I've convinced myself it's up to each of us to make the most of the immeasurable time left to us. Inspired as I am by philosopher Simone de Beauvoir, I am sure the way to achieve full life as we age is to fight for ourselves and not be crushed through our own and others' ageism discrimination. It's up to ourselves to continue to work towards our better lives. Soon I'll be back out there, in training, ready to participate in Masters' marathons. These events may perhaps not be the ultra-events of the past but most certainly still strenuous and demanding, and until Life presents me yet another obstacle whereby this kind of activity is no longer possible, I will continue. And then I'll find another passion to involve myself in. Life is, after all, a long-distance event, where pace must be adjusted to meet the challenges encountered along the way.

THE END

About the author

WENDY GLASSBY may be respectfully labelled a late bloomer, a title aptly fitting with the theme of this, her latest novel 'Forever Young,' influenced by French Philosopher Simone de Beauvoir who says as we age we must fight for ourselves, or be crushed by ageist discrimination; we do so by reconnecting with the person we inwardly know ourselves to be, continuing always to expand and improve ourselves. For Wendy perhaps this is demonstrated by writing a book, despite implied judgements such as, 'What's the point? You are old.'

Although writing short fiction since young, only in retirement did Wendy send her work out for publication, a fruitful decision. This success was followed by a Bachelor of Creative Arts, First Class Honours, and a PhD, and her first novel 'Between' in 2021 at age 76, for which draft versions received three VARUNA The National Writing House awards. And now this one at 79, and more in the pipeline.

Thanks

I thank my family, each and every one – husband, children and siblings – for their support. Overt or covert, and each in their own special way, please know I've noticed and I'm grateful.

A special mention to my daughter Cathie for designing this perfectly beautiful cover.

I thank my mother-in-law Rene, who achieved 101 years, mostly capable, but the last twenty-five or more spent in a retirement home, making it her home and living her own life. Unintentionally, Rene brought me to question why so many of us seem terrified that her life might be in our future.

I'm particularly grateful to my Tai Chi instructor Gil, her generous and valuable contribution so obvious within the narrative.

Last but definitely not least though numerous, I thank my friends for their encouragement and support. I thank them for putting up with my downloads, overloads and overspills.

I am especially grateful to Christine, Lynne, Noelene and John who, like my sisters, read some or all of my early drafts and had the courage to offer comment, a truly precious gift for any writer.

www.ingramcontent.com/pod-product-compliance
Lightning Source LLC
Chambersburg PA
CBHW020005140726

47904CB00018B/1863